Magic Kingdom at War

VOLUMES 1-4

by

Tao Wong

Copyright

This is a work of fiction. Names, characters, businesses, places, events, and incidents are either the products of the author's imagination or used in a fictitious manner. Any resemblance to actual persons, living or dead, or actual events is purely coincidental.

No part of this publication may be reproduced, distributed, or transmitted in any form or by any means, including photocopying, recording, or other electronic or mechanical methods, without the prior written permission of the publisher, except in the case of brief quotations embodied in critical reviews and certain other non-commercial uses permitted by copyright law.

Magic Kingdom at War Volumes 1-4

Published by Starlit Publishing
PO Box 30035
High Park PO
Toronto, ON
M6P 3K0
Canada

www.starlitpublishing.com

Ebook ISBN: 9781778552267
Paperback ISBN: 9781778552274

Books in the Magic Kingdom at War Series

Magic Kingdom at War Volume 1

Magic Kingdom at War Volume 2

Magic Kingdom at War Volume 3

Magic Kingdom at War Volume 4

Magic Kingdom at War Volume 5

Magic Kingdom at War Volume 6

Magic Kingdom at War Volume 7

Magic Kingdom at War Volume 8

Magic Kingdom at War Volume 9

Magic Kingdom at War Volume 10

Magic Kingdom at War Volume 11

Magic Kingdom at War Volume 12

Other Series by Tao Wong

System Apocalypse

System Apocalypse: Australia

System Apocalypse – Relentless

System Apocalypse: Kismet

System Apocalypse: Liberty

A Thousand Li

Adventures on Brad

Climbing the Ranks

Dating Evolution

Hidden Dishes

Hidden Wishes

Table of Contents

Chapter 1

Being called into Kyran's office first thing in the morning was never a good thing. That he had left a message at reception for Matt Fang to come by the moment he arrived for work – five minutes before nine as always – boded ill.

Six months and twenty-three days. Well past his probationary period, at least. Which was a better showing than his last job by a good five months. He'd been careful to leave that job out of his resume. Not that it helped a lot.

Arriving at the partially closed door, Matt rapped on it. A quick scan of the office behind him showed half the desks in the open-plan office filled. Everyone else had arrived early as usual. Mary, mousy Mary with her frizzy brown hair and big brown eyes, ducked her head as he caught her looking, refusing to meet his eyes.

"Come in."

Matt wiped the smirk off his face, made sure he looked serious, and pushed the door open. Kyran within was glowering at the monitor, not even bothering to look up as Matt walked in. He didn't bother sitting, figuring it wasn't worth the energy. Of course, his boss with his carefully tended trendy fade of a haircut didn't bother looking for long minutes.

Childish power plays, but then again, the boy was a child.

"You left early yesterday." Kyran swung his office chair straight, facing the man squarely. "Again."

"I left at five-oh-five," Matt said, not rising to the bait.

"The Rushman project was not finished."

"There's about two hours of work left on it, yes," Matt replied. "I was intending to finish it this morning."

"Don't bother. I gave it to Mary. She got it done, yesterday."

"Okay."

Silence stretched between the two as Matt just waited patiently for what he knew was about to come. He'd done this dance often enough.

"We've discussed the requirements of your job before," Kyran said, leaning forwards and steepling his fingers. He tried to look stern, but it mostly made him look constipated to Matt. "And how your dedication to the company is lacking, especially compared to your peers. Now, an important project was nearly not done on time."

"I informed you about the problems with the project two weeks ago, how the client has not provided answers to pertinent questions. I'd already alerted them about the potential extension of the deadline if we did not receive answers promptly and when it arrived late, I again informed them about the delay," Matt said, shrugging a little. "It's not like everyone involved didn't know what would happen."

"Our job is to make our clients happy!"

"If you wanted the work finished on the original deadline, you should have assigned someone else to help me, as I'd asked."

"Are you saying I am in the wrong?"

Matt chose not to answer that. It was rather obvious after all and there was a slim margin he was not about to get fired.

Very slim.

Silence again, drawn out. After a moment, Kyran cleared his throat. "The Jacobs' file. I'd like you to go over it and get me a summary by tomorrow morning. They're looking to divest some of their poorer performing investments and reinvest in a few new ventures."

"The whole file?" Matt asked carefully. The Jacobs had been working with the firm, making use of their financial service advice, for nearly two decades now. They had over fifty million dollars in holdings, spread out across a variety of industries and companies. There were dozens of contracts and investments to review, from private companies to public shareholdings, ETFs, real estate investments, forex reserves and bonds, and more.

"Of course."

"Who else is on it?"

"No one."

"It won't be done by then," Matt replied firmly. "It just isn't possible. Not if you want a proper review."

"I'm sure it can be, if you're dedicated enough."

"Are you paying overtime then?" Matt said archly.

"You're a salaried employee."

"That a no?"

Kyran let out a long, dramatic sigh. "You know, my father thought you'd be a good fit. He insisted that I give you one last chance, says you've got a great mind on you. Said that the work you do, it's world class. But all I see is a lazy man whose actions are driving a wedge into my company, destroying morale. I won't have it."

"I don't work for free, and I won't work unpaid overtime. It's not my responsibility to manage the schedules and workload. Just the clients and their expectations." Matt shook his head, his smirk making a reappearance. "Which isn't made easier when you won't back us up."

"Your job is to keep them happy!" Kyran slammed a fist on the table as he finished. "Or do you not know how much money they bring in?"

"I do. I also know how much you pay us." Matt shrugged. "And that you can afford the overtime."

"You… you…" Kyran pointed at the door. "Get out!"

"Okay." Matt stepped back, then hesitated. "So, when you said get out, did you mean of the office or the company?"

"You're fired, you idiot!"

"Figured." Grinning now, Matt reached up and tugged on the necktie around his neck, loosening it. He then sauntered over to his desk, pulling open the drawer, grabbing the stash of candy bars he had in there, and stuffing them into his pocket. He scanned the table, searching for anything else he had brought in.

Nope. The single, dismal potted plant had been bought by the company. So had the laptop, which they had hinted he bring home and he had refused to do so. No company phone, of course. They'd been too cheap to buy him one. The pens and other stationery were all from the company store.

He'd stopped bothering with bringing in personal effects a while ago. Since the… fourth? job he'd been let go from. Hauling it all around was annoying.

Satisfied he was leaving nothing behind, he sauntered to the exit. The other employees dared not even look at him, their eyes glued to their screens. Even Mary only glanced at him before looking down, shoulders hunched. His smirk grew even more pronounced.

On a whim, he stopped at the exit, near where the receptionist waited. Raising his voice, he made sure to project so that they could all hear him.

"You know, the job market – especially for qualified CPAs – is really tight right now. Why'd you think half the desks are open? No one is really willing to work for these cheapskates." A crash came from Kyran's office at his words, muffled cursing arising from within, but Matt ignored it. "Is this what you want? To spend the rest of your lives seated at a desk, making rich men richer?"

Silence from the group. That smirk turned into a sneer as Matt regarded his ex-peers, the beaten and scared faces never turning his way. Exasperated, he threw his hands up and added, "At the least, get paid well for doing this shit!"

As soon as he finished, a red-faced figure poked itself out of the office, a finger leveled at Matt. Kyran was bent over, clutching his leg as he growled, "Get the hell out of my office before I call the cops on you!"

"I'm leaving, I'm leaving."

"Don't believe all that bullshit he talked about. You think he knows anything? He'll find that burning bridges with us is a fool's game," Kyran ranted. "A good reference from us…"

Rather than wait for the elevator and listen to the boy's voice a moment more, Matt headed for the stairs. It was only six floors after all. As the door cut off his ex-employer's voice, Matt began to whistle a jaunty tune. Losing a job sucked, but it was all the same anyway, wiling away time doing bullshit work till you died. He'd find something soon enough.

In the meantime, it was a brilliant day outside. Maybe sitting by the beach with some ice cream was called for.

His whistling slowed and came to a halt as he skipped down to the third floor. He put a hand to his head, wincing at a growing pressure. His other hand gripped the railing as the pressure and pain increased. Eventually, he found himself on a knee, vision swimming and a message in his head.

Not a vision, just a message that he somehow knew.

To all humans,

The time of trials is before us. We – your gods – have failed to hold the line. Now, a final test must be enacted. But before this test may begin, we require champions. Will you stand between humanity and the chaos that approaches? Know that in doing so, there is no return, no glory, no acclaim. Just the knowledge that what you do matters.

Will you face this challenge?

The pain subsided, only a single locus point of focus left. A thought that he could push one way or the other to offer an answer. Strangely enough, there was a certainty within Matt that this thought, this message, was real. Perhaps it was a side effect of a stroke or seizure. Or perhaps it was because it was real and true and part of the divine message that it was.

He held no doubt this was real.

He wondered how many had chosen no. How many had refused immediately. Who had quailed at the thought, who had chosen to accept the call. Soldiers, firemen, charity workers. He wondered what kind of trial it might be.

And then, as he made his decision, he wondered why he ever hesitated.

After all, what else had he been waiting for, all his life?

Chapter 2

Transitioning between worlds was rather more of a shock for Matt than he had expected. Rather than a portal opening, or his body transforming into energy or even an unfriendly truck coming along, he instead had a brain hemorrhage.

One moment, he was alive, in pain, and making a decision that would change his fate forever.

The next, he was slumped over on the stairs, bouncing down a couple before coming to a stop. Eyes glassy, nose bleeding a little from the massive brain bleed. His heart kept beating for a little while, his automatic nervous system still functioned. But the man himself was gone.

Snatched away as his soul left his body and was thrown into battle.

***

Matt stumbled, his balance all awry and his vision clouded. There was a white haze over everything and a scream that rang through his ears, stifling all other noise. As he fell, he felt someone grab hold of his body, his arm, holding him up. Even as the pressure around his body held him close, he realized his throat hurt and that the screaming came from himself.

He clamped his mouth shut, stopped screaming, and forced himself to breathe.

"New teeth. That's weird."

Matt kept blinking, the white haze disappearing with each blink. He hurt, not physically – other than his throat, but even that was fading a little – but deeper. He hurt in his soul, a kind of pain that was all encompassing and yet remote at the same time. Like someone had replaced the pain with a memory of the pain, such that he knew he should hurt but he didn't, but it still was there.

His eyes cleared up, enough so that Matt realized that the person gripping him was a brown-skinned, wrinkled, and tusky orc. Perhaps it was another creature, but for Matt, he labelled the one holding him up as orc.

Lurching backwards by pure surprise, he tried to scream, only to find his voice and throat dry. Before he could overbalance in this new unfamiliar body, another hand gripped him on the other side. Looking over, Matt could only see an older man staring back at him, with a wispy long beard and what he could only describe as unfashionably tight pants and a blousy pirate shirt.

"Easy there, my lord. The transfer can be quite tough." Smooth, cultured, though with a tinge of a guttural slur to it. Not the old man but the damn orc was saying this.

"How would you know?" Matt snapped as he pulled himself free, straightening more carefully. His balance was coming to him, slowly.

"We all died to get here." This time, it was the old man speaking. His voice was a surprise too, for it had a broad twang to it that Matt could only think of as belonging to New Orleans and the bayou.

"Shit." Somehow, being told he had died – was dead – was not shocking. Not when he was still dealing with the burgeoning horror of being tossed across unknown dimensions to a new location. More importantly, he touched his face, running unfamiliar fingers over unfamiliar planes. "This isn't my body."

"No," the orc said. "It's a loaner."

"Goddamn unpaid overtime…" Matt cursed, dropping his hand and forcing himself to take in the surroundings. They were in a small grey-brown stone room, the walls constructed with imperfect blocks and mortared together with old cement. Nearby was a wooden table, over which what he could only describe as a hologram hovered. A couple of chairs added to the ambience as did the pair who'd welcomed him.

"Why am I not freaking out more? I just died, got booted over dimensions, and stuck into a new body. I should be in a ball, quivering, right?"

"You should?" the old man asked, confused. "That doesn't make much sense. It's already over and done with, boy."

"No, I get it. It's an irrational response to an irrational situation," the orc rumbled. "Though it does not bode well for our chances."

"Will you two shut up!" Matt snapped, and then glowered at the pair until they did as he said. In the quiet, he took stock of himself further, not just physically but mentally and emotionally. Spiritually too perhaps. After a few moments, he nodded to himself.

That feeling of remoteness, that compartmentalization of his pain. It extended not just to his soul, but it seemed to be cushioning all the other shocks to his system. It was strange, and different, but he was not going to complain at the moment.

"Alright, let's just try to figure this out from the start. Who are you? I'm Matt Fang." He really needed a mirror. He wondered if he even looked Chinese anymore. Certainly his face seemed a little broader and longer, and his hair… He reached up quickly, grabbed a lock, and tugged at it. "Purple? Seriously?"

"It is quite striking, my Lord Fang." The orc slurred the last name a little, so instead of doing a more ph noise for the f, and rhyming the last name with hung, he'd gone with a more f sound with a guttural, dropping -ung. "I am Braskar, your Warlord. And that is Irvine, your Alchemist."

"No last names?"

"We do not recall them any longer," Irvine said.

"That's messed up." Matt frowned. "Why can I?"

"It is likely that they protected your mind with a greater degree of caution than ours," Braskar said. "Your job is more important after all."

"As though being an Alchemist isn't?" Irvine snapped waspishly. "I'll let you know, putting the wrong mix together means death for us all."

"And if I lose, we all die. But still, they took my name." Braskar rumbled, a dissatisfied look crossing the orc's face.

Strange, Matt thought, that it was so easy to read the alien features. Hopefully, that'd stay the same and no weird cross-cultural problems cropped up. But that wasn't the problem, none of that was. Because his memory of the last few moments of his life was returning, and the damn hovering hologram on the table was looking all too familiar.

To start with, why create hexagonal denotations for landspace? Squares made more sense if you were navigating, since you could just give a two-line series of co-ordinates to mark the specific location and there was less confusion. That's the reason why even military maps went with squares.

The only time you had hexagons for map pieces was when you needed to simplify movement in an artificial manner. Like, if you thought of units as pieces on a board that had to be shifted around. Then, you could mark hexagonal terrain areas, make movement cost a specific amount while also indicating minimum or maximum movement speeds of a unit.

That was kind of similar too, since a lot of the terrain denoted was semi-realistic. The hologram displayed the surrounding terrain around the central fort – where he was, he assumed – and the three circles of hexes of space around it. Outside of that, additional hexes could be seen but were shaded grey – two circles of hexes out – and black.

He'd have to ask about that.

Later.

He was a little busy understanding what he was looking at on the map, grabbing pieces of information. He had to admit, they had a pretty damn good strategic location. Right on the water, with a couple of hexes of ocean – or was that sea? – behind them. To the left, hills and mountains, which meant they had a good chance of finding precious metals or gold. Directly ahead, they had a series of plains and to the far right, what looked like a landing shifting down and an isthmus or peninsula – or maybe just a lake? – and a large amount of forests.

Most interestingly, a village marked almost immediately north of them on a straight line across plains. No road between the fort and the village though. There were tiny pennants on the village, grey-brown unlike the dark blue that flew above their keep.

So. A Warlord, an Alchemist, a hexagonal map of the surroundings with a fog of war overlay. And himself, of course.

"I'm supposed to help you build an army, aren't I?" Matt said, looking at Braskar. "This is a damn strategy game, with what? Magical troops that I send out to control land?"

Braskar grinned widely, showing yellowish teeth and a lot of tusk. Irvine sniggered. "Exactly."

Matt palmed his face at the absurdity of it all. Then again, it was probably better for him that this battle for humanity's existence was a damn strategic board game, rather than say a PvP arena. He'd be so much dirt on the ground. At least here, he had a chance.

A good one. It'd been a while since he broke out his board games, but he had been a pretty decent player back in the day.

"Alright, fine. So what kind of troops do I have?" Matt took his hand away from his face, flexing it by his side.

"Touch the keep, boy, and choose," Irvine replied. "And hopefully, you'll choose right. Because I'm not looking forward to dying again."

Well, no pressure there then.

Chapter 3

His fingers brushed the hard light projection, feeling a touch of heat, and then a frisson of energy shot through him. He fell into himself – that was about the only way he could describe it, even now – as information flowed through him. No words, just sense impressions of things that he could choose.

Too much to choose. The first, basic choice was what kind of race he would have, who he would rule. There were multiple species, hundreds of variations available within each species even. As an example, humans were an option but there were a large variety of cultures or civilisations available within.

Someone who had a little more pride in humanity might have stopped there, picked something like the Romans or the Greeks or perhaps the British. Even Tang Dynasty China, where the motherland had been at its medieval peak, before corruption and conquest had driven it away.

That was a thought…

"It's all pre-industrial revolution in here," Matt said out loud. Or at least, he thought he said it out loud. He wasn't sure his mouth was even moving, and his advisors – if they answered – weren't being heard.

Freaky, being both inside his own body and yet, so deep within that he couldn't consciously move anything. But, better to focus. So, no options that were at the industrial revolution stage, which meant that all the fun – and powerful – weaponry that humanity had created was unavailable. No atom bombs to end the fight or multi-kilometer long artillery bombardments.

Pity.

Anyway, humans sucked. Nevermind the ethical complications of what exactly these humans were being pulled into or how they were added to this world. Were they all volunteers like him? Were they people plucked from their lives? Or perhaps, since the gods were in play, drawn from heaven or hell. Or Valhalla?

That'd probably be the most ethically non-dubious resolution. But since he had no idea, he couldn't, wouldn't bet on it.

Also, if he was going to play a damn video game, why go for boring ass humans. And no flouncy, bouncy elves. Well, maybe elf girls, especially if they were Japanese elf girls with their big hearts and love for the protagonist…

Focus!

Saving humanity here.

No elves, no dwarves, no gnomes or small people. In fact, might as well cross out the majority of the basic sapient creatures. Among other things, he wasn't sure he could wait for them to give birth, grow up, and get out there.

That led to another bouncing thought, a question of overall strategy. Was the entire game or set-up a civilization building one or just battle driven? Was he doing civ or total war? That… He needed answers. Whatever all this information flooding into him was, it was not giving him those. Probably what his advisors were for.

But he couldn't ask them.

Pitting will against the damn block that was stopping him from moving was futile, no matter how he struggled. He felt, maybe, a little give, felt his mouth move a little but no words, no sound escaped his lips. Still, he pushed, his head pounding, that fear and anger and confusion that had been blocked off fading a little. As though the more he struggled, the thinner the barrier grew.

Then, another presence, two in his mind.

"My lord, you called?" Braskar's voice in his mind.

"Couldn't even spend two shakes of a rat's tail without us." Irvine now.

Weird, to hear without his ears. Still, that was good. He asked his questions.

"Heroes – like me and Braskar – and you as our Lord are, well, what we are. The servants however are not sentient. They're formations of energy, from what we can tell. Smart enough to take orders, but utterly useless outside of their preprogrammed routes. So choose whatever you want, it's all the same, boy," Irvine replied first.

"And this is a game of conquest and control, my lord. You must build out our keep, form our legions, and conquer the surroundings. Once you find our enemy, we will crush them," Braskar growled, pounding a fist into his hand.

"Oh good…" Matt said.

That simplified his life a lot. A few more quick questions and probing inside the data slew within his mind allowed him to grasp the basics. His initial choice would allow him to create basic troops from the race. It wouldn't make a difference in spawn sizes or whatever, since there was no inherent population cap. So no worries about waiting for children to grow up.

The only limitation was spawn time of the troops he chose to build. He could choose a dragon, for example – and boy were there quite a few different types of dragons available from proto-dragons like wyverns and drakes to real ones coming in all sorts of elements and some weirder variations – but the spawn time of a single unit felt massive. Certainly at least eight to ten times as long as an equivalentish human unit. Maybe more.

Too bad he didn't actually get numbers, but he assumed it had something to do with the variations in unit types and species. Any other time, he would have spent a while more poking around, trying to get more details about the world, but the longer he stewed in the knowledge base, the more the barrier between his emotions and the pain faded. Somehow, he knew he was on a timer – one made up of his life force and sanity.

So, good rather than perfect. His only hope then was that everyone else was going to be stuck doing the same calculus.

In which case, the real question was quality or quantity?

"Evolutions and progression. Can these cultures or species grow stronger? Units change and modify as we go along?" Matt asked suddenly.

"Yes, my lord." A little quieter. "Mostly."

"Purrr-fect."

Then, going for the top end in terms of quality made no sense. That discarded dragons and other massive players like the titans and the like. No need to go for perfection immediately. Especially if evolution was on the table. Better to get something that could build towards it, have pieces on the table and move on.

So, dragonmen and wyrmlings and the like over full-born dragons. There were also elementals in there, along the same line as the dragon creatures.

Or on the opposite end of the table, faster growth creatures. Spinning through the options, he could feel his mind latch onto a few that popped up. Goblins, slimes, ants, and a bunch of semi-sentient insects. Plants too.

Weird. Carnivorous plants made him shudder a little, bringing with it memories of giant, cannibalistic plants singing.

Nope. No plants.

So. Big push and dump a lot of troops out fast, swarming his enemy before they could catch on, or risk a slower build out.

"Is this choice locked in forever then?" Matt asked. Almost always, the quantity species were overtaken by the quality ones in a long-term game. If this entire thing was built out of multiple rounds or he had to conquer an entire world, he was better off – in the long run – with a quality-based purchase.

"Your base choice is always your base," Irvine said. "Why I said choose carefully."

"However, conquests will allow you to pick up additional units." Somehow, Matt could hear the confusion in Braskar's voice. Probably partly due to the hesitation he had while speaking. "It's not all of the units, like a choice? One. Two? Something of that form."

"Good. That gives me more options," Matt replied.

Suddenly, lighter and firmer, Braskar added, "We can get mercenaries."

"And don't forget more Heroes. The kind that can lead fights and aid in expanding the kingdom," Irvine said.

This was becoming more and more familiar to Matt. If they could get additional units and mercenaries, if he could get Heroes, then it seemed that winning the first fight, no matter if they restarted or not, was the safest bet.

Anyway, any balanced game would have ways to balance out even a late game hindrance, if one was smart and could grasp the opportunities as they came up.

The only problem, of course, was that this wasn't a game. As much as it might look like one. Perhaps that's why they killed him to start with. As a stark reminder of the stakes. Worth considering but not an answer to what he wanted to do.

Quantity over quality. Goblins, gremlins, slimes, ants, bees, halflings, ratkin… The options spun through his mind as he enforced his will on the information flow. His head was beginning to throb now, the pain growing with each moment and more as he accessed additional details.

What did he need? Something humanoid was probably best. There were variations of the insect creatures, variations that he could tell meant that he could get humanoid type too. There were disadvantages though, to things that did not have thumbs, that were not bipedal, or had societal building blocks.

Higher recruitment rates, but lower variation in types of units to begin with. Some kind of negative morale modifier for recruited units, in some cases an entire ban on recruiting certain types of other units even. A bunch more negatives that he could feel humming at the corner of his mind.

In the end, he chose not to go with the weird insect or other hive-like creature types. Evolution options, now that he had dipped quickly into a few, showed that they were limited, specialized, and costly. Potentially weird too.

But it wasn't wasted time at least. Because when confronted with the knowledge that these monsters did not have many evolution options, Matt realized he wanted that. Flexibility and volume, those were his watch words.

Pushing his thoughts down that route forced the information flow to shrink, the pain doubling briefly before relief appeared, as he discarded all the other options. Those he had poked at briefly came back to him, and he could not help but look at them, grabbing a quick overview as he skimmed.

Gremlins. Humanoid, tech-oriented later on, able to evolve to different gremlin types. Highly chaotic though, low discipline, low combat morale.

Mimics. Superior number of evolutions. Able to reform themselves into quite possibly the highest number of units. However, extremely aggressive, low discipline, great morale, very slow in progressing actual technology.

Goblins. No, just no.

Slimes. So. Many. Evolutions. No technology options at all. No other negatives or positives off-hand since the specifics depended on the evolution type. Though low damage output to begin with.

Elementals. The base kind were earth elementals. Slow to produce, tough units, not a huge variety. But the evolutionary path from there allowed him to pick at more things. Fewer tech options though in the future, but societal progression was there.

Gnolls. Quite a variety of variations, but they had a decent number of evolutions, though it was the least of the humanoids. Slower unit recruitment, though they did more damage individually. Bonuses for fighting in groups too, which helped, and no negatives in terms of societal or tech structures.

And then there were kobolds. Two kinds. One was the humanoid, scrawny-bodied kind that evolved into demonic things, just like the imps that were another option. And then there were the dragon wannabes. Scaled creatures, slower reproduction than most, though better than the gnolls. More batchy, it seemed. Good variety of units, low damage though and a minor negative on social and tech areas.

He could have kept looking, but the pain was coming back. And Matt knew, instinctively, there were more choices to be made.

No more time. It'd be dumb to die, here and now, before he even got started.

So he made his decision and willed it at the pain, only for it to disappear and then return with a vengeance moments later.

His scream echoed, through this dream world and the next.

Chapter 4

Options. He could feel them pressing down upon his mind, demanding he make a decision. He should have expected something like this, what with the way the damn system loading into his mind worked. He wanted to pick a more esoteric ability, something that looked innocuous at first unless you read a lot of anime or science fiction or fantasy, the kind of game breaking option that would let him overwhelm everyone else.

Except, if it was that easy, why wouldn't everyone else make those choices? Sometimes, the esoteric choices that gave the protagonist an ability that defied the gods were just a trap for everyone else. Stories were great, but what the stories were never about were the million and one fools who tried the same thing and failed.

And since everyone thought they were the heroes in their own story, it meant that you could never really know if making a brave or foolish choice was the point.

More importantly, part of the reason he was going with a fast recruitment species was because he wanted to establish a wide base of power. Esoteric powers might be interesting, but if they also came with finicky uses – like difficulty figuring out how to manipulate gravity or space or time properly – then his entire plan would fail from the start.

So. No weird elementals. Because that was what he had chosen in the end, elementals. More complex than slimes or mimics, but not as straightforward as something like the humanoids. He knew he could even choose or push them towards being humanoid elementals in the future, but that was later.

Right now, he needed to choose an element. It wouldn't be the only one he would ever get to choose. He could feel that. It was just a starting point, until it was time to evolve his species once more. When that happened, maybe he would have time to play with stranger options.

Simple. Time for simple.

"Recommendations?" Matt shot to his advisors. He could tell that they had sensed it when he had made his decision.

"The kobolds, if you had asked before," Irvine grumbled. "But a metal elemental would be good. If you got something semi-precious, we might be able to shore up our treasury immediately."

"At least he did not choose the slimes. Snotty useless things," Braskar rumbled. "This is a decent choice and could give us a significant advantage in the future. Metal is reasonable, but something hard. Earth might be slower, but their strength could be useful."

"Fire?" Matt mused out loud.

"No!" Both advisors shouted the word together.

"Owww. Fine. But why?"

"Undisciplined at best would be my assumption. Most elementals are not smart. The amount of damage a fire elemental could do does not bear thinking about. Without proper discipline, it would be a danger to us," Braskar said.

"I bet they'd burn down the keep before we even get started," Irvine said. "Then what would we do?"

"No water then because we need to expand upwards and we're lacking ships or any naval vessels for now. If this was an island, that might make sense," Matt said, thinking out loud. "Air is too airy." He giggled a little at the pun, the pain driving him a little loopy. "What else is there?"

"Those are the major elements. Earth, air, fire, water." Irvine harrumphed.

"Metal isn't an element in that, of course, but it is a good substitute for earth. Lava has the same problem as fire. Mud perhaps? Ash, smoke, or the other options might make good units though," Braskar said.

"Depends on what those units have to do," Irvine pointed out. "Useless if they need to grab or hold anything."

Matt had grown silent, letting the pair argue about the various merits. His own mind was skimming and skipping, though the comment about major elements… it was wrong. There were five elements, and air was not part of them. In fact, if looked at that way, that might be the best elemental of all.

Then again, he had said no to plant things before. But these weren't really plants, more the concept of a plant, the very element of plants.

It shouldn't have made a difference.

It did.

He made his decision, before his brain leaked out of his ears, hoping he was doing it right. Wood elementals were chosen, and the world twisted around him again. He lurched within his own mind, spinning around as information fled and then returned.

"Wood, my lord? An interesting choice, but I can work with that."

"Red ink! I ask for gold or silver, I get wood."

Matt found no time to answer them for he could feel his mind buckling. More choices again, always more choices. What kind of body? He knew there were arguments that bipedal was not the best option, that there might be variations, but he couldn't remember them. Not right now.

Whatever. Bipedal wood elementals would do.

Gone were the living plants, the balls of living ivy, the crawling ivy, the poisonous spore form, flowering and semi-sapient root vegetables. All those options, gone like tears in the rain, never to come back.

Nevermind.

The pain in his head had faded, the choice of form having relieved a lot of the pressure. All those myriad options had been pressing down on him, and now he had a few less to work with. In fact, there were only three more options, and each of them were connected. Like assigning points on a trigram that tugged and pulled the other points closer as you pulled on one end.

Body, Mind, Spirit.

The yogis were wrong. You couldn't have all three. Had to give up one or the other, at least in this scenario. Nothing for it but decide. Another portion of his mind pulled information that had been shoved into him to the forefront before he could pluck at the data.

Wood elementals – inherently high Body, good Spirit, lousy Mind. The points he was allocating were enhancements on the base, like a multiplication table or something. Assign too low on one thing, and he'd have dumber than rocks tree elementals.

He could almost hear Braskar pleading with him not to do that. Irvine was quiet, probably had given up at this point. Though, maybe a high Body might mean more adaptability.

Oh. It did.

More instinctual knowledge that did not come to the forefront till he actually thought the question. But that might mean he could create fruit-laying tree elementals. Or warp the forest to grow thorns that could explode and kill.

Was he playing the game equivalent of Plant Wars?

No, no. He had humanoid wood elementals that could move. He was safe. Anyway, what were they going to do if he wasn't? Kill him?

Too late.

He really was getting loopy. Needed to make a decision soon. So, increase Mind. Increase Body, because he wanted wood for its adaptability, its ability to change and alter. He wasn't sure what he was giving up, by lowering their Spirit.

Hello weird knowledge?

Nothing?

Fine.

He locked in the decision after shoving the points of the triangle as best he could. Felt a mental jerk – not Al from Physics class who always had the answer – as the information fled him. Leaving him reeling in his own mind before he was catapulted backwards.

Out of his own soul back into the real world. Feeling like twelve miles of bad road, sweating and cursing, head pounding.

They didn't even buy him dinner after using him so roughly.

Chapter 5

Coming to himself, Matt pushed himself upwards. The pain was receding, pulled back behind the shadow curtain around his soul and feelings. He found himself straightening and wiping at his nose, only to stare at the blood that had dribbled from it. A cloth was shoved in his direction by Irvine, which made Matt blink dumbly with painful, crusty eyes.

"Take it. You need to clean that face. It wasn't much of a looker before, but now…" Irvine shuddered.

"Bathroom?"

A finger pointed to a nearby door, and Matt staggered within. He found a familiar looking abode, with an actual toilet and taps, so he yanked on the handle to watch as liquid splashed out. Moments later, he had his face buried in the water, squinting around the cold shock to watch as the water pinked up. Blood had come not just from his nose but his eyes too.

Eventually, the water stopped running red and pink, and he hauled his face upwards. Magical taps and running water, but the mirror they had was a yellow oval of beaten copper that distorted and twisted the face he saw looking back at him.

Another shock to the system, one that sent shivers down his spine.

The person staring back at him over the other side, that wasn't him. Couldn't be, yet he knew it was. At least he looked Asian, the slant of the eyes a little more northern Chinese or Korean than his own southern Chinese roots had been. Taller too – again, like the northern Chinese. That he didn't mind. Not much in terms of muscle mass though, but that was fine.

Old. Mid thirties if he would have guessed, but the body felt fine. No aches, no pains, nothing troubling him at all. He wasn't even hungry. Yet.

Then another thought struck him, and, making sure the door was closed and locked, he made use of the washroom's other facilities. He might have handled it a little longer than strictly necessary, but a man had to have some priorities.

Admittedly, so far the denizens of this keep were an orc, an old man, and a bunch of trees. Not exactly prime dating material, no matter your orientation.

Laughing a little at himself, Matt managed to make his way out. The tunic and draw string pants getup was not too hard to work out, even if the fabric itself was a lot coarser than he preferred. He wasn't even certain what kind of material it was beyond not silk or cotton or polyester.

"My lord, are you feeling better?" Braskar interrupted his thoughts when he strode back out.

"I am."

"Good. Looks like you making the choices has given us more options on our end," Irvine said quickly. "I now have access to information on our resources, income flow, and builds."

"Builds?" Matt said.

"Builds." Irvine nodded. "Units are Braskar, but the buildings needed to build the units are mine."

"I have recommendations on unit builds available, my lord. I would recommend we begin unit production immediately," Braskar said. "We only have a single unit available right now."

"Just be happy we have any at all," Irvine said. "We could have gotten none, and then where would we be?"

"Shit," Matt muttered.

"My lord?" Braskar asked worriedly.

"If I'd known we were guaranteed a unit, I might have gone with a dragon." Matt opened his hand wide. "Can you imagine?"

Braskar followed up with a big grin before his face fell. "Too late now, my lord." He waved to the table, continuing. "But if you'll review the information we have, we can begin."

Matt looked to the table as requested, eyes widening as he noted a new block of hovering information. It wasn't much, but it clarified almost everything that he had chosen. So simple, considering how much pain he had been put through.

Species: Wood Elemental – Bipedal (Least)
Mind: 6
Body: 8
Spirit: 3
Available Units: Woodlings

"Woodlings?" Matt said out loud curiously. As though on command, the table flickered, the map disappearing to be replaced by a rotating figure of a bipedal, wood creature. It looked nothing more than a five-foot tall, thin, ashen sapling with branch arms and two stumpy legs. It had wide, glowing openings for its eyes and mouth but lacked a nose or even a hint of one.

Next to the image, further information in text format appeared.

Unit Name: Woodlings
Type: Wood Elemental
Tier: Lesser Tier I
Number: 8
Movement: 1
Cost: 20 Gold
Melee Attack: 6

Melee Defense: 12

Ranged Attack: 0

Ranged Defense: 18

Hit Points: 8

Speed: 5

Special Abilities: Grow, Harden

Vulnerabilities: Fire (Low)

Growth Potential: Medium

"I…" Matt cast a helpless look at Braskar as he stared at the detailed information. Some of those he understood, though without context he had no idea if a Melee Attack of 6 was good or bad. Was that straight damage? Did that contest Defense then, and thus his own units could not defeat themselves? Did a point in Melee Attack mean a point of Hit Points was removed? And what was the difference between Movement and Speed?

"Ah, interesting," Braskar finished looking it over. "The woodling is our basic unit. Very high defense, mediocre attack." He paused, looking into midair before giving himself a firm nod. "It will be a trend for our units, unless we specialize in that." Eyes flicking downwards, he continued. "Battle statistics are relatively simplistic. Attack contests defense, whatever is left over is applied against resistances and then applied to hit points. Movement is based on hexes, speed is combat speed. The higher the speed rating, the better."

"What about the specials? I get the vulnerability," Matt said.

"Grow is a passive boost. We have eight woodlings per unit. When we lose individual woodlings, eventually the units are replaced through natural replenishment. Grow boosts the rate of replenishment. So long as a unit isn't destroyed entirely, they'll eventually return to full strength," Braskar said. "If we park them inside a location, like a keep, that replenishment rate obviously increases."

Matt nodded. All of that made sense.

"As for Harden, it's a defensive Skill. Doubles their defense for a short period." Braskar stared into space again before nodding slowly. "We don't get to control that unless I'm – or another Hero is – with the unit. Otherwise, they choose."

"So the dumb trees get to choose?" Irvine scoffed.

"Yes," Braskar said repressingly. "It's a good thing our Lord increased their base Mind rating, no?"

Irvine just muttered something under his breath.

"Okay, enough." Matt waved them quiet. A moment later, reacting to the motion of his hands, the unit information disappeared, replaced by the keep once more. Staring at it, Matt spotted a few interesting things, including a new section in the keep itself that he could only describe as a tiny grove.

Reaching out, his fingers touched the grove. For a moment, his fingers felt as though they had touched something. Like a soap bubble, but even more ephemeral. Then, the hologram changed again, the grove increasing in size.

Name: Grove

Building Type: Barracks

Tier: Lesser Tier I

Units Available to Produce: Woodlings (20/4)

Units in Production: None

All self-explanatory except those last numbers. Which he asked about, of course.

"Gold cost and production time." This time it was Irvine who spoke, the thin man grinning at Braskar. "We have two hundred gold right now."

"Nice. So we can produce ten of them." Matt paused. "In four days?"

"Yes."

"Damn, that's fast."

"It seems that everything is accelerated here," Braskar replied, gesturing down at the table where the map used to be. "And weirdly off-scale."

"What do you mean?" Matt said.

"I'm certain that there's no reason it should take the units three days to march to the village," Braskar replied. "But yet, we're forced to allow for that."

"Huh…" Matt blinked, then shook his head. "Whatever." Weirdness was just part of this world.

"Yes, exactly. And before you spend all our gold, you better look at what else we can build."

"We can build more?" Matt said, surprised.

"Yes," Irvine snapped. "If you let me speak, you'd know that."

"Right, right. Sorry." He waved for the crochety old man to go on.

"You have two hundred gold to start. Production of gold is low though. You get five gold a day." As if he could see Matt thinking it, he cut the man off. "Yes, exactly enough to keep putting out one new unit each time it comes up. Now, hush."

"I didn't say anything!" Matt protested.

"You're thinking so loud, I can see it on your face." A slight pause. "Do you play poker?"

"No."

"Probably best for us…" muttered Irvine.

"Irvine," Braskar rumbled.

"I got it, I got it. We got five options for building. I can sense there are more options, but here's what we got." A spotted hand waved at the table, and then it shifted, the map disappearing once more. Five new building types appeared, hovering in the space, even as Irvine muttered, "Got to fix that. Having the map disappear all the time is bad…"

"Agreed. You figure that out…" Matt said, leaning forwards so he could read the unit information better.

Time to see what they could do about improving the keep. And at some point, figuring out what their overall objective was.

If it wasn't *kill them all and let god sort out the innocent.*

Chapter 6

Five floating construction pieces. It was a weird mixture, since on one hand, there was the Grove itself, except this time more robust, more plentiful with bigger trees. And on the opposite spectrum, what he could only describe as a streetside stall. Nature and civilization mashed together.

Upgrade Available: Grove (II)
Building Type: Barracks
Tier: Lesser Tier II
Units Available to Produce: Woodlings (II) (25/5)
Cost: 125
Production Time: 8 days

"Doesn't look like much of an upgrade," Matt said. A quick probe got the map to shift, pulling up the new woodlings II. Longer production time but an overall increase of two points to their attributes. That was it really, other than a graphical change that had them looking bigger. "That it?"

"Yes," Braskar rumbled. "The woodlings will just grow stronger, as we upgrade the Grove."

"The Grove can be upgraded further. I can feel the system, and once we get it high enough, it'll be able to build different unit types," Irvine said.

"Right, right," Matt muttered, turning his attention to the next map by flicking the upgraded woodling away.

He moved on to next floating spot, which was, strangely enough, just an open space. No information on it at the moment. It took Matt prodding it for details to come up. And then he was left with a simple question.

"Squirting cucumber, sandbox trees, or firecracker flowers?" Matt did try to keep a straight face, but the idea of the cucumbers… "Well. It seems to have safe search on."

"What?" Braskar said. Irvine on the other hand was laughing softly.

"I take it where you come from, there's no such thing as the Internet and Rule 34?"

"My lord…"

Matt waved the man's protests away. No. Better to focus. Ranged units would be good for their overall unit strength. In fact, his favorite tactic when playing these games was a strong, highly defensive melee frontline and a powerful ranged group that just tore up the enemy.

Something to consider, but for later. Most importantly, it seemed building a new building itself was going to cost him his entire treasury.

"Expensive…" Matt muttered. If he bought it now, he might not have a lot of funds to actually build a new unit, what with only getting five gold a day. Depending on how fast it took to build, that'd be a real gamble.

"I would recommend later, my lord," Braskar rumbled. "We must gain control of our surroundings first."

"Fair…" Matt said, but he chose to put off making any strategic decisions yet. No. Better to know his options, which meant looking at the other two buildings.

The roadside stall was a surprise. He would never have expected it to be the way to increase monetary production.

Structure Available: Stall

Building Type: Treasury

Tier: Lesser Tier I

Benefit: +5 Gold Per Day

Cost: 100 Gold

Production Time: 5 days

"That's bloody expensive," Matt spluttered.

"More gold is always better," Irvine said. "The earlier we can increase our monetary lead, the better."

"Unless we get crushed beforehand," Braskar rumbled.

"Or we just get crushed later!"

"Enough," Matt snapped, quieting the two. How did people work when everyone wanted their say? He could never understand it, not even in the real world.

One last building. This was a dome, a rather slipshod, murky glass-walled, earth-barricaded greenhouse. It looked like some medieval inventor had heard of the idea of a greenhouse and then threw it all together, even going so far as to have included flues for smoke and heating of the earth itself during winter months.

Did they have winter months here? Was he going to even be alive by the time winter arrived?

Structure Available: Basic Greenhouse

Building Type: Evolutionary

Tier: Lesser Tier I

Benefit: Allows Research into new unit types and evolutions

Cost: 500 Gold

Production Time: 20 days

"Well, that's a wash," Matt said immediately. No point even considering buying that, especially considering how little funds he had. Irvine's point about getting more funds now was beginning to look more and more important.

The smile that Irvine was showcasing said that the man knew his point had been made.

"Alright, so I think it's pretty clear we should get the Stall to begin with. It doesn't wipe our funds entirely and we'd earn back what we spent in twenty days, which is good." Matt paused, then looked at Irvine. "Is there anything else we can do to get funds? Resources?"

The old man nodded, waving his hand at the table. Once more, the buildings collapsed back inwards, the light within the room flickering a little before the map of the surroundings came back once more. More finger wiggling, the man going so far as to chew on the corner of his lips and beard before, suddenly, little dots appeared on the map.

Peering closer, Matt slowly registered that they were resource symbols. Fish on the water, which probably indicated that with the right kind of buildings he would have fish to trade. Or perhaps to eat. Depended on the kind of game they were looking at playing. Then, further up, lumber on the forest hex. Nothing on the plains at all though.

"So, fish and lumber?" Matt asked, pointing at the two symbols respectively.

"Yes. We do not know what that means, though the lumber I assume is the minimum required for production," Irvine said.

"Ah…" Matt hesitated, then bulled on. He didn't need exact details right now, just general overview. "I'm assuming we're at five gold because that's what the keep is producing." He gestured downwards. "Is there any other way to increase gold production?"

"It's possible if the keep grows, so will its base amount." Irvine touched his head. "I've not much information on that, I admit."

"Any idea how we do that?"

Irvine just shrugged. Matt growled, though if he was irritated with the old man or just in general, he was not certain.

"If I had to guess, it is likely available after we reach a number of prerequisite builds, my lord." Braskar rumbled.

"Right. Okay, any other ideas about the resources?"

"Exactly what they are. Food and lumber, of course," Irvine said. "You daft?"

"No. Nor do I like being insulted," Matt snapped. He made sure to meet Irvine's eyes and wait for the irritable old man to break and look away first, muttering a soft apology, before he went on. "I need more than just guesses if you have it. That's your role here, after all."

"Well, I don't know what more I can say. It's not like I have much more information."

"More than me." Matt smiled grimly and then sighed. "Fine, we're stuck with what we have. Forest and plants, all the way. Good position at least."

"It does seem that way, my lord."

"And the village?" Matt pointed at the village hex, which had a single gold coin on it. "Can we build a trade route, increase our gold that way? Or do we have to conquer it."

"We must conquer it, my lord," Braskar said. "It is what I would suggest we do immediately."

"With our single unit?" Matt said. "Can we do that?"

"Only one way to tell." This time, the grin was full of teeth and set Matt shivering. It seemed that his man was just a little on the bloodthirsty side.

"Alright, I think I have it." Matt considered, reviewing everything he had learnt. He'd need to make some decisions very soon, to get things moving. And then, well… Then he'd have to see what else this world had to offer him.

"Let's get working."

Chapter 7

Matt pushed away from the table, choosing to walk. He wasn't sure if it was just because it was his first time being in charge and being able to pace wherever he wanted or because this body was naturally antsy, but he felt the need to move to get his mind working.

"Right. Strategy before purchasing. We're going for fast replication. We want to spread and spread fast, to gain control of as much land and learn as we want. That means we should start building units immediately, nevermind the other concerns and upgrades."

"My lord…"

"Wait, let me talk this out. Then object," Matt said, interrupting Braskar. "We can view up to three hexes away, we seem to be able to move one hex. That means if we start producing right now, there's some minor risk of someone being close by and coming in to attack us, but we can always pull our unit back if we see that happening."

"But we'll have only one unit here. And they might have more than one," Irvine said.

"Yeah, but walls. Those will help." Matt shook his head. "No, building up a unit early and sending the one we have should be safe enough. We might not want to have more than one scouting unit out, but the first can get moving."

"The village?" Braskar rumbled.

"That's not scouting," Irvine pointed out.

"It is gold though."

The older man let out a low hum of agreement.

"Right. Gold. That's got to be our next upgrade. Getting more funds early is a non-brainer," Matt said, then frowned. "It's so obvious, I'm now wondering if there's a trick. A catch…" He stilled, thinking hard as he tried to find a reason why he shouldn't get a Stall now.

"It's possible that upgrading the Grove will provide powerful footsoldiers that will allow us to conquer and contain the surrounding areas," Braskar offered hesitantly. "Especially if they are close."

"Right, doubling down on the fast unit production." Matt nodded. "We don't have a lot of funds either, so if we spend it all there, we'll be forced to wait longer for a return."

"Ranged units would make us a lot safer. Your melee units can't do much for defense," Irvine pointed out.

"Another good point…" Then Matt shook his head. "Still, I think we're going with the obvious. I might be wrong, but I think we need to plan for a longer-term game than a complete blitzkrieg."

"Very well," Braskar said. "We can delay the upgrade and ranged units until later." He hesitated before gesturing at the table. "If we take an aggressive, expansionist stance now, it will suit your initial fast unit production strategy."

"And more gold now is better. We'll know more once we have it built," Irvine said. Then, reluctantly, he added, "I approve."

"Good." Matt strode over, put his hand back on the table and then spent a few minutes working out how to implement his plan. Moving the unit was easy enough and something that Braskar took care of but applying the production recommendation – which even let him queue up two additional units, of which he chose to do one – and beginning construction required his implementation.

Once all of the decisions were made and locked in, Matt frowned. "Hey, this gold."

"Yes?" Irvine said cautiously.

"Where is it?"

"Why?" Irvine grew even more suspicious.

In answer, Matt gave him a wide grin.

***

"Owww… so that's a lot harder than it looks," Matt said, rolling off the piles of coins in the treasury. When he had spotted the gold in sacks on the ground, he had been taken by an impulse to fling himself at it. Perhaps he was still reeling from the earlier brain damage, but not a moment before the thought had arrived that he implemented it, to his now bruised chest's sadness.

"We're doomed," Irvine intoned morosely.

"Lighten up, man," Matt said, standing up. "So, what should we be doing? We have a day left."

Irvine frowned, watching as Matt pocketed one of the coins, slipping it into his pouch before walking out. He coughed into his hand, staring hard at Matt's pouch.

"I'm the Lord, right?"

"Yes."

"Then I should have some walking around money." Matt said the words as though it was a self-evident set of facts.

Irvine looked intensely unhappy, but eventually he swung the treasury door closed, locking it with a large key that he then slipped back under his tunic. Matt frowned as he watched the action, touching his own chest, which had no such key.

"Hey, shouldn't I have one?"

"One what?"

"Key."

Irvine frowned even more, reaching out to tug at the bottom of his wispy beard. He looked around, but since Braskar was downstairs, dealing with the unit of woodlings that was moving out, he was left alone with Matt. Eventually, after one last tug, he released it and let out a long sigh.

"You are the Lord of the keep. You may access any room by just willing it," Irvine said reluctantly.

"Really?" Matt paused, then looked at the door.

It did not open.

"You must will it. Sometimes, vocal commands sharpen the will. Especially useful for the unfocused," Irvine said.

"You calling me unfocused?" Matt growled, continuing to glare at the door.

Silence greeted his challenge, and Matt strained his thoughts, trying to make it open. Face screwed up like he was attempting to dislodge a particularly stubborn dangler, he finally just slapped the door. The motion seemed to be what was required, the door swinging open with a loud click.

"Hah!"

"Yes. Brute force is another method," said Irvine dryly.

Shaking his head, Matt tugged the door close. He didn't even need to will it locked, as a casual shove showed.

"It's good to be king."

"You are the Lord of the keep, not a king," Irvines said repressingly.

"What's the difference?" Matt said, strolling off down the stone hallway they were within. He hoped that whatever upgrades that were needed to the keep were magically induced like everything else, otherwise he could not imagine how they were intending to pull down the stone keep and put up something new. Did it not take multiple years for such things to happen back in medieval times?

Then again, woodlings.

"A king requires a kingdom. A kingdom requires subjects." Irvine gestured around him. "Preferably more than two."

That brought Matt to a stop, and he spun to look at Irvine. "There aren't servants? Cooks? Stablehands? People to tend the Grove?"

Irvine shook his head. "Not in the sense of real individuals like us." The older man's lips thinned. "You'll see when you meet them. I believe only advisors, Heroes, will be truly intelligent."

Frowning, Matt continued to walk the keep. Since he had no true idea of what he needed to do, he assumed that spending some time getting to know the keep itself and the surroundings would be a good start. He certainly did not feel like he had any special abilities, no magical or lordly powers to call upon. Mostly, he just felt human and slightly off-balance. He assumed that last was from dying and then being resurrected in a new body, but it might be the intense pain he had suffered or the travel through whatever dimension.

All in all, not a great experience.

Matt continued to question Irvine as he wandered the keep, noting how the map itself had fooled him in his expectations. The keep had looked much larger on the map, taking up the entirety of the hex it had been placed upon. Yet, walking it, he began to realise that the hex map was but a representation of the world itself, similar to a subway map.

Four floors, his own room just below the map room on the top floor, his own private room a level beneath it along with a washroom and a closet with space for weapons and armour. The second floor had an empty armoury, the treasury room, and four bedrooms along with a shared bathroom, all meant for his advisors. The ground floor was the communal dining room, the kitchen, and the main hall all rolled into one.

It was as he poked his head into one of the empty rooms on the second floor that Matt ran into one of the ghostly servants. They were a strange mixture of wood elemental, humanoid maidenservant, and specter, like a half-shaded caricature that undertook the tasks but that, when Matt attempted to touch, his hand passed right through.

"Overflowing toner…" Matt blinked. "That's creepy."

"This toner…" Irvine said slowly. "What is it?"

"Oh, you know, photocopier toner… Just the bane of my existence at an old job. The damn place was too cheap to get proper toner, so we had to buy cheap replacement ones and then actually fill the toner cartridges ourselves. Stained more than one shirt and they never paid me back for it," Matt said.

"But what is a photocopier?"

That brought Matt to a stop halfway down the stairs to the ground floor. He turned to look up at Irvine, searching the man's face for something, anything. Eventually, he spoke slowly, "You don't know what a photocopier is?"

"No."

"What ummm… year were you taken from Earth?"

"1443, of course."

"They pulled you from nearly six hundred years in the past!" Matt could not help but shout.

The older man could only shrug, leaving Matt stymied. He had no idea what to say about that or do about it. If there was anything to do.

After all, Braskar was an orc, Irvine was a man from the past – who seemed to know modern idioms for the most part – and he… he was the supposed champion of the world.

"We are in soo much trouble."

Then, forcing himself onwards, Matt kept walking. After all, this was the least impressive surprise he'd faced in the last day.

Okay, second least impressive surprise. Who knew that cartoons lied to you about swimming through gold.

Chapter 8

No horses. No barracks or training grounds. Or not a traditional one. Not that Matt knew what traditional barracks looked like, but he was certain they did not consist of a bunch of trees and open pits of churned earth that his units were meant to climb into. By the time he had made his way downstairs, the woodlings weren't even around for him to inspect, having already marched out of the open gates, ghostly figures holding the doors open for them. All he got was a sight of their backs as they tromped down the field, Braskar standing beside the main gates looking longingly after them.

"Not going with them?" Matt said, stepping up onto the ramparts to lean against the wooden palisade walls and question his military advisor.

"My place is with you," Braskar said.

"Seems to me, your place is winning my wars," Matt said, cocking his head to the side. Something he had realized, after spending some time actually getting settled into his mind, was that both Irvine and Braskar had character sheets. Information that he could, if he concentrated on it, call forth.

Braskar (Level 1 Warlord)

Specialty: Military Leadership

Skills: Inspiring Aura, Rage

Experience: 0/100

Attack: 18

Defense: 12

Power: 4

Knowledge: 8

"I should advise you about our next steps," Braskar rumbled.

"Don't need it. We have three more days before we can build anything else, we'll have ummm…"

"Ninety-five gold," Irvine supplied.

"Right, that, and I'll decide what to build next after that. Probably another unit of melee fighters really, so that we have at least two units free. Maybe send the second one to look at those hills in the far side – or set up an outpost to the east," Matt said.

"Why not use our initial unit?" Braskar rumbled.

"Because it'll need to heal up after the fight for the village," Matt said. "We might need them to hold and safeguard the village or to keep them for control anyway."

"And if we don't?" the orc asked.

"Then I'll be wrong and we can make a different decision." Matt shook his head. "Probably send them north then." He jerked a finger backwards, to where the beach was. "At some point, we'll hopefully be able to exploit the sea, possibly after we finish the Stall."

"And my ranged units?" Braskar said, having turned fully to look at Matt.

"Possibly after we get our second melee unit built. I do want them," Matt replied. "But it's expensive, and there's a lot to build. As you said, we're building fast and exploring, so getting more melee units out first is the way to go. If we can control the forest over there to increase our evolution possibilities, that might be the way to go."

Again, the orc fell silent before he spoke up. "So you think I'm better off with the unit?"

"If we lose them, we'll be pushed back even further. I need someone who can make the right call when they reach the village and while I'm assuming I can do so via the map…" Matt shrugged. "I'm not exactly looking forward to hanging out waiting the entire day till I get alerted."

"I see."

Irvine snorted. "He's not wrong. You could also do with the experience too. You don't get it just because you exist, like I do."

That made Matt glance over to Irvine, taking in his details. Similar to the way the information of the races had come to him, he could glean much of the details that showed on his two advisors' status screens. Not that it was particularly complicated.

Irvine (Level 1 Alchemist)
Specialty: Alchemy
Skills: Alchemical Concoction, Burst Production
Experience: 0/100

Attack: 6
Defense: 9
Power: 11
Knowledge: 18

Specialties and Classes were what they did, Skills were just that. Attack and Defense were obviously the same as the unit information – though why there wasn't a ranged option, he was not certain. Perhaps the default was melee and if it was ranged, they'd add something under Skills? That felt right.

Power was magical power, which he wasn't entirely certain about how that played out, but Knowledge tied to magical power and indicated the kinds of things they could do with their magic. In this case, alchemy for Irvine and not much at all for Braskar.

Really, looking at Braskar, it was rather obvious that the man needed to be out there, fighting wars, exploring rather than stuck back in here. At least Irvine could do something in here, though he'd have to poke the man about what Alchemical Concoction and Burst Production were.

But first, the Warlord.

"He's right. Time for you to get going," Matt said, waving his hand outwards. "Go. Level. You'll be more use to me out there. I don't really need an advisor, I got this."

"Are you certain?"

"Yes." Matt touched his hand, before he shook his head. "Morning. We'll talk more again in the morning in the map room. I get the feeling that isn't hard."

Braskar nodded, reluctance clearing once a decision was made. He grinned, lowering himself to the floor of the palisade wall, putting one hand on the edge and then letting himself drop over the side, swinging a little before he let himself fall the rest of the way, absorbing the drop with a flex of his legs. Then, he was off, running, somehow conjuring a massive axe to his back between dropping off the edge of the wall and running out of the gates.

Matt would have questioned it, if not for the entire absurdity of his current situation. He watched the orc lope into the distance before he turned to stare at Irvine.

"So, what's Alchemical Concoction?"

"What, no foreplay, no how am I or what my plans are?" Irvine said.

"No."

Irvine let out a long huff, blowing at the beard around his lips before he threw his hands up. "Fine, fine. Whatever. It's a Skill. I was going to work on it, after you were done today."

Something in the way that Irvine said it, the way he refused to look at him, made Matt think that he really wasn't going to. Making a mental note to keep a closer eye on the man, he continued. "What does it do?"

"Potions. I think."

"You think?"

Another elaborate shrug. "I haven't been here much longer than you, damn it."

"Right, right." Matt considered, then nodded. "Alright, fine. Go and test it out, tell me what the results are. I am going to see if I can figure out what the rest of Braskar's abilities are, though I think I can guess."

"Guess." Irvine shook his head, but he chose not to actually comment further as he hurried away from Matt.

Leaving the ostensible Lord of the keep alone, without a clue what he was supposed to do.

"Now, I wonder if I have a status screen of my own?" Matt mused.

Leaning back against the wall, he started mentally prodding his own mind, trying to figure that one out. Because hell, if it was a game and everyone had special Skills, maybe he did too.

That'd be a nice change.

***

Wandering the keep, poking his nose in everywhere, and then stealing the food that the ghostly servants made satisfied his culinary cravings. However, no matter how he pushed himself, prodded at his mind, and conjured terms, none of it worked.

"No special Skills for me." Matt sighed, leaning against one of the trees that was growing in the Grove, staring outwards. He could almost feel the tree growing, forming behind his back. He was now somewhat at a loss of what to do.

Sure, there was some logic to the point of potentially training himself in a martial art. Except he had sent away the only person who could train him. In addition, scarily enough, he was pretty certain that if he did have the ability to call up his base stats and compared them to the stats of someone like Braskar, he would be significantly overshadowed.

In a world of magic and auras, of Skills and Experience, a normal person would easily be overshadowed and overwhelmed. No matter if he was an Olympic fencer, he would still easily be beaten within a few Levels by everyone else around him. If not before he started.

So, knowing that…

"What else can I do?" There was no answer, not from the tree growing behind him, not from the ghostly apparitions that drifted through the keep on their errands, not from the intrinsic knowledge that had been sunk into his brain.

Well, what was his job? What did he know? He was the Lord of the keep. His job was to beat whatever monsters were out there, win, and keep humanity from dying. It seemed that doing so was via a command and conquer type game with units being created and sent out.

Outside of that, he had Heroes or advisors that he could utilize and…

Well, not much else.

"If that's the case, I guess I should go poke at that map more." After all, it wasn't as though he had anything better to do. If his job was taking care of the map, deciding what and where to deploy his resources, then thinking about that, optimizing his builds with as much information as he could get from whatever sat in his brain and what showed up on the map was the smart thing to do.

With a long sigh, Matt pushed himself off the tree, giving it a pat.

"Time to do more paperwork." A slight hesitation, then he added to the tree, "Not actual paperwork with paper, mind you. So, you know, not killing any of your friends." Then, slower. "Though actual paper for taking notes might be good…"

Deciding perhaps this discussion was best held somewhere else, he hurried off. Just in case he did need to find some paper.

Chapter 9

Days. Three days to be exact before Matt had something more to do than just wait. It took him less than a day to realise that there was little more to be gained from the map or the information available to him. Left with nothing to do, not even a library and certainly no internet connection available, Matt took to walking the keep grounds and surroundings.

It was the morning of the third day, Braskar and the woodlings having arrived near the village the night before, that Matt found himself with a decision to make.

"You're saying that the village won't let you in?" Matt said. "But there's no wall, right?"

"No wall, but there's a militia blocking our way," Braskar said. "If we want to take the village, we'll have to beat them."

"How strong are they?" Matt asked.

"Uncertain," Braskar replied. "You can see what we see."

"Exactly the same?" Matt said, reading out what he saw on the map, the small unit figurine that stood outside the village blinking before him.

Type: Militia Unit

Tier: Lesser Tier I

Number: 6

Movement: 1

Melee Attack: Very Low

Melee Defense: Very Low

Ranged Attack: None

Ranged Defense: Low

Hit Points: Low

Speed: Medium

Special Abilities: Unknown

Vulnerabilities: Unknown

"Yes."

"And what are we?" Matt muttered, though he didn't bother to wait for a reply. He knew Braskar had no more idea than he did. "Nevermind. Can we win, in your estimation?"

"Yes." Very firm, very fast the reply came.

Now, Matt hesitated. His mind could not help but turn to the answer, to the fact that they spoke of conquering an independent village. He would be ordering an attack on a neutral third party – because that was what they were, from everything that the map and Braskar had said – for nothing more than an advantage.

In anything but a game, that would make him the bad guy. But here…

"What of the militia? Are they like our woodlings? Our servants?" Matt asked now, uncertain.

"As best I can tell," Braskar replied. "I can't get too close or else this battle will definitely begin. But they've been standing there since we arrived last night."

"It doesn't matter," Irvine said by my side, hand flat on the table. "We need the gold and resources. We need you to expand the city. So do it."

"And if those are real people?"

"Too bad, so sad."

"What are you, five?" Matt muttered, but even so, he knew Irvine was not wrong. They needed the village, and this contest would likely require him to do more than conquer apparitions conjured by the system before it was done.

This was the easy start.

"Do it," Matt said firmly. Then, lifting his hand off the table to cut the connection, he leaned back in the chair to watch what was to happen.

He could only hope that Braskar was right, and they were about to win this easily.

***

Braskar licked his lips again, his tongue dry. He reached for the water pouch by his side, sipping lightly on the water and swishing it around before spitting the mouthful out. Then he took a longer drink, though not too much. Didn't want to be sloshing around when he started the fight. Same reason he was choosing not to eat either, for you did not want to be dying with half-eaten food falling from you when one was eviscerated. He'd seen that too…

Or thought he did.

His memories were still messy, coming in dribs and drabs. At times, like around a campfire last night, a memory would come to him. Ghostly images of past family or friends, talking and eating as the smell of burning wood and roasted meat filled the air. Other times, he would reach for understanding or the memory that formed the bedrock of his knowledge and find it missing.

Now, he was here, ready for his first real test. Braskar's heart pounded in his chest, faster than it should have for the start of an engagement. Yet, he could not help it. His lips were peeled in anticipation, even as he stood beside the unit of eerily silent woodlings.

They did not speak, they did not argue or fight or call out challenges. Instead, they followed orders impeccably, moving to do battle even now with but a rustle of branches and the fall of leaves. It was not the way mortals did battle, but these were elementals and thus defied such expectations.

If this was their first real battle, Braskar would have worried. But before this, a day ago, they had had their first encounter. A couple of bears, massive creatures twice the size of himself, that had seemed to just appear from nowhere on the rolling plains they marched upon.

The woodlings had charged forward on his command, going to battle without a trace of fear. He himself had held back, content to watch them do battle. He watched as the bears struck and clawed at the lead units, saw bark fly and sap leak from the bodies. For all their massive strength, not a single woodling fell, even as their own attacks landed on the monsters.

The fight had taken much longer than he would have expected, for the woodlings lacked in their ability to harm their opponents and the bears the same. In the end, it came down to the greater defense of their units and his own Command Aura that allowed him to rotate front level units backwards to ensure none of them were loss without purpose.

Now, the very same units stood here, healed entirely thanks to their Grow ability, ready to do battle. And before them, the militia.

He had not lied to his Lord that there was something incongruous about the units before him. The villagers themselves were similar to the keep's servants. Apparitions that had no true sapience, moving through the motions of life. But the units…

They wore a variety of makeshift armour and helms, and they wielded a variety of makeshift weapons from plowshares to spears to pitchforks. They were more alive and more solid. They shifted anxiously, whispered conversations breaking the monotony of guard duty as they waited for Braskar to attack. They almost seemed alive.

At the same time, they had been standing there, on guard, for nearly fourteen hours now. Not once had any left to relieve themselves or sat down. Not once had there been a rotation on watch for food or other refreshments. They might mimic life, but they were not real.

Then again, was he? He could still remember his own death, choking on the spear that had been driven through his neck, dying by the lungful of blood…

Perhaps he was dead, and this was his penance. He had failed to secure victory in his past life, forced to relive endless battles till he won. If so…

"Onward march!" Braskar commanded.

A shiver ran through the woodlings, leaves and branches rattling and swaying, the creak of supple wood filling the air. As one, the elementals moved forwards, golden glow within their trunks intensifying. Braskar let out an involuntary shiver, for there was something unnatural in the way they approached the other unit, the deep intensity and hunger they exhibited.

On the other end, the militia unit reacted, pulling together into a tight formation, three men across, two deep. They chose not to rush the team or even angle themselves around, though perhaps they intended that later. Braskar trotted alongside the woodlings on their left flank, his axe unslung and carried in his hand.

Today, he would let his axe drink deep. He would not hold back like before. Today, he would see if his memories were true and he was a warrior and not a coward…

A hundred meters fell away quickly, becoming ten. At the last moment, the militia let out a ragged cry and charged into the woodlings, choosing to meet the other unit head-on. Fools.

Spears and pitchforks glanced off toughened bark, scraping against wood and leaving shallow lines. The occasional blade caught deep, but others were entangled in long-reaching limbs and pulled aside. In the meantime, the long line of elementals collapsed down, seeking to envelop the militia unit.

Braskar sprinted to come around the end of the fight, ducking sideways as a staff swung towards his neck. He stayed low, his axe held by his side till he swung it upwards. The blade bit into the body with ease, barely slowed by the flesh and bone within his opponent's body.

He remembered that feeling, that slight resistance before a blade moved through. The inexperienced thought that there was more to it, that fresh bone and flesh somehow stopped a sharpened blade. Not true. Fresh blood, fresh bone was soft, pliable. Easy to cut through all but the thickest bones, like the hips and pelvis or skull. And even then, with the right edge alignment, the right push…

Simple.

His blade flew free, the body nearly bisected as the militia unit fell away. His eyes grew red, his breathing sped up, lips peeled away as his tusks showed further. Something swung at him, tore into his shoulder, but he only felt the tug of the spear passing through him. Not the pain.

Not yet.

Around him, the militia unit was surrounded. Big clubbing branches came down, hammering the mortals to the ground, beating them down. They screamed, they cried, they lashed out. They attempted to beat back the horde.

They failed.

Standing over the bodies, watching them pulse and twitch, Braskar threw his head backwards, raised his axe, and roared his victory. Around him, the woodlings moved back into line, silent, implacable, unrelenting. His new horde.

And this world would shake.

***

Status Report

Day 4

Gold: 95 (+6 Gold per day)

Units: 1 Woodling

In Production: 1 Woodling, Stall (3/5)

Structures Completed: Grove

Structures Available: Grove (II), Ranged Copse, Basic Greenhouse

Chapter 10

Back and forth, back and forth. Matt paced the tiny room, watching as the two units engaged, the map flickering again and again as the two units occupied the same spot. The map did not show the actual battle, just the conflict between the two.

Irvine on the other hand was seated, legs up on the edge of the table, eyes half-closed. Between his fingers was a long glass pipe, which let out a harsh acrid smell as smoke rose from one end. Occasionally, he would draw on the pipe, smile to himself in bliss as the smoke hit him, and then let out a long exhale.

"OSHA would really have issues with that..." Matt grumbled, considering demanding the man stop for the eighth time. Then, he dismissed silly thoughts. He was resolved to deal with Irvine, to tell the Alchemist to stop – or at least, report on his progress.

A flicker in the corner of his eye had him seeing that the unit of woodlings and Braskar's tiny icon figurine were standing, uncontested, inside the village now. A moment later, the map table flickered again and further information spiraled outwards.

Battle Report (Woodlings vs Militia)
Results: Victory (0 Units Lost, 1 Unit Defeated)

"Huh." Irvine's eyes had opened, the man leaning forwards as he stared at the map. Matt frowned, surprised he could read it so well from his spot but then shrugged. Magic. Sometimes it was better to just let it be. "Not much information."

"But it's enough, isn't it?" Matt smiled in relief, sagging a little. He had no idea why his heart was beating double-time or why he felt like he had run a marathon himself. It was not as though he had taken part in the fight, after all.

"We won!" Braskar cried out, startling Matt. Not bothering to wait for a reply, he provided a quick report of the fight itself, ending with, "It looks like you are right. Units without a commander in place are foolish and lack any tactical acumen. However, these battles have seen me increase in experience. I now have sixteen points!"

"Only?" Matt frowned, then nodded suddenly. "Right. Two points per unit, then?"

"It seems so."

"Before you get lost patting yourself on the back, have you looked at the other notifications?" Irvine cut in.

"Other notifications?" Matt frowned, waving his hand and dismissing the victory notification. Immediately another showed up.

Village #1 (Small) Conquered

Rewards: +1 Gold, +1 territorial overview

Would you like to rename it?

No need to ask what the territorial overview was as the faded bits of the map disappeared and strengthened, with a one hex range extended. On top of that, two hexes were further revealed, allowing Matt to get shadowy glimpses of those other spaces. More plains and forest for now.

"No need to rename it right now," Matt muttered. Not as though the residents were actual people. So better to move on. Immediately another notification appeared.

New Build Options Available

- **Road (10/+0.25 Gold/increased movement speed by 50%)**
- **Watch Tower (15/+1 hex view)**

"Looks like you were right. The more we conquer and build out, the better for us," Matt said to Irvine. "Thoughts?"

"The Road might be useful to reinforce the village," Braskar said, obviously somehow able to perceive the table himself. "I am getting the feeling that we will need to keep the woodlings here or see the village fall. There's no militia option available."

"Fall to what?" Matt asked.

Quickly, Braskar explained about the random encounter he had experienced.

"So you think you'll see more of that? Raiders and brigands and the like?"

"Yes."

Matt frowned, then rubbed his chin. "Alright, then stick around. I'll send the new woodling unit to take over, build another one here and once it's close you can leave and let them take over. If you are getting experience, it's best for you to keep finding trouble.

"If it's like any of the other games I've played, it's possible that we can offset these brigands and other random encounters by having you on patrol or hunting them down and finding their base."

"Very well. I'll see about securing the village," Braskar trailed off. "I'm getting a sense there are options in here for me, with the units. I'll let you know."

"Thanks." Matt turned to Irvine. "You're quiet."

"Running some numbers…" Irvine said. "Forty days to break even on the gold outlay. But we'd recover the amount spent in a day. And you can begin building it now, which is nice."

"How long to build?" Matt said curiously. "I don't see any information on it."

"One day."

"Huh."

Irvine could only shrug. Magic was after all the only real answer to that. After a moment, Matt nodded. "Let's do it. More gold now is better, especially if we're just building base units."

"Not upgrading the Grove then?" Irvine said.

"Not yet. We'll talk tomorrow, but we don't have a lot of gold left once everything's finished." Then, waving a hand to dismiss the notifications once he had the Road started, he fixed Irvine with a glare. "What's going on with your alchemy?"

"Nothing," Irvine said.

"What does nothing mean?"

"It means a lot of failures, alright?" the old man growled. "I need more experience, more levels. Everything I do keeps failing."

"Is that common then?" Matt couldn't help but wonder if he had a broken Hero. After all, he had initially come to him as the financial advisor. Perhaps that was all he was meant to be?

"At Level 1, sure." Irvine threw his hands up. "I can at least tell you what I'm trying to make."

"Oh?"

"Potions of Strength. Gives a +2 to melee attacks. Once I have the formula correct, then I can produce them in quantity for our units. One set of potions, once a day."

"I assume they're consumables."

"You mean you drink them?" Irvine said.

"And they're gone after you use them," Matt clarified.

"Of course."

"That's great." Matt sighed. "Wait. If we used those potions for Braskar and you, wouldn't it be useful for like twelve fights?"

"No." The older man was waving his glass pipe around. "It locks to the unit the moment you give it to them. Quantity and number shrink."

"That makes no sense."

Another elaborate shrug.

"Fine, fine." Matt rubbed his face. Sometimes, this damn world made utterly no sense to him. "But you have to figure out the formula first. Can you research and produce at the same time?"

Another shake of the head.

"Damn it."

"Maybe in the future?" Irvine said tentatively, brows furrowed. "I think. If I level up."

"And you're leveling right now?"

"Gaining experience, yes." A single finger was held up. "Slowly."

Another long sigh from Matt, before he pointed to the doors leading out. "Then you best get practicing. I'll take any advantage we can get."

Grumbling about micro-managing taskmasters, Irvine stood up and walked to the exit. He stopped right at the doorway, tilting his head to the side.

"What are you going to do?"

Staring at the map, Matt took his time in answering. "The only thing I can do. Strategise."

Irvine hung by the door for a second more before walking away, leaving Matt to continue to stare, fruitlessly, at the map.

***

Status Report

Day 4 (end)

Gold: 86 (+6 Gold per day)

Units: 1 Woodling

In Production: 1 Woodling (3/4), Stall (3/5), Road (0/1)

Structures Completed: Grove

Structures Available: Grove (II), Ranged Copse, Basic Greenhouse, Watch Tower

Chapter 11

The next morning, Matt barely took the time to wash his face and brush his teeth before he jogged up the stairs. As expected, the woodling unit had already finished production. He could see them standing silent and disciplined in ranks, both out the window and on his tactical map. A simple gesture had them start walking out the keep exit, heading for the village.

Then, once he inputted that order, he eyed the map once more. No marauding raiders or other units in play, though he was uncertain how many of them would show up. The bears hadn't. He'd not even known about that encounter till Braskar had told him on a morning briefing.

"Hopefully, there's a difference between random monster generation on travels and units that are allowed to attack keeps." Matt rubbed his hair, forced himself to sigh. "This entire world or game or whatever is just way too weird a mixture. What I'd do for a proper delineation.

"Or a rulebook. I'll take the rulebook any day."

And of course, he was talking to himself. Then again, with only one other person in the entire keep who could hold even the barest of conversations, it was either talk to himself or listen to the sound of the wind blowing. Which he had done.

"Go, woodlings, relieve our Hero!" Waving his hand with a final flourish, Matt confirmed the woodling journey. Then, he drummed his fingers, pulling up the barebones status information of his kingdom.

Status Report

Gold: 92 (+6 Gold per day)

Units: 2 Woodlings

In Production: Stall (4/5)

Structures Completed: Grove, Road

Structures Available: Grove (II), Ranged Copse, Basic Greenhouse, Watch Tower

Well, that was simple enough. He now just had to choose what to build. He discarded the Watch Tower, of course, and the Basic Greenhouse. Neither would serve him right now. And also…

"Commit to building woodlings now before I forget."

A small gesture, and the Grove was filled, leaving him with one more woodling started.

Gold: 72 (+6 Gold per day)

Not a lot that he could afford with that. It would take him just over two days more to begin production of the upgraded Grove. It would take…

"Eleven, twenty-two, forty-four, eighty-eight, ninety-nine." Using his fingers, Matt counted it off. "Seven days to get to ummm, ninety-six plus ninety-nine plus eleven. That's two hundred and eight, right?" He ran the numbers again and nodded. "Right. Two hundred and six. That's nine days to get enough to build a Ranged Copse. Assuming I don't bother with anything else."

He shook his head, staring at the board and then threw his hands up. "Damn it."

As much as he'd like to get moving on things, it seemed he was stuck waiting. Perhaps he could find some paper whilst he waited. Or a clay tablet that he could then scribe on. Because all this mental math was a pain and a half.

***

"One more day…" Humming to himself, Matt ascended the steps again. Braskar had taken to wandering around the village, checking out the locations by himself. Thus far, no fights or any other concerns. His newest made woodling unit was one step closer, and most importantly, the damn Stall was done!

In and of itself, the Stall was not particularly surprising. It was the additional notifications that showed up when it had completed that were exciting.

Upgrade Available: Stall (II)
Building Type: Treasury
Tier: Lesser Tier II
Benefit: +10 Gold Per Day
Cost: 75 Gold
Production Time: 7 days

"Now, is that an additional five more gold, or a total of ten more?" Matt prodded the information a bit more, then shook his head. "Just an additional five. Which is why it's cheaper."

Pretty decent really, fifteen days to break even. And only seven days to get enough funds to build it. Considering he had ninety-six gold right now, with another eleven coming in every day, he'd be able to build this and another woodling too.

On the other hand, there was the other notification that had him interested.

New Build Options Available

- **Tavern (100/Allows Recruitment of Additional Heroes)**
- **Marketplace (200/+10 Gold)**
- **Blacksmith (100/+2 to Damage or Defense of Units)**
- **Harbour (200/+5 Gold)**

"And now we're cooking." Matt could not help but rub his hands together as he stared at the new information. He knew what he wanted, of course, but he also wanted to take a moment to review what options there were.

The Tavern was the obvious option to buy if he had been an Isekaied hero with a cheat ability. Or it would become his cheat ability, where he would find amazing Heroes that would add to his army and make him unconquerable.

And while it was pretty sure he had been isekaied over, or close enough since most portal books didn't have their heroes die from a brain hemorrhage, Matt was still pretty certain that he was not going to get away with it that easily. Among other things, considering how expensive everything else was, hiring a Hero probably was a matter of luck and money.

No. That was for when he had the funds.

The Blacksmith was a nice overall upgrade, and when he had more units – assuming it increased all units in total and not just newly built units – would be incredibly useful. Right now though, he could not see how it would add much more to his fighting prowess when he could spend the same amount and get five more actual woodlings.

Other than the fact that they were on separate production tracks of course. Still… Later.

Which left the two gold producers. Not forgetting everything else he could build of course, but his biggest holdup right now was building up enough gold so that he could punch out new buildings without having to worry about production time.

In that sense, the obvious answer was to save enough money to get a Marketplace. An additional ten gold a day would mean it would pay for itself in another twenty days. Not as good a deal as an upgraded Stall though, so he might want to do that before the Marketplace.

Except, it was rather obvious that building new structures had additional bonuses beyond just the direct line noted here. The Harbour obviously added something else – probably build options to exploit the sea. And the Marketplace might offer something else, whether an upgrade, new build options, or new units being available. He wasn't certain, but it was obvious it was part of this entire structure.

So.

Run a risk of not getting anything good, build something that was rather obvious to continue upgrading his gold production, or go for the all-out risk and get a Tavern?

Choices, choices, choices.

***

Status Report

Day 6 (End of Day)

Gold: 3.25 (+11.25 Gold per day)

Units: 2 Woodlings

In Production: Woodling (1/4)

Structures Completed: Grove, Road, Stall

Structures Available: Grove (II), Ranged Copse, Basic Greenhouse, Watch Tower, Tavern, Marketplace, Blacksmith, Harbour, Stall (II)

Chapter 12

Luckily for Matt, he had a lot of time to think about his choices over the next few days whilst waiting for the units to build and Braskar to report back. Matt thought about what he wanted to do, while jogging up and down the stairs, while moving around heavy rocks or digging into the earth around their keep. He had taken to basic manual labour and exercise, not because he thought it might one day save him in a fight, but because the sheer effort required to ascend and descend the damn tower stairs every day was exhausting.

Also, boredom. At least building the beginning of a trench around their keep or hauling around rocks to put against the wall to throw at invaders gave him something to do. Without books or television or social media to take up his time, finding his own amusement was all that he had on offer.

In the meantime, the world journeyed apace. Irvine appeared once a day or so, promising he was close to a breakthrough. He just needed one more day. Matt figured that one more day was sort of like self-driving cars or nuclear fission – something to expect to happen when it did and not a moment earlier.

Once the new woodling unit was close enough to take over the guarding the next day, Braskar had brought the other woodling unit out of the village. At which point, both he and the unit had been waylaid by another random attack. This time, the battle with the snakes had been significantly simpler, though Braskar himself had nearly died, having been poisoned by one of the creatures as he'd charged in.

That result had seen to a long tirade by Matt, as he let loose repressed emotions of fear, anger, and helplessness at the Hero. The older orc had accepted the tirade without a word, though the situation continued to be frosty between the pair.

Even so, the Hero continued to scout, moving a hex further out from the village and beginning to reveal more of the map to Matt.

Eventually, another major milestone was achieved. The third woodling unit was finally created, which meant that he now had a safeguard for the fort itself too. To Matt's surprise, a level of tension and fear that he had never realised he felt faded away, allowing him to run the numbers with less tension.

A quick flick of the information allowed him to review the information that had changed.

Status Report
Day: 9 (Beginning of Day)
Gold: 37 (+11.25 Gold per day)
Units: 3 Woodlings
In Production: Stall (II) (3/7)

Three woodling units, enough funds to make another. If he picked up another woodling, he would have four. Which meant he could look at scouting to the east or west while having a unit that could keep him safe if raiders came.

Of course, so far, he'd seen none. It was possible that his concerns of attackers on the keep were overblown too. If he did not build a unit now, he could wait for the Stall upgrade to finish, and use the funds to build the next structure soon after. Which one though, he had no idea.

At sixteen and a quarter gold a day once the Stall (II) finished, it was literally a two day wait. Made little sense to wait then, knowing that number. Triggering the production of another unit dropped his gold again to thirty or so gold and left him with four more days before he could make a decision.

That would put him just under a hundred gold, which was pretty damn sweet. Almost like they wanted him to buy the Tavern.

The only other item available at a hundred gold was the Blacksmith, though Grove (II) would see him with upgraded woodlings in two more days after that. Those could do some major damage, though the additional cost was likely to tip the Blacksmith ahead of the upgraded woodlings for now.

At some point, he really did want the Ranged Copse.

No.

Matt shook his head, firming his decision. He would not get distracted by shinies like the Tavern or Grove, or even the Blacksmith. He needed to alter his unit composition or get caught out when a better built army came along and peppered his pure melee army to death.

***

Irvine listened as Matt wandered around the empty keep, muttering to himself. The old man frowned, wondering if his errant 'Lord' was going insane. Or any more insane. Hard to tell sometimes, with the way things were set up. Who could blame him for talking to himself? It was not as though he had access to tomes and tomes of alchemical research to dig into.

Studying the books, practicing his alchemy was a strange sensation for Irvine. It was sort of like learning to dance again, after both your legs had been chopped off, left to heal over and then, a few years later, regrown.

Learning in that sense was nearly as weird as realizing that he had drawn this comparison not from thin air but from a past experience somewhere. Not his own, Irvine was sure. But someone he had known, once, a long time ago.

The fact that he could not put his finger on it drove him mad. He found his thoughts wandering more often than not to things that he half-remembered, formulas and solutions that seemed nearly right, but just weren't.

Ghost memories.

Then there were the ingredients he had access to in this room. Dozens and dozens of bottles lined the shelf, filled with everything from floating eyeballs to petals and what was labeled as 'the first glimpse of morning light on a summer eve.' The fact that such a title even made sense to Irvine was insane, but it was not the worst part of this alchemical lab.

It was that he couldn't actually touch the vast majority of the ingredients. Every time he swiped his hand towards an ingredient he was not meant to have access to, his hand would fall through it. Just like the ghostly attendants that cleaned up after the pair of them.

He had just over two dozen ingredients he was allowed to make use of at his current Level, and that was it. Everything else among the ingredients and two thirds of the equipment, from various cauldrons and alchemical pots to pipettes and distillation equipment, was off-limits to him. His first few days had been a matter of walking back and forth, trying to work out what he could and could not do in this strange location.

But now, he knew. And so long as Irvine chose not to think about how infuriating and insane these restrictions were, he could forge ahead with his attempts at making the potion.

And forge ahead was the right word, since, like so much in this world, things were arbitrary. The exact same methodology, the exact same movements gave him varying degrees of success. Never a full one, but sometimes he would drift closer or further, and not for any discernible reason Irvine could sense.

A little change in the rate of bubbling from the potion brought Irvine's attention back to what he was doing. He stirred the pot five times, counterclockwise. Not five and a quarter or four and a half but five times exactly. Then, he poured in a dram of faux silver, the liquid dripping into the potion to twist it, congealing together and changing colour swiftly from purple to brown. A reddish brown, similar to live flesh after being cut into by a particularly sharp scalpel.

That was no ghost memory. He remembered every moment of cutting into the squirming woman as she screamed, her legs and flesh kicking, muscles straining, blood flowing and piss in the air. If they had to take memories, why couldn't they have taken that one?

Reddish-brown glowing before him. Irvine counted under his breath, got to seven before the colour shifted suddenly, purpling again, darkening to a dark blue and black. Smoke exploded but it did not catch Irvine this time, for he had moved away in anticipation.

The notification came, late as usual.

Potion of Strength Creation: Failure
Success Rate: 92%

His best yet so far. Waving his hand, Irvine wandered over to the window and made sure it was propped open fully before he went to grab a book. Nothing to do but wait. After all, the other annoying notification was still there.

Potion Creation on Cooldown
Cooldown Time Remaining: 29:07

So close, and yet so far. One day, he'd get it. And then, maybe, just maybe, he'd get his hands on more ingredients. Till then, it was a good thing they weren't relying on his skills for safety.

***

Status Report

Day 9

Gold: 19 (+11.25 Gold per day)

Units: 3 Woodlings

In Production: Stall (II) (3/7), Woodling (0/4)

Structures Completed: Grove, Road, Stall

Structures Available: Grove (II), Ranged Copse, Basic Greenhouse, Watch Tower, Tavern, Marketplace, Blacksmith, Harbour

Chapter 13

Dust in the distance, just over the slope of the hill. Braskar frowned as he stood against the rise, the woodling unit halted beside him. The rolling plains with their lightly swaying grass was dappled in a variety of greens, with the occasional stunted tree that had somehow managed to survive marauding goats and herds of sheep poking up from the ground.

Lips peeled back, Braskar ran over their location in his mind. Two hexes north of the village, just far enough away that you could not see them from the village itself, moving to the third hex today. He had been moving in a zig-zag search, which was why they had taken so long to get this far, verifying the search grid and looking outwards.

Now, there was dust. Not like the almost magically appearing random monsters they occasionally fought, but actual dust. Instinct – and some little logic – said that this change of schedule spoke of something more dire than just another set of weirdly-grouped, hyper-aggressive natural monsters.

Which was why he had the woodlings halted on the hill, watching.

Idly, he poked at the mental connection that linked him to the map. No answer from within. No surprise, since outside of their regular morning chats, Matt had taken to wandering the keep or doing other matters to keep himself active.

Perhaps it was a good thing that the Tavern had yet to be built. He could just see his Lord spending all too much time there, rather than thinking about what their next move should be. Strategy and tactics, though he understood his Lord's feelings. Right now, they were stuck, forced to wait as build times grew long and events transpired slowly.

Movement now, just coming over the hill. Braskar narrowed his eyes, for it was low to the rise, like whatever was coming up was doing so carefully. A scout? Possibly, but that indicated a degree of smarts that he had not seen before.

Not good.

Then more movement. One, two, three, and more. More bodies cresting the rise, and the orc realised he was right and wrong. They were smart – or smarter – than the random encounters he'd run into. At the same time, it was no scout. No reason to send so many in that case.

A full unit of creatures that ran on all fours, ears like a dog, long faces, but the full body and muscles of a creature that could stand upright too. Jackals, or something like it, but humanoid. Smaller than a full human though, all wiry power and yipping and angry baying.

Just as interesting was the information lingering over them now that the full unit was in view.

Enemy Unit: Saakal

Type: Creature

Number: 10

Melee Attack: Medium

Melee Defense: Low

Ranged Attack: None

Ranged Defense: Low

Hit Points: Medium

Speed: Medium

Special Abilities: ???

Vulnerabilities: ???

"And now we have found you. And now we shall see you defeated!" Braskar said, his grin widening. He waved his unit of woodlings down the hill at a slow pace, even as the saakal came rushing down the moment the group spotted Braskar and the woodlings.

Red eyes glowing, he took off at a slow jog, unslinging his axe from his back. He gripped it cross-body, trained eyes watching the enemy unit loping down the hill, picking up speed. No set movement, no line, but they were shifting towards an arrow formation. At the same time, a light began to form around every member of the jackals, small dots of red amongst the yellow-brown that began to spark and join together.

"Shit. Special. Must be…" Making a snap decision, Braskar howled out, "Form up, tighten ranks. Brace for impact!"

The woodlings moved as one, stopping and making sure they were lined up before shuffling closer together. To Braskar's surprise, the woodlings stomped their feet into the ground, roots digging into the earth even as the creatures leaned forwards.

By the side, Braskar crouched low too, not too close to the unit but making sure not to get so far away that he couldn't duck behind the unit if the saakal came after him instead of the woodlings. Not too late, when the glow around the unit coalesced. A howling face similar to the saakal's own visages came to the fore just before they crashed into the woodlings.

Howls of pain, sounds of shattering wood, the physical impact of meaty bodies against hardened wood exploded through the hill. Even having crossed their way up half the hill, the saakal barely slowed down, their momentum contained by the magic.

One woodling, two, then a third fell. The glow around the saakal began to fade, the energy of their attack petering out. The woodlings dealt their damage too, smashing down on the saakal, dropping one and then another. But the saakal mixed into the group kept tearing at the woodlings who swung big wooden limbs to strike at the furred opponents.

Braskar shook his head, a little annoyed for he had not been part of the attack at all. Not a single unit of the saakal had come for him, but that at least allowed him to sprint around to the front of the group and come at their enemy from the side.

Over the sound of the crashing and hammering, the yelps and growls, and the meaty thunks, Braskar could see the difference in the battle. The saakal had done more damage than the woodlings had, and though they had lost a pair, they could afford to lose the two with their greater numbers. Another two of his woodlings had been damaged in the initial charge, but now they were laying into the saakal. After the initial charge, the pair of units were on equal ground, losing unit to unit.

That was bad. Very bad.

The first saakal to spot him spun on its back legs, snapping at Braskar. The orc reacted reflexively, stabbing his weapon outwards to bounce the creature away from him with the front of the axe. Then, letting the weight of his weapon drop low, he stepped in close and swung upwards, putting his hips into the attack to cut at the monster, tearing its throat out.

Five saakal now, to their four woodlings.

No. Three.

He watched another woodling, one that was injured before, fall under the fangs of a monster. He watched as unit after unit of his people died, and a part of him snarled and bubbled froth. He threw himself at the enemy, his axe flashing as he caught the creatures from behind. The first sliced deep into the back of one monster, then he elbowed another that tried to take him down. He staggered a bit at the creature's momentum, but he forced himself to stay on his feet.

A red haze fell over his eyes as he no longer worried about the disposition of his troops. No need for that, not when the woodlings pulsed with his own Rage Aura and took the battle to the saakal. The enemy did not flinch, fighting back ferociously and taking down another woodling before they were finally felled.

Braskar was left breathing heavily and in pain, even as the woodlings fell into a proper unit formation, stepping over the slowly fading bodies of their enemies and friends. Not that the Hero thought they actually saw their fellow woodlings as friends.

Probably.

More importantly, this battle had revealed something rather worrying. Something he really needed to talk to his Lord about.

Now, where was the damned fool?

Chapter 14

Matt blinked as he stared at the notifications waiting for him after he reentered the map room later that evening. Tactics room? War room? Kingdom control room? He wasn't certain what to call it though the last seemed a little pretentious. Map room worked for now, at least.

Battle Report (Hero Braskar vs Enemy Units)
Result: Victory! 1 Saakal Defeated, 0 Units Escaped
Rewards: +2 Gold, +1 Reputation

Huh. He got gold for beating the enemy unit. Just as interestingly, there was a possibility for units to flee – on both sides he would assume. That was important to note in the future. A flick of his hand brought up further information, giving him the saakal's unit data and then his people's.

Woodlings Status
Number: 2 Units (Injured)

...

There was more data but he discarded it for later, focusing on the total number remaining.

"Braskar?" Matt called out as he triggered the option to talk to his man on the ground as it were. Not surprisingly, Braskar was quick to answer, providing him with a rundown of the battle itself.

"Our units cannot – as they stand – face our enemies on a one-on-one basis. They just are not strong enough to do so, though if we gain sufficient experience, that might change," Braskar concluded. The orc sounded a little unsure of himself at the end, possibly worried about how Matt would react.

"Why? We're both base units, so why are we doing worse?" Matt muttered, mostly to himself.

"I assume it is an off-balancing between their strengths and speed and ours, my lord."

"Speed?"

"I believe they might have more movement points than we do. I would assume that we are looking at probably two hexes per turn," Braskar said. "Until we are proven wrong, I would want us to assume that."

"So…" Matt trailed off, thinking it over. "No more leaving our villages undefended. We only have a two-unit vision from there. If they can move two… we'd spot them but might not be able to move one in and have them settled for defense before they're attacked. Or am I getting that wrong?"

"Unknown. Do we take turns in turn or at the same time? I would assume at the same time, so your assumption might be correct. Any bonuses for defense might not trigger to the next turn. It certainly would suit the way things work, my lord," Braskar said.

"Crap. Okay. Any other thoughts?"

"We should have an advantage on quantity I believe. Or it's possible that we can win a war of attrition, with our wounded units rotated back for growing between battles."

"Right. So have two-unit groups – or a unit and Hero – so that we can ensure we keep our two units alive and grow them." Matt frowned. "Do we need to do that for our bases?"

"The defense structures in them should be sufficient," Braskar said. "There is another option than just doubling our unit numbers though."

"We could gift them potions," Matt said. "If we ever get them."

"Or get the Blacksmith."

"Would a +2 be enough?"

Silence, then Braskar spoke up suddenly. "Sorry, I shrugged. I do not know but would assume it would be sufficient. The fight was very close."

"Interesting." That put a different spin on things. An immediate boost to their units would make every single unit they made more powerful, along with any upgrades. The problem with waiting for more units is that it would take eight days to get a pair of units running for further scouting options. It helped as well that the Blacksmith only took five days, so it would be a fast build.

Hands twitched and he called up the detailed information on the Blacksmith once more.

Structure Available: Blacksmith

Building Type: Unit Upgrades

Tier: Lesser Tier I

Benefit: +2 Melee Ranged Damage / +1 Ranged Damage (if available) or +2 Defense

Cost: 100 Gold

Production Time: 5 days

"I have only twenty seven gold right now." Matt sighed. "I can't do anything about either of those choices." By the time the next woodling unit was built, he'd have a bunch more. Till then… "You going to keep scouting?"

Hesitation on the other side of the line before Braskar sighed. "Not in the northerly direction. I'll head east. Less chance of running into an attacker and it'll allow me to rebuild the units."

"Alright. Keep reporting in. We'll keep an eye out for more enemy units."

Braskar confirmed the words and then cut the connection, leaving Matt to inform Irvine directly. Now, it was just a question of whether their enemy had sent more units after them. And how many they had. Working in the dark sucked.

Chapter 15

Four days later, both the second level Stall and new woodling unit were finished. Braskar had reported that the woodlings had reformed two units a day, seeming to sprout out from the other units during the night and fast growing through the day till they had become full-sized units themselves. By the time the new woodling and Stall had finished, Braskar was back to full strength and exploring further, though the woodlands he now was moving through offered little beyond random encounters.

No further enemy units were spotted, though on a hunch on the third day, Matt had sent the unit of woodlings waiting in the fort off to reinforce the village. It left it one hex away from his own. More than sufficient safeguard in either case.

Now, Matt had to make another decision on what to do this morning, even as he stared at the map glowing before him.

Status Report

Day 13 (Beginning of Day)

Gold: 64 (+11.25 Gold per day)

Units: 4 Woodlings

In Production: (None)

Structures Completed: Grove, Road, Stall (II)

Structures Available: Grove (II), Ranged Copse, Basic Greenhouse, Watch Tower, Tavern, Marketplace, Blacksmith, Harbour

"Arse. Three days before I can get the Blacksmith if I don't build anything now. Another day on top of that to get another woodling started. Or begin building another woodling immediately, which puts me at forty-four. Then, that is ummm…"

"Four days before you have just enough for a Blacksmith, but you'll have to wait another day before you can start another woodling," Irvine said.

"Irvine."

"That's my name. Don't overuse it or I'll start charging licensing fees."

"That's…" Matt hesitated. "You know about licensing fees?"

"I do." Irvine repeated, incredulously. "I do. I just don't know why…"

"That is… unimportant right now. What are you doing here?"

"Oh, right. I did it."

"Pooed? Found a shoe? Remembered your past?"

"No, no, well yes, but why'd you say that and no."

"You're only wearing one shoe."

"I know that part," Irvine rolled his eyes. "I couldn't find the other. Did you see it?"

"No. But we're off topic again."

"You're the one who's distracting me. The shoe comes later. This is what I have finished." A hand raised, a green sparkly potion in it.

Snatching the potion, Matt cradled it to his chest, a burst of exuberance rolling through him. "You did it! It works?"

"It works. And now I have the potion formula so I should be able to reproduce these much more easily." Irvine smirked. "That change your plans at all?"

"Of course, it does!" Matt said, rubbing his hands together. "How many can you produce?"

"Depends."

"Clarity! What do you mean, man."

"Generally, I can produce a potion once ever three days. However, I have a Skill."

"I know."

Irvine glared. "Will you let me finish?" He waited, saw that Matt wasn't going to interrupt, then continued. "Right. So. A Skill, Burst Production. Means I can make a total of three of these in one day."

"What's the drawback?" Matt said, suspicious.

"I can't use the Skill again for ten days," Irvine replied.

"Not much of a drawback right now," Matt muttered. "Not as though you have another potion to research. Do you?"

"I have three actually," Irvine said. "Potion of Speed, Potion of Growth, and Potion of Defense. Don't think you need an explanation, do you?"

"No." Drumming his fingers on the table, Matt asked. "Does it take the whole day to do production?"

"It does, and I can't research and produce at the same time."

"And you're not very good at research," Matt said. "One chance in… twelve or so days? So either four potions while we wait for you to do research or we get three now, then put you to research and then have you use the Skill again.

"Seems like that's the optimal condition, unless there's another option?"

Irvine stroked his beard, tugging on the wispy hair falling down his chin as he thought before he eventually shook his head. "Nope."

"Okay. So you get me three new Potions of Strength for distribution. We keep one here for the unit, send one up to the village, and another to our current surplus member. That leaves them, theoretically, able to do battle with the enemy."

"So long as they aren't improving too," Irvine said.

"So long as they aren't improving too," Matt confirmed. "That means the Blacksmith isn't necessary right this second." Thinking into the future a little, he grimaced and nodded to himself. "And if we keep trying to play catch up, we might not win. We're ahead for now, I hope, but there's no guarantee we will be in the future. We need the ranged units."

"That's a long time not to be building any new units," Irvine said.

"True." A long breath in and then out before he nodded. "One more now. And then we wait and let it build up, no matter what. We also pull back on the exploration a bit, for now."

"You sure that's the right hand to play?" Irvine said.

"I can't even see my opponent right now," Matt replied. "So, no." He chuckled grimly. "But we can't keep playing for the short-term. At some point, we're going to have to plan for the future. Even if it means risk in the present."

It had always driven him mad, that part of these games. The transition point between early game advantage to mid or late game advantage, and that transitory moment of weakness had always frustrated him a little. Still, it was never sufficient for him to want to build a Watch Tower for the early warning system since he had always felt such purchases useless. If you lost because you got overwhelmed, you just restarted.

Now, when his actual life was on the line, when the fate of the world — hah, how had he almost forgotten that? — was on hand, suddenly that Watch Tower made sense.

If it hadn't cost so damn much of course.

"Well, no use in me hanging around. You can't buy anything anyway," Irvine said. "And I got some potions to make."

"Yeah." Waving the older man away, Matt stared at the table one last time before walking off. Informing Braskar about what to do tomorrow morning would be more than time enough.

***

Status Report

Day 13 (End of Day)

Gold: 44 (+16.25 Gold per day)

Units: 4 Woodlings

In Production: Woodling (0/4)

Structures Completed: Grove, Road, Stall (II)

Structures Available: Grove (II), Ranged Copse, Basic Greenhouse, Watch Tower, Tavern, Marketplace, Blacksmith, Harbour

***

Chapter 16

Two days and of course, things changed. Braskar had pulled back towards the village, both to acquire the potions that were on their way to him and also to ensure they had a redoubt in case of an attack.

In the meantime, Matt continued his work on building improvised defenses around the fort, digging into the ground with very little to show for it. Surprising how much work there was, creating trenches of any appreciable depth. After his first attempt at digging down deep to around six feet and then going sideways, he had started forming a much less deep but wider trench, figuring that would be more useful in the long run. It also meant that the tiny redoubt he created on the other side was easier to reach with his spade as he flung the soil upwards.

Stopping by the tactical map during his midday break with sandwich in hand, Matt noted the rather concerning presence at the edge of the map, three hexes away. He leaned forwards, staring at the unit that had appeared and poking at it with his finger. A moment later, the notification formed.

Enemy Army Sighted!
Quantity: Unknown

"Oh, of all the red tape…" Matt rubbed his face. Then, drawing a deep breath, he bellowed for Irvine, sending a ping to Braskar too at the same time.

"My lord?" Braskar's answer came back fast, the mental connection that existed working faster than Matt's shout. It only took Matt a moment more to realise he could have done the same thing to get the Alchemist to come too.

"Problem." Then, pushing open the channel to Irvine, Matt elaborated on what he was seeing. Not that there was much to relate.

"No idea of number of units?" Braskar muttered. "That is not good. Do you believe it is due to the distance involved?"

"Possibly. You didn't spot the saakal until they were literally upon you."

"If this is the saakal…" Braskar rumbled. "This is bad. How long till they reach you?"

"Depends if they know where we are. On a straight line, assuming they have used all their movement this round… two days. If they don't come directly for us, might be longer," Matt said.

"And if they have more movement?" Irvine asked querulously.

"Then one day. Tomorrow, basically," Matt said.

"When will you know?" Braskar asked.

"Later today, probably." Matt gestured at the map, even though he recognized no one else could see it. "I'll probably be able to track if they shift over."

"I could march back," Braskar offered. "If we leave now, we might be able to make it to the next hex."

"Or you could just tire yourself out, leaving so late, and not be any closer," Irvine said.

"We have Roads now. We should be able to make it," the orc replied.

"Assuming they take into account the half-movement and don't arbitrarily lock you down," Irvine said.

"We should have paid more attention," Matt grumbled to himself, as he considered the way they had shifted woodlings around. They just hadn't been thinking about it, so they had moved the woodlings without noting how fast they moved and how far. The fact that the trip for the fourth woodling had arrived quickly had been something they had known but not really noted.

Now…

"They can move in too, can't they?" Matt muttered.

"Move in where, sir?" Irvine said, his voice coming in startlingly loud.

Jumping a little, Matt looked at the Alchemist who had made his way over in-person from his tower.

"The village. The way they're positioned to the west, three days to either the village or us." Matt shook his head. "Either way, we could be in trouble."

"We have four woodlings and three of them are in the village. I'm sure we could afford to lose at least one coming back," Irvine said.

"And Braskar?" Matt said.

"I would prefer to be with you, my lord. But…"

"But?"

"I might suggest another option," Braskar said. "We know they are not able to see us, not well." Matt nodded, unseen by the orc. "We have the informational advantage."

"You want to take the battle to them," Irvine said.

"Yes."

"That…" Matt trailed off. "Isn't the worst idea. Unless they beat you."

"All war is risk."

"Not helpful, Braskar." Matt rubbed his face, feeling the weight of the decision crashing down on him suddenly. So far, the fear, the worry and pressure of making decisions that would factor into his and the Heroes' lives, had been remote. He could push it aside with a bit of thought, but now it came back all the more forcefully. Such that he was frozen in indecision, his chest constricted as his breathing became harder. If he chose wrong here… If…

"He's right. Anyway, we all died once before. So we know, dying isn't that bad," Irvine said, laying a comforting hand on Matt's shoulder.

"I had a brain haema… hemora… brain bleed!" Matt snapped. "It hurt like hell."

"Then it stopped, didn't it?" Irvine shrugged. "Pain passes, eventually. Then, it's nothing. Or something that we can't remember, which is about the same damn thing."

"But we have another chance now."

"And you'll still make mistakes. That's kind of life. You probably won't even know why you made a mistake when things come crashing down. Not until much later, if at all." Irvine shrugged. "But you still have to make one."

"Mistakes?" Matt said.

"A decision."

"Aye, my lord. I fear not death. And if it comes, I would rather it find me on the field, facing my opponent than waiting behind walls like a coward," Braskar said, his deep voice rumbling.

"That… nothing wrong with a good defense. But I get it," Matt said, shaking his head. "You have the potions of strength, right?"

"We do."

"Then… fine. Take two units with you, head out, and see if you can intercept if they're coming this way. If we have to fight, we fight." Matt tried his best to sound resolved but found his voice shaking a little at the end. If either of his advisors heard it, they ignored him.

"As you say, my lord. May fortune and blood favour us," Braskar rumbled.

***

Status Report

Day 15

Gold: 76.5 (+16.25 Gold per day)

Units: 4 Woodlings

In Production: Woodling (2/4)

Structures Completed: Grove, Road, Stall (II)

Structures Available: Grove (II), Ranged Copse, Basic Greenhouse, Watch Tower, Tavern, Marketplace, Blacksmith, Harbour

Chapter 17

Braskar grinned, letting the handle of his axe fall into his hands. It was a pleasure, fighting with more information than one's opponent. Knowing not just that the opponent was trying to locate them – the twisting route they had taken in the last two days had shown that to be true – but also that they had the advantage of knowledge meant that it was unlikely their upcoming fight was going to be particularly difficult, which had grown his Lord's confidence.

Now, with his opponent coming down this plain hex, they need only march to meet them to finish the battle. The only concern was that they knew that there were more than a single unit of the saakal in play, the further information available on the tactical map informing them of such as the enemy closed in.

An unfortunate thing, that they could not – as yet   tell more than that. Still, two woodling units to their two saakal with their additional potions should be sufficient. Especially since he was here.

He eyed the surroundings quickly, searching for the best suitable spot to have the fight. Not much to look at, this rolling plain. Still, in the distance to the right of him, there was a stream that crept out from under a slight rise with a forest bordering the edge of the minor rise in the plains. If they could get there, and Braskar judged they could, they would channel the forces right up the hill. The advantage of fighting up the hill would be sufficient, he assumed.

"Double-time!" Braskar roared, waving his hand forwards and gesturing for the woodlings to follow his orders. The creatures took to his orders with alacrity, doubling the speed of their movements. He loped alongside the tree elementals, grinning a little.

The woodlings reminded him in a way of the orcs. They were slow, so like the orcs they had few chances of running away. Half the reason why orc armies had gained the reputation of being indomitable had been the realization that their traditional armies – the humans, the dwarves – had the ability to catch them in the quick or outmarch them in the long. Breaking and running was a recipe for disaster for your typical orc army.

No, better to stand and fight, to wage war till the last man and turn the battle around via ferocity and unwillingness to give up. Dying to the last man, rather than being paraded through human cities or slain outright by the dwarves. No orc desired to be a slave, no orc wanted to die on their knees.

The woodlings were not orcs, but without full sentience, spirits that invigorated trees, they also did not quail at being attacked. A good thing too, since for them, like for his own fallen comrades, running was not an option. Not against the much faster saakal.

As they ran, Braskar eyed the incoming units. He frowned as he watched them, realizing after a time that one of the creatures, hidden amidst the ranks, was different. Bigger, wider, with a different colouration of fur and face. It moved on its hind legs mostly, only dropping to its forelegs once in a while to keep up with the much faster moving saakal. The face was more wolf-like than the narrower jackal features of the saakal, its body broader.

And the saakal themselves were changed too, nearly half of them. Bigger, wider in muscles. Their fur a touch darker than their brethren. He might not have noticed it, if not for the direct comparison available in both their leader and the other unit.

All of which lead to a simple conclusion.

"My lord."

He waited, hoping that Matt was there. That he could hear it. Silence for a long moment, even as he urged the woodlings onwards. The enemy units were speeding up, much faster than he had anticipated. No way for them to make the rise. He would either have to have the woodlings dig in now, or...

"To the woods!"

Perhaps fighting within the woods would confuse them. The woodlings looked like trees after all, perhaps the change in pace, the twisted ranks would allow them some advantage. They would need it, after all.

"Braskar. What is it?" His Lord's voice now, worried. Probably picked up the tension in his voice. Braskar tried to modulate it, though it was hard while running.

"We have met the enemy, sire. Two units, as expected. But one is an upgraded saakal unit, and there's also a Hero."

"Shit."

"Succinctly put, my lord. I do not know if we can win this." Braskar hesitated, then added, "If not, we will do our best to winnow down our enemies. If I fail, dispatch the rest of the units and finish them off. Run the enemy down, before they can heal."

"Don't die on me now, you big green oaf," Matt said fiercely. "I'm not done with you yet, and you with me. I won't have you giving up on me. You've got the potions; you've got the woodlings. Win. Or run."

"I'll do my best. Now, I must focus."

The creatures were howling now, the saakal letting out their strange yip howl. Not great, but the woodlings were now in the trees, spreading out. Their formation had broken, but that was fine. Time for another command, for the last major one he had to offer them.

"Drink potions!" He roared, suiting action to words.

The woodlings crunched down within themselves, crushing bottles held within their trunks, broken glass cracking apart as liquid seeped into slow moving sap within themselves. Braskar was no fool. He popped the cork off his own drink and glugged it down rather than try to copy his own units' actions. The wood elementals might not care for the changes, but he was only flesh and blood.

Immediately, he could feel the potion working on him. Making him stronger, toughening hide and bulking up the elementals. A low-level glow seemed to appear on the creatures, even as they shifted and dug in for the incoming saakal.

Just before the first wave – the bigger, bulkier of the jackal creatures – began their charge, having pulled away from their smaller brethren, the enemy Hero acted.

A single, long howl sounded as he stood to his full eight feet tall height and threw his lupine head back. A howl that shook Braskar to the core, acting upon primal urges within his body and freezing him. The woodlings froze too, the magic within the roar taking effect on them, even as the upgraded saakal units burst into a charge.

Disaster, rushing across open ground, mouth slavering as they were caught in the fear effect and frozen.

Chapter 18

Braskar fought the primal fear, bottling it up within himself, pushing against the magical effect as he tried to command his own forces. He failed, but to his surprise, the woodlings shook the effects off first. Their lack of earthly bodies gave them an advantage, one that their opponent had failed to take into account. Straightening out from the immobility moments before the first wave of saakal arrived, the woodlings wielded their clubbed hands against the bigger, bulkier monsters.

Almost immediately, the woodlings started falling, the glowing, energy-laden charge slamming into wooden bodies. Four of the woodlings came apart, their bodies shattering as the saakal leapt at them and sent branches and leaves and sap flying through the air. Another two innocent trees befell the same fate, while other saakal had to break their direct charge to weave through the trees before making the leap, allowing the elementals to dodge and suffer less fatal wounds.

Not that the upgraded saakal were doing much better. Stronger and faster they were, but it seemed they had lacked any major upgrade to their defences. The additional damage done by the stronger, enchanted limbs began to take their toll, six of the saakal dying in the first wave as they were impaled on wooden limbs or bodies booted into trees and across the clearing.

Even as the blood red colour of their charged attack faded and they ran onwards through the woods to meet the second unit, the second wave arrived, having triggered their own charge.

Braskar had no time to review all this though, for he found himself shaken free of his own paralysis as a saakal bore him to the ground. Only his axe, held stiffly before him, saved him from having his throat torn out. As he fell, he regained control of his limbs, allowing him to roll backwards and heave the creature away from him, to bounce away behind.

No time to check whether it was still alive, for the orc Hero rolled to the side and onto his feet, ears filled with the crack and boom of the magically enhanced charge crashing into wooden bodies, over and over again.

His first troop unit was gone, completely shattered but for a single member that somehow, somehow, had managed to survive untouched. Now, the second unit was dealing with a combined mixture of the surviving saakal.

Striding forwards, Braskar laid into one of the bigger saakal, his axe catching the back of its leg as it leapt away from one of his woodlings. His weapon bit deep into the body, crushing bone and leaving the monster crippled even as it struggled to draw itself away.

With a brief moment to review it, the orc took the time to take in the unit details.

Enemy Unit: Saakal (II)
Type: Creature
Number: 4/10
Melee Attack: Medium+
Melee Defense: Low
Ranged Attack: None
Ranged Defense: Low
Hit Points: Medium
Speed: Medium+
Special Abilities: Charge
Vulnerabilities: ???

Not much new, not at all. Rather than finish off the crippled creature, Braskar moved away. He knew he had bigger prey to hunt.

The battle through the trees was chaos. He had to congratulate himself on choosing to fight here at the last minute. In fact, he was somewhat certain that the woodlings were benefiting from the environment, both potentially on a statistical basis but also from the confusion. In the gloom, it was all too easy to mistake a tree for a woodling or vice versa. And a moment's hesitation was all it took for death or injury to occur.

In the meantime, he wove through the group, searching for the other Hero. He knew he was here somewhere, the question was, where?

Instinct had Braskar jump backwards from an unseen attack. He was a touch too slow, the blow catching him in the side and spinning him around. Only his axe, swung at the same time, kept his opponent from following up, leaving him to tumble and right himself, to stare at the lolling tongue from a wide-open, predatory mouth to stare at him.

"Fool orc. You think you can beat me?" his opponent said.

Rather than speak, Braskar watched the other as details floated to the surface.

Rerturms (Level 2 Warlord)

Specialty: Warrior

Skills: Howl of the Predator

Experience: 04/200

Attack: 26

Defense: 11

Power: 6

Knowledge: 4

"You see it, don't you, you pitiful Level 1?" Laughing, Rerturms let his long hands hang down from his body, sharp claws clipping the ground as he hunched forwards. "Give up. Humanity is doomed."

"I care not for humanity," Braskar rumbled. "I am an orc. And I do not give up."

"Then die!" Howling, the Hero lunged forwards, claws glinting in the gloom.

Reacting entirely on instinct, Braskar swung his axe, blocking the lunge attack. He barely moved his feet in time to dodge the majority of the other arm swiping at him, though the attack tore through his armour with surprising ease and cut into his torso, leaving strips of pain and hot blood flowing.

Reversing the swing, he cut backwards into the retreating arm, watching it clip the limb. He felt the axe bite deep, even as Rerturms lunged at him, shouldering him with his greater bulk and strength backwards. Pushed off his feet, he flew backwards to bounce off the ground and roll over, a bone in his chest cracking under the force of the assault.

Rerturms gave him no chance to recover, the orc Warlord finding himself swinging his axe defensively, feet paddling backwards constantly as he deflected and struck at his opponent, trying to find a gap. Even the few pauses in tempo that were forced upon the werewolf were insufficient, only giving Braskar enough time to plant his feet.

He was losing. Slowly, thankfully, but losing nonetheless.

Around him, the sounds of battle continued. He had no time to review how things were, but from the slowly decreasing number of clashes, of the crack of branches and startled and pained yips of the saakal, the units were whittling themselves down.

"Gather and hold!" Braskar shouted, desperately. Hoping that his units could do so, could pull together and win.

Then, Rerturms was on him again, claws flashing as they sought his lifeblood. Except… they weren't. Braskar realised soon enough, the creature was playing with him. Just like a wolf would wear down its prey before going in for the kill, Rerturms was wearing him down.

It was smart, fighting like this in the wild. Braskar's only chance of winning was crippling his opponent, cutting into those arms that kept coming at him, chipping away. If not for the faint glow around the arms, if not for the strengthened fur of his body, he might even have succeeded. But combined with careful strikes that never went too far, that allowed the werewolf to pull back when his axe threatened, his opponent was winning.

As the battle waged on, Braskar could feel his lifeblood slip from his numerous wounds. An anger rose within him, with each laboured breath, each cut and taunting feint or snap of a jaw. He felt that Rage pulse within him, combining with the alchemical concoction flowing through him and a growing realization.

One last swipe, this one tearing at his helmet, leaving it hanging off his head with a strap to the side. He had no more time nor care for this slow battle. Roaring his determination, Braskar threw himself forwards, rolling to the side as he flew through the air to let a swinging claw glance off the remnants of his armour as it tore into his chest.

His axe sank deep into Rerturms body, cutting through collarborne and nearly separating one arm entirely. With a twist of his body, in furious pain, his opponent picked up Braskar and threw him away to crash into a tree, bones and hip breaking.

Slumping to the ground, consciousness slipping, he watched as Rerturms pulled the axe from his body, blood pooling around him before stalking forwards. His last gambit had failed. The Rage Skill might have given him one last opportunity, but he had wasted it.

Now, it was the end.

Chapter 19

"Shit, shit, shit…" Matt paced the floor, staring at the intermingled units on the tactical map. His hand clenched and released, clenched and released behind his back the whole time as he tried to figure out something, anything that he could do.

Ever since the pair were in conflict, he could see the information appearing. The details and the inevitable result. He could see that Braskar would lose, that he would die, and eventually the pair of units would end too. Somehow, he still had two units, a single woodling unit managing to survive through this fight, even as the rest of the woodlings in the other unit were killed.

"There's nothing you can do. We need to have you, we need… troops. Moving, now. To make the choices," Irvine said, stuttering at the end.

"There's got to be a way," Matt snarled, walking back to the map. He slapped his hands on the table, leaning closer as he stared at the units, watching as another unit died.

"There's nothing. You've tried, haven't you? You must have," Irvine said. "He'll win. Or not."

"There's got to be something, something I can do. If not, how the hell are we supposed to win? The hell am I supposed to do beyond just sitting here, staring, as fights go on?" Matt replied. "If there's nothing I can do, this is fucked."

"It's always been a mess."

"Well, I refuse to have it end this way." Hand coming down on the table again, striking it hard such that his hands hurt, his body hurt. He stabbed a finger at the units fighting in rage, trying to grasp at it. And startled when new information flicked into life before him as his hands pulled back.

Units Engaged: 2 Woodlings, 1 Hero

Spells Available: Regeneration

"What the hell?" Matt stumbled backwards, staring at the information that glowed before him. Surprisingly, even to him, his hand was moving, grabbing at the Regeneration before he consciously realised what he was doing.

The motion of grabbing and pulling it backwards seemed to make the words expand, the Regeneration widening to fill his vision just like every other text method did. The details that came across his vision were quickly read over, even as his mind spun over the best options.

Spell: Regeneration

Casting time: Instantaneous

Range: 3 hexes

Duration: Instantaneous

Effect: Instantly heals 24 Hit Points worth of damage to targeted unit

Cooldown: 7 days

"One cast. And only one thing to heal." He could help Braskar. Save his friend, save the Hero. Give him a fighting chance against the enemy Hero who was kicking his ass. But he wasn't sure it was enough, not really. The damn Hero was a whole Level above him. One cast, upgrading his man might not be enough. Not at all.

On the other hand, fixing a unit, healing them entirely might be enough to win the fight. The Hero might run, rather than face a healed unit. 24 hit points meant three more units, putting the woodlings, which were on the backfoot and barely hanging on, against the saakal.

Then again, three units weren't a lot. Not really. Might not be enough to pull things out, not when there was an enemy Hero on hand. Maybe nothing they could do was enough, and the enemy would come for them next. And he'd need the Regeneration for when they came then.

How was he supposed to choose?

The crushing burden of command poured down upon Matt once more, and he trembled, licking his lips in hesitation.

"My lord. You must decide," Irvine's voice rasped out as he stared at the glowing information.

It seemed like he was frozen for hours, but in reality only seconds had passed before Irvine had spoken to him. "How can I?"

"The same way you make every decision from now until the end of time. Choose what you can live with, what will allow you to look into the mirror, boy. Because you never want to hate the face looking back at you, especially if you grow to be as old as me. Trust me." Irvine's voice turned wry and hateful, though the hate was turned inwards. "I know all too well."

Matt looked over to the man, then found himself nodding. He instinctively knew how to apply the Regeneration now that the damn mechanic was revealed to him. All he had to do was grab it and then slam it down on the target, pouring intent and will into the action.

All he had to do was hope he wasn't too late, and his friend was not already too far gone.

***

Rerturms was standing over Braskar, the axe – his axe – held in one hand contemptuously. He let it dangle from the fingers of his injured arm, as though even touching the weapon was an affront to the werewolf. After all, he required nothing so crude to kill. Lips were peeled back, and the hot stink of the creature's mouth poured down over him as Braskar lay prone and bleeding. Warm and sticky, he could swear he could see the gristle from a previous meal in the creature's mouth.

Taking his time, Rerturms bent low, blood still dribbling from the deep wound on his body. But it was already healing, the damn creature making his own axe jump in its fingers.

"Axe or claw, axe or claw. Choose your death."

"I'll see you in hell first," Braskar growled, even his words too weak to come out as more than a slur. He could feel his life slipping away from him, the damage too great to survive. It mattered not, axe or claw. He was done for.

"So rude…" Rerturms laughed. "I shall teach you a lesson then."

Arm raised, a pair of fingers pointed. They descended towards the orc's eyes. He shifted, trying to get away and turn aside. A little howling laugh, even as the sounds of battle continued around them, as the werewolf dropped his axe and used his mangled other arm to grip and turn Braskar's face back.

Claws descended further, inches disappearing, and Braskar could only stare, letting his courage gather as he scrambled for the dropped axe. Unable to find the hilt, unable to lift it even if he found it. Inches. Millimeters.

Then, light.

Filling him, surrounding him. Strength followed the light, just as quickly, even as Rerturms jerked backwards, long claws around his face tearing into green skin, opening up his skin as they did so. Only for the claw wounds to close, as did the rest of his wounds.

Body jerking with the sudden rush of power, Braskar was already sitting up. Hand searching for his axe handle, finding it nearer to him than he had believed. The arm numb from lack of blood had missed its presence till now.

Pushing with one hand his opponent who was already reacting, Rerturms swung one arm against his own upraised one. But his axe was turning, coming in and chopping to the side. And something else, Braskar realised. Something perhaps the system had not realised.

That Rage, that additional strength that had been granted to him from the pain and injury and weakness of his body, had not left him. He pushed, and Rerturms moved backwards, waving claw leaving a raking attack on his arm. He pushed and swung, and the axe bit into the body above him. Sinking into his opponent's side and arcing upwards, cutting through ribs into lung and ribcage.

Braskar held on as Rerturms lunged and turned the rest of the way away, nearly pulling his axe from his body. Both Heroes staggered away, getting their feet under them, the wounded werewolf staring at the now uninjured Hero.

"Fool. Your Lord is a fool to heal you." Mouth falling open, Rerturms snarled, "I shall feast on your body and then show him his foolishness."

Braskar saw no reason to prolong the discussion. He could sense his units dying, falling by the wayside. No. Better to finish this, here and now. He threw himself forwards, axe swinging in a feint. Rerturms did not fall for the feint, instead leaning back only a little to give himself more space. So that when Braskar pushed the axe forward in a straight thrust, it was insufficient to do more than scrape the werewolf.

Savage grin swinging, aiming for Braskar's side. But the orc chose not to dodge, instead stepping into the attack with his axe cocking backwards as he did so, staying in roughly the same position. He took the blow hard, but without the full extent of the swing, it only dug into flesh and armour.

Then, Braskar twisted, hips and body flowing in one motion to pour strength into the swing to take his opponent in the center of the body. It tore sideways and upwards, carving another deep furrow into flesh. Not content, the orc kept shoving forwards, using his feet to power the attack till he was past the werewolf, the creature already turning away, attacking hand trailing behind.

A butterfly return, a swing downwards caught the arm as it pulled back, lopping it off. The werewolf staggered backwards, pain and surprise in his eyes. Braskar was panting, adrenaline and Rage carrying him on as he threw his body forward, letting the axe go over his head and out of his hands, the weapon crossing the last few feet to catch the werewolf by surprise.

He watched the axe bury itself in the other side of the body from his first, Rage-filled attack. Watched Rerturms sink to his knees, blood bubbling from pierced lungs and throat, discontent and disbelief in red eyes. The orc staggered forwards, grabbing the axe from the body and tearing it out, before spinning on his heels and beheading the Hero.

For a second, he stood there, victorious and exultant. Raising his axe above his head, he roared his victory; his Command Aura pulsed as it empowered his own units. Then, having rejoiced long enough, he ran.

After all, the battle was not over yet.

Chapter 20

Long minutes watching the dots flicker and numbers drop. A woodling unit, that last member, had disappeared somewhere before Braskar had finished his own fight. Then the enemy Hero had finally died. Now, more members in the second woodling unit had disappeared, even as the saakal fell, one after the other. Until they broke, running for it.

The battle report was simple and stark, if worrying.

Battle Report (Hero Braskar vs Enemy Units)
Result: Victory! 1 Saakal Unit & 1 Enemy Hero Defeated, 1 Saakal Unit Escaped
Units Lost: 1 Woodling
Rewards: +27 Gold, +3 Reputation

The pair in the tactical room stared at one another for a long moment, neither daring to breathe as they read and re-read the notification. Irvine was the first one to let out a long whoop, dancing around and waving his thin, spindly arms around his head, the old man offering a sudden burst of joy. Matt followed him a moment later, pounding the table in joy before grabbing Irvine and swinging him around.

"We did it. We did it!" Matt shouted.

"He did it. That green fool lived," Irvine replied.

"Showed them, we did." Laughing, Matt finally released Irvine. His cheeks were beginning to hurt, so wide was his smile.

"My lord," Braskar's voice came, causing the pair to shout his name in greeting. When they finally quietened after exclaiming their surprise and congratulations, he continued, "I thank you for your aid. It was well timed."

"You're welcome," Matt said. A sudden flash of honesty ran through him, and he almost confided in his desire to heal the units instead of Braskar. Then, good sense returned. "I'm glad you lived."

"As am I." The low rumble was full of satisfaction. "I have further good news to provide, however."

"Oh? You managed to grow some hair down below?" Irvine replied.

"No. Why would an orc need to grow hair on their legs?" Braskar said, confused.

"Not their legs, your privates!"

"Woodlings have bark, not hair. What have you been drinking, Irvine?"

"You know what I mean!"

"I surely do not."

Matt thumped the table, jarring the pair shouting into the air at one another across their magical connection into remembering he was around. "The good news. And stop annoying him, Irvine."

"I didn't…"

"I have Leveled up. As has my woodling unit."

"Ooooh!" That distracted the pair so sufficiently that they yanked and grabbed at the information. First was Braskar's, the two of them hungrily eyeing his character information.

Braskar (Level 2 Warlord)

Specialty: Military Leadership

Skills: Inspiring Aura, Rage

Experience: 27/100

Attack: 27

Defense: 18

Power: 6

Knowledge: 12

"Half again increase." Irvine was the first one to note the increase in Braskar's strength. Definitely a major increase, though Matt wondered if the increases would continue to scale in that manner. Exactly how powerful could Heroes get?

"No new Skills though. I wonder if that's common, or just staggered or…?" Matt trailed off, since the truth was, none of them had any idea.

"Have you stared enough?" Braskar asked, his voice filled with amusement.

"Just about," Matt said after a moment, flicking his hand away to call up the surviving woodling unit. This should be interesting.

Unit Name: Blooded Woodlings

Type: Wood Elemental

Tier: Lesser Tier I

Number: 8* (2 remaining)

Movement: 1

Cost: 20 Gold*

Melee Attack: 8

Melee Defense: 14

Ranged Attack: 0

Ranged Defense: 20

Hit Points: 9

Speed: 6

Special Abilities: Grow, Harden

Vulnerabilities: Fire (Low)

Growth Potential: Medium

"That's it?" Matt said, when he read over the notification. After a moment, he shook his head. Of course, that was it. What did he expect? This was a unit, not a Hero. And even a two-point increase, over eight units, was a sixteen-point total increase in attack. Much more than a single Hero gained. Even if the Hero could, one-on-one, take out any individual unit.

Something that might change though, once Braskar got a few more levels.

"So now what?" Irvine said.

Matt blinked, cocking his head at his advisor. After a moment, he realised what the man meant and sat back down himself, biting his lip in thought. Now what indeed?

"We keep going. Kicking ass. Growing stronger. Winning this insane game," Matt said eventually, sitting up. "We win. And then we find the assholes who started all this and get some answers."

"But first we win," Braskar rumbled.

"That's right. First we win," Matt confirmed, grinning grimly. Time to start.

***

Status Report

Day 16 (End of Day)

Gold: 119.75 (+16.25 Gold per day)

Units: 3 Woodlings

In Production: Woodling (3/4)

Structures Completed: Grove, Road, Stall (II)

Structures Available: Grove (II), Ranged Copse, Basic Greenhouse, Watch Tower, Tavern, Marketplace, Blacksmith, Harbour

Chapter 21

For Matt Fang, former fired accountant of Earth, life had taken a strange turn. Seventeen days ago, he had just been let go from another job for refusing to bow to a petty middle manager. Now, he was a champion of Earth, having agreed to become the frontline in an interdimensional war that he had neither understanding, knowledge, nor even grasp of.

Joining had been on a whim, a burning desire to matter as more than just another cog in the machine. Spending days logging into work and being time- and video-tracked, having his work questioned, and the number of times he went to the washroom counted.

Now, he ruled a kingdom, a magical kingdom with elemental woodlings, and had a pair of trusty advisors. An irritable Alchemist and an orc Warlord that he had nearly killed during their most recent skirmish. It was this very skirmish and the end results that he looked into now, taking full stock of the situation the very next day.

"Do you think it's wise for us to keep him so far forwards?" Irvine muttered, lips thin as he eyed the tactical map floating right before them. The tactical room was on the top floor of their small keep, a room where the hexagon map that portrayed the land around them floated.

"We've got a woodling unit moving up to him. We have another already in the village and he's got the damaged unit with him. That puts him with three units, compared to the single one we have here right now," Matt said. "I'd be more worried about us than him."

"Eh. Aren't we already dead, what with the brain bleed and all that," Irvine said.

"Don't remind me." Matt touched his forehead, remembering the massive pain that he had faced, the stroke he likely had just before he was transferred over. Who knew? Maybe this entire thing was just another hallucination before he died.

"And I do worry about us. And want to know what you plan," Irvine said.

"As do I, my lord." Braskar's voice, the hoarse rumbling tones of the orc, came floating through space. Just another part of the magic, allowing the Hero to connect to them in this room. And only this room, which led to a whole bunch of rather frustrating situations.

Still, a routine meeting every morning was perfect. As was a check-in during the day when Matt or Irvine were free to swing by. And one more at night. Before, they'd only done one once a day, but recent events had seen them decide on something a little more regular.

Recent events being finally locating their opponent, the hyena-humanoid hybrid creatures he called the saakal and the Level 2 werewolf Hero that they'd managed to kill. Thankfully, the enemy Hero had not had much beyond a terrifying roar and a sped-up healing factor it seemed, for it had fallen to Braskar eventually. With a little help from Matt.

"I don't know, alright." Matt sighed. "I spent most of last night celebrating and I've still got a pounding headache. Whatever magical world we're in, you'd think they'd have found a cure for a hangover."

"Orcs have a traditional cure for hangovers."

"What's that?" Matt said, perking up.

"A five-mile run."

"Pass."

Irvine laughed softly. "I told you to stop drinking, did I not?"

"Oh, and you're any better? I remember you red-faced and drunker than a skunk." Matt paused, then frowned. "Hey! How come you don't have a hangover. Are you holding out on me?"

"Nothing of the sort. Side effect of being an Alchemist," Irvine said, smirking a little. "Poison resistance is a minor perk."

"Oh." Matt sighed after a moment, rubbing at his temples. "I got nothing, guys. We could keep to our plan and build out for ranged upgrades, or we could put ourselves back a few days and start a woodling unit. Even if we get a ranged upgrade, we still need to save up enough to build a ranged unit."

"You sound doubtful, my lord," Braskar rumbled.

"I do. I mean, our opponent has upgraded melee units already. Shouldn't we try to at least match them?" Matt said.

"Fighting strength to strength seems like a bad idea." Irvine twitched his hand and pulled up the ranged upgrade and the barracks upgrade, showcasing them both to Matt. "Perhaps reviewing the information again would be a good idea."

Upgrade Available: Grove (II)

Building Type: Barracks

Tier: Lesser Tier II

Units Available to Produce: Woodlings (II) (25/5)

Cost: 125

Production Time: 8 days

Structure Available: Ranged Copse

Building Type: Barracks

Tier: Lesser Tier I

Units Available to Produce: *Squirting cucumber, sandbox trees, or firecracker flowers*

Cost: 200

Production time: 5 days

"Huh," Matt said, staring at the information. "I'd forgotten that it took eight days to build the new Grove upgrade." Then he hesitated. "Wait. If the saakal were already upgraded, and they weren't an evolution – which they might be, mind you – does that mean our opponent has a headstart on us?"

"That would make sense," Braskar rumbled. "We were – humanity that is – the defeated group as per the announcement you relayed to us. If so, we would be fighting at a disadvantage."

"Arse. I should have thought of that…" The 'Lord' rubbed his face. "If I'd known, perhaps a mass production method was the wrong way to go."

"Perhaps. Though, if not for that, we might have been overwhelmed already, my lord," Braskar said.

"Coulda, woulda, shoulda. Enough watching the potion boil. We have decisions to make," Irvine snapped. "What are you going to do? Add more woodlings, keep to your original plan? Do something else stupid?"

"Like what?" Matt said.

"I don't know, build the Tavern?" Irvine replied.

"More Heroes might help…" Matt said quietly. "We certainly have seen the advantage of having Braskar on the field. Without him, I don't think the woodlings would have survived as long."

"No, my lord. My Command Aura Skill provides a sizeable bonus to their unit cohesion and strength," the orc confirmed.

"But what would it cost to hire a Hero?" Irvine said. "Also, we've seen what happens when you drink. Adding another location for you to be even more useless is a bad idea."

"That's really hurtful," Matt said, sniffing. "Learning to relax when appropriate is important for the long-term happiness of an individual and reduces burnout. Management 101."

"I'm sure that's the reason entirely for your drinking."

"Well, I'm not a saint."

"All the better. We do not have enough personnel to sacrifice," Braskar rumbled.

"Wait. Sacrifice?" Matt said, confused.

"Of course. Once a month, a sacrifice must be made to the Old Gods for their favour, so that they do not rise against the New Gods and wage war. In return, the Saint may continue to utilize their favour." Braskar paused, a considering tone entering his voice. "I know humans did not have the same religion, but I remember there being many such sacrifices in village squares. Though burning their sacrifices alive always seemed barbaric."

"Uhhh…." Matt said slowly.

"We do not do that!" Irvine was nowhere as hesitant at rebuking the orc. "At most, we might offer them a cup of poison if they are that heretical. But we make no sacrifices to our gods beyond a bushel of wheat and a cup of poured wine."

"No. I'm sure there were human burnings. On one memorable raid, they were so focused on the process they did not hear us coming till we were nearly on them. The slaughter was mighty and wonderful," Braskar rumbled, happiness in his voice.

"Maybe in your barbaric world. Not mine," Irvine snapped.

"Perhaps. And yours, my lord?"

"Uhh…"

"You were that barbaric too?" Irvine said, shrinking away from Matt.

"Not me. Or my people. And certainly not my culture. But, across the world and in the past?" Matt made a face. "Let's just say we've progressed."

"Oh, the past!" Irvine relaxed. "Those were barbarous times. Why, they refused to even use leeches back then."

Matt snapped his jaw shut, making a side note not to avail himself of the physicking services Irvine might offer in the future. He definitely wasn't going to let anyone punch holes in his head to 'cure' him. Even if he was already hearing voices in his head.

"Well, my lord. Do we have a plan?" Braskar said after a moment. "Or do you want quiet to nurse your headache further?"

"Not so much a plan, but a decision."

***

Status Report

Day 17 (Beginning of Day)

Gold: 136 (+16.25 Gold per day)

Units: 4 Woodlings

In Production: (None)

Structures Completed: Grove, Road, Stall (II)

Structures Available: Grove (II), Ranged Copse, Basic Greenhouse, Watch Tower, Tavern, Marketplace, Blacksmith, Harbour

Cooldown: 6 days to spell casting, 6 days to Burst Production

Chapter 22

"Nothing to report, my lord," Braskar rumbled, four days later. "No sign of our enemies. The injured woodling unit has regenerated an additional member today, putting us at six out of eight in total. I feel that it is time for us to begin scouting once more."

"You think?" Matt said, biting his lip. "Which direction?"

"Northwest."

"Right into the teeth of our enemy, you mean."

"Yes."

"How many do you plan to bring?" Matt could not help but ask.

"Both spare units, my lord."

"Leaving only a single woodling unit in the village." Irvine shook his head. "And I can't do much to help. We got an extra potion here, but you don't have it and I can't run it up to you in time."

"The unit you sent has a potion," Braskar said. "I can bring that with me."

"And you're sure you can't take the one from the woodling unit that's in the village?" Matt asked.

"I cannot. Once assigned, it seems such things are locked to the unit."

"Arse."

"Yes, my lord."

Matt drummed his fingers on the table. They had been safe so far, but he could not help but think that they were risking it. Four days without any sign of their enemy meant that they could have produced another unit in that time. Maybe finished production of another upgraded building. Hired a Hero.

Something.

On the other hand, he knew part of the reason he was so concerned was because they had no information. If they could get further details, he could at least work with that information. Even if it was nothing more than a scouting tower, he could at least tell when the damn fools were coming. He needed more money, more time, more everything.

"Take the last unit," Matt said suddenly, resolve tightening.

"That would leave the village undefended, my lord," Braskar protested.

"They're not real people, right?" Matt said. "And there's a militia?"

"I believe there might be, though we have yet to test it. But it would be insufficient against the forces we've noted."

"Exactly. So what's the point of a single unit?" Matt shook his head. "An upgraded saakal unit will kick our woodling's ass anyway. Unless they get a bonus for defending the village-"

"They do not," Irvine said, having poked at the village again.

"-there's no way they'd hold. So we shouldn't bother trying. Bring the unit with you, be safer," Matt said. "Worst case, we lose a village and get informed that our enemies are coming for us."

"As you command, my lord," Braskar said finally.

Silence filled the room now, as both parties across the enchanted voice communication waited for the other to say something. The silence lingered for a time, before Irvine let out a loud harumph.

"So, are you going to buy it or not?" he said.

"Buy what?" Matt said innocently.

"The copse!" Irvine snapped.

"Fine, fine." Laughing a little, Matt called up the information. Once more, he selected the Ranged Copse, only for the previous details about the ranged options to arrive.

Unit Name: Squirting Cucumber

Type: Wood Elemental

Tier: Lesser Tier I

Number: 12

Movement: 1

Cost: 25 Gold

Melee Attack: 2

Melee Defense: 6

Ranged Attack: 6

Ranged Defense: 4

Hit Points: 4

Speed: 9

Special Abilities: Entangle, Ranged

Vulnerabilities: Fire (Low)

Growth Potential: Medium

Eyes skipped over the information, then just to have something to compare it to, Matt grabbed at the next notification.

Unit Name: Sandbox Trees

Type: Wood Elemental

Tier: Lesser Tier I

Number: 4

Movement: 1

Cost: 25 Gold

Melee Attack: 3

Melee Defense: 8

Ranged Attack: 7

Ranged Defense: 8

Hit Points: 6

Speed: 2

Special Abilities: Ranged (Short), Explosive

Vulnerabilities: Fire (High)

Growth Potential: High

"Damn, these guys look almost better than our normal woodlings," Matt said, eyeing the overall higher Melee and Ranged stats. Not that high for hit points though, and much lower speed. Still, speed was only an issue if they got in range.

"Low range though."

"Yeah, I wonder what they mean by short?"

Irvine shrugged.

Braskar rumbled, luckily being able to see the notifications they pulled up even from far away. Probably something to do with him being Matt's technical military advisor. "I would prefer to see the final option before we make a decision."

Unit Name: Firecracker Flowers

Type: Wood Elemental

Tier: Lesser Tier I

Number: 8

Movement: 1

Cost: 25 Gold

Melee Attack: 1

Melee Defense: 5

Ranged Attack: 10

Ranged Defense: 5

Hit Points: 6

Speed: 12

Special Abilities: Ranged, Explosive

Growth Potential: Low

"We? Pretty sure it's a me decision," Matt replied, half smiling.

"Then you do not require my advice, my lord?" Braskar said, not sounding offended but hurried instead.

"No, no. I'll listen." Waving his hand around, knowing the orc probably was pulling his leg anyway, Matt added, "So, speak."

"I believe the most important thing to note is what role you decide your units will play in battle. The cucumbers will entangle your opponent, allowing you to pin them down and wear away at them with additional ranged attacks, or for your fast-moving units to conduct hit and run tactics."

"Gotcha. But we are lacking other ranged units. Or fast-moving ones."

"Exactly, my lord." Braskar continued next, "The sandbox trees offer an interesting compromise as tough melee additions. We would devolve to significantly closer battles, but the explosion from the trees could likely give us an element of surprise. Especially on first encounters."

"But less so afterwards." Matt rubbed his chin. "And they're tough enough to stand in line, so we could have them bolster our melee fights as we go along. Makes for a tough army to handle close-up."

"Yes, my lord."

"And the final one?"

"A pure ranged unit. High explosive damage, long range but very weak to attacks," Braskar said.

"Yeah, I spotted that. Super weak."

"Do we need more weak units?" Irvine complained. "It seems all we have are weak buildings."

"So your vote is for the sandbox trees?" Matt said.

"Obviously."

"What about you, Braskar, my Warlord?"

"I concur. My preference is for close combat and strengthening our close-range combat, when our opponent has shown the lack in ranged units seems the best option." Matt could swear he heard a tiny purr in his Warlord's voice, one that came from being called Warlord. Or perhaps just having his advice solicited. Or both.

"Well, that's good to know. Both of you." Matt fell silent, eyes narrowing in thought. Then, he straightened, decision made. "But if I'm running this, we're playing this my way. And I've always felt that going for contrast is better. So, if we've got a slow-moving front line that's decently tough, we're not going to add to it, but play synergies."

"Oh…" Irvine said, seeming to get it.

"My lord?"

Rather than answer directly, Matt's fingers stabbed outwards, confirming details on the copse. Moments later, he watched his gold account drain, along with the new, confirmed building information appearing.

Structure Under Construction: Ranged Copse

Building Type: Barracks

Tier: Lesser Tier I

Units Available to Produce: Firecracker Flowers

Cost: 200

Production time: 5 days

"Well, at least we have a decision." Irvine sighed. "I just hope you get it right."

"Hey, I got us this far, haven't I?" Matt said with a devilish grin.

"Yes. And everyone's alive. Till they're not." So saying, Irvine waved goodbye and wandered off, leaving Matt to frown into the distance. To his surprise, Braskar did not say anything either, leaving him alone.

Sometimes, being the guy who made the decisions just meant everyone else got to be upset with you.

***

Status Report

Day 21 (End of Day)

Gold: 1 (+16.25 Gold per day)

Units: 4 Woodlings

In Production: Ranged Copse (0/5)

Structures Completed: Grove, Road, Stall (II)

Structures Available: Grove (II), Basic Greenhouse, Watch Tower, Tavern, Marketplace, Blacksmith, Harbour

Cooldown: 2 days to spell casting, 2 days to Burst Production

Chapter 23

Rather than deal with his advisors, knowing that Irvine was continuing to make potions to offer to the fighting units and Braskar was scouting, Matt made his way out of the tactical room to eye his own building. The entire thing was a single hold with a wooden wall, the keep itself on a hill. Sort of a motte and bailey kind of construction rather than anything more elaborate, though there wasn't a separate bailey around. At least, Matt thought that was what it was called. It'd been a while and the vast majority of his knowledge about the various kinds of castles out there came from video games, which really was not the best source of knowledge.

Outside, the settlement was made up of the forming Ranged Copse down one side of the wide – very wide – open ground between walls and hold, with the copse basically being a bunch of sprouting bushes growing from the ground up. Unlike what he'd assumed a real archery range might look like, the Ranged Copse for his wood elementals was just a grove. A garden? What did you call a bunch of bushes?

Anyway, it kind of made sense. Not much training was needed for accuracy, he assumed. There was an earthen embankment down one side, so he guessed they'd just practise a couple of times lobbing their explosives in that direction. But beyond that, he was literally growing his fighters.

Sort of like the 'barracks' that grew the woodlings. Now, the Grove here was his favourite spot. Not only did the trees that made up the barracks offer shade, but there was also something calming about leaning against a big tree and just letting his mind rest.

Of course, that was when he was actively producing a woodling. Right now, the Grove was empty, just some smaller bushes and pathways showcasing where the woodlings would grow. Made the place look pretty empty, really.

Outside of that, he had the Stall which generated revenue for him, though how it did beyond 'magic' made no sense to Matt. After all, it wasn't as though anyone actually ever bought anything from the Stall, nor did the Stall sell any goods.

Sort of like the Road that connected them to the village.

Stupid magic, stupid made-up rules, stupid war waged for humanity's existence without explanation or even sense. Stupid brain, for actually finding the last few weeks of life more livable than the past decade or so of corporate drudgery, college, and school. Which kind of fool thought that working for the rest of your life, doing menial, meaningless things, just to make someone else rich was the way to exist?

Oh, right. Billionaires.

Maybe when he got back, he'd sic his woodlings on them all and see how they liked it.

And Matt was very, very careful to believe deep within that he would get back. Thinking he might fail, that he might die was a bad way to go and something he intended to avoid at all costs. Despair – even if the odds were stacked against him – was a powerful drug and would leave him senseless, curled up in an uncomfortable, too hard bed all too easily.

On that note, with little more to do for the next few days, Matt chose to tackle his other major project. The only other major project he had and his own attempt at gaming the system. Just because the damn system didn't create options to make traps or build a moat or really allow him to do anything useful with his time, that didn't mean he couldn't do it on his own.

It just required a shovel, a pickaxe, a wheelbarrow, and a lot of time. All of which Matt had. Now, building deep pit traps, which would eventually turn into a moat in front of the city along the sides of the road, was his main objective.

If nothing else, it kept him busy, made him stronger, and meant he wasn't just sitting around, waiting for something, anything to happen.

***

Irvine watched as the precipitate from his latest solution gathered, dripping down the distillation tube to collect further down his assembly. He eyed the yellow liquid, and the level gained for a moment more before he nodded to himself and moved away, turning to the next item on his list. While he knew they needed more of the Potion of Strength, there were only two more days before Burst Production came off cooldown. Better to spend that time attempting to make another potion rather than waste it attempting to make a single use of that potion.

At least in his view.

Good thing that was all that mattered right now. Obviously, Matt might have something else to say about it, if he had thought to give Irvine an order, but having assumed that the other was going to keep producing potions, he had left the Alchemist alone. And what the man didn't know wouldn't hurt him. Or cause him to go into another spiral of analysis paralysis, trying to work out the best method.

That's the thing Irvine had realised, working with alchemical potions a long time ago. You could control for everything possible, whether it was the kind of equipment one used or the quality of ingredients, but there were always going to be hidden aspects of the world that one could not fully grasp. Was the moonlight that shone on the celestial nodding flowers strong enough to affect their growth? Did the plant face east or west when it first grew?

Most of the time, none of that mattered. Most of the time, you could control for the majority of important aspects in the growth of a plant or herb or ingredient, and the potion that you produced would come out fine. But on occasion, a series of unknown changes would affect the ingredients, combining together to make a potion you'd made a thousand times fail.

That was life though. You could worry about the known aspects all you wanted, but it was the unknown that would get you every time. And worrying about the unknown was a fool's game. So best just to get on with the making and stack up the advantages as best you could.

In Irvine's case, that meant trying to produce new potion formulas. Because those gave a much better boost to his experience gain than reproducing the same damn potion over and over again. Nevermind the utility of having more potions in play too.

Which was why he was focused on working out a new formula. The Potion of Strength had been what he had started out with, but once he had learnt it, he now had a pair of new potion formulas to work on. A Potion of Defense and a Potion of Stealth.

Really, he didn't even need to talk to Matt to choose which one to research. Stealth was so not the Warlord's style, nor was it his Lord's.

Turning back to the dripping potion, he switched out the flash and carefully poured it into the waiting purplish mixture. This was the final ingredient. Careful stirring with a glass pipette set the colour of the mixture to change, yellow and purple combining to make… grey sludge.

Irvine didn't even need to look at the notification to know this was another failure.

Potion of Defense Creation: Failure
Success Rate: 27%

Well. Better than before. Now, time to go over his notes and try to figure out what he did wrong, before trying again.

Chapter 24

Three days in and Matt was on his afternoon break, ripping into the chicken and potato meal that he'd taken from the kitchens. Magical kitchens were great and all, what with the ability of his semi-corporeal, semi-sentient servants to take his dirty dishes and do his laundry, but it also meant that they lacked a certain flexibility humans had. Like more than a half-dozen recipes. He had grown desperate enough at one point to try making his own meal, but Matt had quickly found out that many of the resources that worked for the servants just didn't for him.

"Braskar," Matt called out, leg slung over the tactical table. "Anything new to report?"

"No, my lord. We are three hexes north of the village and are just beginning to cover new ground," Braskar replied. "More plains at the moment, though I believe there might be a forest to the east of me. It could just be another stand of trees though."

Matt nodded. "Great. You headed further north first or going west?"

"Northwest, yes. I believe that's where we'll find our enemy."

"And you're just going to do a hit-and-run, right, if you see any outposts? No trying to lock down into a real fight. I doubt we have the might to win against a fort right now, not unless they emptied out their hold."

"Unlikely, I agree. But we can not know this till we try, my lord."

"Just don't go getting yourself killed. You just leveled up after all."

"Your concern is touching."

"I can't tell if you're being sarcastic or not," Matt groused.

Silence just greeted his words and Matt chuckled, glad that the orc was beginning to lighten up and josh him too. He needed Braskar. The man — orc, Hero — was his main fighting force and one of two others he could talk to here. Frankly, he was also a lot less prickly than Irvine.

"Keep me informed, will you?"

"Of course."

Mentally willing the connection closed, Matt continued to tear into his food. He ignored the dirt that tumbled to the floor or the greasy mess it made of his hands. One would be dealt with by the automated servants, the other would wipe away in the ground when he got to it.

In the meantime, he let his gaze dance over the surroundings, checking the map once more for problems. He frowned as something to the east appeared, along the edges of the coast that he could see, and poked at it. With the entire fort built up against the water, he had always been a little worried about how open the entire thing was to an attack from the water, but so far, it had been a non-issue.

He hadn't thought of someone running along the coast to map everything out. Which, in this case, the new unit was doing he'd guess.

"Oh shit." Rubbing greasy hands on his face and picking up even more dirt and sweat, all of which he hadn't noticed, he called out to his advisors. Of course, things weren't going to go so easy.

***

"This does not seem to be the same as the previous attackers," Irvine said, poking at the unit. Once again, the tactical table provided exactly the same information as before. Which was, for all practical purposes, zip.

Enemy Army Sighted!
Quantity: Unknown

"Why do you say that?" Braskar asked, not having access to the tactical map due to being multiple hexes away. He could only hear their reports, though Matt could picture the large orc Warlord pacing along the woodling units impatiently.

"The flag they're using and the icon are all different. The last time, they were shaded a yellow-green colour. Now, it's just brown," Matt answered. "Flag is super plain looking too." Then, a thought struck him. "Do we have a flag? Why haven't I seen one."

"You mean the flag flying above our hold?" Irvine said, staring at Matt. "Exactly how did you miss that?"

"There's a flag flying above us?" Matt said, surprised. He frowned heavily, trying to recall the look of the keep and then grimaced. Oh, there had been something on the topmost tower, something flapping along. He had just ignored it because it hadn't seemed important and after that, he'd promptly forgotten about the matter.

"We're going to die," Irvine complained.

"Yeah, yeah…" Matt waved his hand, dismissing the matter both because they had something more important to discuss and also because he was rather embarrassed. If there was a little niggle of worry about what else he had missed, he kept that hidden. "So, brown unit flag. Another opponent?"

"That would be entirely unfair, my lord," Braskar rumbled.

"Killing us and dumping us into a weird ass RTS game with no instruction manual doesn't seem exactly fair either, does it?" Matt said sarcastically.

"No, it does not, my lord."

"The orc's right though, this seems different. Putting us in multiple fights doesn't seem to be the way they intend to build this. And even if we are at a disadvantage, if there was no chance for us to win – and moultiple opponents leans towards low or no chances – then, why bother with this at all?" Irvine said. "Anyway, the colours we saw before, yellow-green and our own blue-white are… colourful. This isn't."

"So, you think it might be what?" Matt said.

"Raiders?" Braskar offered. "The system-controlled enemies that we were worried about initially."

"Like the village," Matt said, recalling the weird militia units that Braskar had to fight to win. Sort of like the random encounters his fighting unit had to deal with occasionally. Not that Braskar even bothered to report those anymore. With multiple woodling units and himself, fighting the random overly aggressive wildlife was barely an inconvenience.

"So, do you think they'd be like the random encounters?" Matt asked rhetorically.

"Unlikely," Irvine said. "I'd assume they're a more difficult challenge. They have to assault our walls, after all."

"Yeah…" Matt sighed. "So, one hex a day, you think?"

"Most likely. If they move more, we will know by tomorrow," Irvine replied.

"Then the only question is if we are going to fight them behind our walls or go straight out to meet them."

"Behind the walls," both of his advisors chimed in at the same time.

"But the village…" Matt gestured down at the small settlement that lay below and outside the walls. More village than anything else right now, but it was his.

"It is unlikely to be touched. They'll come for the keep first. And if they don't, you can sally forth and take them from behind," Braskar rumbled.

"I don't know…"

"I do," the orc replied firmly and Matt found himself hunching a little at the tone of command, feeling like a naughty five year old. After a second, he sighed and nodded.

"Fine. We wait. Again."

Satisfied, Braskar cut the connection and Irvine left, muttering about getting more potions together. All well and good, but it did leave Matt to stew in his worries again, his cold lunch beside him and his appetite gone. Glancing at the information, at the single unit of woodlings at home, and how much they were earning, he came to a resolution.

Needs must and a woodling came first. The ranged units could come later.

Because for the first time, he was going to have to fight. And in truth, he was not looking forward to it. Not at all.

***

Status Report

Day 24 (End of Day)

Gold: 29.75 (+16.25 Gold per day)

Units: 4 Woodlings

In Production: Ranged Copse (3/5), Woodling (0/4)

Structures Completed: Grove, Road, Stall (II)

Structures Available: Grove (II), Basic Greenhouse, Watch Tower, Tavern, Marketplace, Blacksmith, Harbour

Cooldown: None

Chapter 25

Two days later and Matt was bouncing on his feet, watching the Ranged Copse finally complete itself. In the tactical room, additional data was streaming in, though he was alone. Irvine was outside, physically watching for the enemy unit that was on its way. Best to make sure they were ready for them, rather than all crowding around. The moment the bell chimed and the copse fully resolved in the tactical unit, Matt called the information to him.

Name: Ranged Copse
Building Type: Barracks
Tier: Lesser Tier I
Units Available to Produce: Firecracker Flowers (25/5)
Units in Production: None

Nothing surprising there. What was a little surprising – when it really shouldn't have been – was the upgrade option.

Upgrade Available: Ranged Copse (II)
Building Type: Barracks
Tier: Lesser Tier II
Units Available to Produce: Firecracker Flowers (II) (35/5)
Cost: 150
Production Time: 10 days

Matt barely glanced at the details before discarding them. No point in worrying about it, even if the upgraded firecracker flowers might be useful. He neither had the gold nor the time to utilize them. Glancing at the unit information again, he confirmed that they were the same as before. No random mutations for him.

Twenty-five gold was not expensive, and he had enough, so Matt confirmed the purchase, watching the copse begin sprouting the flowers. It would still take five days before they formed, so it was utterly useless to him, and in between he'd have to figure out what else he was going to do with his funds.

Mostly, he was leaning towards the Harbour rather than the Marketplace. He desperately needed more income, but the potential utilization of the water, including perhaps defenses from waterborne attacks, was very tempting. Nevermind whatever potential new buildings that could appear when he finished the production.

Problem was…

Gold: 37.25 (+16.25 Gold per day)

Another ten days before he was ready to build the Marketplace at two hundred gold. Could he wait that long? Or was a Blacksmith, which could get him immediate results, more important? He could get that built in four days, a third of the time or so.

Now that he was adding more and more units, a flat increase to all his units would mean a major change in overall strength if he built the Blacksmith immediately. On the other hand, his opponents had upgraded basic units. Even getting an upgrade on his combat strength would not put them ahead of the upgraded enemy units. He still needed two units to one, or three to two it seemed. With the Potion of Strength though, maybe they might just about equal another unit.

Maybe. Annoying that there were no specific numbers to check against, but leadership and Skills, like Commanding Aura from Braskar, made a difference he assumed.

Oh, and it wasn't just ten days. He still needed to build more woodlings and the firecracker flowers units. Those would push the timeline even further back. And while he might not want too many more units till he could get ahead, he needed at least one more of each. So figure another fifty-five gold required, or the equivalent of three and a half days. Four because the income didn't stream in but reset at the start of the day.

Fourteen days of not building anything but more units. Was that viable? Or would it be better to wait the nine days, and a few more days after that, before he built the next unit? He also had to worry about the timeline and how long it'd take for any structure he created to be completed too.

Risk, in all the ways.

Right now though, he couldn't make any further decisions. He neither had enough money to build anything more, nor the options. Right now, he could only wait, but at least having weighed his options, he could make a choice when he did have the gold in a few days.

In the meantime, he just had to wait for Braskar to find their enemy and the raiders to arrive. A shake of his head, and then Matt turned and left the building. It was time to join Irvine, for there was nothing else to do up here.

Not at this time.

***

"More water," Braskar growled. After the trees he had noticed in the distance had turned out to be the beginning of a series of forested hills, he had chosen to head west. That had allowed him to follow the plains further north a little, hoping to skirt around the hills itself. That had been a mistake though, for though there had been no hills before him, there was water.

Lakes, a giant lake that they had skirted around and then bypassed before having to avoid again when they tried to go around the hills. Now they had found the source of the lake – or at least, the source of the current one. The lake stretched as far as they could see, certainly far enough that there was no crossing it without a boat.

To the west, they could see more water. Maybe it would disappear in time, that they could go around it. Most settlements were built near water sources, so it was quite possible their enemy was on the other side of the lake. If they followed its shores, they could eventually find their enemy.

A good choice perhaps. But there was no clue to how big the lake was.

The other option was to go east, retrace their steps, and enter the hills he could see there. They would move slower though. How much slower, Braskar knew not. Thus far, they had only gone through forests or plains.

Braskar hummed to himself, fingers drumming against his thigh. He could wait and ask his Lord, but his Lord was both a great man and a lousy one. He trusted in Braskar to make the decisions on the ground, but that also meant that he had to make the decisions.

Go west and test the lake or go right, get slowed by the hill, and potentially lose what little hint they had of where their enemy had come from. After all, all they knew was that their enemy had come from the northwest.

East or west?

***

"You shouldn't be here," Irvine groused, tilting his head to the right as Matt joined him on the wall.

"Where else would I be?"

"Safe in the tactics room."

"Where I can't see or do anything?" Matt touched the sword he had belted on, the small buckler strapped to his arm, and the long spear he had picked up. Since he had very little actual training, he figured something to keep him at a distance was his best option.

If they had a single bow in the damn keep, he'd use it. But he had no idea how to make a bow or any arrows, so spear it was.

"Where you can use your spell," Irvine said. "You know, the one that heals us?" Irvine said. "The one that saved Braskar?"

"I remember it," Matt's lip curled up. "Do you think I'll need it? If we can hold without it…"

"It'd be best, yes. But if you die, we lose."

"Are you certain of that?"

"Are you certain that it isn't?" Irvine said.

No answer to that. Then, dust in the distance. The pair watched it grow, along with the small dots against the horizon. Matt's lip thinned, annoyance increasing as he realised he had no binoculars here. Had no way of acquiring some.

All he could do was wait. Watch as they grow closer, wait and watch as they chose which to attack.

Seemed like waiting was his entire thing in this game.

***

Status Report

Day 26

Gold: 37.25 (+16.25 Gold per day)

Units: 4 Woodlings

In Production: Woodling (2/4), Firecracker Flowers (0/4)

Structures Completed: Grove, Road, Stall (II), Ranged Copse

Structures Available: Grove (II), Basic Greenhouse, Watch Tower, Tavern, Marketplace, Blacksmith, Harbour, Ranged Copse (II)

Cooldown: None

Chapter 26

Cavalry. A dozen men on horses. How the heck the brigands had cavalry when he was stuck with infantry, Matt had no idea. So bloody frustrating. Then again, the entire game was biased anyway, he knew that. So bitching about it further had no point. Not really.

"A dozen. That's not great…" The more he squinted, the more he waited for the unit information to come up. Braskar had related how that information had come up for him, so he just needed to wait for it to appear. They had a single unit of woodlings, eight members only.

"Depends on how tough a lot they are, no?" Irvine said. "Scousers like that, you never know. Might just fall over with a good wallop."

"Yes…" Matt's eyes narrowed in thought before he added, "Definitely not meeting them in the clear, if we can choose otherwise."

"No, no we're not," Irvine confirmed. "Or you'd be doing that by yourself, my lord."

Matt snorted, noting that the man finally had chosen to call him by his title. Not at all being sarcastic there, was he. Nope. Not at all. It did, however, help distract him long enough for the system to finally decide he could see enough of their opponents to get a proper read.

Type: Raider Unit

Tier: Lesser Tier I

Number: 12

Movement: 2

Melee Attack: High / Very Low

Melee Defense: Low

Ranged Attack: None

Ranged Defense: Low

Hit Points: Low

Speed: High

Special Abilities: Charge, Unknown

Vulnerabilities: Unknown

"What's with the weird melee attack?" Matt groused. Not that he really needed an answer. Probably a question of whether they were in a charge and moving on their horses or stuck in melee or even on foot. It would have been nice to have confirmation, but since they seemed to be ignoring the village and coming straight for their fort, he assumed he'd find out soon enough.

"Alright, you had your look. Time to go back," Irvine said, turning to look at Matt.

"Not just yet."

"You dying because you were curious and got hit by an accidental attack would be a stupid way to lose," Irvine said.

Matt kept his gaze locked on the raiders, sweeping his gaze over each individual to let the system trigger if something was being hidden. Or if a Hero or something else showed up. Not finding anything, he verified they all had the almost same features that the pre-generated creatures had before he finally answered the Alchemist.

"They don't have ranged attacks. But I'll leave before they start throwing things or trying to hammer our front gate down." Matt paused. "We did close the door, right?"

"It's closed and locked." Irvine hesitated, then added, "I think."

"Maybe check on that?" Matt said sweetly, though he couldn't help the thread of tension in his voice.

"Yeah, yeah…" But Irvine moved his feet, scrambling over to the ladder that took him down to the ground floor.

Matt turned away from his advisor, leaning on the wall. He found himself biting his lower lip in anticipation as they kept riding forwards, only pulling up a little when they hit the latest of his pits. He had not had time to cover it, so it was rather obvious. Slower now, the group rode around it, guiding themselves and their horses around before continuing to close.

"Well, that's one theory out," Matt said. It was a low percentage theory anyway, that the raiders were dumb enough to fall into open pits. While the programming or whatever it was that drove some of his opponents and the units were not particularly sophisticated, they weren't entirely dumb either. At least in the parts that mattered.

So.

Eyes narrowed, he waited. They guided themselves around the open pits, heading in deeper. They were even smart enough to go around the pits that had rushes placed on them, that were semi-camouflaged but not entirely hidden. Another test failed.

Damn. The raider pathing and AI was definitely smarter than he'd hoped. Either that or his skills at hiding things were entirely crap. Of course, they might actually be AI, but for Matt, it made more sense for him to believe they were not truly real than devolve into an existential crisis of whether he was killing actual people with each of his decisions. As much as the movies might make light of it, actually killing someone was an act that froze your average person and sent more of them into therapy than he cared to consider.

"Come on, come on. One last try." These pits were the last of his attempts, woven pieces of wood and rushes along with dirt and carefully extracted sods of land and earth. Basically, his best attempt at hiding the pits. Those pits weren't even that big to begin with. He had one attempt. Not even enough to actually take out the units. But then again, he had never planned on his traps doing all the hard work.

Five. Four. Three. At one meter, the rider at the front slowed a little, but the push from behind kept the man moving. A step, then another, and the horse put its foot through the simple planks. It tumbled, dropping forwards and throwing the rider over even as the horse neighed and whinnied in surprise and pain. The soldier, tossed over, slammed face first into the ground even as the others pulled to a stop immediately.

"Huh. So… that works."

"Is that what you've been looking forward to?" Irvine said, causing Matt to leap upwards in surprise.

"Don't do that!" he snarled, glaring at Irvine.

"Doors are closed. They were already closed." He shook his head. "Which is for the best really. Where do you want the woodlings anyway? On the doors or the wall?"

"Can't we split them?" Matt said.

"No." The Alchemist shook his head. "Braskar might, but I don't have that kind of control over these."

"His Command Aura, eh?" Matt hesitated, looking back and forth. "Start them up here. It'll take them a bit to break through. We have things to help with a siege, right?" Looking around, Matt saw no rocks, no boiling oil. No catapults or bows.

"Not with me, but…" Irvine shrugged. "I'm sure there's got to be something, right? Or what's the point of a fort?"

"Exactly my thoughts." Matt caught the pointed look the Alchemist was giving him and sighed. "I know, I know. I'm going. Hiding away…"

Grabbing the spear he had brought along, he went down the stairs further down the wall rather than the ladder that Irvine had used. After all, he had no reason to rush. Much. Not as tough a cavalry charge could take down a barred gate.

***

Irvine watched Matt disappear down the stairs and let out a long sigh. Moments later, the woodling units swarmed upwards at his command. The woodlings each took position along the wall facing their enemy. Once they stopped moving, piles of stones appeared next to them, making Irvine let out a long breath.

"Oh good, we were right." He had ways of getting around that, if necessary. A couple of alchemical potions that could explode, an irritating dust… but he'd rather not make use of them unless he had to. Which, he assumed, would be any moment in the next thirty minutes.

The cavalry trotted near the walls, rode up and down for a bit, and then, not actually having carried siege weaponry with them or even ladders, got off their horses. Irvine's eyes narrowed in thought as he wondered what they'd do now. Would whatever insane system that was in play create ladders for them to ascend?

The answer was more mundane than that. They rushed the doors, a trio in the front having axes that they wielded above their heads.

"Gather up at the doors!" Irvine shouted, trying to encourage the woodlings to congregate. Unfortunately, just as before, they took no notice of his specific orders, instead just standing at their assigned spots. It still left two right above the gate, and potentially two more at the sides who could lob or swing their stones at their opponents, but nowhere the numbers he wished for.

Better than nothing.

The shouts of the cavalry raiders were mechanical to Irvine's ears. He wondered if it was just his imagination or they truly were just mechanical. It did not matter to him, in a sense, since the roars of aggression soon turned to cries of pain. The woodlings might not be the most inventive of units, nor the fastest, but they were strong. Each woodling standing above the gate hefted a sizable stone and then dropped it with ease, targeting the cluster of raiders below.

From the sides, he noted the woodlings throwing their rocks. Those were more badly aimed, what with the need to actually get the angle right. Of the four rocks tossed, the two from above had struck, cracking against arms and shoulders, bouncing off light hardened leather armour, and one had ended up skipping along, knocking into the foot of a raider. The other had missed entirely.

No casualties yet, surprisingly. Irvine knew if he had been struck by one of those rocks in another time, he'd be on the ground. These raiders did not look that much stronger than him, and yet they took the dropping stones well.

Worse, they seemed to be tearing into the gate at a rate that should have been impossible with three basic axes and a bunch of swords. Irvine could hear the crack and thud of splintering wood, as though they'd shored the doors up with rotten trunks rather than… Magical wood that had been here before?

Okay, so maybe he should not expect much from the door.

"I'm getting alerts here, saying the gates are already at 82%. What the hell, are they using a ram or something? How'd they carry that?" Matt said over the connection, sounding incredibly stressed. "Are they using magic? It's magic, isn't it?"

"No magic. Just some axes."

"Axes? Who are they, Paul Bunyan?"

"Who?"

Irvine could imagine Matt shaking his head aggressively, pushing the question aside. "So what are we doing about it?"

"Can you not see the damage the woodlings are doing?"

"Uhh…" A pause, then his voice returned, a little sheepish. "Yeah. So they're stabbing them or something?"

"Rocks. We were right, the fort generated the rocks when the unit arrived," Irvine said. He eyed the woodlings, tossing their third round of stones over the parapet. The same poor raider got hit in the opposite leg, sending him sprawling to the ground. When he struggled upwards, he did so slowly. Not so two others of those swinging at the gates, one of whom was wielding an axe.

"Fifty-five percent. But they lost two so far. And the others are accumulating injuries. What do you think? We can take them all down before the walls fall?" Matt asked curiously.

"Unlikely."

"Didn't think so either. Do you think they'll run?"

Irvine stared at the figures below, and then sighed. "No. I do not. But the fight won't be as one-sided as you'd think."

"What do you mean?" Matt said.

"We'll have to pull the woodlings off the walls to face them at the entrance."

"Shit. You're right."

"I know." Irvine eyed the rocks, the raiders, and his woodlings, gauging the timing. "Now, if you'll let me do my job…"

"Sorry, sorry. I'll… get ready to use my spell, I guess."

"Do that."

Feeling the connection close, Irvine could not help but let out a long sigh. Matt was not the best Lord, but his nerves were rather grating. You'd think it was the first time his life was threatened.

Chapter 27

Matt rocked back and forth on his feet, drummed fingers on the tabletop, and opened his mouth again and again before shutting it. He shook his head firmly, forcing himself not to bother the Alchemist. He was in charge of the woodlings. Not Matt. No jostling his elbow. Still…

Fort Under Siege!
Gates at 18%

That damn alert kept flashing up each couple of points at regular intervals. He could see it bleeding down, and even as more units fell, it didn't seem to slow down the rate of the destruction. Stupid really. You'd think the amount of damage being done would decrease, but nope.

Finally, he saw the woodlings begin to move from out the window. They were streaming down the stairs, gathering in front of the gate. Interestingly enough, he could see Irvine himself moving to take position above the gate on the wall, peering down. The way he kept leaning over, Matt was treated to the knowledge that the robe the man wore was rather a little too threadbare around the buttocks.

"What the hell are you doing?" Matt muttered to himself. He was clear that he wasn't going to activate the connection though.

Alert! Gates Breached!

The klaxon that went off in the room made Matt and Irvine jump. The Alchemist wavered for a second, nearly falling off the wall as he got his balance, cursing loud enough that even Matt could hear him in his tower. Balance restored, the Alchemist then seemed to pour something downwards.

Now, Matt couldn't help but ask, especially since Irvine had dropped back to a safer position. "What was that?"

"Itching powder. It'll distract them, put a debuff. It's short-acting, which is why I didn't use it till now, but that damn alarm made me miss half of them," Irvine groused. "Now let me watch."

"Right, right. Sorry!"

Matt moved away from the wall, eyeing the seven members of the cavalry raiders who were charging into the jaws of his eight, uninjured woodlings. Well, seven charging members and one deeply limping one who seemed to be having trouble walking and was busy scratching himself too.

Matt had liked watching action movies in the past. He didn't even mind horror movies and torture porn, while not his preferred horror type, was something he'd suffered through for an ex. He had considered himself innured to the kind of mess that the human body could experience. Or so he thought.

There was something very different about seeing it – even at a remove – in person. Something about the screams, the rictus of pain, the sudden and sharp snap of bones or the spurting of blood in the air that made it all kinds of immediate. The way the rage in those eyes went from all too present to suddenly absent and lost as a woodling speared a cavalry member in the chest.

And the woodlings themselves, his friends, the ones he had leaned upon…

Well, somehow, it didn't seem as bad seeing them die. Perhaps it was because they never talked, they were just trees. And you didn't have the same level of feelings for the death of a tree as you would a person, and the raiders were people, even if they had slightly more sloped foreheads and a distinctly strange length of limbs.

Maybe it was that, or maybe because Matt knew the woodlings were elementals and thus not really living. Or he thought they weren't living. Had to believe that, otherwise he was not sure he could keep sending them out to die. Just trees animated by the system, vegetation that moved but weren't really real.

Yup, just animated vegetation.

That spurted sap like blood. That had glowing eyes that were so kind, which disappeared when they were struck too often and they fell over. Who reacted to breaking branches like they were arms or legs. That flinched from axes stuck in trunks or swords stabbed into knotty mouth holes.

Just animated vegetation. Sure.

Another body crushed, another cavalry member down. Another woodling staggering around, looking damaged and tired. But he could do the math, could see the difference. They were winning, doing more damage and dropping raiders faster than woodlings were going down.

It helped that at least half the raiders were fighting distracted, itching or grabbing at their faces. A rash, a nasty rash with puss and boils rising from their face and along any exposed skin. Being rubbed where skin and armour met.

One, then another, fell and Matt turned away. He had a way of affecting this, of helping make sure they really won. All he had to do was use his one spell, his one way of affecting battles. But that came with a cost, a cooldown that might be needed for a real fight. One where they might lose.

No. As painful as it might be to watch, as gruesome as this was, he would wait. He would not make it easier, guarantee his survival just because he was a little afraid of the outcome, of random chance making things worse. He would wait.

And watch.

***

"The battle is over? How bad is the damage?" Braskar's voice erupted from around them in the tactics room, making Matt wince.

"Yeah, like we told you, you foolish orc," Irvine snapped. "And we didn't have to waste a precious spell either."

"You faced a single raiders unit. We've faced more than that!" Braskar rumbled.

"We?" Matt said.

"My units and me, of course."

"Oh, right. Gotcha."

"What're our losses then?" Braskar said.

"We have three woodlings left. One was pretty injured but it's healing fast," Matt said. "We should have most of our units back in a few days with the way they heal."

"Also, I got experience as did the woodlings. Not enough by far to upgrade our levels, but I wouldn't mind another attack." A slight pause, then Irvine added, "After our unit comes back into play."

"We got six gold too. It's not much, but better than nothing. It'd be easier if we had a ranged unit though, when the next attack comes." Matt quickly relayed their findings about the siege and the magical weapons along with the raiders' behaviour. "The only problem was how fast our gate was going down."

"Only problem?" Braskar rumbled. "I can think of one more."

"What's that?" Irvine said. "And if you say anything about me being useless, I'm going to kick your ass when you're back."

"Nothing like that. It's the lack of other defences. No militia, no castle guards. If we hadn't left a woodling unit, you'd have been defenseless."

"Careful!" Irvine grumbled.

"Nearly defenseless." Then, with a grin that could be heard over the magical communicator, he added, "Might as well be, really, with an Alchemist."

"Itching powder in your underwear," Irvine warned.

Matt snorted, though he did make a note not to annoy Irvine. He had seen the effects of the 'itching' powder. Just imagining what that would do to his privates had him hunching over a little and crossing his legs. There just were things you did not do to a man.

"Well, we have less than two days before another woodling unit comes. We'll have them to back us up, and maybe send them out scouting," Matt said.

"Scouting?" Irvine said, curious.

"East." Matt gestured down at the map. "We know they came from the east along the coast. So we should check it out."

"I do not understand why you are splitting our forces, especially as we seek battle with our main opponent," Braskar rumbled.

"Two reasons." Matt held up one finger before realizing Braskar could not see him. Then, he decided to just go with it. After all, Irvine was here. "Firstly, we want to stop more attacks, right? So we should check them out. I bet there's a base or something, so if we can find that, we can destroy it. Earn ourselves some coin too."

"And the second?" Matt had fallen silent for too long.

"Oh, the second? No guarantee we only have one opponent. It's best to get an idea of what we might be facing faster, I figure."

There was silence that greeted his words, before Irvine eventually sighed. "It sounds reasonable. But I don't like the idea of sending just one unit out. Especially when they take so long to produce."

"Yeah, be nicer to have actual scouts, but this system doesn't seem intent on letting us build them yet." Matt shrugged. "C'est la vie."

"What?"

"So be it," Matt explained, then winced as his stomach let out a loud rumbling noise. He touched it and then shrugged. "I think that's my cue to eat. I'm strangely hungry. Who'd have thought that nearly dying would make you hungry?" Chuckling to himself, he bade the pair goodbye. Time enough for other concerns in the future. After all, he was stuck doing the one thing he hated most of all.

Waiting.

***

Status Report

Day 26 (End of Day)

Gold: 43.25 (+16.25 Gold per day)

Units: 4 Woodlings

In Production: Woodling (2/4), Firecracker Flowers (0/5)

Structures Completed: Grove, Road, Stall (II), Ranged Copse

Structures Available: Grove (II), Basic Greenhouse, Watch Tower, Tavern, Marketplace, Blacksmith, Harbour, Ranged Copse (II)

Cooldown: None

Chapter 28

Braskar growled a little, staring at the water. Two days of going further west. He had hoped to find a gap in the water, but the lake before him stretched for miles. The one place where the lake narrowed to a river, the ground had dipped dangerously before the river narrowed amongst the canyon, such that crossing it was too risky.

Two days spent moving further west, in hopes of finding a crossing, and he had nothing to show for it but more frustration. He thought, like he had the day before, he'd found a potential narrowing further west of him. In fact, he was certain that looking west, he could see the beginnings of hills and lakes and then the looming mountain range.

He surely knew that there was nothing to return to if he went east, not unless he wanted to retrace his steps. What worried him was that the mountains were rising and if this world had something like normal geography, more rivers were ahead. Perhaps the hills would break up the rivers, give him a way to go through the massive lakes.

Of course, the giant river that fed these lakes might split further upwards. Going from highly inadvisable to cross to just inadvisable. And slow. He had no idea how long it might take to trek across the ground further west. If he went that way, were the hills just rises amongst deep lakes and unfordable rivers, or was there a way past?

Then again, perhaps if he kept heading west, he might find a bridge or a river crossing that would have been simple to ford. After all, stranger things had happened.

Nevermind however the system worked. He knew his people could move faster if he could just work out how to give them the right command. A forced march was a common tactic, and with the innate strength and regeneration of his troops, it should have been common practice.

Yet, no matter what kind of orders he had given, the woodlings continued to move at their own sedate pace. Even the few times he managed to get them to pick up speed, they eventually slowed down to the same routine. And, strangely enough, they never seemed to cover more ground than before.

It almost made him wonder if when they reached the mountains, they would suddenly be able to move the same amount of distance anyway. A part of Braskar was interested in attempting to test that, to see the limits of this strange world. A larger part worried more about leaving his Lord and the castle alone. Taking himself and his army so far away was dangerous.

Perhaps the worst part for the orc was the fact that Matt did not seem to care. He weighed the benefit and loss of either option and had chosen to allow Braskar to make the final decision, leaving the Warlord to figure it all out on his own.

If it was not for the fact that his Lord occasionally made an actual decision and stuck to it, Braskar would worry about their eventual fate. As it stood, it seemed that his Lord felt that he should listen to the experts in the matter, something he called 'not paying accountants to be managers.'

Whatever that meant.

Now, here he was, trying to decide if he should keep moving onwards or if he should turn back and retreat. Given a choice, the orc felt that he should forge ahead. And he would have, if Lord Matt stopped making noises about sending a scouting party further east to find the cause of the raider attack. If they ran into another enemy because he did that...

Braskar was out of position. He could not help his Lord. And while Irvine might be a good Alchemist, he was a useless Warlord.

Perhaps it was time for them to recruit another Hero? It was clear that a Warlord with Command Aura could make inflexible units much more effective. He had hints of that with the fight with the militia but the battle against those raiders had made it all too clear.

Even if his Lord did not see that lack as clearly as he did.

Now the orc was dithering. Even the woodlings were looking at him, awaiting instructions. Strange how even featureless tree trunks with slashes for noses and gaping, glowing knotholes for eyes and mouths could be so expressive. Creepy expressive perhaps, but expressive.

"We go west," Braskar decided suddenly.

Immediately, the woodlings turned as one and began marching, forcing the orc to hurry to catch up. Those creatures were deceptively fast, for moving trees.

Perhaps he was overthinking things. If his Lord could trust in him to make the right decisions, Braskar could trust in him to do the same.

***

"What are you doing?" Irvine's voice rose, startling Matt.

Jerking backwards, the rope that the dead-then-reborn human had been winding spun out, causing him to curse as the bow limb that he had been pulling backwards snapped forwards. The motion was too fast, and the bent limbs actually shattered, sending splinters flying everywhere. One even went upwards to strike Matt in the face, only bouncing off the open-faced helm which had been covered – roughly – by a semi-clear piece of glass.

"Don't. Do. That!" Matt snapped, standing up from the shattered remnants of the crossbow – well, wannabe crossbow – and turning to the Alchemist. The man pulled the helmet off, struggling a little with a newly bleeding hand and the strap before it freed up, at which point the man stuck his wounded hand in his mouth and started sucking on it.

"Then don't do whatever you're doing!" Irvine said. "And that is so not hygienic. You know I have ways of fixing that."

"Antiseptics that suck and burn," Matt muttered around his hand. "I know. After I get…" Searching with his tongue, he found the splinter and then bit down on it. He had to try twice before he latched onto the right piece and yanked it out, spitting wooden splinter and blood out and waving his hand around in renewed pain. "That."

"I have tweezers too," Irvine said pedantically.

"Whatever. I got it, right?" Matt raised his freely bleeding hand, grateful it had stopped aching mostly. On the other hand, prying with his dirty fingers, he tried to spot additional splinters. Eventually, he just prodded the wound with his fingers, hissing a little.

Fed up, Irvine yanked Matt's dirty hand away and pressed a bandage around it. Matt hissed, but the older Alchemist's grip was surprisingly strong, refusing to let him go. "Now, what were you doing?"

"Trying to build a crossbow. I realised we have all the things I need to do it," Matt said. "Theoretically, at least."

"Not a bow?" Irvine said.

"I have very little experience with ranged weaponry," Matt replied. And the little he had included going out shooting with some highschool, redneck friends one summer evening with some rifles in an abandoned gorge and one toy crossbow. Everything he knew about archery said that was a lot more difficult to learn than pointing and shooting with a crossbow. "And I figured this is easier, right?"

"Easier." The degree of doubt in Irvine's voice was significant.

Not that Matt disagreed. But after finding himself incredibly reliant on the units and the Hero, he had felt the need to figure out something. That feeling of helplessness had been really uncomfortable, sort of like the way he had tried out bondage for the first time. And while that had been fun, in a sexy and why was she holding that paddle kind of way, this was really not.

So.

Crossbows. Or at least a few attempts at making one. Who would have thought that something that was basically a bent piece of wood, cord, and a stock could be so difficult to build, without it either barely being able to shoot a bolt or worse, it exploding on him.

Then again, maybe that was the reason bowyer had been an entire profession in the Middle Ages.

"Braskar informed me that he's going to go west," Irvine said, choosing to ignore his Lord after all. "Are you still intent on your foolishness?"

"In two days, yes." Matt tossed the modified helmet aside, grateful that he was smart enough to be careful. Didn't save his hands, but those would heal fast enough. "We get the ranged unit up and running, and the firecracker flowers can take guard up top. We'll then send a woodling out scouting." Lips pursed, Matt then shook his head. "Or I'll send it out in two days. Probably just before the flowers are ready."

"Because you trust in our ability to see dangers before they arrive."

"I do." Matt shrugged. "If there are stealth units, we haven't seen them." Then, he grinned at the unintentional play on words. "And we have a unit guarding us anyway. We'll be fine."

"I do not like it."

"I don't like any of this either, but as the SAS says, who dares, wins." Matt shrugged. "It's time we started being a little more daring, eh?"

"I do not know this Ass-Aye-Ass. But it sounds like a group you would like." Irvine stepped away after a moment, gesturing for Matt to continue. "Let us dare it, then. And see if we are sufficiently assed."

***

Status Report

Day 28 (End of Day)

Gold: 55.75 (+16.25 Gold per day)

Units: 5 Woodlings

In Production: Firecracker Flowers (2/5), Woodling (0/4)

Structures Completed: Grove, Road, Stall (II), Ranged Copse

Structures Available: Grove (II), Basic Greenhouse, Watch Tower, Tavern, Marketplace, Blacksmith, Harbour, Ranged Copse (II)

Cooldown: None

***

Chapter 29

"Where is he now?" Irvine muttered, staring at the glowing map before them. Another two days, and the day of great leaving was upon them. At the same time, before any further decisions were to be made, Matt figured it was best for them to get a gauge of what his intrepid explorer, Braskar, was up to.

"Just north of the first lake. He managed to head north and west the day before, but he says there's no crossing further east, so he's been forced further north and west. If he's right, he'll be able to go east tomorrow though," Matt said, gesturing to the map before them.

One of the aspects of the tactical map was that it had a tendency to shadow itself once there were no units nearby. However, at least the terrain that they had spotted continued to glow, so it was easy enough to see where Braskar had gone. It still left a large path of darkness right above their own area and to the east of them. And frankly, to the west.

In truth, there were more dark patches than light on their map.

"I don't like having him so far. He's what?" Irvine's lips moved as he did the count, trying to gauge how far the orc was away from them. "Seven days?"

"Seven days to the village, yes." Matt nodded. "Add another day along the Roads." He sighed. "At some point, we'll find an upgrade to make more Roads, I'm sure. Till then, we're stuck with slower movements."

"Seven days. And we have at best two days of warning if they attack the village."

"And three to this city." Matt shrugged. "I could build a Watch Tower, but I need my money for other things." He frowned. "Frankly, I probably could just make a woodling and march it upwards. If it dies, we know something is coming."

"Cold." Irvine nodded firmly. "But effective."

"Thanks. Anyway, they're just elementals." Matt shrugged. "I don't think they care if they get broken."

"Perhaps."

"Anyway." Matt pushed on, looking at the map. "We got our firecracker flowers tomorrow."

"Yes, you do. Are you sending a unit east then?" Irvine said.

"I will." Matt hesitated, looking at the gold he had left. At eighty-eight and a quarter gold, that would put him in another… "Seven days?"

"To reach two hundred for your Harbour?" Irvine replied, doing the same math himself. "I believe that is correct. If you do not waste any more gold."

"You agreed having the firecracker flowers was important."

"I was speaking of the sixth woodling unit you created," Irvine said.

"Planning for the loss of the one I'm sending out." Matt drummed his fingers on the table, spinning options through his mind before he sighed. "One more firecracker flower unit to build once we get the new one. We can send it upwards to the village later if need be, or keep it here. But then, we stop."

"Stop?"

"Yeah, stop." Matt shook his head. "We need that Harbour. And adding another ranged unit puts us two more days behind. We'll never get there if I don't commit."

No answer to that from his Alchemist, though the way his disapproving gaze was fixed upon him, Matt could read every single word he likely had to say in them. Either that or it was his doubtful mind supplying that information.

Another pause, then Matt gestured. Moments later, the woodling unit began peeling itself off the walls where they had been stationed, going down the staircases to the doors, which were now swinging open. Matt's gaze trekked over to his pits, some of which were looking worse for wear since the recent rains. He wondered how they did those in the past times. Or hell, how graves managed to not fold in on themselves.

Who'd have thought digging pits required deep knowledge? It was a hole in the ground. You dug straight down and pressed the earth to the side a bit. But when rain came along and filled the bottom or washed the earth sideways, your hole became more of a long slope. And some of the earth you'd piled into an embankment started washing back in.

All in all, Matt was just lucky the pits had lasted as long as they had.

Which was half the reason he'd gone and started with the crossbow making. At least that, he assumed, would actually work well enough. And if not, well, it gave him something to do that wasn't destroyed by the first hard rain they had.

"If that's all?" Irvine rumbled, startling Matt.

The man waved his hand, let the grumpy Alchemist get nearly most of the way out before he asked, "How's the research going? And the potion making?"

"Slowly. We have enough made that we can provide for the units we have now, even the upcoming one. But I have only started to look into other forms of potions." Another shrug. "The process takes a while, as you know."

"I do. Just, you know, keep at it, eh?"

A nod, and Matt left him to go. Instead, he turned back to the tactical map, tracing his finger along the proposed route for his woodling. East along the coast was the best option as far as he could tell, such that if there was another city along the water, he'd know.

There had to be something to the water, he knew. Couldn't just be water, all alone, without a point. Or so he felt. That was why the Harbour was important. Also, any defenses from the water, even if it was a big chain strung across the entrance.

But to get that far, he'd need a boat and right now, he had nothing. Which was all kinds of dumb, if naught for the fact that even the supposed people down in the town were no more real than the woodlings. It hurt his head, sometimes, to deal with the NPCs, but that's why he avoided thinking about it as best he could.

Nothing he could do but keep pushing on. And hope that when he finally did get enough money to get a Tavern, the new Heroes were like his old ones.

Alive.

***

Status Report

Day 30 (End of Day)

Gold: 88.25 (+16 Gold per day)

Units: 5 Woodlings

In Production: Firecracker Flowers (4/5), Woodling (2/4)

Structures Completed: Grove, Road, Stall (II), Ranged Copse

Structures Available: Grove (II), Basic Greenhouse, Watch Tower, Tavern, Marketplace, Blacksmith, Harbour, Ranged Copse (II)

Cooldown: None

Chapter 30

Matt had arrived late to the morning's meeting since he'd spent it watching the newly formed firecracker flowers practice firing down their range. His new ranged unit had formed in the morning, and he had to admit, he'd been excited to see exactly what they could do.

First thing that struck him was that they were weird looking. The plants themselves were extremely thin, with long and broad leaves that shielded their main stems. These leaves wrapped all around them, with a quartet of long arms which each had the seed pods that gave the firecracker flowers their name. At the end of the seed pods, the occasional pale salmon and orange flower with drooping petals sat. These petals when present hid the seed pods and the vines that ran down the arm. As for a head – it was pretty much non-existent. They just reached upwards, ending in a nub or a couple of branches that he assumed would eventually form into new arms.

Perhaps an upgraded firecracker flower unit had six arms instead of four? And then eight? Now that'd be a sight to behold.

So was the sight of the entire unit loosing attacks. It seemed those vines that ran across their backs along their arms were filled with water, for they would pump them into their swaying seed pods at the ends of their arms. Once the water contacted the pods, the pods themselves would explode, scattering vegetable matter shrapnel all over the surroundings. The explosion was rather loud, like a man slamming a heavy dictionary down on a wooden table, but not loud like gunfire.

No snipers these firecracker flowers but closer to a shotgun round, except with smaller spread. Or something like that. At least, he thought so. Realistically, Matt's understanding of shotguns was mostly from 80's action films and even he knew that people didn't fly through the air from shotgun blasts. So all of it was suspect. What he did know was that the ranged attacks could pepper an area about forty feet away with shells around the size of his torso. Further than that, and the effectiveness seemed to drop off pretty badly.

Not really what he had been imagining when he'd picked the firecracker flowers. Perhaps the squirting cucumbers would have been better and more focused, but here he was with what he had. Anyway, having them lean over the walls and unleash an armful of seed shrapnel was something he was rather looking forward to seeing.

"Any news, Braskar?" Matt called out, dithering a little before making the purchase he knew he was going to make anyway. Just in case his Warlord found something up there. Not that he had that many choices he could make.

That was the thing about these kinds of games. Once you started down a path, it was really hard to course correct at speed. Perhaps in the future, when he had a lot more building options, a lot more units, a lot more gold. But right now, his options were just tiny.

"I am traversing the land between some rivers. These feed into the lake that I have managed to make my way past. I will chart out the edges of the lake itself for our map before heading north once more. No signs of the enemy." Braskar hesitated, then added, "I do not like being so far from you."

"Nor we you." Matt added, "Oh, thanks for the gold and the monster hunting."

"They attacked us."

"What were they?"

"A hydra-like creature. Only two heads, and it lacked the massive regeneration of its storied cousin. It still injured one of my units badly, though they have recovered already," Braskar said.

"Wait, you guys have hydras?" Matt said, frowning.

"Do you not?"

"We do, of course we do. That's why I'm surprised you do."

"Interesting. A case of parallel mythological evolution?" Braskar hummed. "Or is the translation different?"

"Different?"

"The creature I think of as a hydra is a legendary creature, once a beautiful woman transformed into a monstrous creature. She was cursed, to grow as many heads as the women she seduced away from their husbands, reforming those heads every time one was chopped off."

"Uhhh…." Matt scratched his cheek. "That's not the legend we have." Quickly, he explained about the Greeks, Heracles, and the multiplying heads.

When he was done, silence filled the room until Braskar spoke. "I dislike your legend. There is no moral to your story."

"Oh, and what's the moral of your hydra?" Matt said, stung. Not that he was Greek, and it wasn't really his legend, but somehow, he found himself personally affronted. "Be careful of your wife having pretty female friends?"

"No. An orc must do his utmost to satisfy the needs of his companion or they will find comfort among other women," Braskar said. "And when that happens, the scorn of the women folk will require a legendary hero to overcome."

"Well, that's… well." Matt trailed off, then shook his head. "Whatever. Keep doing what you're doing. I'm going to buy myself another ranged unit and then do my thing."

"Of course, my lord."

Matt narrowed his eyes since he was sure there was a smirk in that voice. Then again, he couldn't help but admit the man had a point. It was a rather better legend than Hercules and the hydra. Even if the hydra itself was one part of a bigger story and not the story in itself.

Then again, he didn't think the Greeks had much of a thematic or moralistic point to their legends. Except perhaps that the gods were horny, vengeful, and likely to shit on you when they had a chance.

Huh.

Maybe they were right.

***

Status Report

Day 31 (End of Day)

Gold: 79.5 (+16.25 Gold per day)

Units: 5 Woodlings, 1 Firecracker Flower

In Production: Firecracker Flowers (0/5), Woodling (3/4)

Structures Completed: Grove, Road, Stall (II), Ranged Copse

Structures Available: Grove (II), Basic Greenhouse, Watch Tower, Tavern, Marketplace, Blacksmith, Harbour, Ranged Copse (II)

Cooldown: None

Chapter 31

Days passed quickly, what with the lack of combat. The woodling exploring to the east had naught to show for its exploration beyond a lot more coast, including a peninsula and forest. Braskar had managed to chart out the edges of the lake – except for a couple of hexes south since that would have him backtracking – and was now heading north and west once more, covering more ground in search of their attackers.

Outside of the occasional random monster encounter that added a minor trickle of random gold to their coffers, the scouting pair had nothing to report.

Overall, other than some minor tension and worry, things had grown quiet. Matt continued to try to figure out how to build a proper crossbow, scavenging pieces of wood – the one thing his wood elemental-filled holding did not lack – and cordage to work out a proper design. More than once, he'd spent time sketching out his memories of crossbows glimpsed in museums and the occasional movie, hoping it gave him some further insight.

In the meantime, Irvine ignored everyone and hid in his laboratory, testing new alchemical potions. The few times Matt had poked his head in, he'd been shouted at.

As for the new units, outside of sending the extra woodling unit they had hanging around the keep away, leaving the keep guarded by both firecrackers and one woodling, not much had changed. No additional attacks, not in the eight days it took for him to get enough funds to build a Harbour.

It annoyed Matt, as he stared around the empty tactical room, that Irvine would not even bother come out to speak with him. But it was what it was, and he did not need to speak with anyone to make this decision.

Not at all.

Structure Under Construction: Harbour

Building Type: Naval

Tier: Lesser Tier I

Benefit: +5 Gold Per Day

Cost: 200

Production time: 5 days

And done.

Matt waited, and waited, and when the room chose not to pop up any further information, started poking the tactical map. After a few futile minutes, he had to give that up too since no new options had generated during that period.

"I really, really want a manual. I'd RTFM even." Not getting any answer, Matt shook his head and started to turn away, heading out. Only to be startled when Braskar's rather hurried voice came erupting from all around him.

"My lord. Are you there?" Braskar said.

"I am!" Matt hesitated, hearing the tension. "What's wrong?"

"I seem to have located our enemy." A slight pause. "Again."

"Army or settlement?" Matt cursed under his breath at the timing. Still, at least he wasn't out of the room. Which meant he could help with the fight if it came to that. He hurried back to the tactical map and leaned in close, curious to see what it showed him.

"Settlement. I'm staring at the fort in the distance," Braskar said. "It's a little big, my lord."

"What do you mea…" Matt trailed off as he managed to make it to the map and see what the problem was. He cursed internally, realizing they had literally been walking one hex away from finding the fort for a few days. But they had failed to head north which meant they had missed it all.

Until now.

More startling was the size of the enemy settlement. Compared to the tiny single motte and the bailey construction surrounding their small village that made up his own place, the enemy was significantly larger. It had a moat around the upraised Stone Keep, which had been built up with three additional floors, with the external palisade having enough space between the courtyard and the keep to fit the entirety of his own simple fort inside it with space to spare.

"Well, at least that answers that question," Matt said, trying to go for light and unworried.

"What question, my lord?"

"Can the settlement upgrade? Yes. Yes, it can…"

"I am glad to see that we were able to answer some of your questions, my lord, but I believe I can see the gates opening and an army emerging."

"Shit. Sorry," Matt said. "Retreat. Now."

"My thoughts exactly." Matt listened as Braskar issued a series of orders that had the woodlings with him pulling back. He watched the units do the same on the tactical map for a bit before the orc returned to speaking with him. "It seems, my lord, that we were a tad too ambitious."

"You're not dead yet, man," Matt replied. "Keep running. We'll try to get some reinforcements."

"I fear that will be a foolish attempt. We know our enemies are faster than us."

"In a fight, sure. But maybe not across the terrain."

"We can hope."

The pair fell silent, while Matt stared at the map. Something was nagging him, and it took him a bit to realise what it was. When it finally occurred to him, he could not help but ask, "Why didn't they attack you before?"

"My lord?"

"I can see at least two hexes away. And I've got the smaller settlement. They should have been able to spot you at that range, at the minimum, you'd think."

"That follows."

"Then, why didn't they attack you? You were blundering around in front of them for a while, and they did nothing."

"Ah, I see your point." Silence filled Braskar's end of the line. Eventually, he had to admit, "I do not know."

"Neither do I. But it is interesting, isn't it?" Matt hummed to himself, then mused out loud. "Most obvious reason – they wanted you close so you can't run away. Second option, they didn't have enough units to confidently take you down. So they held off, till they built what they needed and are now going to beat you. Thirdly, they don't have enough units and are making a show of force just to drive you back because there's something they don't want you to see."

"I like that third option," Braskar rumbled, his voice just a touch breathless.

"You running?"

"Yes."

Matt chose to keep his mouth shut, instead going around the table to peer closer at the enemy settlement. He poked at it, and then let out a yelp of surprise when it expanded, a new notification appearing before him.

Enemy Settlement Located!

Congratulations!

Type: Stone Keep with Bailey

Structures Built: Barracks (II), Tavern (I), Wall (I), Temple (I), Stall (I)

"Problem, my lord?"

"Just got details about our friends. They went Tavern along with an upgraded Barracks, but they only got the basest item for gold development." Matt hesitated, then added, "I think they might not be as far ahead of us as I thought."

"But an upgraded Barracks and a Tavern means they likely have a Hero and powerful units."

"We killed one of their Heroes. It is possible they might not have gotten a new Warlord yet," Matt mused. "If that's the case, their units might not be that powerful. In fact…"

Matt leaned to the side and poked again, this time at the unit exiting the keep.

Enemy Army Sighted!

Quantity: 3 Melee Units

Not a lot of information, but this was better than nothing. Three units. Figure they were all upgrades, which meant that the two units with Braskar were not going to be enough. He drew a breath again and then let it out. Sometimes, you just had to give the bad news as it came.

"So, first things first. I'm going to camp here, to use my spell when I can. I just…" He shook his head. "If they're risking it, I'm going to assume they have a spell too." He exhaled. "But I'll do my best."

"Thank you, my lord."

"Alright, here's what I know. Good news, no Hero. Bad news…"

***

Status Report

Day 39 (End of Day)

Gold: 12.5 (+16.25 Gold per day)

Units: 6 Woodlings, 2 Firecracker Flowers

In Production: Harbour (0/5)

Structures Completed: Grove, Road, Stall (II), Ranged Copse

Structures Available: Grove (II), Basic Greenhouse, Watch Tower, Tavern, Marketplace, Blacksmith, Ranged Copse (II)

Cooldown: None

Chapter 32

A day was twenty-four hours; one thousand, four hundred and forty minutes; eighty-six thousand, four hundred seconds. Not a long time. You could just count them off, one after the other, in your mind if you were willing to do it and didn't get bored. Even more, it was not as though it was the start of the day when they ran.

So why did all that time feel like an eternity?

Matt had no answer to it, beyond the belief that all those physicists who said that time was not a linear progression were in the right. Every second was an age, every minute an eternity. The hours crawled past so slowly with nothing to do but wait, poking at the tactical map over and over again, hoping to find something, anything, new.

Failing, of course. He'd spent so much time doing that, he'd lost count of it. But Matt refused to leave, not even to grab a bite to eat. The damn ghostly servitors would bring water without a problem, but food? Not somehow part of their routine.

No wonder he fell upon Irvine like a starved wolf and tore into the meal with ravenous hunger. The Alchemist had stayed for a short while, but Matt's pacing, his inane blather had driven the other man away eventually.

Not as though there was a point for the Hero to be here. He had no Skills that could affect the battle so far away. Except, of course, there was no battle.

Matt sort of knew there would not be. They were a hex away. Even if they made the move now, they should not make it to the next hex till the next day. Probably. So that meant the battle was meant to start tomorrow.

But that was only for his own troops with their paltry single hex movement. If his opponents moved two hexes at a time, which he knew they did, then perhaps, just perhaps decamping did not take up both movement pieces.

And battle would be brought on that day itself.

Luckily, it seemed, that it did not work that way. Decamping, even for faster moving pieces, took a minimum of a day. Which meant that the enemy needed to cross a full hex plus to catch them.

Delay began to make more sense then, since decamping and moving to a new hex was one day. That put Braskar one hex away. If both parties moved only a single hex, it was literally impossible to catch a fleeing enemy unless they wanted to fight.

However, with a speed advantage, his opponents would catch Braskar the very next day. No question about it. The only real question was when and where.

"You sure you want to move into the forest?" Doubt filled Matt's voice, as he regarded the position that his Hero had taken. Rather than heading south and retreating immediately, he had gone east. Heading towards the forest he'd spotted in the distance.

"We had an advantage the last time, fighting within one. I expect that advantage will increase further, now that there is no Hero to disrupt our attacks," Braskar said, guiding his people deeper into the forest. "We might even be able to lose our pursuers within."

"You think that's viable?" Matt said.

"No."

"I'm going to get you a mug, and it's going to say 'World's Greatest Pessimist.'"

Braskar snorted, the noise ripping through the room. Matt sighed and turned away, looking out the window to stare at the slowly rising light. Early dawn, probably a few more hours before the battle would commence. Maybe more than that, depending on how fast the saakal would catch up.

Time crawled on, the units on the tactical map merging onto the same hex. Matt watched, licking his lips over and over again, fist squeezing and releasing as his heart raced. Nothing that he could do, even as he stared hungrily at the damage counter.

Something, anything would happen.

Any moment now.

Any moment.

Now?

***

"Typical," Braskar growled, shaking his head. The saakal had caught up with them just before noon. The orc had chosen not to run his people – or himself – ragged and pulled them into a stacked defensive formation. Rather than a hill or a rise though, he'd made use of the boggy ground, finding the muddiest, most difficult terrain to run through and put his people near the center of it.

A part of the Hero wondered how much any of this mattered. Their lives were weirdly governed by abstract laws on movement, on combat, and fighting ability as evidenced by the fight at the Lord's keep. And yet, minor alterations could be made, the rules could be pushed. And Braskar believed, had to believe, that these decisions mattered.

If nothing else, why give him the Skill Commanding Aura if not to allow him to command his troops as best he could?

Now, watching the saakal come, their footsteps pulling as they waded through the mud, sinking halfway to the deeper ends of their feet, he had a chance to test his theories. Because as they spotted him, that blue light that had infused the enemies before formed around them.

They charged, pounding forwards, covering the ground faster than ever. Immediately, the orc could tell his choice had made a difference. They were slower, unable to gain the same speed as their charge against his people from before. And without the crippling effects of a howl, his woodlings were properly set, hunkered down or near other trees, bracing against one another for the explosive crash.

They'd all downed what potions they had. A pity that Irvine hadn't been able to fully restock his group, but that was partly his fault for coming out scouting without a full inventory. Maybe next time, he'd wait.

Probably not.

Grinning, Braskar watched as they hit his people, watched as woodlings splintered and cracked, blood sap flying through the air as limbs were torn apart, trunks shattered, and saakal were impaled on raised staked arms.

Six units down within moments. Not great. But the damn creatures had fallen too, their charge slowed down. And it could have been worse, for more than a few innocent tree trunks had exploded. That was the initial charge, but there were two more units coming in, right behind.

And it was his turn, in the second line, to face the oncoming enemies.

The first monster, howling and panting, leapt at him. The stink of their unwashed fur swept over him as he ducked low, his axe dragging through the air and cutting apart that blue light, spilled viscera joining the musky stink and muddy earth.

Even as he recovered upwards, another monster hit him hard from the side. The orc snarled, spinning sideways, nearly losing his axe but still managing to sink the spike at the back of it into the monster's back leg. Not a kill but crippling at least.

More blue bodies, more shattered tree trunks, splintering wounds, and the pained howl of his enemies filling the air. A deep bruise forming on one arm, the taste of blood as he realised he'd cut his lips on the inside of his own mouth during the impact.

And more woodlings fallen. More saakal too, but it was not enough.

"Braskar!"

"Not yet."

The charge was over, so now it was time for the killing.

"Rally!" Braskar roared, waving his axe around above his head. "Rally to me!"

Attracting attention in a fight like this was never a good idea. Even as the woodlings fell back, gathered around him, the orc had to deal with more saakal. Another came low, forcing him to split his head with his axe. He never saw the creature that hamstrung him, taking him to his knees even as another saakal threatened to take his face.

The orc managed to get a mail-coiffed arm in the way of that lunging face, a woodling dealing with the attacker from behind. Red light filled his body, his other ability triggering now. Rage, threatening to take his reason, but giving him a trump card.

"I'm going to heal you."

"No!" Braskar growled, eyes flicking over his people. Reading the numbers, judging even as he pounded the side of his axe into the body of the saakal hanging onto his arm, even as he managed to dislodge it long enough for it to try to limp away. Only for another woodling to kill it as they rallied. "Heal the upgraded woodling unit. On my command."

Struggling to his feet, leaning against a woodling unit, Braskar watched as the saakal pulled back a little. Getting ready for another charge. Unaided this time. But they were still coming.

"Braskar…"

"On. My. Command."

***

Status Report

Day 40 (Beginning of Day)

Gold: 28.75 (+16.25 Gold per day)

Units: 6 Woodlings, 2 Firecracker Flowers

In Production: Harbour (1/5)

Structures Completed: Grove, Road, Stall (II), Ranged Copse

Structures Available: Grove (II), Basic Greenhouse, Watch Tower, Tavern, Marketplace, Blacksmith, Ranged Copse (II)

Cooldown: None

Chapter 33

"Now!"

Matt's fingers flew through the air, tapping out the commands. He cast the spell, the only spell that he had, watching it strike the woodling unit. Watched as the cooldown triggered again, the units springing back to life and new units literally reforming on the tiny map.

He couldn't tell much from the fight, it was no tiny map of the fight, just indicators when saplings fell from his woodlings, when people got hurt. When the enemy got hurt.

That initial charge had done a ton of damage. They'd lost nearly two thirds of all their saplings, a single woodling left in the unboosted original unit put in front. Matt knew it could have been worse. Three units against their two, the three all presumably upgraded.

Not great.

Yet, they had survived, and they'd taken out nearly a full unit of the saakal themselves too and damaged a few of the individual members in the other groups. Braskar was taking a beating too, but he had a lot more health this time around it seemed. Benefits of leveling up.

A flicker, then a whole saakal unit disappeared, another four of the enemy blipping off other units. Matt's jaw dropped, mind only catching up with the surprise moments later. Braskar must have triggered his Rage ability right after the woodlings had regrown.

And now, the fight was on.

Biting his lip, Matt could only hope it went well.

***

A wave of exhaustion ran through Braskar after he finished swinging his axe. He would have held on a little longer, but the group of five saakal had clumped together so well, he could not help but swing away. Didn't help that he was bleeding like a stuck frosfka serpent.

"Charge!" Braskar dropped his hand and the axe. Partly to indicate the charge, partly because he lacked the strength to hold it up.

Either way, the woodlings charged. The ones gathered with him. And, most importantly, the ones that had reformed behind the enemy units, the units that had ringed his people, thinking they were the ones in control.

Stupid tactics, lousy understanding of the lay of the land. Fighting in this bog, the saakal were slow. So were his people, but being slow was not a major problem for them. For the enemy, it was. Now that they were bogged down, the losses began to accumulate on the enemy side, even as the surprise attack took further saakal out.

On his side, Braskar did not charge. Instead, he was wrapping his leg up, tying tight the damn wound that kept bleeding, trying to stem the blood and get himself moving. He was no use to the battle, standing alone.

Worst, he could tell from watching, they were losing. He'd done a lot of damage, the terrain, the surprise, his abilities. They had done a lot of damage. But the numbers had never been in their favour, and those numbers were finally beginning to tell.

Woodlings fought on, without care, without emotion. They plunged splintered branch hands into bodies, had limb feet and bodies torn apart by swiping claws and ripping mouths. And still, they kept swinging till they could not.

They were going to lose, and there was no escape for his people. Braskar knew that, deep in his soul. Always had.

The only question worth asking now was if he was going to die with them.

Or find another way to survive.

***

"SEVERANCE PACKAGES MY ASS!" Snarling, Matt stared at the tactical map. At the results it was showing. Woodlings he had healed all wiped out. Not a single woodling unit left in fact, every single one of them gone.

They had done well. Taken out two entire saakal units, leaving the third one damaged. They were outnumbered, outleveled. They had lost, from the start. But he had hoped, just a little, for another miracle. Yet the system had no desire to be that kind, not today.

Battle Report (Hero Braskar vs Enemy Units)
Result: Defeat! 2 Saakal (II) Units Defeated, 2 Woodling Units Lost.
Penalties: -5 Gold, -2 Reputation

Eyes locked on the words defeat, Matt sunk down. He mostly missed the chair, ended up bruising his back as he pushed it aside and slumped on the ground. Tears welled up in his eyes, and he found himself pressing the palms of his hands into them to stop the tears that threatened to spill outwards. Even so, some leaked out, as he felt the deep sting of loss.

Braskar was dead. Gone. Finished.

He had let the man go out, fight for him, scout, because the orc had insisted, sure. But in the end, it had been his decision. Who dares wins, but also, who dares loses and loses badly. Because if you rolled the dice often enough, you lost.

And his friend had lost.

He had lost.

A deep darkness rose up within Matt, threatened to pull him downwards. It was an old friend, this darkness, a familiar feature of his life. He'd pushed it aside, been thrilled by the new world, by the insanity and strangeness of everything, that he had managed to avoid thinking about it, managed to avoid dealing with it.

But it was always lurking. Waiting in the depths of his heart.

Matt wasn't sure when it had arrived. Back in school, going through classes that no one liked or wanted to do. Listening to teachers strained to the breaking point trying to control a classroom full of children no smarter than a bag of bricks? Or was it when he entered the work force for real, taking orders from petty tyrants while working a minimum wage job and being screamed at by men and women about food that was a touch cold, service a little too slow, ketchup packed wrong…

Or perhaps it was his first office job. With the shininess of getting a degree and thinking he was finally, finally going to get a proper chance at making his way through this world. Only to find that the bureaucratic, brain-dead managers were still there, that any sign of initiative was either stamped out or exploited to drive fresh-faced interns to work unnecessarily long hours.

And the only reward was a pat on the head and a promise of a job.

Maybe next year.

Old friend, dear friend, it took him and wrapped him in its senseless arms, drew him down and left him on the ground, curled up on his side even as the light faded and the shadows darkened. Until he was just there, lying on a stone floor, heat leaching out of him.

Quiet. Cold. Like the grave.

Peaceful.

***

Irvine walked up the staircase, dreading what he would find. He was smart enough – hah! Genius was its own curse – to know that if the orc had survived, his Lord would have trumpeted the news from the rooftop long ago. Since that was no longer the case, it was pretty clear which way things had gone.

He'd held out hope, long enough till the sun had set. Then, there was no more hope left from the hourglass, and he found himself walking up these stairs. The boy, if he was here, was likely looking over the map, trying to figure out how to game the system, how to recover. Maybe grieving a little from the orc's death.

Not that there was much to grieve. They were all dead men given a second chance. Much better than his family, who'd died on him over the years. Some from accidents, some from disease and illnesses and injuries. Some by the blade, of the raiders, or on the sea as they travelled. His first wife in childbirth. The second ran away with a suave young armsman, only to be hanged years later for banditry. His third wife… he could not even recall. Illness or disease, it had happened while he was away, that he recalled. And the last had lasted him till she grew old and faded in her sleep, not long before he would go too.

He'd seen a lot of death in his time. Problems of having a large family and a long life. You grew old, you saw friends and family die. Enemies too, which was surprisingly not as satisfying as you'd think. Mostly, it left him empty, where the hate or rage or jealousy had lived, still lashing out but nowhere to go but spiral outwards into him.

Empty.

He'd known as soon as he spotted him when he arrived that the kid knew little about that emptiness. Whatever world the boy had come from was a soft world. Soft enough at least to allow a boy to grow to manhood and more and not see death around every corner, to not hug a child hard when given a chance or to pronounce their love at every opportunity.

Because you never knew who wouldn't come back that night.

A soft world. Irvine wished he'd grown up in a soft world.

But now that softness was going to get them killed.

Staring at the boy, turned on his side, unmoving, Irvine poked him. Once. And then again. Called his name.

Got no answer.

"Angel's tears and medusa's tits," Irvine growled. "You best get up. Or I'm going to brew something so hideous, you'll be shitting it out for a month and wondering why all of it is still purple."

No answer. He hadn't expected one.

"Come on, boy. It's one death. He was a good man. Orc. But not worth crying to death over," Irvine bent down, yanking him upwards. "Now come on. Let's grab some food, get some beer into you. You'll feel better, after you get properly sloshed." The Alchemist hesitated, then added, "You can even tell me all about your woes."

"Why bother?" Matt said finally. Softly.

"What?" Irvine frowned, staring at the man who'd managed to sit up, but now had his legs wrapped up in his arms.

"Why bother?"

"Got a fight to win, of course," Irvine said, then smirked. "Why, you going to give up already?"

"Yes."

Shit. That was not the answer Irvine had expected.

"You serious? All this talk of beating the game, winning for humanity. And you're giving up now?" Irvine leaned forwards, pushing his face into the other's space. Making sure he looked into those soulless, empty eyes. Searching for something. "Where's all that resolution, that strength from before, eh?"

"Gone. I was just faking it, mostly. I'm an office worker. A lousy office worker. What am I supposed to do?"

"Do? Well, fight and win, of course. You got us moving, you keep us moving ahead."

"No us." Matt laughed, his laughter a little wild. "No us anymore. Braskar's dead."

"And so what? I'm still here. So are you." Irvine shook his head. "It ain't no matter whether he's dead. We still got to push on. It's what the orc would have wanted."

Before Matt could answer, another voice interrupted them. "You know, I do prefer to speak for myself. If you don't mind, Alchemist." A slight pause. "My lord."

The scream that erupted from Matt at that voice was enough to make Irvine reel backwards, clamping a hand over his ears in pain and slam into the edge of the table, leaving him writhing in pain. Even as Matt kept screaming.

Chapter 34

"I climbed a tree, once I realised the battle was lost," Braskar was saying, now that Matt had managed to stop screaming. Rather embarrassing that, though at least the adrenaline dump into his system had helped a little with the bleakness. It was still there, threatening to drag him under. But alongside all that was the bubbling joy that his friend was alive.

Somehow.

"And they just left you alone?" Irvine said, incredulous.

"Yes. I think it's a restriction on their minds. Once I left the ground and climbed high enough, I think the system, the game, thought I had retreated far enough away that I was out of combat. Once that happened, and all the woodlings had been killed, the saakal just pulled themselves together and left."

"All the woodlings are gone?" Matt said tentatively. He knew that was likely true, after all, but he had to ask.

"Yes." There was a trace of sadness in Braskar's voice as he said that. "Not a single unit left."

"Blasted potions," Irvine growled. "We had an upgraded one with you too, didn't we?"

"Yes. They did well for themselves, but outnumbered as we were, we had no chance, not from the start," Braskar said.

"At least…" Matt started then trailed off.

"At least what?" Irvine asked.

Matt shrugged. He could not say it, since it was so obvious.

"I live. And we know that they have no Warlord," Braskar rumbled.

"We do?" Irvine said, surprised.

"If they had one, I feel they would have sent them. Especially as I was vulnerable," Braskar said. "It's clear that Heroes can make a significant difference on the battlefield. Otherwise…"

"Otherwise, they wander off into the middle of nowhere and all you get is a report of the final results," Matt said morosely.

"What now?" Irvine said, exasperated as he spun around to stare at the man. He shut his mouth when he noticed that Matt was staring at a new notification he had pulled up, one that Irvine had not noticed himself.

Battle Report (Woodling vs Enemy Units)
Result: Defeat! 1 Woodling Unit Lost
Penalties: -2 Gold, -1 Reputation

"At some point, we're going to figure out what reputation does," Matt said idly to the air as he read the notification for the third time.

"What is going on?" Braskar asked impatiently. Irvine quickly explained the loss, causing the Warlord to let out a little harumph.

"Well, not as though you weren't expecting that at some point," Irvine offered when he was done explaining to Braskar their latest defeat.

"I know. I'd just hoped for more than the basics," Matt said. "And if I'd known we'd lose so many…" He shook his head, discarding that thought. It was what it was, and now at least, they had a little more balanced numbers in terms of the kinds of units they had.

It did ask for a revision on how they sorted their men though, something he'd have to think about. And what kind of things he bought, though…

"We took out two of their three units, right?"

"Yes, my lord."

"Then, we're not as far behind as I'd feared," Matt said slowly. "And I don't think, if they waited until you got that close, that they've got much more people than we do."

"That… makes sense," Irvine said.

"And there is one more piece of good news, my lord."

"Oh good, I could use that." Unspoken was the fact that, as much as the words might be a little humorous, he really did need it. He scrubbed at his face, staring down at the peninsula and coast he'd sent his people on, wondering what kind of danger lurked to the east.

Maybe best not to stir that hornets' nest for now.

"Click on my information, my lord."

It took Matt a moment to find the portion of the tactical map that pulled up his Hero information, a process that made Matt kick himself for not looking for it before. He shuddered, pushing back the recriminations forcefully, knowing cursing himself out was not going to be helpful.

Instead, he stared at Braskar's details that had now appeared, trying to work out what had changed.

Braskar (Level 2 Warlord)
Specialty: Military Leadership
Skills: Inspiring Aura, Rage
Experience: 87/100

Attack: 27

Defense: 18

Power: 6

Knowledge: 12

"That's cheating," Irvine grumbled after a moment.

"What is?" Matt asked.

"He's nearly Level 3." Irvine gestured at the map, making Matt startle.

Out of curiosity, he could not help but poke at Irvine's information too, bringing up the Alchemist's own information.

Irvine (Level 1 Alchemist)

Specialty: Alchemy

Skills: Alchemical Concoction, Burst Production

Experience: 98/100

Attack: 6

Defense: 9

Power: 11

Knowledge: 18

"Oh hey! You're nearly there too," Matt said.

"Nearly. To Level 2." The disgust in the Alchemist's voice was all too clear. "As I said, we could use more attacks."

"I'd… prefer not."

"My lord?" Braskar interrupted, making Matt focus. "I believe I should return, rather than stay out."

"Yeah, I think… I think you're right." Matt hesitated, then added, "I'm going to send the village units out to meet you." He almost added 'if you don't mind,' but realised he did not really care if Braskar minded. He was not going to leave the Warlord out to hang.

"I would be grateful. It's… sobering how lacking it feels to be alone without additional aid."

Matt nodded, then glanced at Irvine to see if he had any input. Only to find the Alchemist standing there, arms folded, sulking.

"What? Don't bother asking me. I'm just a Level 1."

Sadly for the pouting Hero, Matt had neither the energy nor desire to deal with him. Instead, he waved Irvine away while he finished charting the orders for the next day. That'd start with the production of a new woodling tomorrow when he actually had funds,.

Especially since there was nothing else he could do beyond begin the replacement of his units. Not without more gold.

"Get back here, will you?" Matt said, before killing the connection and following the Alchemist down. If nothing else, he needed food too.

***

Status Report

Day 40

Gold: 21.75 (+15.25 Gold per day)

Units: 3 Woodlings, 2 Firecracker Flowers

In Production: Harbour (1/5)

Structures Completed: Grove, Road, Stall (II), Ranged Copse

Structures Available: Grove (II), Basic Greenhouse, Watch Tower, Tavern, Marketplace, Blacksmith, Ranged Copse (II)

Cooldown: 5 days to spell casting

Chapter 35

Tense. And tiring. Those were the two words Matt would use to describe the next three days as Braskar hurried south to meet with the units. No sign of any additional enemy units, though that didn't stop Matt from purchasing the production of another woodling the moment he could afford it the next day. He held off on another firecracker flower though, since a new plan was forming in his mind.

Of course, things never played out the way he thought they should. Almost immediately upon meeting the units, his enterprising Hero decided to drop a new nugget of information on Matt.

"There's another village up north?" Matt said slowly. "And you want to take the units to take it over."

"Yes, my lord."

"After you nearly got killed and lost both other units with you."

"Yes, my lord."

"Are you insane?" Matt shouted, pounding his fist downwards as his emotions escaped him, that cold lump of fear for his friend rising up, even as the black dog of his mind whispered that it didn't matter. All of them were going to die anyway.

"I am not, my lord. It is a perfect staging ground. And you constantly complain about the lack of gold. A new village will see that change."

"It'll also put you in easy reaching distance for when they decide to swat you," Matt snapped. "And if you didn't realise it, we're kind of low on units."

"Yes. But as you said, who dares wins."

"That's…" Matt threw his hand up. "And we just dared and lost."

"That doesn't mean we should stop taking risks."

"You, no. Just no." Matt crossed his arms, glaring at the tactical map and the icon that showed Braskar's icon.

There was silence on the other side of the line, as he waited for the Hero to answer him. The silence lengthened, such that Matt found himself gulping and shifting from foot-to-foot. As he waited, his eyes could not help but be drawn to the dot for the village. Almost reflexively, he tapped on it, finding as usual the tactical map had little to offer him. The only difference was that there were two coins on this one.

Then, he flicked his way through the tactical map till he found the log of the initial victory. The one that had made him think he could win this.

Village #1 (Small) Conquered

Rewards: +1 Gold, +1 territorial overview

Would you like to rename it?

He was right. It was likely this new place would get him two pieces of gold. Nothing amazing, but it was better than nothing. And if he recalled, it also let him build Roads – hah! As though he needed the enemy to get to him faster – and a Watch Tower.

Watch Tower.

Eyes narrowed, Matt leaned forwards as his fingers shifted over the map and what he could see. With the village, he had two hexes from around it. If he had two hexes of clear view from the village…

"Shit."

"My lord?" Braskar said promptly.

"The map. Did you see it?"

"No, my lord. I do have a sketch of my own, but not the main map."

So the Warlord did not know the advantage that having two hexes of the fog of war pushed back granted them then. He just wanted to hit things. Typical orc.

But he was not wrong either. If they had the space, if they could set themselves up for the fight and know what was coming…

Wars were won because of logistics and information. You needed not just one but both. In this case, the second village would give them both, if he let Braskar take it.

But it also meant that his man, his friend, was right next to the enemy. If they caught him out, sent a Hero to hunt him down, or they sent armies straight down to attack them, he only had a few units here, not enough perhaps to defend everything.

Could he risk it? Should he risk it?

"My lord?" Braskar rumbled.

"This is not advisable, not at all," Matt said. "If we lose…"

"Then we lose. But we're already on the defensive."

"Blinking powerpoints. Do it."

"My lord." This time, that answer was firmer, filled with respect.

Matt could only hope that he was not wrong. That the fight was the right choice. If he took the village, he had view of the most likely route down south for the enemy. If they took it fast enough, it meant that when the enemy made a move on him, he'd know.

And that information could be, might be, more precious than he could imagine.

If Braskar could win.

For once, he realised how much of a pain having an insubordinate subordinate was, and he felt a little for his previous managers.

Just a little.

***

Status Report

Day 43 (End of the Day)

Gold: 50.5 (+16.25 Gold per day)

Units: 3 Woodlings, 2 Firecracker Flowers

In Production: Harbour (4/5), Woodling (2/4)

Structures Completed: Grove, Road, Stall (II), Ranged Copse

Structures Available: Grove (II), Basic Greenhouse, Watch Tower, Tavern, Marketplace, Blacksmith, Ranged Copse (II)

Chapter 36

One more day and finally, the Harbour was done. A tense time, as Braskar headed north once more. In the end, nothing he could do there, so Matt focused on what he could control. The Harbour. Which meant pulling up details and actually reviewing whether any of his burgeoning plans would hold any water.

Hah. Pun.

First things first, he pulled up the newly completed Harbour information.

Harbour

Building Type: Naval

Tier: Lesser Tier I

Benefit: +5 Gold Per Day

Not much useful information there, but on the other hand, it was all the other notifications that had Matt excited.

Upgrade Available: Stone Harbour (II)

Building Type: Navy

Tier: Lesser Tier II

Benefit: +10 Gold Per Day

Cost: 400 Gold

Production Time: 12 days

Yeesh. That was one heck of a jump and nothing that made sense to Matt to acquire. He might as well get the Marketplace, which was half the cost and the same amount of gold. But, of course, the Stone Harbour wasn't just a gold-making upgrade. It was what they needed to access a whole new slew of upgrades, like he'd suspected.

A flick of his hand pulled up the summary option, one of two last notifications he had available.

New Build Options Available

- Fishing Dock (100/+5 Gold)

- Shipyard (200/Creation of Naval Units)

- Trading Post (250/+? Gold)

- Temple (200/Recruitment of New Hero Types)

"Well, that's insane. But why did they have a Temple to start?" Matt muttered, recalling the enemy base. He had no answer, of course, though at a guess different starting races and locations might dictate different base options.

If that wasn't right, he had no idea what it might be.

Pushing that aside for the moment, he plucked at the very last notification available to him. And felt his jaw drop.

Requirements Met for Coastal Village Upgrade!

- Stall

- Grove

- Harbour

- Minimum 5 Units Created

Begin upgrade? (Y/N)

"Lost staplers and bad internet connections…" Matt rubbed his face. Was that all it required? That seemed a little too simple, a little too easy. But there it was, no further notes, no further requirements. Just sitting there, waiting.

He really wanted to say yes. A small flicker of the joy that he had felt when he'd been thrust into this insane world reappeared, and his fingers twitched.

Why the hell not, eh?

He selected Yes, curious to see what would happen.

Of course, that's when all hell broke loose.

***

Status Report

Day 44 (Beginning of the Day)

Gold: 66.75 (+21.25 Gold per day)

Units: 3 Woodlings, 2 Firecracker Flowers

In Production: Woodling (3/4)

Structures Completed: Grove, Road, Stall (II), Ranged Copse, Harbour

Structures Available: Grove (II), Basic Greenhouse, Watch Tower, Tavern, Marketplace, Blacksmith, Ranged Copse (II), Stone Harbour, Fishing Dock, Shipyard, Trading Outpost, Temple

Cooldown: 1 day to spell casting, 1 day to Burst Production

Chapter 37

"How was I supposed to know it was going to do that?" Matt said, shrinking away from the Alchemist who had a potion in hand, shaking it back and forth as he ranted. Now, Matt normally wasn't particularly afraid of bottles of liquid. Except, this one seemed to be making the grass under their feet hiss and die each time a drop fell out of the beaker, even if it didn't seem to do much to the Alchemist himself.

"You could have warned us!" Irvine snarled.

"They don't seem to care," Matt said, gesturing back at the woodlings and firecracker flowers. That was all too true. Their fighting units seemed to be riding the bucking earth and twisting, flowing wood and metal without any issue.

Of course, Matt secretly understood what had gotten Irvine all worked up. Having the entire structure buckle and twist under one's feet, growing and shifting, was rather disconcerting. He'd only managed to make it out of the building unharmed through luck. Well, mostly unharmed. He had a number of bruises on him – some in places that were entirely undignified – but nothing was broken.

Unlike Irvine's latest series of experiments, or so he'd been informed.

"Great. You get them to make your potions," Irvine snapped. "I'll just go stand around and stare into the distance, why don't I?"

Matt muttered another apology, but he knew it would have been a lot more sincere if he was not grinning like a loon. Watching the wooden keep transform into a stone one, just like his opponent's, had buoyed his mood, half-banishing all his earlier sadness. It made him think that they had a chance, even if they'd taken a beating recently.

Especially with the new options they had.

"Are you even listening to me?"

"Not exactly," Matt said. "What'd you say?"

"What exactly did you do to make this happen?"

Matt turned and pointed down to the water where the village extended into the water and where the Harbour had widened and reformed deeper.

"That's it?"

"There were other options, like building enough units. But we'd done that, so yes, that's it." Matt rubbed his chin. "There're also a bunch of other options that came about."

"Like what?"

"Look for yourself, when it's done." Matt bounced a little on his feet. "I need some quiet, got to think about what we need to do."

"That good then?"

Matt offered a single nod, before he walked off. He had to think about what else he could do, what else they had to offer. The Temple was an immediate discard. Too much risk to get it, especially if it didn't come with a new Hero to use immediately. Even if he was interested in that, he would have to wait.

Same problem with the Shipyard and Trading Outpost, what with his lack of need for naval units and an unknown boost from the outpost. There was a time to gamble, but it certainly wasn't right now when they were down three units.

That left the Fishing Dock, which would give him the one thing he liked the most of all. Gold. But could he afford to wait, to build up enough to get more gold for a future advantage, when they were already behind?

On the other hand, if he didn't try to leapfrog ahead with more gold, sooner or later, he would lose.

Nevermind his other plan, his other goal. A way to make sure they would stop losing units, what with their inability to handle the damn monsters that kept coming at them? The Blacksmith was the way to go. It might only add a few points in combat strength, but that was just the first level. And as it stood, they were already coming close to winning most of their fights, so a few points might be all that was needed to tip the scales.

Not that he could do anything today. He didn't have enough gold right now. Two days and he could make a decision, though he could also start out a firecracker flower. That'd put him four days behind, what with the cost of the firecrackers pushing him just under.

Better to wait in that sense, so long as they didn't need the unit. And thus far, he would guess it wasn't needed.

"Should I send another unit north?" Matt said suddenly to Irvine when he came back to ask.

"Oh, you talking to me now?" Irvine grumped.

"Yes."

The Alchemist noticed the lack of humour in the other man's voice and dropped the teasing. Instead, he hummed to himself idly, thinking about their options. "We have two woodlings here, one firecracker flower. The new Stone Keep might have more options for defense." He rubbed his chin and the wispy beard he still sported. "You'd hope."

"Yeah."

"One woodling. At least our village will be guarded then," Irvine said. "That's what I'd suggest."

"My thoughts too." Matt's fingers itched to make the commands, but it seemed it was not to be. Even now, there was still shifting and creaking in the building ahead of them. "How long do you think this is going to take?"

Irvine shrugged and Matt sighed, looking around till he found a nice tree to flop under. Well, if he had nothing to do, he might as well just wait. He certainly wasn't going near the building, not with the way everything kept moving.

For now, he'd wait. Hold off on purchasing anything, until Braskar either won or lost and they got some more details. But finally, things were looking up once more.

Chapter 38

For all his worries, the battle was over faster than he could have imagined. There wasn't even much of a start to it, though from what Braskar told him, the firecracker flowers had done nearly half the work. They might not have the range he had wanted, but against the unarmoured militia, the shrapnel of the seedlings sent at them had taken the militia units down with ease. After that, the woodlings and Braskar had waded in to finish the fight.

Now, he was just staring at the notification that had appeared for him. None of it was particularly surprising, though it was nice to get the confirmation.

Village #2 (Small) Conquered

Rewards: +2 Gold, +1 territorial overview, Reputation +1

Would you like to rename it?

No. He really did not want to rename it.

Additional Build Options Available

- **Road (20/+0.25 Gold/increased movement speed by 50%)**
- **Watch Tower (15/+1 hex view)**

And there it was. What he'd wanted and sent Braskar all the way north for. Matt wanted to start the Watch Tower right now, to get the extra overview of space. It would cost him a day of getting the next building upgrade, but he had no idea how long the Watch Tower would take to build.

He held himself back though, wanting to take a moment to think it over once more. However, he couldn't think of a reason not to. It would get him the overview he needed to make sure the enemy could not sneak past him —

not unless they headed west by quite a few hexes and avoided the roads, coming up just like Braskar had around the lakes.

He did not think that was likely. No, if his enemy was going to send anyone down, it'd be via the most direct method, which was going to come right across his newly expanded view.

So. Watch Tower it was.

Structure Under Construction: Watch Tower

Building Type: Surveillance

Tier: N/A – Base Upgrade

Cost: 15

Production time: 1 day

"Damn. That's fast." Good thing too. "Congratulations, Braskar. You were right," Matt hesitated, then added, "What's the next plan?"

"I am uncertain, my lord. Do you see movement?" Braskar rumbled.

"None," Matt said.

"Then we have a little time."

"A little," Matt acknowledged. His enemy was likely building up its forces, and even if they did not have the revenue that he did, there was no doubt they were likely going to be coming down soon. If there was a limitation, it was in how fast the Groves or the Barracks could output new units. If he assumed it took them five days, then two more units were ten days away from when they last fought. Assuming they had enough funds – and that was a good assumption to make considering they had a Stall – then, they would likely have at least one more unit.

That put them at two upgraded saakal at the least. Maybe more.

If he was the enemy, he might not wait much longer than one more, which put them at five days of time to wait before the enemy sent their army down. Assuming they noticed how badly their own units had fared without a Warlord, he could also assume they were waiting to get one.

Maybe they even had one already. After all, getting ten gold a day and spending only twenty-five of them every five days meant they had twenty-five extra. Depending on how much it cost to hire a Hero, it could easily be enough.

So…

"Stay for a day, we'll have you move out one square tomorrow and camp. The closer you are to the enemy, the better," Matt said. "If we have to have you all the way out there, we might as well have you be useful. And with the new Watch Tower, we'll be able to tell if they come."

"Yes, my lord." Braskar sounded happy at that, which was good. Matt knew he wouldn't be, if he was asked to camp for an unknown amount of time. But it was what it was after all, and the orc was a hardier soul than the ex-office worker.

In the meantime…

"Irvine, how go the potions?"

"Close!" the Alchemist said, unhappiness at being interrupted lacing his voice. The fact that the Alchemist had thrown himself into his lab for the last few days might have been his way of coping with stress, Matt figured. Just like he'd been working on his crossbow when he had nothing better to do. "In a few days, we should have it ready."

"Good. Keep at it." Matt hesitated, looking down at his options. He had a lot of money, but not a lot of reasons to use it. Not yet. "Then we keep doing what we're doing. And hope they aren't going to jump on us any time soon."

"My lord."

Strange, how a pair of words could be laced with so much meaning.

***

Status Report

Day 44 (End of Day)

Gold: 53.75 (+22.25 Gold per day)

Units: 3 Woodlings, 2 Firecrcker Flowers

In Production: Woodling (3/4), Village #2 – Watch Tower (0/1)

Structures Completed: Grove, Road, Stall (II), Ranged Copse, Harbour

Structures Available: Grove (II), Basic Greenhouse, Watch Tower, Tavern, Marketplace, Blacksmith, Ranged Copse (II), Stone Harbour, Fishing Dock, Shipyard, Trading Outpost, Temple

Cooldown: 1 day to spell casting, 1 day to Burst Production

Chapter 39

Watching the Watch Tower come up the day after was perfect. It gave him the overview he needed, though there were no enemy units moving around. Good news, overall, though all that new information made Matt more paranoid, not less.

What was he doing?

Given that he got no answer, Matt could only go on.

Another three days passed quickly, and he bought the Blacksmith, which was the obvious choice. He had to make a selection of whether to go for more damage or defense, and considering he had wood elementals; he leaned for more damage. Later, he would pick up the defense option.

Later.

Whatever else he might want to do, the fact stood that they both knew where the other was. And it was time to finish the fight. There was also a little lurking worry that if and when he won this battle, he might be transported to a whole new map. And if that was the case, then building too much of a gold base here was a fool's game.

Blacksmith purchased and Braskar having left the conquered village meant that Matt was once more bored and with very little gold. That meant back to trying to make a functional crossbow. The fact that he had to make do with whatever knife, awl, and clam he could scrounge up or build was half the reason everything was taking so long.

Sometimes, he wondered if he should have just spent some time making himself a slingshot and learning how to use that. Then again, if he was close enough to be using a slingshot, Matt really, really was in the wrong place.

Same reason why learning to use a spear or sword was a bad idea. He knew better than to believe he could walk onto a battlefield and John Wick his way through the army. After all, he had neither the training nor armour.

Man, he'd like a stylish, magically bulletproof suit.

Sadly, all that peace and quiet was interrupted not long afterwards by the damn enemy. He projected a gentle prod to his heroes as he stared at the map.

"My lord?" Braskar rumbled.

"I have sight of enemy units. They're two hexes south of where we know the enemy fort is," Matt said, his voice tense.

"Coming for us?" Irvine said, a touch of concern in his voice.

"That'd be the obvious deduction," Matt said.

"Do we have more details?" Braskar said.

"Surprisingly, yes." Matt tapped on the icon, grateful that the Watch Tower seemed to not just add to their ability to see things but also give additional details.

Enemy Army Sighted!
Quantity: 4 Saakal, 2 Heroes

"That's… bad," Irvine said, after Matt had read the details out to the two Heroes.

"Yeah…" Matt replied weakly. Very weakly. He had expected one Hero perhaps, a Warlord. Not two. Definitely not four saakal units. He wished there was more information on the kinds of Heroes involved. But nothing was coming up, no details, no information, no way to tell how damn doomed they were.

"This is not ideal, no. What do we do, my lord?" Braskar rumbled.

"I don't know. I… don't know." Matt rubbed at his face, feeling the numbness creeping over him, the desire to just sit down there and let it happen. He fought it, speaking out loud. "What do you suggest?"

"I could meet them. I have the firecracker flowers. They have no ranged unit. If we catch them right, I might be able to damage them sufficiently to force them to retreat," Braskar said. "Allow you to build up your units further."

"Good idea!" Irvine said. "We could get more ranged units. With that, we could chase them upwards and hit them."

"No. I'm not sacrificing you," Matt said firmly.

"My lord…"

"It's not happening."

"The orc has made a good suggestion. If you don't have a better one, boy, perhaps you should consider it," Irvine said.

"I won't just let ourselves get killed for nothing," Matt said. "Anyway, there's no guarantee they'll win. We got the Keep. We got a firecracker flower unit. We got time enough to build another unit." He leaned over the tactical map, doing a quick count. "I think. Depends on how long it'd take to take the village…"

"You mean there's not enough time?" Irvine said. "Boiling potions. I'm coming up."

Matt did the count again, going one, two again and again. "Four days with two hex movement. Damn, that's really unfair."

Out of breath, Irvine arrived, pushing Matt aside and doing the same count. In the end, the man let out a long, unhappy breath.

"Will the Blacksmith not be ready by then?" Braskar asked.

A quick glance at the icon and Matt could confirm that that at least was going for them. Still… "It will. Upgraded units with the Blacksmith behind the Keep, I'm not sure that's enough. I'd feel better if we had more ranged units on the wall."

"So would I," Irvine said.

"My lord…"

"You're not going to do the sacrifice play. We have options. Like… a pincer attack…" Matt trailed off at the end, then shook his head. Wouldn't work. Their own units were too slow. The enemy would be at their gates long before Braskar could catch them. In fact… "Your sacrifice play won't work if they won't take your bait."

"I…" Braskar hesitated, obviously counting off the hexes too. "You are right, my lord."

"So what do we do?" Irvine said.

"I don't know." Matt stared at the tactical map, at the units shining before him, and then down at the map again. Irvine was staring at him, deep lines on his face as concern etched them. In the end, Matt could only say one thing.

"I don't know. But I do know one thing."

"What's that?" Irvine said.

"This is the end of the beginning. One way or the other."

***

Status Report

Day 48 (Mid-Day)

Gold: 42.75 (+22.25 Gold per day)

Units: 4 Woodlings, 2 Firecracker Flowers

In Production: Blacksmith (1/4)

Structures Completed: Grove, Road, Stall (II), Ranged Copse, Harbour, Village #2 – Watch Tower

Structures Available: Grove (II), Basic Greenhouse, Watch Tower, Tavern, Marketplace, Ranged Copse (II), Stone Harbour, Fishing Dock, Shipyard, Trading Outpost, Temple, Blacksmith (Upgrade)

Cooldown: None

Chapter 40

That's the thing about inspirational speeches and sayings. They're inspiring. But at the end of the day, they are just words. And words, without action, are often meaningless. You can talk to a pair of sticks on the ground till your face was blue, but till you started rubbing them together, you weren't going to get a fire.

And what Matt needed right now was a fire.

Preferably one emanating from the barrel of a gun. A machine gun if he could help it.

Unfortunately, all he really had was a half-working crossbow made of twisted rope and bent wood that could send a bolt of wood a dozen feet before falling to the ground. He could injure someone with it, but he might as well just grab a hunk of wood and throw it. It'd be not much weaker and a heck of a lot easier.

Matt kind of figured that was pretty much the theme of his life in this new world after dying. Everything he could do might as well be done by someone or something else, easier and faster. He was superfluous in everything but his ability to actually make decisions.

It was that thought that brought Matt to a complete stop, freezing in utter astonishment as his fingers were playing over the tactical map.

Irvine, Alchemist Hero and one of Matt's two sapient companions, frowned deeply at his Lord. Though he might have grown used to his Lord's random antics, a factor of his upbringing in a soft world, the Alchemist was still not entirely happy when he saw him freeze.

A bony finger from the older man, still steady even if it was liver-spotted, came over and poked Matt in the side, causing the man to jump up in surprise.

"What was that for!"

"You froze. What is wrong?" Irvine said. "Another attack? Some other calamity that we have not planned for?"

"No. Nothing like that," Matt said. "I just realised I'm the worst thing in the world."

"A man who expects others to read his mind?"

"A middle manager."

Matt paused, expecting a reaction. A chuckle, maybe even full laughter. He'd have settled for a groan. Instead, all he received was a blank look.

"Middle manager. You know, the guys who take shit from the people above them and the complaints of the people below? Who have no real power but still have to make decisions?" Matt paused, still getting a blank look, and he sighed. Well, it was clear that whatever world Irvine had come from, his world had not reached the industrial revolution yet or the wonderful world of international, faceless corporations.

Lucky bastard.

"Whatever. Sorry, I was, uhhh…." Matt paused, looking back at the tactical map. What the hell had he been doing?

"Planning how we could win against the army coming for us?"

"Right!" Matt said brightly. Then, he sighed. Right. They had an enemy army coming – if you could call four upgraded saakal units and two Heroes an army. At some point, if he survived, he'd probably laugh at the idea of such a small 'army,' but right now… "We got what? One woodling unit in Village 1, two woodlings and a Firecracker Flower here. And of course, the Stone Keep."

"Yes."

"That's not so bad, right?" Matt said, trying for cheerful. "We pull the woodling we have back, hope they hit the village and get slowed down and if that's the case, we get the Blacksmith upgrade that'll put us sort of in-play. After all, they've only got what? Four days to get here."

"Four days if they do not stop, which should allow us time to get the Blacksmith one way or the other. Not another unit, unfortunately."

"Yeah, sucks that our guys all take five." Matt exhaled, shaking his head. If they had a little more time, a little more warning, he could have spent his funds to get some new units. As it was, they would be a couple of days behind when the enemy arrived. "Doesn't mean we shouldn't consider getting more anyway."

"Why?" Irvine said, eyeing the man.

"For when we survive, of course," Matt replied cheerily.

Irvine was giving him a look, which Matt had to admit was more than fair. After all, the Alchemist had found him curled up in a ball of despair a bare few days ago. He probably was wondering how he could be so calm, so collected, so perfectly fine. There was a simple answer to that, of course.

He wasn't.

Deep within — if you considered a fingernail's width deep — he was a gibbering ball of terror and despair. The two bleak emotions were waging a war within him, which was all that was needed to give him some kind of insane adrenaline dump, leaving him grinning a little too wide, making jokes and, mostly, spinning around. Trying to figure out what the hell he was doing.

In truth, he had no idea. He couldn't build anything right now to make a difference. Still, buying a firecracker flower — just like this! — was at least a nice little dopamine hit.

"There!" Matt said, finishing up with clicking things through.

"I think, my lord, you might be best served to take a break," Irvine said slowly.

Matt snorted. "Sure, sure. Though, I wonder if we should pull our man back?"

"Man?"

"Orc. Braskar." Matt waved upwards, to where the orc and the remaining units of their makeshift army — a single woodling and firecracker flower unit each — rested, up north and east a little near the second village they had conquered. The village whose Watch Tower had given them the necessary information to tell them the enemy was coming. "Should we build a Watch Tower here?"

"Stop, Matt."

"It's fine, it's fine," Matt said with a grin. "There's no more gold anyway. But more information is better than none right now, and it's not as though I can do much with my gold. We're either going to win or not."

"And what about the future?" Irvine said. "That's why you're building that ranged unit now, isn't it?"

"Not going to be one if we don't win." Matt chuckled, a little darkly.

Irvine stepped closer again, leaning in to fix Matt right in the eyes. So close, Matt could see the little grey flecks that moved in the man's blue pupils. He could see the lines around the man's face. And he definitely could smell the pastrami the man just had for breakfast. Nose wrinkling, he began to lean backwards, only for Irvine to grab him and pull him forward, so that their noses were touching.

"You are not touching anything else, my lord. You are going to go downstairs, have a good meal. Maybe a stiff drink or five. And then you are going to go to sleep. If you cannot sleep, my lord, you will drink till you can. Do we understand one another?"

"I'm not sure you should be giving me orders here. Pretty sure that's not the way it works."

"Do we understand one another, my lord? Or should I be dosing you with one of my potions, so that you won't be thinking of anything but my potion?" A slight pause, then Irvine grinned. It was not a nice grin. In fact, it was the kind of grin that reminded Matt of the sight of the Alchemist dosing a bunch of raiders with one of his concoctions, making boils and red skins and other nastiness appear.

"Uhhh…"

"So. Do we have an understanding. My lord."

"I really don't like it when you use my title…" Matt muttered, pulling at the arm. Thankfully, for all the intimidation factor the Alchemist had, he really was not that strong and his grip was easily removed. Not that the other man was fighting him that much. "I'll just take a break, why don't I?"

"Marvelous idea. My lord."

Turning around, Matt moved to the exit, pausing at the doorway and the staircase leading downstairs to glance back at Irvine. The Alchemist was just standing in the same spot, turned to face him, arms crossed, giving him a smile.

Offering a weak one in return, Matt kept walking down.

Damn Alchemist was scary. Nearly made Walter White look downright friendly.

***

Status Report

Day 48

Gold: 17.75 (+22.25 Gold per day)

Units: 4 Woodlings, 2 Firecracker Flowers

In Production: Blacksmith (1/4), Firecracker Flower (0/5)

Structures Completed: Grove, Road, Stall (II), Ranged Copse, Harbour, Village #2 – Watch Tower

Structures Available: Grove (II), Basic Greenhouse, Watch Tower, Tavern, Marketplace, Ranged Copse (II), Stone Harbour, Fishing Dock, Shipyard, Trading Post, Temple, Blacksmith (Upgrade)

Cooldown: None

Chapter 41

Irvine watched the boy walk down the stairs, his eyes flat and humorless, until the majority of his footsteps had faded. Then the Alchemist walked over to the doorway and the staircase, took a few steps down, and poked his head around. Content to see that Matt really had left, he nodded to himself in a self-satisfied manner, walked back to the tactical room, closed the door, and then ended up leaning against it on the other side.

Over-boiled potions and rotten ingredients.

The older man found his knees shaking a little, and rather than fight it, he let himself sink to the ground. He exhaled roughly, eyes half-closing. Manhandling the boy could have gone really badly. Possibly could be a really bad thing in the future.

Most men didn't take well to that. Took a good healthy ego to suffer a bruising like that and not scar, and when it did scar, it often came up at the most inconvenient times. Like in the middle of his second wedding ceremony. Or whilst he was fucking his best friend's son's bride.

Well, maybe that blowup had other reasons.

"Braskar," Irvine spoke up slowly. He needed to talk to someone, and since the options were himself, the orc, and Matt, it really was not much of a choice.

"Irvine?" Braskar rumbled. "Trouble?"

"Why's everyone saying that?" Irvine said. "I might just be calling to catch up."

"Nothing immediate then."

Irvine sighed, rubbing his lined face. He was feeling every inch of his eighty-three years now. Not that this new body was eighty-three. Thank the gods for that. By that point in his life, he was having trouble going for longer than an hour before needing to take a piss and that'd made making potions a real pain. The kind of accidents that happened when you spilled the wrong thing down the loo did not bear thinking about.

"No, nothing urgent," Irvine reluctantly agreed. "It's more Matt."

"What is wrong with our Lord?"

"He's cracking," Irvine said flatly. "I don't think he's doing well, with the strain of being, well…"

"The Lord?"

"In charge and in danger."

Braskar let out a long sigh. "I did worry that he seemed soft. I doubt he ever faced the blood trials."

"I doubt most non-orcs have faced the blood trials," Irvine replied. He didn't even know what the blood trials were, but he could guess it involved a lot of pain and fear and blood. If Braskar's orcs were anything like his own world's – and they seemed, at least in the overall picture, to be similar if a little more civilized – then that'd be true.

"More the loss for them." Braskar sighed. "I shall make sure to correct that mistake when I return."

"Yeah…" Irvine hesitated, then decided to leave that comment alone. First they had to survive today. "Point being, he isn't analysing the situation anymore. I think between the raiders and his inability to actually do anything beyond make decisions, he's not handling it well. He called himself a… middle manager."

"What is that?"

"I do not know," Irvine said. "It did not sound good, and it certainly sounded like a powerless and thankless role."

"Mmm, what do you suggest then? With a child who faced such fears, I would take them out to do battle in the wilds, facing a dire wolf alpha or other creature alone. When they had found their courage from defeating their opponent, then I would know they are ready."

"That sounds like your blood trials."

"Hah! If only those were so simple."

Irvine shook his head, discarding his curiosity. "Well, you're not here."

"You must have dealt with your share of failing apprentices."

Irvine grimaced. "I just threw them out of my tower. Well, except for my second son."

"And what did you do with him?"

"Let him bumble around long enough till he blew off half the fingers of one hand and then regrew them. Was a good lesson in being careless."

"You are a horrible father and trainer."

Irvine just shrugged. "Well, I don't hear a better suggestion coming from you."

"I do not believe we have one. Support him as best you can, temper his rash impulses. But this is our Lord's Blood Trial to face, I fear."

"With our lives on the line."

"We have died before. It was not so bad," Braskar said. "Except the dying part. That was horrible."

"You can remember your death?"

"Impalement. Hopefully our enemy is not as vicious as my previous ones." Then Braskar fell silent, though somehow it felt like the silence was pointed.

Irvine could not help but ask. "What?"

"Just remembering those I left behind. I can only hope they survived after my defeat and capture." There was a slight tremble in the stoic orc's voice as he continued, "I would not wish them to suffer like I did."

"Family?"

"Yes."

Silence, this time darker and more tempered, filled the room. In the end, Irvine shook his head, speaking softly, "Well, at least the saakal look like they're likely to just tear us to pieces. And I'll make sure to make a few Death Embrace Potions, just in case."

"You do that. And you support our Lord. He will need your advice and wisdom."

"Yeah, yeah." Irvine shook his head, looking one last time at the tactical map before walking towards the door. He stopped just before he exited, adding one last sentence. "You best take care yourself, orc. It'd be boring without you."

Then, not bothering to wait for the orc to reply, Irvine made his way downstairs to make sure Matt actually was taking his advice and resting. If he wasn't settled, at least he had enough control to continue masking his emotions.

Chapter 42

Matt woke with a pounding headache. Thankfully, Irvine had left behind one of his hangover potions when the old man had guided him back into his bed after drinking him under the table. Memories of the night before were spotty, but he was sure he'd poured out his misgivings, his worries and fears and pain, during the evening as the glasses of alcohol kept getting filled.

Drinking down the hangover potion, marveling at the fact that it tasted like citrus-and-chocolate this time, he perked right up. The headache and overall bodyache faded as did the pain behind his eyes, though he still felt the need to freshen up further.

Still. His mind was clearer, some of the darkness that had threatened to pull him under released. Not gone entirely, but enough for him to function at least. And really, that was all that he could ask for most days.

After cleaning up, he pocketed the vial that the hangover cure had come from and started for the map room. The tactical map awaited, along with further thoughts about what he could do. Or should do. Halfway out of the door, his stomach rumbled loudly enough to remind him that he hadn't fed it, and Matt detoured long enough to pick up a meal.

A bad idea, it turned out, since that was where Irvine found him.

"Returning to the control room?" Irvine said, raising a single eyebrow even as he reached over and snatched the vial that was sticking out of Matt's pocket.

Matt shifted a little to get away from the fast-moving grabbing hand, though he was too late. After all, he was currently carrying a heavy plate laden with food and a mug, which reduced his ability to avoid the other.

"Yeah."

"Good. I'll come with you."

"No, you won't."

Irvine's eyes narrowed.

Matt lifted his chin. "Don't start. I'm fine. And you have something better to do with your time."

"I do?"

"Finishing your potion recipe. Which one did you choose anyway?" Matt said. He couldn't even recall which one they'd discussed, if they'd ever discussed it.

"Defense." Irvine shrugged. "Speed did not seem necessary, considering how fast our units move. Growth is a long-term advantage, but our units already heal quicker. Unless it means experience growth, and we'd need units that last longer than a few fights. So Defense."

"Makes sense." Matt jerked his chin. "So get to it. Also, if you get your next Level, we might get something good."

"I doubt it."

"Me too. But anything is better than nothing and that's all we got."

"Even so…"

"I'm fine." Matt waved his hand. "If I'm going to be the boss, I'm going to be the boss. And your marching orders are to get brewing. I got other ideas, including an ass-pull of one."

"You have the strangest sayings," Irvine said, but he did turn aside and head back to his rooms. "I hope it is as good an idea as the ones you've had before."

"Oh, it's better," Matt called out after Irvine. After the other man had shut his door, Matt added, "I hope."

Climbing the stairs the rest of the way up the tower, Matt idly noted how much fitter he had gotten. Was? Maybe his body had always been this fit. Nah, he remembered feeling a little out of breath the first time he came up here.

Now, climbing the tower was easy. Not happy making, but easy. Setting his meal aside, Matt looked at the map, doing the count again. The thought had arrived early this morning when he woke up between bouts of nightmares and pleasant dreams, but he wanted to make sure his count was right before he made the call.

Yup. Three.

Of course, it'd take the other army only two days to turn around and chase them back.

So this was the gamble. Wait another day, let the other army move away. Then, they'd be too far away to protect their own fort. Negative – they'd be too far away so they'd probably attack them anyway.

Or…

Send Braskar out now. Then, it'd put the ball in his foe's court. They could turn around, hit Braskar, weaken themselves and let him build up further. Except, of course, he'd lose Braskar and certainly not win anything.

If he waited, they'd have to face the oncoming army. There was no way the other army would turn back, rather banking on beating him first. Did it matter who beat who first if both of them lost their keeps on the same day? Were units left to roam and keep fighting or would they disappear?

He had no idea. Maybe they did stick around, and if that was the case, then he'd be facing an attack anyway when the army arrived.

It would be ironic and show exactly how tilted this game was to their enemy, if that happened. Which probably meant they'd be forced into a battle whether he wanted it or not.

Still, there was a small chance they could disappear if he hit the enemy's keep first. Assuming Braskar could win, they could end this part of the battle. The only real reason he was willing to risk that was the number of saakal units being sent too.

Four.

That was the kicker. Just one too many for there to be any left behind, or so he believed. He'd done the math.

Kids, don't let them fool you. Math is important.

If there was anything back there, it was minimal. A single unit at most.

"Braskar," Matt said, choosing to speak to his Warlord. He was the strategic genius supposedly. Or at least, his war help. Might as well make use of him, even if he was beginning to wonder exactly how much of the 'lord' part of the Warlord title Braskar really held.

"My lord?" Commanding, but questioning. Matt couldn't help but wonder what – if anything – Irvine had said to the other. Might just be worry about a fight he couldn't control.

"I've got an idea. Hear me out, before you interrupt, will you?" Matt said, then quickly laid out the plan to hit the enemy fortress while the other army was away. "I know you don't have much in terms of units. But, I figure, they probably don't either."

"Why?"

"Four units. Two Heroes. I can't believe that we're that badly outnumbered. So they've got to have stripped their fortress."

"Got to," Braskar said, doubtfully.

"Well, I'm guessing, but I think it's a good guess." Matt forced himself to stay positive. He mostly believed he was right, but he had to admit that all this was educated guessing right now. Still, part of fighting on this level, Matt was realizing, was that it was as much a game of mind reading as it was controlling – and understanding – the logistics of the other party.

Forty-nine days. Figure production time required at least four days for a unit, that meant you could at most produce twelve units at intervals of four days. Considering he was running upgraded saakal units, which, if they were like the woodlings, took an extra day, he should have even fewer than that. Nine units maximum of upgraded units. And considering they'd started moving a few days ago, that'd actually be eleven and nine. Now, taking into account inefficiencies in unit production and waiting for gold to come about, you'd have to say they ran on the lower end of that.

He'd destroyed two units of the saakal in their initial meeting. Another two in the most recent confrontation. That put them at four units destroyed and four units showing. So, eight units total. Butting right up on the lower end of the calculation.

That, of course, was assuming they'd started at the same time. He doubted that was true – or his opponent had started with stronger Heroes and more gold to begin with – but everything he'd seen showed that they didn't have that much more of an advantage.

The only question was how much more – five days? Ten? An extra hundred gold and one upgraded Hero? He just did not know. But if it was too one-sided, they'd have steamrolled them already and this entire thing would have been over.

So.

An educated guess.

More importantly, he had to think about what his opponent was thinking. Or why he'd send so many men, so fast. The kind of individual who would pour all his resources into creating a ton of units, not bother with things like Treasury buildings, and, most importantly, used the saakal – slavering, nasty creatures that they were – as their people.

Once he explained it all to Braskar, Matt waited. He found himself holding his breath a little, as he waited for the other man to make a pronouncement on his ideas, on his thinking.

"I cannot fault your logic, nor what you said about our enemy. You are still making assumptions-"

"But good ones!"

"-but I believe them to be sound. I will ready the units and begin the assault immediately," Braskar said, sounding almost eager. Probably was.

To Matt's surprise, having said it all, the man found himself resolved, a clear understanding having awoken in him. One that he was a little surprised to have come to, but it was resolute and bedrock firm.

"Not yet. You move tomorrow," Matt said.

"My lord?"

"If you leave now, they'll cut you off as I said. You have to wait, until it makes no sense for them to try to hit you. Not without you beating them entirely first anyway," Matt said. "That means, waiting one more day."

"That would put them at your walls, my lord."

"I know." Matt breathed out, finding his heart beating a little wildly. Even so, he found himself speaking firmly. "Even so."

"I do not like this, but if you are resolved…"

"I am. We wait, let them get closer, and you hit them from behind." Matt hesitated, then added, "I might not speak with you much over the next few days. Got to see what I can do to prepare here. But if I don't…"

"Yes, my lord?"

"Good luck."

"To you too, my lord."

Matt smiled grimly, flicked his hand, and cut off the connection. Tension from speaking with the orc ran out of him, leaving him a little boneless. Finding a seat, he slumped into it for a few minutes, before he pushed himself upwards.

Time to see how else he could tilt the field in their favour.

***

Status Report

Day 49

Gold: 40 (+22.25 Gold per day)

Units: 4 Woodlings, 2 Firecracker Flowers

In Production: Blacksmith (2/4), Firecracker Flower (1/5)

Structures Completed: Grove, Road, Stall (II), Ranged Copse, Harbour, Village #2 – Watch Tower

Structures Available: Grove (II), Basic Greenhouse, Watch Tower, Tavern, Marketplace, Ranged Copse (II), Stone Harbour, Fishing Dock, Shipyard, Trading Post, Temple, Blacksmith (Upgrade)

Cooldown: None

Chapter 43

First things first. Gold. Forty. Not a lot, though he was now getting twenty-two and a quarter a day. A little frustrating, that things were beginning to come to the head just as his little gold engine was beginning to really get going.

But that was life, wasn't it? It cut you off, just as you were getting your feet under you. The only thing you could do was learn to roll with the falls and maybe, if you anticipated it well enough, you'd do a drop and roll and come right back up like a tumbler in an acrobatic performance.

Not that he'd ever seen a proper Cirque one. Those were too expensive, but local troupes were just as good, and less expensive. Made for fun dates too, when you could get someone willing.

He had a ranged fella coming along, which was good, but nowhere near complete in time. The Blacksmith would be a bonus, it'd be here beforehand. No way to speed up production yet, though he'd bet there was an option later on.

Seemed to be the way these things worked, hiding such options when he needed them most. So, assuming the fight was bad, what were his best uses of his gold?

A quick flick of his hand brought up all the options that he could buy.

Structures Available: Grove (II), Basic Greenhouse, Watch Tower, Tavern, Marketplace, Ranged Copse (II), Stone Harbour, Fishing Dock, Shipyard, Trading Post, Temple

No Groves or Ranged Copses. Those were not useful in the current period. Stone Harbour, Fishing Dock, Marketplace, Shipyard, or even the Trading Post were all non-pertinent to the fight. Same with the Watch Tower or Basic Greenhouse or the Tavern.

Tavern.

A glimmer of hope at that idea. Maybe he could find a personal bodyguard or something in there. Then, he shook his head. Even if he managed to get the gold for it – and quick calculations showed that he would have enough, barely – it still would need to be built.

Damn building time requirements.

Anyway, if he was saving money, maybe he should save money for that Greenhouse. He was a little limited on his units, and if he was going to win the next fight, having the gold and options for another might just give him the advantage he'd need.

"I really don't think there's anything I can do, in the short term," Matt muttered, going over the numbers again. It was the build time that was killing him here. Nothing he could build could save him, not in time at least.

So. Plan for the future.

What would he need in the future? More money. Always.

The Greenhouse for more options.

The Tavern because Heroes seemed to be rather important. If he lost Braskar, he'd need a Warlord. Even if he didn't lose his orc, at some point, he'd need to expand outwards, fight in the east – whatever the hell was that way – and explore north. And west. And south. Right into the water.

Yeah, maybe a naval Hero was needed.

Oh boy. He really needed to figure out what the heck was going to come from the water. Otherwise, he'd wake up one day and find the Vikings at his door, wanting to split his chest and give him the blood eagle, and he just was not into that as a fashion statement.

Long-term, he needed a lot. Right now, perhaps most importantly, whatever happened, units were going to die. Which really meant he had about one option, all things considered.

Still, he put a little mental pin in the idea of buying the Tavern or Greenhouse. One or the other, sooner rather than later. Even if nothing else, picking up something like the Greenhouse and getting its long build time going before picking up a Tavern or, hell, the Fishing Dock was not a bad idea.

For now - woodling.

***

Irvine made sure the boy was out of the tactical room, whittling away and muttering about maximal torsion and scrap metal in the room he'd taken over as his workshop, before he snuck up to talk to Braskar. Not that he was defying orders, exactly. He had potions on the boil, so this conversation would have to be short anyway. But a man had to check.

"What do you think?" Irvine said, not bothering with pleasantries the moment he got into the room.

"He's on edge, but better. His ideas were sound, if a little desperate."

"We're pretty desperate right now."

"I did not say it was a bad thing," Braskar said. "When blood is spilt, the ones who want to live the most are the ones who come back. The ones who seek death often find it."

"Very philosophical for a bloodthirsty barbarian."

"A successful – mostly – barbarian. The rumor of berserkers and crazed fighters are only partly true. Those units we keep in reserve and utilize when we have to, but the majority of us know better than to throw ourselves onto the pikes of the humans."

"Now, we're letting an orc run the war," Irvine said with a huff. "But the plan is sound. Just risky. I'd love to know what kind of Heroes are coming."

"Warlord and one other," Braskar said immediately.

"The other is my concern. If there was a Mage or something else…" Irvine shook his head, though he knew the orc could not see him. "Did you have Mages?"

"Paltry creatures. They were, mostly, useless with their cantrips and tricks."

"Same for the most part. Except a few." Irvine licked his lips. "Those, those were dangerous. There was one – the Blue Wizard they called him. He took down the walls of the hot gates, allowing the armies of Krius to stream in and finish the Great War."

"Let us hope, then, that there are no mages of that caliber then."

"Your words, committed to the everlasting flame."

Braskar let out a little huff but did not object to the heresy. The pair stood in silence for a time, one staring at the tactical map that laid out their fate in glowing, hard light and the other at the fading sunlight filtering through tree leaves, the smell of growing vegetation and fresh rain filling the air.

"I should get back to my potions," Irvine said reluctantly. "If there's nothing else."

"No."

"Right. Goodbye then."

"Goodbye, Alchemist."

Turning around in slippered feet, Irvine headed out the doorway, not looking back. There was no point. There was nothing back there to see.

***

Status Report

Day 49

Gold: 20 (+22.25 Gold per day)

Units: 4 Woodlings, 2 Firecracker Flowers

In Production: Blacksmith (2/4), Firecracker Flower (1/5), Woodling (0/4)

Structures Completed: Grove, Road, Stall (II), Ranged Copse, Harbour, Village #2 – Watch Tower

Structures Available: Grove (II), Basic Greenhouse, Watch Tower, Tavern, Marketplace, Ranged Copse (II), Stone Harbour, Fishing Dock, Shipyard, Trading Post, Temple, Blacksmith (Upgrade)

Cooldown: None

Chapter 44

Matt called an all hands meeting two days later. One day before the army was supposed to arrive, a day after Braskar had started moving. A lot was riding on today. Everything from seeing if their opponent was going to call off the attack to chase down Braskar to whether they were going to hit the village at all and take away some of the gold they had. On top of that, the new Blacksmith was finished which meant he had more to review.

Of course, calling the meeting in the morning when choices had yet to be made and played out meant that they were mostly just watching the tactical map, but it was why Matt had resolved to send Irvine away as soon as he could.

"You got the potion recipe, you old coot?" Braskar rumbled. "Why did you not tell me?"

"Potion recipe and Level. And why would we?" Irvine sniffed. "I completed it last night, and it's not as though anything we do can help you."

"I would still like to be informed."

"Yeah, that's my fault," Matt said. "I figured you sleeping well for a night was better than us waking you." He hid a yawn of his own as he glared at the Alchemist a little. It wasn't a very heated glare, what with the man's success, but it was still there. "What Irvine didn't tell you was exactly how late he managed to get it. And how much of a commotion he made when he did."

"So you are now Level 2?"

"Yes."

Matt leaned over and poked at the Hero portraits by the side of the tactical map, calling up further information. It had been way too late in the day for him to even consider ascending the stairs – nevermind how creepy wandering around in the flickering lamplight at night was in the Stone Keep. Also, cold. No one ever talked about how balls freezing cold these castles were. Made sense, of course, when you thought about it. Stone conducted very well and dragged away heat. Anyone who ever sat against a concrete wall or floor knew that. Of course, the building was cold. He just never thought about it. Never had a reason to.

Matt was not looking forward to winter.

If he managed to make it.

Maybe he could skin a bear or something.

In the meantime, he distracted himself from thoughts of freezing toes and other appendages by staring at Irvine's new character sheet.

Irvine (Level 2 Alchemist)

Specialty: Alchemy

Skills: Alchemical Concoction (II), Burst Production

Experience: 2/200

Attack: 8

Defense: 9

Power: 15

Knowledge: 24

"You got an upgrade to a skill," Matt noted.

"He did?" Braskar said, surprised.

"Alchemical Concoction II," Matt said. "No idea what it does."

"It's nothing major. Just a few more techniques that I can now use and a few more potion recipes I can research," Irvine said, trying for casual. He couldn't hide the small, self-satisfied smile that graced his lips though.

"Which ones?" Matt said.

"Well, I finished the Potion of Defense. Have an upgrade to that called Hardened Skin. And there's of course Growth and Speed still, but also there's an upgrade to the Potion of Strength. It's called Potion of Greater Strength," Irvine said.

"Not very inventive naming sense, eh?" Matt said.

"Is that all?" Braskar spoke at the same time. Then, realizing he had spoken over Matt, added, "My apologies, my lord."

Irvine spoke up before Matt could tell the man it was no issue. "That's it. Better than nothing."

"Any other changes? How you feel? Think?" Matt asked curiously. He was still somewhat amused by the stats, but it was worth checking.

"I feel mostly the same." Irvine tapped the top of his head. "I do have more recollection of the various potions I used to make. Like memories returning. I've found I have access to a few more ingredients and equipment below and can make some short-lived alchemical tools.

"Similar to my itching dust."

"Short-lived?"

"Yes. Can't hand them around because they'd break down too fast," Irvine said.

"Damn."

The older man shrugged.

"My lord, should I continue my march?" Braskar spoke up. "We are packed and ready to travel."

Matt hesitated before answering, leaning over to poke at the tactical map. He couldn't see details, unfortunately, about their enemy, even if they were literally next to his village. Just an icon, sitting next to the settlement.

He'd feel bad about leaving it entirely undefended but since pillaging and sacking was not a thing, or if it was, it was to non-sapient figures, his guilt was mostly mollified. Such a weird and bloodless war.

"Can't see any changes. So I say go for it."

"Very well, my lord." Braskar hesitated. "Is there anything else?"

"Yeah. Blacksmith. Any changes you see?" Matt said. "You're the one who knows the woodlings and firecracker flowers best."

There was a long pause, a few grunts. Then a solid thunk, followed by a growl of pain. The pair listening in a room tens of miles away looked at one another, confusion ringing their faces but neither choosing to break the silence.

After the cursing ended, Braskar spoke up. "They're still as tough as before, but I think the woodlings' arms have changed colour a little. A darker wood, I think. The seeds around the flowers are all glinting a little in the light, like there's metal in them."

"Oooh, metal splinters. Nice!" Matt said.

"Not if they hit you," Irvine said, though he was grinning a little too.

"Is that all, my lord?" Braskar said. "I would like to make sure we make it to the fort by tomorrow."

"Yeah, go ahead." Matt waved his hand imperiously even if Braskar couldn't see it. He was not sure there was much else he could do but wait up here. Wait to figure out which way they were going. Even his own preparations were as complete as they were going to get. Fiddling further, especially doing something like digging rather obvious holes, would be of little use.

You never realized how much wok it was, to dig a pit till you had to do it.

Especially when you considered exactly how much work a single man could do in a day. There was a reason they had work crews for all that. Even so, he'd spent some portion of the last few days trying his best to cover up his traps, or at least make them less obvious.

Not that it helped. Camouflage was hard to do when you didn't really have much to work with. Some basic planking, some turf he'd cut out from around the other side of the hill to help cover the difference. It wasn't half bad, but unless the enemy intended to attack at night or were half-blind, his efforts weren't going to do much.

"I'm going to go too then," Irvine said, turning away.

"Just confirming. You're hitting Burst Production, right?" Matt said, eyes narrowing.

"Yes. Three Defense Potions, done today." Irvine grimaced. "I'll be wrung out after this, but it should be worth it."

"Good." Matt paused, then cocked his head to the side. "What's the duration, anyway?"

"Of the potions? Around an hour." Irvine waggled his hands side-to-side. "In most humanoids. The elementals…"

"Are not exactly the same. But I figure whatever is making this work will make it work for them too," Matt said, nodding. "Good enough. Potions of Strength and Defense for most." He considered, then added, "You should keep one of the Potions of Defense."

"The woodlings…"

"Will get them both. The firecracker flowers should be on the wall and safe enough, at least for the initial charge. If we keep the woodlings just behind the doors, when they break through, the flowers can fire down. Cause even more trouble."

"Sound tactics." Then Irvine sighed. "If we can make them understand it."

"Yeah, your word to HR."

Again, Irvine gave Matt a look.

He shrugged. "Anyway. That's it. Get to it."

Irvine snorted but hurried off. Leaving Matt alone in the room again to stare at the tactical map, find out what their enemy was doing, and finish any planning he might have.

Also known as waiting.

Again.

***

Status Report

Day 51 (Beginning of Day)

Gold: 64.5 (+22.25 Gold per day)

Units: 4 Woodlings, 2 Firecracker Flowers

In Production: Firecracker Flower (3/5), Woodling (2/4)

Structures Completed: Grove, Road, Stall (II), Ranged Copse, Harbour, Village #2 – Watch Tower, Blacksmith

Structures Available: Grove (II), Basic Greenhouse, Watch Tower, Tavern, Marketplace, Ranged Copse (II), Stone Harbour, Fishing Dock, Shipyard, Trading Post, Temple, Blacksmith (Upgrade)

Cooldown: None

Chapter 45

It was nearly four hours later, when half the day had passed, that the damn unit icons moved. During that period, Matt had prodded at the information on the tactical map twice over, tried to see if there was anything he could do to speed up production and then, when that failed, finally went down, got himself a second breakfast, an early lunch, and his makeshift crossbow.

That, amongst all the things, was his greatest pride and joy. He'd test fired it just the day before and it managed to send a crudely fletched bolt tipped with stolen metal through a chair back at a distance of twenty feet.

Overall a success as far as Matt figured. He also had stored the four bolts he'd managed to make in the tactical room along with the spear and basic shield he'd used before. Matt rather expected he would have little chance to fire more than one bolt – especially considering he was hauling the bolt back by sheer force. One shot. And then, well.

He'd get to try putting the pointy bit into the opponent.

"Braskar, confirmed. They aren't going after you," Matt said, recalling the fact that he should have mentioned this to the man. Then, willing the channel open to Irvine, he added, "They skipped the village. They're on the way to us."

"Do you think that would have slowed them, fighting in it?" Braskar asked, curious. It was never an option for them, what with their ability to only move one hex at a time. So they had no way of knowing what the choices were for their opponent.

"Maybe. Or they just don't want to risk losing even a single one of their units. The saakal aren't the most disciplined, you know," Matt replied.

"If you two can stop bothering me, making potions isn't exactly easy. Especially when you're multi-batching!" Irvine groused. Then, the Alchemist forced close the connection, leaving Matt feeling a little ashamed.

"He's just stressed, my lord."

Matt startled and glared at the unit icon, wondering if the orc could read his mind. Not that it was that complicated but...

"Aren't we all?" Matt said softly. "This isn't exactly the easiest thing in the world, waiting for someone to kill you, is it?"

"You will not fall, my lord. And I will succeed, securing our first full victory over our opponent."

"What if we don't?"

"Then we die. But whilst it is prudent to plan for defeat, you cannot go into battle thinking of it. You must fight with all your heart, my lord. Claw for every second of breath, watch for every opportunity. It is those who do not give up who prevail," Braskar said. "So long as you keep your sense of caution, you will survive and win."

Matt shut his eyes for a second then opened them, letting out a long thready breath. "Okay. Yeah, you're right. I'm just not used to this kind of thing. The worst I ever had to worry about was a project deadline that my boss was definitely certain we couldn't meet but had to. Otherwise we'd lose a ten-million-dollar client. And even then..."

"Even then?"

"Even then, I never cared. It was not my business. It was just a job. And while I did my job, I wasn't about to kill myself for them. Figuratively speaking." Matt laughed softly. "Except it's not so figurative right now, is it? And it's not just me who's going to die if we fail."

"Yes, my lord. But you forget one thing."

"What's that?" Matt said, curiously.

"We are all dead men already. Dying is no stranger to us."

At that reminder, Matt held a hand up to his head, remembering the agonizing pain, the headache and his collapse as the brain aneurysm finished him off. The worst pain he'd ever felt in that life, bar none. Which was fitting, since it was the one that ended it.

"Yeah, don't remind me. It sucked."

"But then, it was over. And we began again. So perhaps that is what awaits us next."

"A never-ending game on repeat, with stacked odds and no indoor plumbing?" Matt shuddered. "Yeah, okay. For hells, this isn't the worst that I could think of. At least they're not playing bagpipes."

"You are a very strange man, my lord."

"So I've been told." Matt traced his fingers over the table, watching the display ripple before he pushed the other thoughts aside. "Can you see them yet?"

"I can, my lord. It's in the distance, but we can see them."

"Let me know if you see any units. If there are any other problems." Matt exhaled harshly. "Hopefully, they can't have built up any either, so you should be clear."

"So you've said." Doubt filled the orc's tone, but Matt chose to ignore it. He understood why he doubted Matt's estimations. But Braskar was right, you could choose to stew in your worries or you could push ahead, once the dice were thrown.

"I'll leave you to it then. I'm going to see if I can raid the larder for food for tomorrow," Matt said. "Food and water. Maybe a bucket."

"Of course."

Matt turned away, walking to the door, only to be brought to a stop as Braskar's voice cut in.

"My lord. Tonight."

"Yes?"

"Drink sparingly. Water the wine beforehand, and then put the wine aside. You will want your mind clear."

"Yeah, I get that." Matt chuckled. "And I'm sure Irvine's got better things to do than offer me hangover potions."

"Yes, he does." Then, a pause before Braskar's voice, tinged with outrage, came shouting through. "What kind of potions!?!"

Chapter 46

"Did you have to tell him?" Irvine said grumpily the next morning. In fact, the Alchemist was overall just pissy, deep bags under his eyes speaking of a very long night brewing the potions that they needed. Still, the man had scurried downstairs when he was done, handing them out to the various units and watching a single potion magically multiply such that each individual member of the woodlings had a potion of their own. Which they'd promptly then stored in their mouths. Or what Matt figured was their mouth.

"How was I to know you hadn't told Braskar that you had a hangover potion?" Matt said.

"Logic and understanding of human nature," Irvine said promptly. "Why give up a chance for torturing a friend when you can?"

"That's… well, I was going to say, not how friendship works. But I guess it does, for some kinds of relationships," Matt said, recalling his own time in college. Sometimes he wondered exactly how healthy those relationships had been, what with the sheer volume of alcohol imbibed.

Then again, whose fault was that? The people he hung out with, the overall atmosphere, or just teenage hormones?

"Are you daydreaming again?" Irvine snapped. "That kind of thing will get you killed in a lab, you know. Or a fight."

"We're not in a lab. Or a fight. Furthest place we could be for a fight," Matt said, waving around the tactical room they'd met within. He'd not slept well, so he had added a last-minute twist to his usual pit trap plans, brushing them down a little and then adding the simple roadblock of a bunch of the training pells and an overturned wagon on the main road up. Thankfully, the woodlings were more than happy to help him with such simple manual labor.

"At yours and Braskar's insistence, I might point out. I am fine with the idea of joining the battle, for a bit of time. At least until I fired off most of my bolts."

"And risk having you fried by a magic user?" Irvine shook his head. "Not a good idea."

"We don't know they have one."

"We don't know they don't."

"Are you always this cautious?" Matt grumped.

"Yes. That's why I have all my fingers and other, more careless and less paranoid, Alchemists don't."

"Didn't you get a new body?"

"Not the point. I still had all my fingers in my old body." Irvine sniffed, though he was careful not to mention the scars along one thigh and the missing little toes of his left foot. That hadn't been his fault. Mostly. How was he supposed to know that the Proska grains had grown a mold in the month since their collection? It had never happened before and no one had ever mentioned that possibility.

"Well look at old 'ten-fingers Irvine' here, proudly waving all his digits in my face," Matt said with a little smirk. "I still think you're worried about nothing. We haven't even seen an option for Mages. And if Temples are required to get Clerics or Acolytes or whatever else you call them, then it's pretty clear that you'd need a Mage Tower to get a Mage."

"Or so you believe."

"That's how these games work," Matt said.

"Yet, we're not in a game. And you've said it before, this is not exactly the same, no?"

Matt had to shrug, not wanting to admit defeat directly even if the man was right. "Anyway, why aren't you catching a nap?" He waved down to the screen and then the window. "I can always wake you, later. I'm pretty sure falling asleep on your feet is just as likely to get one killed."

Irvine smirked, reaching into his robes and pulling out a purple potion with sparkling yellow lights drifting through it. "I have a solution for that."

"And what is it?"

"A solution." He waited, then let out a long sigh, obviously annoyed at Matt missing – or in his case, ignoring – the obvious pun. "You've spoken of this coffee you miss. That gives you energy?" Matt nodded, looking very interested in the potion now. "This is similar. If a little more powerful."

Something in the way the Alchemist said that had Matt asking, "Exactly how little?"

"Guaranteed to put even the mortally wounded on their feet and ready to fight for the next four hours. After that, they'll probably fall over dead, but it'll get them on their feet for sure," Irvine said.

"Yeah, just a little more powerful than coffee," Matt said. "Still, sounds like the kind of potion would be good for someone like Braskar to have."

"Can't," Irvine said. "It needs to be brewed on the day and will only hold efficacy for another eight hours. After that, it goes from a stimulant to a poison."

"Well… that could be useful too."

"Not if the poison itself breaks down within the next seven days, at unknown rates, depending on the environmental conditions, and there's no easy method of delivery," Irvine said. "Unless you expect our enemies to hold still while we pour the poison down their throat."

"Unlikely," Matt said, looking around the table, then grinned. "I could invite them in for a meal…"

"You're not serious, correct?"

"I really am not."

"My lord, we're closing in on the keep. I, unfortunately, have to report that your estimation of a complete lack of resistance is wrong," Braskar's voice cut in, interrupting the conversation.

Matt whipped around, his back straightening and the light joviality he had been wielding to keep himself from panicking about the upcoming battle disappearing. His heart had sped up, and, for a second, his throat closed off as he tried to speak. He forced himself to breathe, clenching and unclenching his fist even as he felt a sweaty dampness form.

"How many? What kind?" Irvine spoke before Matt managed to regain control.

"Too many," Braskar paused, "of us to be stopped."

"You overboiled orc," Irvine snapped, staring at the pale-looking Matt who had swayed a little at the orc's initial words. He put a hand to his own chest, his earlier fatigue wiped away as well by a shot of adrenaline of his own. "This is not the time for fun and games."

"But you were allowed to joke?" Braskar said. "Unfair."

"Life's unfair."

"Enough," Matt growled. "What kind of opposition are we talking about? Seriously."

"One unit of saakal. They're standing on the walls, running back and forth and howling." Braskar laughed darkly. "I do not think they have any ability to strike at us."

"Stones and boiling oil," Matt said, glancing outside of the window where the woodlings stood along with the firecracker flowers. The boiling oil was a new addition, added right above the gates. "I'm not sure how they will wield it, but the keep's defenses might be the biggest concern."

"We shall keep it in mind." Braskar hesitated. "If we bring the firecracker flowers within range, we could pelt them initially for a while. But…"

"But what?" Matt asked.

"I fear your opponents will be at the gates before us," Braskar replied. "We still have a distance to march."

"And if you hold back too long, you think we'll lose, but if you rush it, you think you might be able to save us before they break through," Matt said, clarifying what he assumed the man was talking about. He wasn't necessarily wrong, though… "Not much faith in our defenses here, do you?"

"My apologies, my lord, but…"

"He's teasing you, you fool of an orc," Irvine said. "And you should know better anyway."

"Better?" Matt cocked his head to the side, confused as well by the Alchemist. "What are you talking about?"

"That army that's coming, the one just outside the window?" Matt jerked, hurrying over to peer out the window, eyes narrowed as he realised that, yup, there really were figures moving closer. At a damn good pace too, which was why he hadn't really noticed them before when he glanced out. Meanwhile, Irvine kept talking. "That ones going to tear through us long before you're ready to fight your battle. Or we'll beat them. Either way, you're superfluous if we die."

"If you lose, I shall avenge you," Braskar rumbled, sounding a little angry at Irvine's callous words.

"That's nice. That and a leaving of bread will get me across the river of death," Irvine said.

"Stop poking at the orc," Matt said. "You should get going down. Even if you can't control them well, it's better than nothing."

"Which is what our enemies have," Braskar said. "Over here, that is."

"Yeah, yeah, I'm going." Irvine paused, took back out the potion, drank it down, and let out a long burp. Almost immediately, his face grew red, his pupils started dilating, and a wide grin appeared on the Alchemist's face. He pocketed the vial, then bounced down the stairs, moving like a man half his age.

"Man, Irvine really does hide the good stuff. I really want to try that," Matt complained, watching the older man disappear before turning back to the tactical map. He drew another breath, noted his heart was still beating like a drum, then spoke simply, "Do what you think best, Braskar. I trust you. And if I think we're going to lose… I'll let you know."

"Strength and blood, my lord."

Matt nodded absently at the words, waving his hand sideways and cutting off the connection before sagging a little.

Well, the ball was rolling at last.

***

Status Report

Day 52 (Beginning of Day)

Gold: 86.75 (+22.25 Gold per day)

Units: 4 Woodlings, 2 Firecracker Flowers

In Production: Firecracker Flower (4/5), Woodling (3/4)

Structures Completed: Grove, Road, Stall (II), Ranged Copse, Harbour, Village #2 – Watch Tower, Blacksmith

Structures Available: Grove (II), Basic Greenhouse, Watch Tower, Tavern, Marketplace, Ranged Copse (II), Stone Harbour, Fishing Dock, Shipyard, Trading Post, Temple, , Blacksmith (Upgrade)

Cooldown: Burst Production (10 days)

Chapter 47

Irvine stood before the walls, the firecracker flowers beside him. The majority were arrayed in front of the gate and a few along the remainder of the wall. The woodlings were all across the front wall and the other walls, spread out to cover any gaps. Not that Irvine thought there were going to be any multi-wall sieges. Even if they had a Warlord, their enemies were still missing one important aspect of launching a siege: Siege equipment.

Also, hands. Those paw-hands that the saakal had were nasty, but even a glimpse of them and the way they ran across the ground told Irvine enough to know that there were not going to be any exceptional Alchemists coming from that group. Thumbs – nice long and flexible ones – were kind of important in that regard.

Watching the four units of saakal – all of them but one upgraded units with the darker fur and larger bodies – Irvine could not help but pull their information to him.

Enemy Unit: Saakal (II)

Type: Creature

Number: 10

Melee Attack: Medium+

Melee Defense: Low

Ranged Attack: None

Ranged Defense: Low

Hit Points: Medium

Speed: Medium+

Special Abilities: Charge

Vulnerabilities: ???

Forty total units that they had to kill. Stacked against that, they had twenty-four of their own. Not exactly double, at most one and a half times in number, which wasn't great at all. On the other hand, they had the walls and the ability to fire down on the enemy, so that was an advantage.

Of course, the big question marks were the enemy Heroes. Those were whom Irvine was curious about right now, his gaze locked on the two figures on horses. His lips pursed, considering. How did they get the horses? There was no option here and Braskar certainly had no mare of his own.

Was that a factor of their units? Did the horses just appear for their opponent? Was their lack because their units were too slow otherwise? More puzzles.

He was beginning to think like his lord in a way, questioning everything. Then again, a good Alchemist always questioned things. That's how you made better potions.

He pushed it aside for now.

Instead his gaze locked on the pair of Heroes as he drank in their details. The first, riding a little ahead, was clad in metal armour. Light, just enough to cover the basics of the shoulders, legs, and body. There was a term for it, but Irvine had never bothered to remember those things. The Warlord – he assumed the only Hero in armour was the Warlord – was carrying a long spear in one hand and had a mace stuck on the side of their steed. The face was impossible to pick out, what with it being covered by a close-faced visored helmet.

So. Warlord. Or perhaps Warrior. Braskar had mentioned that, the difference perhaps being in how well they ran their units. If this was a Warrior, that might work better for them. Especially if he managed to catch the Warrior by surprise.

They were still a little far, but squinting, he managed to pull up the information.

Nirae (Level 1 Warlord)

Specialty: Tactical Maneuvering

Skills: Redeploy, Rally

Experience: 3/100

Attack: 11

Defense: 14

Power: 6

Knowledge: 12

Nope. Warlord. Those Skills…

"Matt, word of caution. The Warlord has the Skills of Redeploy and Rally." Irvine frowned. "I don't know what that means."

"Rally is probably to make units hold and not run," Matt said, then doubt filled his voice. "Though, I've never seen a unit break. Braskar has never mentioned it."

"Maybe not something that Elementals have to worry about?" Irvine offered.

"Makes sense. And the saakal don't look particularly smart, so not running makes sense," Matt added. "What about the other Hero?"

Irvine had shifted his attention in the meantime, eyeing the other figure. This one was more interesting. They were wearing a simple cloth getup that was wound around their torso, though they were a pair of pants. Made sense, considering they had to ride the horse, though it showed quite the amount of mud-splattered leg. Meaty leg too, since even without armour, this figure was larger than the Warlord.

A weird-dressing mage? Or something else? Rather than guess, Irvine just pulled their info.

Sawyer (Level 1 Acolyte)

Specialty: Theology

Skills: Minor Blessing, Minor Healing

Experience: 3/100

Attack: 7

Defense: 8

Power: 11

Knowledge: 17

"Good news, it's not a Mage," Irvine said. "Bad news, it's a Priest."

"Skills?" Matt asked, voice filled with tension.

"Minor Blessing and Healing."

"Is that Healing, or Minor Healing?" Matt asked tersely.

"Minor Healing."

"Oh… good." Matt exhaled. "Also, fudged signatures. This is going to be a pain." There was a long pause, while Irvine waited for the man to explain himself. They had time, for a bit, while the boy rallied his thoughts. As much as it chaffed Irvine to rely on someone so young and inexperienced, he had to admit, the boy had taken to the idea of this game better than he would have if he was left in charge. If nothing else, some of his assumptions about the game had panned out better than Irvine's own stumbling.

"Right. Here's the powerpoint slide answer to everything. Redeploy is probably the Warlord's way of moving troops around. Probably shifts his units, potentially a minor teleport. Might be a problem, especially if he starts splitting his troops. In fact, I'd bet on that, if they had a way to get up the walls. As it stands, they might still try to trick us to redeploying our own units."

"We don't have that control," Irvine said.

"They don't know that. They might even be thinking Braskar's here, giving us that ability. Or were thinking it…" Matt shook his head, realizing the error. "Maybe not. But either way, if they split up, won't matter for us. It's more if they use it to hit a weakness in our defenses."

"The gates."

"Yeah, the gates," Matt said. "Rally we talked about, but it might also be a targeting command. Be careful about the saakal swarming you, Irvine. Don't put yourself in a position where that might happen."

"I'll mind the potions."

"Minor Blessing is just a buff, so that's a non-issue. Makes them something; stronger, faster, tougher. Maybe all three, but low-grade. Not much we can do about it. I'd keep an eye on her casting the spell, but otherwise, it won't matter," Matt said. "The Minor Healing is the problem. Depending on how often she can use that, it could really change the fight."

"I can see that," Irvine said, recalling how their own spells had done the same in other battles.

"So, here's what you're going to do." Matt hesitated, then added, "Kill her first."

"What!?"

"Kill the healer. Basic RPG tactics. You never let them live," Matt said firmly. "Always take them out. Otherwise, they can just keep the DPS up running."

"I have no idea what you're saying."

"It's fine. Just kill the healer." Matt frowned, considering. "In fact, if you can, ignore the tank."

"What tank? I see no tank." Irvine peered closer. "Are they bringing a storage vessel of oil to burn the doors down? I do not see that…"

"No, no. The Warlord. Leave them alone. You probably won't be able to take them down, with their armour, and you're better off finishing off the other units."

"You do recall, I only have minimal control over the units," Irvine said.

"Yeah, yeah. I got you. But we do our best to follow the strategy."

"As you say, my lord."

"I really don't like how you say those words."

Irvine could only smile while he focused his gaze on the upcoming pair. There really was not much more to say, even as the saakal loped closer and the Heroes cantered after them. Their enemies certainly were not taking their time in arriving.

Chapter 48

Matt stared at the map, then flicked his hand sideways, calling up the tactical information. He watched it birth, eyes narrowed. He blinked, seeing something new.

Units Engaged: 2 Woodlings, 1 Firecracker Flower, 1 Hero vs 4 Saakal, 2 Enemy Heroes

Spells Available: Regeneration, Lightning Bolt

"Oh shit. Braskar."

Words spoken into the air, reply coming soon after. "My lord?"

"New information," Matt said softly. "Tactical map just called up new details. A new spell. It's got a very short range, two hexes only."

"That is very short." A slight pause, and then Braskar sighed. "But long enough for me. What is the spell?"

"Lightning bolt."

"Ah. Any details?"

"Not a lot. But here's what I have," Matt said, reading it out.

Spell: Lightning Bolt

Casting time: Instantaneous

Range: 2 hexes

Duration: Instantaneous

Effect: Deals 12 points of damage to one unit

Cooldown: 5 days

There was a grunt from Braskar when he heard that before the orc fell silent. A moment later, he spoke again, his voice filled with fierce determination. "I will endeavor not to die. I think if I had not my Level…"

"You might?" Matt made a face. "Let's hope it's not a one shot, but there's no indication of how much life you actually have."

"No, there isn't."

Matt looked away back out the window. The army had closed in further, riding past the now quiet village and the simple walls thrown around it. Ignoring the Harbour, the way in, and the lack of units guarding the village but going straight for them.

The enemy had the saakal ranging outwards, just the lower Level, unupgraded members. Nothing too surprising in that, but what was interesting was when the pair of units roving ahead actually fell into his pit traps.

Jaw dropping, Matt rushed to the window, only to see one of the saakal that fell climb out. Long whining noises reached him, even as the enemy Warlord started waving his hands around, drawing the scouts back. Obviously agitated, they slowed a little as they approached the first of his half-dozen holes in the ground.

"I can't believe they fell for that," Matt said. Not when the enemy Warlord was actually there.

"Neither can I," Irvine muttered.

Matt jumped a little, before he realised he'd opened the channel when he was speaking with Braskar about the Lightning Bolt's abilities to the Alchemist, figuring the other Hero should know too.

"What happened, my lord?" Braskar asked.

"Pit trap." Matt shook his head. "Concentrate on your fight. We're doing well." He laughed a little, seeing how the pair of Heroes were now arguing, with the Warlord having gotten off their horse. They were waving their hand at the other, gesticulating quite aggressively. "Who knows, if they keep going this slow and you hurry, you might get done before them."

Silence, and Matt cocked his head to the side, trying to check the connection. Satisfied that it was closed, he returned to watching the enemy Heroes as the Warlord began the process of chivying the group through the randomly scattered pit traps.

Really, it shouldn't have been hard. If not for the fact that they had to move away from the main, blocked road, none of his pit traps would have mattered. Now, they had to decide if they were going to move things out of the way or just continue clambering up the hill.

And one thing Matt had realised, the saakal, for all their speed, just did not have his woodlings' sheer strength. The barriers that had taken the woodlings less than an hour to put out would take a lot longer for the others to shift. Easier, much easier to move around.

If more dangerous.

Now, they wove upwards, going around and prodding at the occasional clump of extra dirt and collected greenery. Matt watched and cursed himself, making note that he really should look at creating mini-decoy areas, rather than trusting into the irregular shape of the motte to throw them off.

"What's the range on the firecracker flowers anyway?" Matt asked, curious. He had never tested the ranged units on the walls, but even office worker that he was, he knew that the angle and greater height would add to the distance they could reach.

"Soon," Irvine replied. "Should we wait till they're closer? Accuracy at those ranges…"

Matt hesitated, thinking. He knew that volley fire was a thing, meant to catch the enemy by surprise at the start, meant to extract the greatest toll upon firing. Something about breaking morale too, he assumed. He knew, then, that he should probably wait a little. Not fire at the maximum distance, especially since the enemy were taking no effort to cover themselves.

"Let's wait a little. Get them, say, three quarters of the way in. We want to hit them hard when they're still clustered like this," Matt said. "We've got a few more traps, no?"

"You should know."

Matt grinned, a little proud. He hadn't thought of that, that the simple act of the pits being there when the ranged attackers opened fire would cause mayhem. Force them to keep close and bunched up, even when they might want to split apart.

"Then, let's wait." Matt held his breath, waiting as the firecracker flowers stood on the walls, awaiting a command. Thankfully, they had that much control over the units at least.

He watched as the enemies progressed, slowly edging upwards, testing the ground and moving around suspected traps. In particular, the Warlord kept looking up, frowning as they stared at the firecracker flowers, uncertain about their presence. He chivied the group, trying to make them move faster while still being safe, an oxymoron that was obviously making the saakal - never the most disciplined units- upset.

"Nearly there. In… five."

"Four."

Matt listened to the countdown, till the "One" was almost whispered before the sudden roar of 'Loose!" rang out. The firecracker flowers raised their hands, even as the Warlord's head snapped up, shouting a warning.

Not that it mattered. The saakal wore no armour, held no protection to stop the explosive projectiles coming at them. The repeated crack of firecrackers going off as water, pumped through ivy vines along the back, struck the seeds and expelled the plant projectiles, the explosive splotch echoing through the keep.

Matt watched the glint of light the seedlings carried, the metal tips making it look like a hail of needles flying through the air. Saakal, far below and grouped together, had started running, dispersing at the Warlord's command. They could not, however, keep up with the speed of the flung needles.

Blood flew through the air, misting the surroundings as they struck hardened fur. Matt could barely see the damage, though he could spot the creatures dancing to the side, some falling to the ground as they took the full brunt of a blast or two. Others— most of them — twisted and shrunk away, but kept coming, injured in varying degrees but still functional.

That was the danger, the problem of the firecracker flowers and their seedlings. Not enough punching power, dispersed attacks at a distance. It was a problem that would rectify itself, as the enemy closed. But for now, the flowers switched arms, even as new buds and seed pods grew on the expended arms at speed.

More yelps, more chaos. Matt watched as some of the saakal, in their haste to run from the ranged attacks, found themselves crashing into the pits. They tumbled within, clawed their way out, some dragging broken arms or legs. Most came out, injured or not, though Matt could swear he saw one with a stripe of white fur along its eyes never emerge.

"Fire at the Hero. The Hero!" Irvine's voice, barking orders.

Explosions once more, just as loud as before. Matt winced, hoping that Irvine had some good ear protection. Even as far away as he was, the continuing explosions still hurt his ears. He could only imagine what it was like nearby.

More fire raking the saakal who were nearest. Matt sighed, not needing Irvine to report their failure at attempting to control their ranged units. They were firing, but they were certainly not aiming at the Heroes. Instead, they targeted the saakal closest to the walls, multiple attacks at times burrowing into individual saakal to drop them permanently.

In fact, as their enemy climbed, Matt could see more corpses left behind. Three, no, four saakal dead. Unmoving bodies, even as the entire group clawed their way up. Not a complete victory, not yet.

But a good start.

That was when the healer raised her hands.

Chapter 49

Matt snarled, darting back to the tactical table. His mind resolved itself, even as his fingers played across the map. He had hoped to contain his spell usage, not knowing if he could use one or two. If both spells could be triggered or was he limited?

Damn game and its lack of an instruction manual.

He barely even paid attention to the new information that came up, his fingers darting to the Lightning Bolt icon. He triggered it, pointing at the Hero icon for the healer. Too late though, as he watched numbers flicker and change on the map.

No need to know what had happened. She must have cast her Healing spell. All their efforts, gone. He couldn't, didn't have time to look at the dead.

Matt's finger moved to hit the icon, to push the lightning bolt hovering on his finger towards her. Then, he froze. He blinked, stared at his hand. Pushed. Or tried to. But it rejected his commands, a portion of him unwilling to commit.

"What the hell?"

"My lord?" Braskar asked.

"What, boy?" Irvine said.

"I…" How could he explain his failure, explain why he stopped from launching the lightning bolt? How could he explain the sudden surge of wrongness that stopped his movements, that refused to let him commit to the action? "This…"

For the first time, Matt realised, he was going to kill someone. Really kill someone. Or at least harm them. And for all his life, he had never even punched another person. Why would he? He was taught not to, that's what civilized people did. What good people did. He didn't consider himself a saint, but he was a good person.

And now…

"Lightning bolt. Healer. I need, I should use it…" He trailed off.

"This isn't the time, boy. Make a choice, live or die," Irvine snarled. "But she just healed most of the damage done to one of their units. She's raising her hand again."

"This is your Blood Trial, my lord. Kill or be killed. And in so choosing, doom us or yourself."

"Myself?"

"The boy who faces the trial never lives. Either he dies or a true orc emerges."

"A true orc, eh?" Matt said. He shut his eyes, reaching within. He had died once. He did not want to die again. He had lived a life of mediocrity, wanting something, anything, more than work to happen. He had burnt out, grown so depressed he never cared. Till he had been given a choice.

And he'd made it. Got himself killed, but he had thrown himself wholesale into it. Without thought, without care. This was a new world, a new existence.

Was he going to half-ass the job again or commit? Perhaps, committing to this world wasn't just about taking half-hearted attempts at optimizing the builds, or trying to build cheats through the system. It meant accepting all of it, the savagery, the wrongness, the need to make decisions.

And be bad. Be a true orc if you would.

Eyes still closed, he stabbed the floating icon.

There was only the barest tactile sensation. Even then, the world shook.

***

Matt opened his eyes reflexively, catching himself on the table as the roar of thunder continued to echo. So long, so close, his ears hurt as he stumbled over to the window, ignoring the flashing tactical map. This was something he had to see with his own eyes, rather than trusting in the magical nature of the table.

Outside, smoke rose in the distance. He traced the smoke downwards, the aftermath of the lightning bolt and the loud rumble of thunder that had followed the attack fading. Saakal had cried and bolted, moving aside and some even going so far as to flee the lightning strike and running into the pits once again. The Warlord, the closest to the attack, had been tossed aside and was standing up, shaking their helmeted head as though to clear their head.

Matt's own units were doing better. They barely looked shaken, though Irvine was picking himself off the floor of the wall. The ranged units were reloading their arms and had begun to shower the disrupted attackers. If there was one thing that you had to give the elementals, they were hard to scare.

Finally, finally, Matt turned to regard the cause of the rising smoke, the strike point of the lightning bolt. He was grateful he had not been looking in that direction, for the sheer volume of thunder spoke of a lightning bolt rather more powerful than he had expected. Or perhaps it was just the proximity of the strike that had made it seem so much louder.

In either case, the healer who had been so vital, so alive, was lying on the ground. From this distance, other than some minor smoke coming from her, Matt thought she might even have been sleeping. Certainly not a shrivelled or blackened corpse like the movies had made him come to expect, just a still figure. Unconscious even, perhaps.

If not for the way the Warlord had rushed over, shaken the body, and then looked upwards, to his tower. He could not see their eyes, yet he found himself unconsciously moving backwards, shivering at the glare that was shot towards him.

"Braskar," Matt said as he backed away from the window. No more reason to look out, not right this moment. And he didn't want to think about the death he had caused, could not afford to break down or deal with the revulsion that was twisting his stomach.

"My lord."

"Try not to get hit by that Lightning Bolt. I just used it and… well, she's down."

"She?"

"Enemy Hero healer," Matt clarified.

Successful, it seemed, at least in taking care of the healer. Now, the question was what their enemy was going to do next?

Chapter 50

The answer was that their opponents kept charging. Which was kind of good, for Matt and his people at least. Even as Matt watched, the Hero glowed and slammed a hand forwards, a luminescent little flag appearing a couple of dozen feet ahead of them. All the saakal's attention was drawn to it, their jaws dropping low. Even those in the midst of running away slowed and stopped and then began to move towards the glowing flag.

"And that's the Rally ability in play," Matt said, nodding to himself. That was good. It meant their enemies had to make use of at least one of their abilities already, which was an advantage to their side. The fewer abilities they had, the better. Even if they could reuse the ability, it still meant that it was one less surprise to be sprung on them.

More importantly, it was clear that their enemy was not going to turn around and leave them alone. No big surprise there, but it did mean that they took the withering fire of the firecracker flowers to the face, even as they climbed higher.

One after the other, the saakal fell. Some never even managed to make it back to the rally point, taken out by ranged units further along the wall. However, as the enemy kept climbing, they encountered these firecracker flowers at new angles and closer distances.

"I wonder what the optimal angle is?" Matt muttered as he peered out the window. He'd taken to using his eyes rather than the tactical map as it continued to be useless for detailed information. "Looks like this is just about it." He rubbed his chin, trying to mark the location in his mind. It could come in useful in a later battle, knowing how far and what angle his units could concentrate fire. If nothing else, if he could figure out a way to build ways to slow down the opponents more in this location, he should.

As he watched, a saakal in the lead jerked its head to the side, a spray of blood and viscera erupting from its face. A lucky hit, Matt assumed, to take out the eyeball and plunge deeper, for the creature dropped not too long after, ignoring the rest of the attack that had peppered its body. The carnage was sufficient enough that rivulets of blood were beginning to flow down the hill, in trickles perhaps, but enough.

"How many have they lost, boy?" Irvine growled over the open communication line.

Matt hesitated, then scurried back to the tactical table.

"Well?"

"Just wait," Matt said, looking at the information. "One unit, the unupgraded one, I believe, is down to three units left. No. Two. And there's umm… two, ten minus seven… three and uhh… two. That makes nine more on top of that down."

"Fourteen total."

"Nearly a third of the force." Matt blinked, surprised. "That seems high. Does that seem high to you, because that seems really high to me."

"It's unusual, yes," Irvine said, satisfied. "Those traps of yours forced them in close. They might not have done much before, but this time, with the ranged units, it's splitting the elements." Then, the Alchemist sighed. "Too bad the easy boil is over."

"What!?"

"They're at a bad angle now," Irvine replied. Those words had Matt turning back to the window. He realised he could hear the difference even before he could see it, the slowdown in the pop-crackle of the firecracker seeds going off. Those ranged units on the side, at the far ends of the wall, no longer fired. And the cluster above the gate were firing slower too, almost leaning over.

That was the other thing. He could no longer see their enemy. Too many, too close, the wall in the way and his own people. Which probably meant…

He heard it moments later. The hammering noise on the door. Unlike the rhythmic slamming of the militia that had attacked them, the attacks were more sporadic. On the other hand, the noise was significantly louder, such that each thud made Matt wince even from his position in the tower.

"What's going on down there?" Matt could not help but ask.

"They're throwing themselves at the gates," Irvine said. "The woodlings have begun throwing stones down, but we've got too many here."

"We do?"

"I'm sending one unit down. They can't all throw the stones or use the oil, so we might as well keep one in the courtyard," Irvine said.

"Your call," Matt said.

He watched the gate as they talked, waiting for the durability pop-up to appear as he wandered back to the table. Soon enough it showed up, making him grimace. Good news, their gates had doubled in durability.

Bad news? The saakal were doing more than double the damage each time they hit. If not for the fact that they were forced to run back and throw themselves at the door, or so he assumed, they'd likely have taken the doors down faster. As it was, he was not certain the additional durability was helping that much. At least in lengthening the battle.

"When should we deploy the oil?" Matt asked, curious. He knew that was one of their best methods of taking down their attackers, but it was also better used when there was an actual battering ram in play. In this case, a crowd of saakal loping forward and throwing themselves against the doors was not optimal.

"Just wait," Irvine muttered. "We want them bunched up. When the doors are close to falling, they'll start to gather to rush us. That's when we'll use it."

"Oh, that makes sense," Matt said. A lot of sense. He cursed himself for not thinking of something so simple. So many little things to learn.

Another deep thump, the durability shooting down. Without anything better to do and realizing that even if the saakal were dying to the stones, to the attacks of the firecracker flowers who were leaning almost right over the wall, they weren't dying fast enough, Matt moved over to his weapons. He grabbed the makeshift crossbow he had made and began the long process of cranking it back.

Because of that, he managed to miss the real drama at the gates.

Chapter 51

Braskar waved the woodlings forward, holding back as he had promised Matt. He wanted to rush in, to join them at the forefront, but the orc managed to keep himself in check. The terror and concern in Matt's voice still rang through the orc's head. Losing now would be a fool's move. While the others might have indicated that what he did was of little consequence, he still had to believe that his attack, his siege, was at least a minor distraction to their enemy.

Up the hill the group climbed, following the road that led away from the rest of the village. They had bypassed the village as planned, giving the buildings a quick glance as they went along but not stopping. Though there were no people on the walls surrounding the village, Braskar still chose to keep a half-eye on them.

The road upwards was smooth, untouched. Nothing blocking the way, no traps laid out for them. Still, Braskar was careful to let the woodlings sweep the area first with one of their members and then the rest of the team before he and the firecracker flowers made their way up. Still, no new surprises played out, which left Braskar smiling grimly.

It seemed not all Lords were the same, willing to throw themselves into random work to improve their chances. An advantage to their side, it seemed.

Two thirds done with their ascent Braskar ordered the firecracker flowers to the front. A simple barked order had them loose their attacks at the saakal who weren't even smart enough to hide before the rather obvious ranged units attacked. They did flinch and move away when the loud crack of the shattered seeds erupted, but it was a too little too late.

Lucky for them, the difference in height and angle meant that the attacks were mostly at the near maximum of the firecracker flowers, such that the seedlings that struck them – while painful – were not immediately fatal.

"Damn. Closer then," Braskar complained. A waste of a good surprise attack, especially now that the damn animals were hiding. Still, it was his first time using the flowers and guesstimating the angle was tricky. It was not as though he had a huge amount of skill with ranged units. His people had used javelins mostly, and those you did not throw at castle walls. Usual orc tactics were to pillage the village, burn the fields and then make their enemies meet them on the field. Or hide, till they starved. "Advance and loose!"

He would have to stop them at some point, Braskar judged. Not a good idea to try to fire nearly directly upwards. When, however, was going to be the question. More learning as he went along. Sometimes, Braskar wished that his Lord had chosen some good orcs as his race to build from. He knew what to do with a good orc.

As the woodlings advanced, shifting around their own people with minimal fuss, he also noted how their hands were changing. Growing thicker and wider as they neared the doors. The orc had to grin. It seemed that the ability of the units to change to do damage to siege buildings was not entirely restricted to just militia or raiders. That would help.

That would help a lot.

"Halt!" Braskar roared, and then he proceeded to chivy the firecracker flowers into a line. Not too spread out, but far enough apart that they would unlikely be taken out by some new spell or surprise attack or cause trouble to one another.

By the time he was done, the woodlings were at the gate, stones raining down on them. Even as the first blows began to land, he noted how the falling rocks were knocking the woodlings about, though the damage done was…

Not negligible, but certainly not as worrying as if these were orcs. Wood bark and tough trunks cared less about being struck by a falling stone, especially when the titular 'head' of a woodling was more for aesthetics than use. Even now, after so many weeks, Braskar wasn't exactly sure how they sensed anything beyond 'magic.'

"Try that on for size," Braskar said, smirking. It also didn't help that the saakal were really bad at actually managing the stones that they were attempting to use. Picking them up and dropping them over the edge of the wall seemed more work than they were used to doing, possibly because of their lack of opposable thumbs.

Now that they were here, the actual siege was going very well. Each booming strike from the woodlings was dropping the durability of the gates by a significant and visible degree. The firecracker flowers, held further back and angled upwards so that they could not hit their own friends, were injuring and even killing the occasional saakal. The smell of new sap and fresh growth filled the air around Braskar causing his nose to itch a little as he waited.

The siege was a success, and if they had not been on a deadline, Braskar would be grinning. As it was, he found himself shifting from foot to foot, wanting to run forward and contribute to the attack with his axe, but having to force himself to calm.

A good thing too.

Braskar watched as the saakal switched tactics. Boiling oil above the gate tipped over, splashing down amongst his units. It caught nearly half of the units gathered beneath, splashing the others with the hot liquid. Twisted screams of breaking bark and snapping wooden limbs echoed as the woodlings dealt with the attack.

Still, it was less effective on the wood elementals than it would be on a fleshy humanoid. Braskar was beginning to grin in relief, forgetting there was one other card to be played.

There was no warning. No indication of what might happen. It was, in Braskar's view, very similar to what happened when his Lord had cast his own magic healing. One second, the woodlings were hammering on the door, shaking the oil off their body with each movement. The next a spark appeared, which quickly became a rolling fireball that covered the group.

A fireball that, once caught on the oil, kept burning. Rather than dying off like any other spell would have, this flame kept burning, caught on hot oil and the wood that lay beneath the liquid. As ready sources of fuel, the woodlings lit up with more shrill and piercing screams as they continued to hammer at the door, creating an unearthly and sickening melody.

Braskar snarled, eyeing the gate itself that seemed to refuse to catch fire too. Nearly all his woodlings were now on fire. Just as suddenly as it began, the siege that had been going so was in real danger.

After all, there was still another spell the enemy could utilize.

Chapter 52

"Shit. I should have known," Matt muttered once Braskar finished reporting in. He'd demanded an answer when he caught sight of the change in units, the suddenly burning figurine right in front of him. "Asymmetric spells and units of equivalent strength was a known factor."

"I do not believe you should have, my lord. But we will strive on. The gates are nearly down. If I must stride over the bodies of our unit and destroy the gates myself, I shall do so."

"Watch yourself, Braskar. We can't lose you to foolishness. And there're still the saakal inside."

"I shall not fall," Braskar rumbled.

Matt shook his head, not entirely certain he agreed with the orc but loath to argue with him. Especially considering he had his own problems to deal with. Turning away from the hex units much further up, he regarded the gates of his own fight and winced.

Twenty-something durability left. Not a long time at all.

Just as he was about to call out to Irvine, a rending, shattering noise echoed through the surroundings once again. The gate durability disappeared, dropping down to zero in one moment and leaving Matt with his jaw hanging. He was torn, unsure of which direction he should look before he ran for the window.

He was just in time to see the front ranks of the remaining saakal pour around the Warlord Hero who stood before the shattered doorways, sword smoking, weaving a little from whatever ability or action it had taken to destroy the door. Even as he tried to grasp what happened, the first saakal struck the first ranks of the woodlings standing before the doors, their bodies glowing as they activated the charge ability.

"Oh shit…" Matt whispered.

At the same time, Irvine was shouting, ordering the firecracker flowers to tip the boiling oil over. To kill the Hero or to slow down the attack, he was not certain. He waved his hands, shouting other orders for the rest of the woodlings to join the other unit on the ground, watching as the wood elementals slowly pulled themselves away from the wall.

All too slow.

Matt could tell it was going to be too slow. The damn woodlings were falling as the saakal hit them in a flurry of fur and claws. Half of them went down, falling to the ground or splintering apart, their wooden arms swinging. Everything was happening so fast, like a movie utilizing jump cuts. He couldn't understand how his people had died so fast, even if they were leaving saakal bodies on the ground as the wood elementals fell back.

Big, heavy hands swung down, smaller limbs swung upwards, and metallic tips pierced bodies. They struck again and again as they fell back, leaving corpses even as other saakal streamed outwards to the staircases, racing for to the walls to take woodlings that were on the way down.

It was chaos down in the courtyard, the howling and screaming of the saakal, the silent battle that the woodlings fought, and the continued crack of firecracker flowers firing down at the few opponents still outside. The oil tipped over at last, and Matt smiled grimly.

At least they got the Hero.

At least...

Shit.

Where was the Hero? Eyes searched the milling bodies, hunting for the armoured figure. When had they recovered? When had they moved out of the way? He could not tell, having been too enthralled by the battle and chaos beneath.

There. He could see it, could see his enemy. See them striding past the too busy woodlings, see them come for the doors to the keep itself. He watched as they disappeared out of his sight and found himself leaning far out to try to get a glimpse. Catching just enough of a sight to see them swing backwards with their sword in preparation to strike the main doors.

That was when realization struck. That was when he realised what the Hero was doing. He remembered then that burning gaze that they hard turned on him, the unspoken promise.

And Matt knew, with the certainty of annual reports, what was coming for him.

***

Irvine shook his head, his ears still ringing. The cotton he had stuffed into them when the firecracker flowers had started firing had done little to muffle the explosive attack that Hero had used. Irvine was still wondering what that attack had been. How had they managed to miss that on the Skills?

"Move, move, move! Take the saakal down," Irvine finished ordering the woodlings, tossing one last packet of dust over the side of the wall. He watched it strike the oil on the other side, the entire mixture suddenly exploding and catching the last of the enemies that were attempting to enter the building, throwing them down and scattering their bodies and limbs around. He could smell the twisted, burnt oil and hair odor reaching up to him, the delectable aroma of roasting flesh and the stomach twisting knowledge that it was somewhat living creatures that he was salivating over.

Then, he pushed it all aside.

"Open fire inside. Inside, you idiots!" Irvine snarled at the firecracker flowers, watching the units slowly turn. Too damn slowly, as far as he was concerned. At least the ranged units on the other walls had started firing already, though the wide spray of their pellets was catching their own people as often as it was hitting the saakal.

Good thing the woodlings didn't seem to mind, and their hardened bark managed to deflect the majority of the metallic seeds. Also a good thing – sort of – was the fact that there just weren't that many of the woodlings to be struck. Of course, the reason for that was because they were a giant mess of splinters and shattered wood all across the courtyard.

A sweeping review of the monsters below told Irvine that there were just over a dozen of the saakal there. Maybe a couple more on the way up, but those were struggling to win against the woodlings coming down. One on one, without their boost to movement, the saakal were finding that the woodlings were a tougher battle than before. Most died, one-on-one or soon after they took down a woodling.

If he had as many woodlings left, that would be a good thing. He didn't. As it stood, once they took out all the woodlings, the firecracker flowers were likely going to be overwhelmed. Which meant it was time for him to add to the fight.

Pulling out a batch of potions, Irvine prepared to cast them into the courtyard and at the monsters. Only to hesitate when he realised that he'd forgotten someone. The hammering and splintering noise that interrupted his thoughts drew his gaze to the enemy Hero standing before the doors of the keep, wielding their sword as they smashed their way in.

For a long moment, Irvine was caught between saving Matt or winning the battle. Because he knew, intuitively, he could not do both.

Chapter 53

Braskar watched as the last of the woodlings fell, stumbling through the open and shattered doors and crumbling under the charging form of the assaulting saakal. This one, at least, had taken the saakal with it, the entire body collapsing on top and trapping the creature beneath it. Unlike the other two woodlings who had managed to survive long enough to take the door down.

That left seven saakal, some of them injured but mostly not, facing his full rank of uninjured firecracker flowers through the opening of the door. And, of course, himself.

"Loose!"

Growling the order, Braskar watched as the regrouped firecracker flowers opened fire at the loping semi-humanoid jackal-like creatures that rushed the entrance. They came, head down, into the withering fire. For once, Braskar saw the full strength of the ranged units.

It was not the ranged fire at an angle that the firecracker flowers excelled at, nor sniping off defenders. No, what they were meant for, what they excelled at, was this range – the mid-range where a unit was in the midst of a charge, seeking to close in on you. And in those few moments, when they were crossing the intervening ground, packed together cheek to jowl, withering fire would erupt.

The first rank of saakal fell, the glow around them never fully realizing as seedling shards tore into muscles and fur, burst eyes, and entered open howling mouths. Footsteps staggered, twisted as balance was disrupted and monsters fell, limbs peppered and robbed of strength. The rank behind leapt, jumping over their fallen brethren to make it only another half-dozen steps before the second round of fire arrived, tearing into the group and dropping even more of the monsters.

Two dead in the first rank, the other two injured and struggling upwards. Three more leapt over, only for all three to fall. Then, the firecracker flowers no longer had any additional arms and had to wait, their seeds reloading. Even the fact that they had all four arms was a matter of training, Braskar having ordered them to gather and stop firing earlier.

Now, only two enemies were left, limping forwards. These, Braskar chose to fight directly, rushing the pair. Confused and injured, they were not in a line, and it was a simple matter for the orc to step aside when the first monster lunged at him, wielding his axe to tear open its stomach and detach one of its legs with a swing.

The second saakal, its body glowing with power, threw itself forward. It carried the orc backwards, tumbling him over, but the axe haft was in the way of the slavering mouth; the Warlord heaved and tossed the monster behind him. The creature landed, crying piteously as it bounced off its injured torso before the firecracker flowers fell upon it, wielding spindly arms like clubs.

Braskar ignored them, hopping back to his feet and discounting the twinge of pain in his lower back. Instead, he rushed into the keep, ducking through the broken doorway and searching for additional enemies. Seeing nothing, he waved the remainder of his army forward to the central building even as he trotted over to it himself.

Without opposition, it was a simple matter to begin pounding on the door with his axe, tearing chunks of wood from the impediment. Each strike saw his axe sink in a good few inches, even the hardwood of the door unable to stop the muscular orc.

It was only a matter of time before he'd break through. His lips pulled apart, Braskar grinned in victory as he swung, putting all of his considerable muscle into the movement.

***

Matt listened to the rhythmic thump of sword on wood. He winced, wondering what it was doing to the Hero's weapon. It could not be good. Then again, he had never asked Braskar if the weapon he used needed maintenance. He'd seen the orc do it, but that could be a matter of routine, of trained instinct rather than actual need. The world they lived in was weird enough that it restocked the training pells and the wooden weapons down in the yard without him seeing anyone do it. Same with their stores of food and clean linen.

Thump.

Licking his lips, he listened as the cries of the saakal, the thump and cackle of burning bodies, and the shuffling of creatures reached him from the window, the smell of new sap, spilled blood, and innards mixing together such that he wanted to retch.

Thump.

Or that could just be the tension in his stomach, the way it knotted tighter with each strike. He took a hand off the crossbow, careful not to jostle the trigger as he wiped sweaty palms on his pants again. His throat was unconscionably dry and he took a sip of the mug of water he had set out. Only a sip. He didn't want to need to pee when the Hero came. Not again.

Thump.

He'd taken Irvine's advice earlier that day, made sure to eat little, pee a lot, and empty his bowels. No reason to let other, nastier things into his body if he got stabbed or shot in the stomach. And that had been quite the conversation.

Thump.

Or was that conversation the last time they had a fight? He couldn't remember. Time, memory was warping, his thoughts scattering with each strike. He glanced at the map again, but there was nothing he could do. No spells to use – at least that was an answer. One spell per battle, it seemed. With a cooldown for a period of time after that. Worth knowing, because you'd have to be careful about when you deployed an attack. Got to remember…

Thump.

Crack.

He jumped. Matt was not too proud to say he was startled when the rhythmic attack changed. He flinched, almost pulling the trigger, but he stopped himself. There was still one more door after all, a whole lot of stairs and places for their enemy to look.

Unless they chose to come up here directly.

Matt suddenly wondered why he was here. Why he was guarding the map. If he was not, if he had gone somewhere else, would they have 'won' because he was still alive, hiding somewhere like down the garderobe? Or would they lose, automatically, because the enemy Hero reached this table and touched it, and then everything would end and he'd die from another stroke, all the while gripping the sides of a shitter and trying to juggle a weapon he barely cobbled together in his hands...

No more noise. Or, well, a lot of noise, but no more rhythmic noise of a door being assaulted. They were probably fumbling around, trying to get the bar out of the way, pushing the door open to get inside and finish the job.

One door, a lot of stairs, and then he was going to have to learn if his crossbow, cobbled together or not, was going to punch through actual armour.

No surprise his hands were trembling. No surprise at all.

Chapter 54

Fool. Fool. Fool.

Irvine cursed himself as he hurried towards the staircase that led off the walls. No jumping down the ladder or attempting to head down that way. For one thing, the nearest ladder had a pair of saakal fighting one another, tearing into each other as the hallucinatory potion he'd tossed took effect. No idea what they were seeing, or how they'd see him if he went down.

At the same time, his fingers flew over the four potions and two satchels left strapped to him. Two of the vials were Healing Potions, one a satchel of clotting dust. Not particularly useful for the fight, but necessary. Which left him with two remaining potions for offensive use and a single dust satchel. The itching powder was something he would have wielded when they were outside, but inside the courtyard; it'd stick around too long. He had no desire to face the consequences of that deployment himself.

Potion of Giant Strength was useful, but better for someone like Braskar. He was no fighter, so pounding a staff or spear into an opponent's face was for others. No, the only potion that was at all directly useful was the Potion of Greater Dispersal. In other words, an acid. A very powerful acid.

He really wanted to keep that one for the Hero. So he ran, keeping his shoulders hunched a little as he watched the woodlings and firecracker flowers fight, his minor contribution seeming to have brought the fight towards a more stable condition. Only one saakal ahead of him, fighting the last woodling holding the staircases. They'd met halfway down, the saakal tearing into the woodling with abandon even as a pair of firecracker flowers stood above, trying to pepper the pair.

Not a great idea to jump in there, but it was still safer…

Booted feet slipping on slick stone walls, he hurried forward and managed a few steps down before the crack and tumble that he had grown used to hearing appeared. The woodling, standing so tall before, suddenly crumpled, falling downwards.

No luck, the damn saakal managed to back off and press its body against the wall so that the falling tree managed to miss it. It slid downwards, joining the mess of fallen bodies of its other comrades, all of it intermixed with corpses of the saakal themselves.

Fool…

He clutched the potion by his side, hand held down. He could throw it, catch the monster as it jumped. But if he did that, he'd have nothing to deal with the Hero. And deal with him, he would need to do so, if Matt managed to survive long enough. Hopefully that fool boy had hidden himself.

The saakal was glowing. Enough time had passed, it seemed, that it had recharged its charge attack. Throwing itself forward, it blurred up the stairs.

Rather than face it or waste his potion, Irvine cast himself off the stairs. He had noted the tree trunk corpse of a woodling, leaning over precariously. Too unstable to slide down against, but if he grabbed it as he fell and hit it right…

The crash, the pain of his arm gripping a broken wooden limb, the tree trunk body tumbling down and slamming into the wooden outer walls and edge of the stairs. It made the old man wince, even as he bounced sideways and came to a sudden stop as he landed on the soft, meaty corpse of a fallen saakal.

The saakal having charged right by him, unable to stop, was now on the top of the stairs. And the rest of the firecracker flowers on this side of the wall were firing at it, tearing it to shreds. Good. Maybe they'd survive long enough to deal with the rest of the enemy racing along the edge, intent on taking them from behind.

For Irvine, that was all academic for now. They should win, could win, he felt. They'd taken enough of the saakal down, whittling fire from their ranged units sufficiently to end this battle. Especially with the enemy Hero not taking part in the fight.

If they had been, it might have been a very different proposition. Then again, as he scrambled across the courtyard, slipping and scurrying in the blood, ignoring the torn branches of the woodlings and the choking smell of burnt flesh and cracked wood, the inside of his lip bleeding into his mouth from where he'd hit it, he could not help but think that maybe they'd made the right choice.

After all, the front door was open and he must be upstairs now. Tearing at the final door.

Boiling potions, he hoped the boy was smart enough to hide.

He'd bet everything on it.

***

"You know, at times like this, you should be monologuing. Telling me if I come out, you'll spare my life. Or perhaps, that this doesn't have to be this way," Matt said, licking his lips and forcing his voice to be calm. It wasn't doing that well, what with the minor tremble that he could hear, but it was better than he'd thought. Talking, even if it was just talking, was better than nothing.

Rather than answer, the door was struck again. He watched the door planks tremble, wood dust shivering outwards, the metal holding it closed shivering. Matt really wished he'd taken the time to reinforce this final door, drop a plank or something between it. Right now, only a simple – if thick –

metal latch was doing all the work, and it was halfway bent now. Footsteps retreated as they got ready to ram into the door once more.

"No, we're not doing the evil overlord monologue now? Oh wait, am I the evil overlord in your scenario? Am I the guy who killed your mother or father or other family and then sent you on a path of vengeance?" Matt shook his head. "I'm pretty sure I didn't do that. I did kill that healer though. Maybe that counts?"

The next thump was even louder, the door latch twisting even harder. He winced, realizing it would only take another hit, maybe two, before it gave way. Shifting his position a little so that he could get a good angle when the door flew open but wouldn't be standing right in front of it, he continued talking.

"Sorry, sorry. I mean, for killing her. And for touching a sore subject. But all's fair, right, in love and war? And I'm not saying we're in love, but we're surely at war. You did come here to kill me and my people." Matt hesitated as he listened to the footsteps end, the slight pause as the enemy Hero got ready to throw themselves at the door. "You wanna tell me why?"

Heavy footsteps moving fast, then a loud thump and shriek, his door bursting open as the latch gave up even the ghost of resistance. The hulking figure on the other side of the door loomed in the shadow, for a moment stunned and recovering their balance.

Crossbow up by his lower ribs, Matt pulled the trigger of the weapon. He'd have it on his shoulder, except he was not entirely trusting of the contraption even now. No idea if the cords he had wrapped around one another, pulled tight, would give way. No idea if the twisted metal and wood arms that provided the tension and energy might snap. No idea if the bolt might shatter when it was thrown forwards, because he had put too much strain on it.

No, better not to risk having the entire thing exploding in his face.

Surprisingly, nothing like that happened. The trigger depressed, the portion holding string and bolt in place disappearing into the wood, and the bolt was thrown forwards. Bolt thrower for sure. Blink – and Matt had blinked – and you'd miss the projectile crossing the intervening space, hitting the armoured figure almost directly in the center of their chestplate and then, having imparted a large portion of its energy, deflect off the curve to the side.

The bolt flew down the rest of the way, plate armour not pierced. The enemy Hero got their feet under them, weapon rising to swing at Matt, and instinct had him throwing the weapon at the face. The crossbow, hours of work in it, was parried with casual contempt, the wooden block flying away and bouncing off the floor.

However, unexpectedly, behind the crossbow was a fast-moving Matt. Head down, shoulder leading the way, he hit the enemy Hero in a similar manner to how they'd taken down the door. Except, there was no more door. Just a small landing and a lot of steps.

They staggered backwards, once, and then a foot reached for balance and found none. Instinct had them grabbing for the wall with one hand and swinging the sword with the other, catching a recovering and surprised Matt across the chest, even as they tumbled down the stairs.

"Point to me…" Matt breathed, even as he staggered back, clutching the bleeding cut across his chest. Of course, now he had to figure out what to do about his enemy when they climbed all the way back up. Unless they broke their neck on the way down.

Nah. He wasn't that lucky.

Chapter 55

Braskar surged through the door, looking up and down the entrance hallway. He waved the firecracker flowers in after himself as he took the exit to the right, heading for the tower staircase. The keep looked exactly the same as their own, so he assumed the staircases were the same. He would go for the tactical room, finish this fight before his Lord died. The flowers would check out the rest of the keep, just in case the enemy Lord was hiding.

The orc took the stairs two at a time, loping upwards with casual ease. His heart thudded in his rib cage, faster than it should have for the slight degree of danger he had been in. Tension kept his heart beating fast, his breathing a little quicker than it should have. Even so, the extremely fit orc found himself at the top of the tower facing the only door available to him in all too quick a time, just a little out of breath.

He pushed against the door with one hand, figuring that he might as well try. Only to find himself thrown backwards, his body shocked and rigid as lightning raced through him. He crashed into the wall behind him, glancing off the circular wall and tumbling down the stairs.

Finally, Braskar fetched up against the edge of one landing a floor down, his head ringing, his ribs aching, a pair of fingers that had been caught on the tumble down dislocated backwards. A deep cut over one side of his head pumped blood down his jaw and around his ear, even as he saw stars.

Fingers trembled and shook, his body felt as though it was on fire. His heart had stopped, the orc swore, for a second or two before the impact against the wall had restarted it. It had hurt, in a strange dissociative way. Entirely unlike the pain he felt right now, as his body throbbed from the numerous bruises and broken bones he felt.

Lying on the ground, Braskar allowed himself a few more seconds before pushing himself to his feet. He tilted his head to the side, one way and then the other, the world spinning a little with each movement. Not too bad, the orc figured.

He'd had worse.

Next were the fingers that were hurting with each breath. He took hold of them with his other hand and tugged quickly, not giving himself time to brace or think about it. The first would end up damaging his tendons and fingers worse, the second would make him hesitate.

He neither had time nor patience to lie on the ground or bemoan his injuries. As he levered himself upwards, the orc frowned because he realised he was missing his axe. Looking around, he could not see it anywhere near here.

Hopefully it was upstairs.

A firecracker flower unit came along even as Braskar managed to get himself to his feet.

"Good timing. Up the stairs. Take the door down," Braskar growled.

He watched as the firecracker flowers turned without a word and started ascending. Once the unit had managed a half-dozen stairs, Braskar gripped the side of the wall and began to limp after it. Each movement was agony, his ribs throbbing against his side with each breath, his left ankle twisted and refusing to bear his weight properly.

He was halfway up before the thump of wood against wood echoed above. The orc cocked his head to the side, not hearing the sizzle of lightning. He sniffed, then grimaced, realizing he could barely smell anything right now. Were the nerves in his nostrils completely burnt out, fried by the lightning in one sudden surge? Or was the reek of his own cooked flesh, his barely washed body with sweat and the stink of fear blocking everything else out?

Hard to tell.

Each step, making his way up. Each step, braced against the wall, panting breath. A part of Braskar wondered about the magic on the door. What had created it, what had caused it? Why had it only struck him and not the firecracker flowers?

He did not know, but certainty ran through him, as he finally managed to make his way up, picking his axe that had fallen down a short distance from where he had first impacted the wall, that it would matter. The answer to the question might be the answer to victory or defeat.

***

Irvine slowed his headlong rush, sagging against the nearby wall of the staircase as he tried to control his breathing. Every breath was like sucking through a straw, his heart beating faster than the first time he'd concocted his first Fire Breath Potion, hands shaking as his master watched over the side protected – unlike him – by the shielding they'd propped up. Of course, like his wives, by the fourth one he'd done, his hands had stopped shaking and his fingers were a lot defter.

Wiping at his sweaty face, the old man looked up the staircase once again and winced. It was a long way up and running was more than he could do. A fact that the Alchemist had realised after making it a third of the way there.

Ahead, he could hear the crank and thud of metal shod boots on stone. It moved slowly with slight hesitations and interruptions between each movement, as though the walker was struggling to ascend. Surprising, since Irvine did not recall there being a woodling unit inside the building at all to have done damage to the enemy Hero or delay them.

Some internal defences they did not know about triggering? Perhaps a guard or two that formed to help defend the keep, just like the militia units had been created? If so, that would make Braskar's life more difficult too, but that was less of a concern than keeping the boy alive.

Precipitating potion, he hoped the boy was hiding downstairs.

Drag, thump. Pause. Metal clashing and moving and then another pause. Then, another drag and thump. Rhythmic at least in the way the enemy Hero was moving upwards.

Irvine pushed himself off the wall, forcing himself to climb now that his breathing had settled a bit. He slowed a little, as he tried to move silently. Even slower, he felt his heart still beating all too fast, his breathing a little too loud and harsh. He could hear his blood pounding in his ears, sweat staining the back of his clothing. Tension bleeding into every movement, even as he tried to work out what to do.

He had his potion still. Acidic, but if they were wearing armour, it might not do much. He'd have to get it into the face or under the armour. Difficult…

Thoughts came to a crashing halt as he saw the small pool of blood. Then, more splatters going up. Irvine bent low, reaching out to touch the red fluid before stopping himself. Right, right. Don't touch random liquids. You never know what they might be. Even if it smelled and looked all too familiar.

Irvine straightened, a slight rush of adrenaline in him making him smile grimly. Perhaps this might not be as difficult as he envisaged. If his opponent was injured enough, he could catch the enemy by surprise and finish the battle.

Now, all he had to do was get up the tower. Problem was, he was exhausted, the adrenaline that had carried him past the saakal and through the initial fight draining out of him, leaving his legs quivering and his breathing coming in heaving gasps. It did not help that he had to take things slowly, in fear of alerting his opponent and getting caught out.

As he neared the top, Irvine found himself moving faster. No point in surprising the enemy if they were killing the boy. As though the thought had summoned the specter of failure, voices came to him, along with the clash of weapons and wood.

Cursing, Irvine started running up the stairs as a fresh surge of adrenaline took ahold of him.

Chapter 56

"Try two. Let's not fight, right?" Matt said, jabbing his spear forwards. His opponent did not even shift, letting the point come to a stop a good three inches from their armoured body. Instead, they edged a foot forward and Matt instinctively backed away again.

"I mean, look at you. You're not in a position to fight. Not at all, right?" In fact, Matt was wondering how the enemy Hero was managing to stand at all. They were on their feet, moving forwards slowly but one leg was obviously dragging behind, something wrong with the foot or hip itself. There was a significant dent down one side of the armour and along the helmet, skewing it slightly to the right. Even so, they kept advancing and that sword was still gripped tight and pointed in his general direction.

"You know, this terminator thing is… heeyah!" Punctuating his last words with a shout, Matt lunged forward and attempted to skewer his opponent in the chest with the spearhead. He'd aim for the head, but it was actually hard hitting a head especially at over a six foot plus distance with a tip that was moving really fast and gripped near the end.

He certainly would have better co-ordination if he actually stepped closer and jabbed while holding onto more of the spear. Doing so would put him all too close to his opponent, a factor that he was really not looking forward to. That sword might have less range, but it could still take off an arm.

Instead of backing away or even letting the armour take the attack, the sword swept up from the bottom right to crash against the spear, throwing it off-course. It was hit so hard it nearly tore the weapon out of his hands, forcing the point completely out of line and leaving Matt vulnerable.

Knowing that, his enemy pushed closer. They managed one full step, landing on their good leg and yanking their injured leg forward before they faltered, unable to cross the remaining distance properly as they tried to propel themselves onward with the injured leg and instead crumpled.

It would have been a great time for Matt to attack. Even the inexperienced fighter knew that much. Unfortunately, by the time he managed to get his own spear under control, pulled back to his arm and pointed in the right direction – with just a slight amount of fumbling as his hands refused to move properly – the opponent was back on their feet, sword pointed at him.

"Come on, I can see it hurts. That sucks. But why do you keep pushing yourself. Just stop," Matt said. "You can't want to kill me that bad."

"I. Really. Do."

Matt froze, surprise widening his eyes. He nearly missed the hand that moved, that grabbed at the spear just behind the tip and yanked the weapon forward. He moved a couple of steps closer, then his feet started pushing backwards, only releasing the weapon at the last moment as the sword came swinging towards his hands. A touch too slow, the weapon slicing through the edge of his arm with just a slight tug as he fell back.

No pain, not just yet, though he knew it would come. The cut on his chest had pulsed as he'd pushed back, body hurting. The hasty bandages he'd pushed into the wound and then wrapped with bandages he'd wound all around him had been the same.

More importantly… "You're a girl!"

"Woman!" the enemy Hero snarled, taking another dragging step forwards. She was not moving carefully now that he was missing his spear. Instead, she attempted to cross the distance as quickly as possible, even as Matt backed off to the table finally. He grabbed at the crossbow he'd reloaded while his opponent had made their slow way back up, raising it towards her once more.

"Shit. Did I kill your lover? I'm sorry if I did. I really didn't mean to do that," Matt said.

"You didn't mean…?" She pushed forwards, tossing the spear behind her and raising her sword to her shoulder, growling. "You called lightning on her!"

"Yeah… but you guys are trying to kill me." Weapon near his chest again, braced. He really did not want to use it. He'd seen the crossbow fail once before, and now, he was trusting that he would manage to put the bolt somewhere where her armour wasn't. Even with something that wasn't entirely makeshift, he wouldn't have trusted that of himself.

"Trying. I'm going to succeed. Then I'm going to kill all your Heroes and your Lords and when we're done, your Earth will be ours."

"My Earth…?" Matt hesitated again, his brain spinning out as he realised what she was saying. Or guessed from what she had said. "I… shit, back off." He tried to move away, but could not do so, the edge of the table butting up against his butt. Instead, he pulled the trigger on the weapon, watching the bolt loose even as the string finally snapped.

The bolt spun through the air, smashed into her chest, and deflected off the plate, heading up her chest and glancing off her full-face helm. She staggered back, head twisted to the side. Even as she flinched, Matt rushed, ignoring the burning pain where the whiplash of the broken string hurt his hands, the crossbow body still held tightly.

He swung the crossbow downwards, catching her sword by the edge. He pushed against it and felt the blade tear into his forearm as she twisted. But he had the body of the crossbow against her sword and he slammed it into the guard, moments before his shoulder took her. Together, the pair tipped backwards even as the sword crashed to the ground.

He bounced off the hard body, wincing as unforgiving metal bruised his shoulder further. He rolled sideways a little, reaching upwards and smashing the hand gripping the sword with the crossbow body as his opponent tried to bring the weapon to bear. Once, twice, gauntleted fingers twisting and locking in place under the repeated attacks.

Then…

He did it.

Her sword released, fingers too pulped to hold on.

He grinned triumphantly, moments before she thrust her hips and tossed him off her, moving as she rocked upwards to follow him. In moments, she had straddled him, one big meaty and metallic hand resting on his body, the other gauntleted arm rising in the air.

Chapter 57

Braskar stepped inside the cracked and broken doorway, cocking his head as he regarded the place. He watched as the firecracker flower unit was bathed in white fire, flames rolling over their body. Now, he saw a problem, for while the unit tried to fire, the flames dried out the seeds and those seeds needed to be wet, needed the liquid to work. Without that reaction, even though the unit attempted to, it could do nothing but stand there.

As for the creator of the flames, it was a man. A man with a stick pointed at the firecracker flower. Even as the wood elemental attempted to close the distance, he backed off, grinning wide. A goatee, dark eyes, a flash of gold on his tunic. Smirking.

Until he saw Braskar.

The orc did not waste time. He could not run or tackle his opponent. But he did have his Rage ability and an axe. He threw it, sideways this time, one-handed, watching it arced through the air to strike his opponent in the center of the body, just above where the staff was held.

Flames spluttered for a moment, fingers slipping off of the grip. The Lord staggered back a little, stared at the axe head that was buried most of the way into his body and blinked.

Then he slumped to the ground, staff clattering to the floor.

Through the smoke and choking smell of burning wood and cracking sap, Braskar stumbled the rest of the way in. He stared down at the body, yanked his axe out of the corpse – and it was definitely a corpse now – and grinned.

Then he spoke, directing his thoughts to his Lord.

***

"My lord?"

Braskar's words, echoing from all around the room, distracted the swinging enemy Hero for a fraction of a second as she swung her fist down. Enough that she did not correct in time when Matt pulled his head out of the way. Mostly. Even so, metal gauntlets tore at the skin of his head, opened a deep cut in his cheek and sent stars spinning. The loud impact of metal on stone rang through the room, even as Matt tried to push his opponent off.

Only to fail, pain coursing through him as the wound on his chest flared and robbed him of strength.

The gauntleted hand retracted and Matt realised he could have grabbed it. Maybe pulled her close so she couldn't strike him. That should have worked, right? Hard to say, when you had a heavy body sitting on your lower body, putting over two hundred plus pounds of weight onto you and intending to punch you. Repeatedly.

Instead, he'd missed his chance. And now that she had reared back again, hand coming up to punch him, he wasn't sure he had another opportunity to head her off. One hand rose and pushed against her, trying to tip her backwards and away from him, only for his sweaty palms to slip against slick metal.

Rather than let him continue to annoy her, the enemy Hero grabbed hold of his arm with the one she had used to pin him down, shifting it over. He squirmed, and for a few moments, the pair struggled. It was made harder for her with the damage to her gauntlet and fingers, such that she let out pained grunts. At which point she just dropped her weight forward and slammed her other forearm onto his chest.

Breath driven out, ribs creaking and definitely bruised, Matt stopped struggling for a precious few seconds. Long enough for her to get a good grip and place her weight down on his arm, to rear back so that he had nowhere to go, and then swing.

Once again, Matt stared at the huge, gauntleted hand coming for his face, intent on pulverizing him.

***

"Not so fast!" Irvine snarled, tackling the enemy Hero off Matt and disrupting their swing. The pair tumbled off Matt, just over his shoulder as the fist came slamming down next to the poor man, though the Alchemist was a touch too busy to pay attention to that. So long as the boy lived, that was all that mattered.

The pair hit the ground with him nearly on her back, both of them sideways. One arm was wrapped around her shoulders, the one holding the vial of acid. He gripped it tight, trying to yank her helmet off or shift the gorget such that he could get to her face or throat. Either would work.

In the meantime, she'd started bucking, trying to throw him. Kicking legs caught Matt in the side and stomach, the boy having been turned as the pair tumbled. Now, he was curling up on his side clutching his chest from pain, a little breathless cry all that he had managed. At the same time, she was grabbing at his other hand with her own damaged one, trying to stop him from holding onto her entirely.

This – wrestling on the ground with an armed and armoured warrior – was not something Irvine was particularly good at. On the other hand, it was not as though he had much of a choice. He either managed to finish this, or she was going to kill them both.

Which was why, concentrated as he was on trying to get her helmet off to get the vial aimed in the right direction or at least down a gap where it could spill in, he never saw her shift enough to put the back of her helmeted head before his before slamming it into his face.

Irvine felt his nose break. He pulled away, or tried to, but there wasn't much space to move. Not with both of his own hands around her still, even as he automatically relaxed a little. Not far enough for a second jerk to not catch him on the lips, tearing up the insides of his mouth as his teeth cut his own flesh.

Then… she was free. One hand, the one attempting to grab his, latched on as she scrambled to her knees, keeping him close. It twisted him around, pulling the vial away from her to the opposite side of his body, giving her control.

Removing his only weapon.

Enough that she could bring up her other hand and swing, striking his torso. Irvine let out a cry of pain, bending over as the enemy took control of the fight again.

And all the while, a voice called out, never getting an answer.

***

Thrice more, Braskar called out. He received no answer each time. A shiver ran through his soul at what that meant, at the possibility. Rather than wait around, he chose to act.

If the enemy was not stopped by the death of the Lord, then it was the tactical map. He strode over to the table, frowning. There was nothing to indicate how he was meant to take control of the table, of the kingdom.

Should he destroy it? He stared at the axe he had retrieved, then decided to use that as the final option. Instead, he did what he had seen Matt do before so often.

He poked the table.

Surprise of surprises, information flowed upwards from the table, replacing the tactical map that had been displayed.

Battle Report (Saakal vs Enemy Units)
Result: Defeat! 1 Saakal Unit Lost, 1 Lord Lost
Penalties: -5 Gold, -4 Reputation

Opposition Unit Detected!
Would You Like To Claim Stone Keep?
Y/N?

"Yes!" Braskar snapped out. Nothing happened, so he did the next option, poking at the letter Y. It flickered and flowed, the text disappearing and new notifications appearing in its place. It hurt Braskar's head to deal with so much text. He had defeated the enemy, why did it not just acknowledge his victory?

Stone Keep Claimed!
To Claim Complete Ownership, Keep In Contact of Control Table for a Period of 30 Seconds

Braskar frowned, but placed his hand back on the table. New numbers appeared, counting down the time. As he stood there, he realised there was something he could offer.

"My lord, just stay alive. I am claiming the keep right now!"

*****

All three opponents scrambling on the ground, a bloody and tired Alchemist whose hand had dropped his offensive potion, the enemy Hero Warlord, and the ruler of the keep all startled at the voice's words. They froze, before they reacted in different ways.

Irvine tried – again – to wrench his hand free. Blood and sweat and mangled fingers managed to provide sufficient leverage that he was able to throw himself away from the incoming strike, even as he felt something in his wrist twist and tear.

The enemy Hero swung, and though they missed the Alchemist, ignored their own injuries and struggled to stand as they searched for the enemy Lord. Whether they had lost or not, she intended to finish off Matt before she ran out of time.

As for Matt…

He'd recovered enough – and lucked out enough – to be near the spear which had been tossed aside. Grabbing hold of it to help himself stand, he had been in the midst of trying to find a location to stab the armoured Hero when Braskar had spoken.

Now, with the enemy on their feet, he charged. Time seemed to slow down for him, her body twisted to the side, offering him a glimpse of what he needed. A gap, right in the armpit beneath the arm that she had used to swing at Irvine. A space cut out in her breastplate so that she could move easily and not chafe.

An opening that he shifted the spearhead to point towards.

He ran into her, not trusting in his ability to target it properly, felt as the spear sank into her side after deflecting off the metal a little. It surprised Matt how little effort it took to push the spear into her, barely an impediment. Until he hit the other side, skewering her all the way through and butting up against the metal of her breastplate on the other end.

Because of that, because of how much energy he'd put into rushing her, he bowled the two over into the side of the table, her body pushed up against and bending over the edge. He held her close, stared into her eyes as she struggled weakly, striking him in the sides and chest as she choked on her blood.

Saw the last glimmer of hope and life disappear.

And then, because he was at the table, saw the notice as it appeared above it.

Chapter 58

Battle Report (Stone Keep vs Enemy Units)
Result: Victory! 1 Woodling Unit Lost, 0 Units Escaped
Rewards: +14 Gold, +3 Reputation

Just as quickly as that appeared, more information appeared.

Battle Report (Hero Braskar vs Enemy Units)
Result: Victory! 1 Units Lost, 0 Units Escaped
Rewards: +4 Gold, +1 Reputation

One notification after the other.

Territory Occupation Granted!
Hero Braskar has acquired enemy territory of Baron Mexaon for Baron Fang.
Acquired: 1 Stone Keep
Rewards: +99 Gold, +5 Reputation

"My lord?" Hesitantly, Braskar spoke up. "Are you… do you live?"

"I do," Matt said softly. "Thank you. And good job."

"You're welcome, my lord."

"What am I? A chemical hazard?" Irvine groused from his position slumped against a nearby wall. When he noticed Matt looking at him, he waved languidly at the last potion on the ground. "Don't touch that. It'll burn your face off. Like it should have hers, if I had ever gotten it on her."

"You have done well, Alchemist," Braskar rumbled. "Our Lord still lives and we have true victory."

"Yeah, it sure looks like that, doesn't it?" Matt said softly. Then, he backed off the body that he was still holding aloft, watching it slump down the table before falling to the ground, blood leaking out of the wound onto the ground. He looked down at his chest, at the blood that stained it, the smell of iron and vomit and something worse coming from the body next to him and suddenly he turned as the contents of his stomach rose up.

It took him a while to recover, to get ahold of his mind and control his reaction, for him to stop dry heaving and for the shakes that had come right after that to end. Neither Hero chose to interrupt that process, Irvine dealing with his own issues and the orc knowing better.

After battle shakes were all too common.

So was crying. Sobbing. Lamenting their fates.

All common, all normal. As were the nightmares.

Eventually, Matt managed to recover sufficiently to push himself upwards. It took a little longer to fix up the bandages around himself and then do the same to Irvine, to check what was happening outside and to watch, rather bemused, as the keep started to repair itself.

Among other things, the bodies of the fallen were disappearing, the door to the tower room began to rebuild itself, and splotches of blood and wounds disappeared.

Finally, Matt made his way over to the tactical map once more. He leaned over, staring at the new map that had formed, showcasing the land between the two villages, the two keeps, and the land that they had sight of from their new settlements.

He stared at the unit marker for Braskar, and then the one near him. And he found, through the roiling stomach, the pain in his chest that still throbbed, and the incipient headache, a new feeling.

Relief, of course, but more importantly…

Joy.

He'd won. It was only one battle, and the fact that no further notifications or his sudden disappearance told him that this war was not over. But now, he knew. There was a world to explore, more enemies to battle, and more victories to be won. A long road to travel.

Yet, here, now, he had won.

And Matt grinned, knowing then that he really could do this. He had won. And he would continue winning. Beat his opponents, figure out why this was happening, and, most importantly, save Earth.

***

End of Volume 3 Status Report

Status Report (Town 1 Only)
Day 52
Gold: 203.75 (+22.25 Gold per day)
Units: 2 Woodlings, 2 Firecracker Flower
In Production: Firecracker Flower (4/5), Woodling (3/4)
Structures Completed: Grove, Road, Stall (II), Ranged Copse, Harbour, Village #2 – Watch Tower, Blacksmith
Structures Available: Grove (II), Basic Greenhouse, Watch Tower, Tavern, Marketplace, Ranged Copse (II), Stone Harbour, Fishing Dock, Shipyard, Trading Post, Temple, Blacksmith (Upgrade)

Cooldown: 10 Days to Burst Production, 5 Days to Spell Casting

Chapter 59

The only thing sadder than a battle won was the paperwork afterward. Or in this case, since there was no actual paper and instead a bunch of glowing lines across his map, it was mostly Matt Fang seated with his legs up on a chair and waving his hands around like a mad conductor.

Every once in a while, he'd grimace and stop, the pain from the beating just a day ago coursing through his body. He hadn't realised until later, when the adrenaline had faded sufficiently, that he'd bruised his ribs. Then, of course, there were the torn skin and cuts across his face and arms that he hadn't even realised had happened during the scuffle, along with numerous other bruises.

And he didn't even want to discuss the hanging piece of skin on the side of his face or the giant cut across his body that he'd had to have stitched up.

Who'd have thought that a minute or two of fighting could end with so many bruises, even when you were the winner?

Probably quite a few people, really, if Matt was being truthful. Bouncers, bodyguards, policemen, some army personnel. The ones who actually did physical things rather than paperwork or logistics or, you know, the vast majority of other jobs. Martial artists too, he guessed.

None of them described the ex-accountant of course. The most strenuous thing he'd done physically was a game of ultimate frisbee about six months ago. Or, well, six months before his transfer, he guessed. He was kind of losing his sense of time, his mind split between the day he'd died and, well, everything that had happened after.

Still, he at least knew how to check how long it had been since he'd arrived here. A flicker of his hands was enough to pull up the status report.

Global Status Report

Day 53

Pooled Gold: 236 (+32.25 Gold per day)

Total Units: 4 Woodlings, 3 Firecracker Flowers

Cooldown: 9 Days to Burst Production, 4 Days to Spell Casting

Fifty-three days. Nearly two months since he had arrived, give or take a few days depending on how you counted what a month was. More importantly, the Global Status Report was the biggest change in his reports since he'd managed to take over the second town. Now, if he wanted to – had to – he'd be able to dig down into each town for individual management.

On the other hand, the fact that he actually had a global pooled treasury and gold increase meant that he could build out towns differently. Specialise them if you would. Make one just a gold producer, make the other place where he got units.

At least in theory, but naturally, when theory met reality, things went to hell. Part of that was, of course, the devil in the details when one went into individual town reports.

Town 1 Status Report

In Production: None

Structures Completed: Grove, Road, Stall (II), Ranged Copse, Harbour, Village #2 – Watch Tower, Blacksmith

Structures Available: Grove (II), Basic Greenhouse, Watch Tower, Tavern, Marketplace, Ranged Copse (II), Stone Harbour, Fishing Dock, Shipyard, Trading Post, Temple, Blacksmith (Upgrade)

Town 2 Status Report

In Production: None

Structures Completed: Den (II), Tavern, Wall, Temple, Stall

Structures Available: Den (III), Javelin Range, Training House, Watch Tower, Blacksmith, Stall (II), Temple (II)

Both towns were quite different, at least in what they had concentrated upon. Some, like the Den and Javelin Range or Grove and Ranged Copse, were just different names for the same thing. And the addition of the new town added more gold to his coffers, even though it also meant he had more places to spend all that new money on.

Mostly, Matt had spent this morning on verifying the basics of his original and new settlements, making sure his guesses, like what the Training House was, were correct. There were enough differences that he had wanted to deal with them with a clear head, even if he did lose a day or two of production, rather than engaging in it immediately following the battle the day before.

He had to admit, after getting beaten up and maybe even mildly concussed, he had not been in any mental state to make big decisions. Nevermind the fact that a part of him had still wondered if he would wake up in a new location after going to bed.

Stranger things had happened.

Now that he had done that, he needed to verify the unknown. In this case, the two buildings he hadn't himself purchased before but were available to him now – the Tavern and the Temple.

Matt had to admit, he was most excited to see what the Tavern was.

Name: Tavern

Building Type: Hero Management

Tier: Lesser Tier I

Heroes Available to Recruit: Bard, Warlord

Number of Available Hero Slots: 1

Matt blinked, staring at the building information. As usual, there was less to go on than he'd like. What other options were there in Hero Management? Could he train Heroes if he upgraded the Tavern further? A quick perusal of his available buildings list showed there was nothing like that right now. So was that a no or just a possibility he had yet to find?

He – obviously – poked at the Hero types, but, unfortunately, there was no information available on them either. Now, he sort of knew what Bards did, in theory. Except, of course, they might not be the same here. If they were though, he could not see himself recruiting a singer.

Would you like to recruit a Bard?

Cost: 200 Gold

Declining that option, Matt leaned back. He only had one available slot and the previous opponent had commanded a Healer of some form. And that came from the Temple. He should look at that rather than pick up a weird singer and lousy mage combination.

On that note, time to look at the Temple.

Name: Temple

Building Type: Hero Management

Tier: Lesser Tier I

Heroes Available to Recruit: Priest

Number of Available Hero Slots: 1

Matt pulled up the upgrades too, just to get an eye on them. Not that he was planning on upgrading it right now, but getting a healer was never a bad idea. And he'd only seen a small amount of what the other Hero was able to do after all.

Upgrade Available: Temple (II)

Building Type: Religious

Tier: Lesser Tier II

Cost: 350 Gold

Production Time: 12 days

Expensive and no indication of what he'd get. If he had to assume, some bonus to morale perhaps and more Priest options. The only question was how expensive it would be to pick up the Priest.

Would you like to recruit a Priest?

Cost: 200 Gold

Wincing, Matt shook his head. As good as it sounded, he had a lot more to consider before he went spending his limited funds.

After all, he once again had to balance his immediate needs with long-term growth. He no longer had an enemy directly in front of him, but they were out there. Somewhere.

All of which meant reviewing his units in play.

Chapter 60

Total Units: 4 Woodlings, 3 Firecracker Flowers

On one hand, that seemed like a lot. On the other hand, it really wasn't, not with his army split and needing to care for multiple villages. Braskar had no woodlings with him and a single firecracker flower. The rest were here, having been pulled back to guard Matt and Irvine. Well, except the Woodling in the last village.

Of course, other than the newly formed woodling and firecracker units, all of his units in town were damaged. He literally had one woodling in town that had only a single unit left. If not for pure luck, he would have lost two units entirely. As for his firecracker flowers, only half of the units remained here, though Braskar still had two thirds of his sole unit. As it was, it would take days before the units regenerated.

Now that he had two villages, he needed to reinforce them just in case they were destroyed or taken over by roving bandits. He assumed that was coming since most of these games had such hindrances. So he'd have to move at least one of his units away to guard the furthest village at some point. If his opponent had not been in such a hurry, they might have taken his village first, depriving him of the gold while he got ready.

Good news was that he had access to the saakal. A flick of his finger brought up the info on the Den.

Name: Den (II)

Building Type: Barracks

Tier: Lesser Tier II

Units Available to Produce: Saakal (II) (25/5)

Not much information there. The saakal units were interesting, though the details were obviously not too surprising after scanning them before in battle.

Unit Name: Saakal

Type: Beastkin

Tier: Lesser Tier II

Number: 6

Movement: 2

Cost: 25 Gold

Melee Attack: 15

Melee Defense: 8

Ranged Attack: 0

Ranged Defense: 10

Hit Points: 6

Speed: 12

Special Abilities: Charge (II)

Vulnerabilities: Sonic (Low), Fire (Medium)

Growth Potential: High

High melee attack, lousy defense. Almost the opposite of his own woodlings. Skirmishers rather than front line fighters. Matt was actually looking forward to seeing how they combined with his woodlings. Adding the saakal pretty much put him in the optimal configuration for a starting battle – heavy infantry, skirmishers, and ranged units. Of course, he'd love to upgrade them and maybe get some cavalry, but for a start it was damn decent.

Which reminded him.

"Braskar," Matt called out into the air, trusting the magic to send the notification to his Hero, even if he was in the other town.

"My lord," the formal orc Warlord replied immediately. Matt could almost imagine the orc coming to attention, even if he'd never actually seen him do that.

"I'm thinking first things first, get at least a saakal building. What do you think?" Matt said. "We've got to know how they work with our units. See if the stupid system has any surprises hidden."

"Surprises, my lord?"

"Morale problems, issues with combining various troops of different species," Matt offered. "I don't think there'll be issues, but I'm not really willing to bet on it."

"Wise choice, my lord." Braskar hesitated. "And the disposition of the rest of the units?"

"Something I was going to ask about too." Matt gestured, pulling up the map. There were multiple hexes between the two towns. Something he could fix with purchasing roadworks between the pair, increasing both his gold income and speed of travel. However, the bigger question was the northwestern village, which had no guards right now and was their most vulnerable acquisition. Assuming, of course, there were not even more enemies further north.

Right now, all they knew was that there was a potential enemy to the west.

"We should not leave the recent conquest unattended. We know that doing so will not spawn automatic defenders like the villages," Braskar rumbled. "And new towns offer us the greatest increase in strength."

"Agreed, though the militias the villages create are useless right now. They're barely a speedbump to the forces being produced."

"True, my lord. Are you thinking of sending a unit over to reinforce the northwestern village?"

"Seems like it's the same problem, isn't it?" Matt said grumpily. "If we don't send enough people, they're barely useful either."

"Unless it is a scouting unit."

"Truth. The militia can't beat scouting units, but leaving a single unit can." Matt hesitated. "Is that what you're suggesting?"

"You have multiple units on hand, my lord. I think reinforcing the new village would be wisest. You have damaged units, do you not, my lord?"

"Fine." Matt sent the most damaged unit to the nearest village and then had the unit in that village head for Village 2. It would shorten the travel time for both. Even then, it would take a few days before it arrived, but better to get it started now. While he was at it, he quickly confirmed production of the saakal. As they had discussed, that seemed the best option after all.

While he was at it, he chose to start pushing a Woodling and Firecracker Flower up to Braskar. It would make him weaker than he'd like here, but it would offer aid to his main fighting force.

He could, if he wanted to, hire a Hero. But while Heroes were a multiplier, when you had nearly nothing to work with, they weren't really worth buying. As such, hiring one was not high on his agenda right now. Replacing his units and upgrading the settlements seemed the best course of action.

"Is that all, my lord?" Braskar rumbled, interrupting his thoughts.

"Yeah, for now. Keep…" Matt hesitated, then asked, "What are you doing?"

"Looking over the Stone Keep. I have not seen one before, not being there when our own capital transformed," Braskar replied. "I also intend to review the units and the remainder of the buildings here, my lord." A slight pause, then he added, "And rest. Something I recommend you do too. Such a battle and its aftermath can be taxing on the mind."

"You mean nearly dying?" Matt said, tracing the crusted blood on his face. "Yeah, I bet. I will, but working is keeping me going right now. Not as though I slept well last night." Nightmares had kept waking him, even as his body had lulled him back to sleep soon after as exhaustion, injuries, and adrenaline had taken their toll. "But this is like playing a video game, and that was restful for me. Back then."

"I see, my lord." Matt knew Braskar only had the vaguest idea of what he meant by video game, what with coming from a more primitive world. But the orc was willing to take his word for it, which was the point. "Just… be careful. I am sure the Alchemist is already resting."

"You'd have won that bet," Matt said, chuckling. He'd poked his head in on Irvine. The older Hero had been splayed on his bed, jugs of wine next to him and completely dead to the world. "Tah for now."

Killing the connection before Braskar pursued the questioning further, Matt focused on his next steps. Having over two hundred gold gave him options, including more units, the Fishing Dock, the Trading Post, the Blacksmith, and a Stall upgrade.

A quick check showed no further information on the Blacksmith, so no guarantee that it'd stack upgrades across towns. Buying the next level of the Blacksmith for defence was cheap – relatively speaking – at fifty gold. On further consideration, Matt was pretty certain the Blacksmith only worked on units built within the Town. It wouldn't make sense to have the option in each town otherwise.

So…

Units or gold? Or both?

As usual, it seemed to come down to security now versus more options in the future.

Chapter 61

Security or gold, which was more important? Nevermind the fact that Matt had been attacked from the east, what else could he buy? And what, if any, concerns should he have about the monsters coming from the west and the south?

He could go all in, buy a ton of gold-producing buildings. The Fishing Dock was only a hundred, the Stall upgrade seventy-five. It'd mean all his gold would be used, but then next day he could just buy two units. Or he could start the units immediately and then add the buildings later.

A quick flick to pull up details on the Fishing Dock had him regarding the details.

Structure Available: Fishing Dock
Building Type: Treasury
Tier: Lesser Tier I
Benefit: +5 Gold Per Day
Cost: 100 Gold
Production Time: 3 days

Not much information in there, almost exactly the same as the Stall except a little bit faster to build. The upgraded Stall would take even longer but had the advantage of being cheaper, of course. Which was not a consideration to be ignored since the return on investment for upgrading would make it available within fifteen days rather than the twenty that the dock had.

All well and good, and three days was not a long time. In fact, there was an argument that he was spending too much time debating this, what with the degree of optimization in play probably being overly inflated in his mind. After all, he could see far enough out that it was unlikely for an enemy unit to sneak up on him and as such, he could debate whether to buy gold producers versus units now or later.

On the other hand, having an idea of which to prioritize – military or gold – was likely going to mean less debate in the long-term.

"Military or gold?" Matt drummed his fingers on the table. "Considering how long it takes to build units, there's something to be said about frontloading unit production. I could even double my purchase, pick up all three units available across all the settlements."

It would take a total of forty-five more gold, putting him down to a hundred sixty-one. He could still get the Fishing Dock then but not the upgraded Stall. Or any of the other gold producers, though those two were the cheapest and most efficient. He'd complain about lack of flexibility, but thus far, it wasn't as though he could hurry production. So he'd have to just suck it up anyway.

That was probably the sticking point. Since he couldn't hurry production, units probably were the most important aspect to get moving, what with the need for further protection. His greatest danger was having someone wander in and start a fight right after he sent off all his units.

"Get more units up, just in case I get attacked. And then worry about gold later." Matt listened to his words rebound off the stone walls, waiting to see if doing so would reveal any foolish ideas expressed. Since no random voice shouted at him, he locked in the changes and leaned back.

Done and done. He bought the two units, watched his gold drain, and smiled to himself.

He even had a plan for tomorrow, after which he'd have to start sorting out what else he would build. There were a number of interesting, unknown buildings and options left, like the Temple and its upgrade, the Priest, and the Trading Post.

Though…

Maybe at some point he should also add the Road to his list of things to add. Building roads didn't seem to increase much in terms of gold, but the ability to quickly move armies between locations was important. Wasn't there something about how Rome managed their empire because of their roads?

Though that had failed them eventually. Then again, they also didn't have a magic telephone system and hovering tactical maps. If Octavius wouldn't hang him for a heretic or witch or whatever, he'd probably be showered in praise if he ever showed them this.

Or, hell, Shih Huang Di. Though that was one tyrant that Matt had no desire to provide additional aid to. That was not a nice man, not at all, even if he had managed to build a society that had lasted centuries.

"Right, how much for a Road then?" Matt said. "Or Roads."

Ten gold to Village 2 from here. Twenty for the Road to the other town. Only worth half a gold per turn in addition. More than that, it looked like he'd have to pay another ten gold to connect Town 2 to Village 2. So, in total he'd be looking at forty gold.

"Ouch…" Matt grumbled. He flicked the options up on the board, then frowned as he spotted a potential sidestep.

"You little cheaters…"

A quick adjustment had him highlighting the movement from Town 2 to Village 1. Ten gold. A quarter gold increase. But now, he had a full Road between both towns that pushed through the village rather than be a separate circuit. That was fine. It wasn't any different from the town to town road, just…

"No additional half gold. Which I can live with." And then if he added Roads to Village 2, he'd have a full setup running for thirty gold. Cheaper by a bit, though it would mean he couldn't purchase a Stall upgrade.

"Army logistics first. Money second…" Matt chanted to himself, confirming the choices. He took a breath, then added the Fishing Dock. A hundred gold and a three day start now was important. It was the right choice, he knew it. Or so he assured himself at least.

Nothing left to do, he dismissed the map and stood up. Braskar was right. Whatever else, he needed a day off. Maybe a few days. After all, he had made the necessary decisions. Now, it was just a matter of seeing how it played out.

Damn turn-based games really were better left as actual games.

***

Global Status Report

Day 53 (End of Day)

Pooled Gold: 36 (+32.25 Gold per day)

Total Units: 4 Woodlings, 3 Firecracker Flowers

Cooldown: 9 Days to Burst Production, 4 Days to Spell Casting

Unit Organisation

Town 1: Irvine, 1 Woodling, 1 Firecracker Flowers

Town 2: Braskar, 1 Firecracker Flower, 1 Woodling and 1 Firecracker Flower (en-route)

Village 1: 1 Woodling (en-route from Town)

Village 2: 1 Woodling (en-route from Village 1)

Town 1 Status Report

In Production: 1 Woodling (0/4), 1 Firecracker Flower (0/5), Road to Village #2 (0/3), Fishing Dock (0/3)

Structures Completed: Grove, Road, Stall (II), Ranged Copse, Harbour, Village #2 – Watch Tower, Blacksmith

Structures Available: Grove (II), Basic Greenhouse, Watch Tower, Tavern, Marketplace, Ranged Copse (II), Stone Harbour, Shipyard, Trading Post, Temple, Blacksmith (Upgrade)

Town 2 Status Report

In Production: Saakal II (0/5), Road to Village 1 (0/3)

Structures Completed: Den (II), Tavern, Wall, Temple, Stall

Structures Available: Den (III), Javelin Range, Training House, Watch Tower, Blacksmith, Stall (II), Temple (II)

Chapter 62

To Matt's surprise, right after he finished making the decisions and having a late brunch, he'd found himself suddenly weary beyond belief. Crashing in his makeshift workplace had caused him to wake up with a crick in the neck, helped a little by more food for dinner and a long soak.

The next day, he'd checked the map over cursorily. Without anything better to do and with little enough gold, he moved on to taking a slow, careful review of the Stone Keep, his pit traps that were entirely non-standard, and his crossbow. Fixing all that – or at least, getting the materials to fix it all – had taken the majority of the day, what with his body still exhausted and aching. He had to admit, he'd not been particularly vigorous or enthused with his chores. It sucked when even breathing was a pain.

Now, two days later, the team was having their very first all-hands meeting. Irvine had returned to working on creating batches of potions due to the units having nothing to their name. Since the Potions of Strength and Defense had been so intrinsic to their battles, Matt was all for the man working on those.

"Do you have options for more potions?" Matt said. A foolish hope for Irvine, what with his recent leveling, but he had to ask. "New levels maybe?"

Both Heroes declined, though Braskar was moving at a decent clip to his second. So was Irvine, now that he had returned to making potions.

"Do you think you're better off doing Burst Production to get some Potions of Defense or Strength for our units here and then getting back to research?" Matt asked Irvine, curious. "When you have it back, that is."

The wiry, old Hero frowned. Like Matt, he was human, though his world had been one filled with magic and wonder, unlike Matt's own dull, paper-clipped, spreadsheet-filled existence. On the other hand, indoor plumbing and proper ventilation were wonders that Matt was never going to discount, even if the magical equivalents in the Stone Keep were doing better than their previous fort.

"I could, my lord, but I get more experience creating potions directly, and my chances of failure have dropped significantly," Irvine said.

"Yeah, but you make them faster with Burst, right?"

"Yes." Irvine hesitated, then added, "If you order me, I shall do so."

"If." Matt drawled the word out, then waved away the Alchemist's protests. "Later. Can't do anything now anyway. Braskar, anything to report?"

"Nothing, my lord. I wish to ask for the right to begin further exploration north," the orc rumbled. Matt could almost imagine the grey-skinned, tusked figure speaking to him at attention or maybe standing on the walls of the Stone Keep, staring wistfully into the distance.

"Not east," Matt said, surprised.

"I believe there is much to see north of us," Braskar said. "And while we know of a threat to the east, that threat is, we believe, automated."

"The raiders aren't real, so they're less dangerous, eh?" Matt could see the logic in that. Certainly, a thinking and active opponent was more dangerous as they'd just experienced. Of course, they were also prone to mistakes and overconfidence. If they hadn't rushed the attack on his own capital, it might have taken his team a lot more effort to grind them down.

"We also know that we have the sea to the south. Perhaps there might be a similar obstacle further north," Braskar said.

"Isthmus or peninsula or island, you think? Rather than just the edge of a continent?" Matt hummed. He had to explain the terms to Irvine, though it did give him time to consider the suggestion further. It would help to know the lay of the land though… "I'd still prefer if we kept you closer on hand. We've seen the difference a good Warlord makes in battle. You also need more units."

"And if we find another village, we could create a new line of defense," Braskar said.

"Not much defense, really, the villages."

"Visibility then."

"What do you think?" Matt asked Irvine, who had been quiet thus far.

"Seems to me like we're rushing. We don't even have enough units to guard everything," the Alchemist grumbled, waving a hand at the tactical map hovering before them. "If we expand even further, who knows what we'll encounter? What if the opponent to the north decides to chase us down?"

"Instead, we wait for them to find us?" Braskar said. "Waiting to be prey is not how orcs behave."

"Good thing I'm not an orc."

"I am."

"You think heading north is the best option?" Matt said softly.

"I do, my lord."

"With what units?"

"The saakal will be available in three days and we know nothing is within range now," Braskar said. "I can be back long before there is an issue, if so."

"I don't like it," Matt said. "But okay. Go for it." He paused, then added, "I want you to plan a route to link up with the saakal when it's done. I'll build a second one immediately after. Once we have them, I'll start moving a woodling and firecracker up to the town."

"A good plan, my lord."

"That's going to leave us a little short here..." Irvine protested.

"Same reasoning though," Matt said. "We'll see any problems long before they arrive. Or should, at least. And we have other units building now."

He reached out to the map, tracing his fingers along the roads. "Almost makes sense to start considering building a reactionary force in the first village. It's close enough to this town to offer almost immediate help and if it's large enough, we could use it to intercept enemies."

"When we have enough units, sure…" Irvine said pointedly.

"One step at a time."

"I shall set out then, my lord. Unless there is anything further to discuss?" Braskar said.

A quick glance at the Alchemist, who was also standing and getting ready to leave, answered that question for Matt. Bidding the pair of Heroes farewell, Matt pulled up the town information and sighed. There really never were enough funds. But at least he could get moving on the upgraded Stall.

Soon, they'd have some real money.

Now, if things could continue staying quiet, it'd be perfect.

***

Global Status Report

Day 56 (End of Day)

Pooled Gold: 57.75 (+32.25 Gold per day)

Total Units: 4 Woodlings, 3 Firecracker Flowers

Cooldown: 6 Days to Burst Production, 1 Day to Spell Casting

Unit Organisation

Town 1: Irvine, 1 Woodling, 1 Firecracker Flowers

Town 2: Braskar, 1 Firecracker Flower, 1 Firecracker Flower and 1 Woodling (en-route)

Village 1: 1 Woodling

Village 2: 1 Woodling (en-route from Village 1)

Town 1 Status Report

In Production: 1 Woodling (3/4), 1 Firecracker Flower (3/5)

Structures Completed: Grove, Road, Stall (II), Ranged Copse, Harbour, Village #2 – Watch Tower, Blacksmith, Road to Village #2, Fishing Dock

Structures Available: Grove (II), Basic Greenhouse, Watch Tower, Tavern, Marketplace, Ranged Copse (II), Stone Harbour, Shipyard, Trading Post, Temple, Blacksmith (Upgrade)

Town 2 Status Report

In Production: Saakal II (3/5), Stall (II) (0/7)

Structures Completed: Den (II), Tavern, Wall, Temple, Stall, Road to Village 1

Structures Available: Den (III), Javelin Range, Training House, Watch Tower, Blacksmith, Temple (II)

Chapter 63

Travel was slow, but travel was at least progress as far as Braskar was concerned. His people were nomads and staying still in a fort while unknown enemies ranged afield sat ill with him. Better to journey forth and confront them.

The fact that the saakal were fast-moving was just a bonus. They could catch up and reinforce his army whilst he was moving, and out here the random encounters his units faced would allow them to grow. Himself as well. The fact that his units were damaged and still healing did not matter since their own losses during the battle had been mostly insignificant other than the woodling unit. And that had been a complete loss, so nothing to heal there.

More importantly, up here for the first couple of hexes – hah, how strange to consider terrain as hexes, even if the entire world was based on it – the ground was featureless, minorly rolling plains. He knew better than to assume that he could spot everyone, for even minor changes in terrain could hide a wily opponent.

It did mean that travel so far had been less torturous than movement through a forest. The forest that was coming up would soon slow them down, and linking up with the saakal unit would be interesting. He had a feeling that some degree of magical adjustments would occur to ensure they actually met.

If not, well, that too was new information, as his lord would say.

Braskar chuckled, stretching his back as he turned to regard his unit. Strange plant creatures, these tottering, multi-limbed 'flowers' that followed. His little army, made even stranger when the saakal – loping, beast-like creatures – would join in the future.

"If I was to make this even vaguely normal, I would situate enemies on either side, and away, in a ring. So, the question is whether this would be in a direct line or further apart?" Braskar asked the air, knowing there was no one to speak to. Which was for the best. He was not sure he liked giving in to the weird logic of this universe, though in-world, of course, there was some logic to settlements being separated too.

That logic, of settlements forming a distance from one another, was often dictated by the amount of resources available – or the position of specific resources. In his world, mining camps and the towns and villages that made use of natural resources would appear, farming villages in the plains, fishing villages next to rivers and lakes. You could tell where to raid or where villages would likely be if you knew the terrain or could read the way a land formed itself.

Nothing like that in this new world, where towns were plopped down by some unseen force.

No, the town they had just left had been in the center of the plains, but there had been fields to farm the land around it. Any reasonable settler would have chosen the lakes a short distance away for access to fresh water rather than the drier land.

Raiding logic was of less use here. But the creator logic, that might make sense. If discussions with his lord had any sense, then this entire world was meant to be a challenge. Not much of a challenge if you overwhelmed the fighters immediately, so he expected – though he didn't tell his lord – to find their opponent a distance away.

Still, no guarantee there were no scouts. If anything, that was likely what he would find. If not more raiders.

What those were, he did not know. His lord had said it was a feature of these games, to add difficulty in the early stages. Destroying them gave bonuses, allowing each opponent to develop somewhat before they clashed.

Yet, that logic had fouled as they'd located their first enemy almost immediately, so that seemed foolish to believe.

No, the raiders, as far as Braskar was concerned, were a different thing. Perhaps a chance to gain greater strength. In either case, it was not his task to aid his lord in that endeavour but to focus on finding their true enemies.

Now, if only they could cover more ground.

***

Irvine stretched, feeling the muscles in his shoulders shift. He winced as he felt the back of his head, his torso, and his arms all twinge. Thankfully, this world seemed to help him heal faster than ever, such that he was less injured already than he should be.

Not so his lord, of course, but Irvine and Braskar seemed to be more suited to this existence. Perhaps it would be a not-so-subtle hint for his lord to stay out of the direct battles. Which, all due given, he had tried. Unfortunately, matters had progressed beyond that, forcing him to do battle.

Looking around his room, Irvine smiled. He could not help but feel a surge of pride at the alchemical laboratory that was his. Even at the height of his success, he had never had as many tools, instruments, and ingredients on hand. Certainly not glass that was so clear, burners that were so well made that he could try the flame with such exactness. A moment later, that pride dimmed a little. So many of the tools and ingredients were still locked out, forcing him to only stare at them.

It was the height of idiocy that the world system forced him to only use certain items and refused to open drawers or unscrew caps. He'd even tried breaking a few bottles, only to find them unbreakable. Which could have been useful, if not for the fact that they could not be removed from the room. His hands still ached from the bruising they had taken when he'd used a stone club on one of those jars.

Still… ever since his level increase, he'd had more access than ever. While he would have preferred to focus on the research of new recipes – or recreate the very same potions he had once gained fame for in his previous life – this world and the ingredients were strange. Different enough that he knew better than to assume anything.

Right now, his job was to create the potions for the rest of their remaining units. Matt had never verified what he had decided upon, which meant Irvine could do what he thought best – gain experience making new potions. Each time he went through the process, he felt himself getting better, more experienced.

Every day, a new potion, or every two days if he failed one day. A decent production speed, no matter what his lord said. Especially since it seemed that each unit could only carry a single potion.

No chance of loading down a single unit with multiples of the same kind or multiple potions at all. It was an 'exploit' that his lord had attempted recently, one that had just resulted with the woodling in question staring back at Matt blankly as he offered the vial to it.

Now, that had been an amusing sight.

Irvine stretched. Proper stretching was part and parcel of long-term survivorship of Alchemists. He had seen all too many of his compatriots blow themselves up or poison themselves because of a bad cramp. Fools, all of them.

Done, he leaned over the cauldron, checking its content. Purple and yellow. Just right. Except… why were there flecks of grey in there?

Improper stirring or a new contaminant?

Humming to himself, Irvine got to work. This is what he enjoyed, and after decades of work, he still found a love for the process of alchemical creation. After growing so decrepit he'd no longer been able to – reliably – work in his own laboratory, this was a pleasure.

Almost worth dying for.

Chapter 64

The next few days passed by in a blur for Matt. The moment the saakal had been created, he had sent it after Braskar as promised. Immediately after, he'd started the process of training another. At the very worst, he figured he'd at least continue producing the strange creatures, since they were his closest equivalent to the cavalry the raiders had sent.

He also kept running additional units because he knew he needed more fighting power, especially front-line fighters. Getting another one up immediately was a bit of a drain on his resources because he was still incredibly poor. Braskar needed another, the new town needed another, and he wanted more himself.

Then, of course, there was the firecracker flowers to deal with, but in this case, he knew better than to split the units off. Better to have a larger contingent in his fort than otherwise. And if there was perhaps a touch of paranoia and fear in that decision, who could blame him?

While he couldn't say he didn't exactly not volunteer to get attacked, he certainly hadn't chosen to do so on purpose.

After that, with insufficient gold to do much more than wait, he did just that. He figured after this last build, he would have enough for the army he needed to scout the east. The ranged units survived longer than their melee ones after all.

Another new building or an upgrade or perhaps enough gold for a Hero was now the focus. He still had concerns about hiring another Hero, though he could see how important they were in the overall scheme of things.

If anything, he almost wished for another Warlord. Pity that he had only one slot and no idea how to increase the number available. Or whether he always had three slots or what he could have triggered to increase that allocation. He had guesses – the Temple acquisition, the Tavern, the new town. But it all had come at the same time, offering no further information.

The Fishing Dock, when it had finally been completed, had offered only a minor upgrade.

Structure Available: Fishing Wharf
Building Type: Treasury
Tier: Lesser Tier II
Benefit: +10 Gold Per Day
Cost: 250 Gold
Production Time: 7 days

No new buildings. Matt had a feeling that if he wanted to pursue additional upgrades along the water, he needed to build the Shipyard. Might even get a naval unit out of that. Sadly, he did not have the funds to pursue such a project at this moment.

After all, he had known enemies coming from the west.

It was that belief that had him considering pouring more funds into unit building, hoping to create a force that could match whatever was coming. He figured at least three units, potentially four with a saakal unit added to it, would be sufficient even without a Hero. Two woodlings, a firecracker flower, and a saakal would be perfect. Or swap a woodling for a firecracker flower in the hope that they had enough stopping power?

Of course, that would leave him nearly destitute again with significant unit production and no more buildings. He was also constrained by the speed that units could come out. Which had him thinking that upgrading the next town would be the way to go.

With all this idle time, Matt took his time rebuilding his crossbow. It hadn't worked very well against the plate mail, which meant it hadn't worked well at all.

With the Blacksmith in play and the wood from the woodling and the Grove, it was a simple matter to get the base materials. Thankfully, taking simple tools from the Blacksmith was a non-issue. The problem, more than anything else, was figuring out how to build it. It wasn't as though he had spent any real time in a machine shop back on Earth or even spent time looking at crossbows. Even if he did manage to make one, the bolts it threw were another problem. Certainly, getting actual metal points on his bolts would help with the penetration power.

Still, becoming a semi-competent bowyer was at least a project he could pursue right now. Unlike the pit traps, where even a brief attempt at digging with bruised ribs and a giant wound that was barely stitched together had informed Matt that that was a foolish idea. Brief, in this case, was the first sinking of a shovel into the earth.

It took another four days before another major change occurred, just over twelve days since the end of their big battle. That was when the Stall upgrade was finished, adding another five gold to his gold production, but most importantly, access to new buildings. In this case, not just the Marketplace that had appeared before but also a Granary.

Structure Available: Granary
Building Type: Unit Upgrade
Tier: Lesser Tier II
Benefit: -1 Day to Production Speed of Units
Cost: 250 Gold
Production Time: 7 days

"Holy staples on a Wednesday." Matt flopped into his chair. "That's, well, a game changer? Maybe?" He really was not sure, but it certainly was quite the difference.

"Braskar."

The answer came back almost immediately. "My lord?"

"Busy?"

"No, my lord. Scouting but there is not much to report. Is there a problem?"

"Nah, just a new structure." A short while later, after Braskar was up to speed, Matt added, "What do you think?"

"It seems to me that this is quite the change. Is there a way to replicate this in our own town?" Braskar asked.

"No idea. I got it after the Stall upgrade, but we already have that. Maybe if we purchase the Marketplace. Might be a town-exclusive in the plains since they don't have a Harbour," Matt said. "In fact, I'd lean towards that. Maybe the Granary would come in much later at best."

"I see, my lord. Do you intend to purchase this upgrade?"

"You'd think so, wouldn't you?" Matt said softly. "But I think it might be a trap."

"A trap?"

"Not in the traditional sense, but an early production trap. What happens if we purchase it?"

Braskar sounded truly puzzled. "We are able to produce units faster."

"Right, but units aren't any cheaper. And what's our biggest problem?"

"Lack of gold."

"Exactly. We'd fall into the same production trap as our previous opponent. He was so focused on building units, he didn't ever increase his gold production. In the short-term, that gives you more units to throw at your opponents, but the moment opponents get their production going, you're hosed. If we had even another ten days, I bet we'd have beaten them without a worry," Matt said.

"So you're worried this is a similar problem. We will get caught up in producing units only, falling behind on gold production," Braskar said.

"Exactly."

"I see." Braskar fell silent for such a long time that Matt thought he had gone offline. When he did speak, Matt nearly jumped out of his chair, having returned to poking at the interface to see if he could replicate the Granary in their original town. "You are right, I believe. Well done, my lord."

"Yeah…" Matt said, holding a hand to his chest. "Right. Well, you get back to… scouting. And I'll get back to being smart and strategic, eh?"

"Yes, my lord." There was amusement in the orc's voice as though he could sense Matt's true thoughts. Perhaps he could. In either case, the office worker waited for a long time to make sure that Braskar really was done and gone before he returned to perusing the build table.

No Granary. Two hundred and seventy gold and change. A decent amount of gold production now actually, though it could be better. Truth be told, he'd left it to run a little long, but he had been wanting to see what the Stall would create, nevermind the Fishing Dock. Now, he had options to make more gold or to buy a Hero or begin the Marketplace or Trading Post.

One area he had not perused was the equivalent of the unit upgrades. He did seriously wonder if the time had come for him to do so. In particular, Matt could not help but turn his attention to the Basic Greenhouse. The fact that it had cost five hundred gold before had stopped him from considering that as an option, but now…

Before he made up his mind, Matt flipped the unit information on again.

Structure Available: Basic Greenhouse

Building Type: Evolutionary

Tier: Lesser Tier I

Benefit: Allows Research into new unit types and evolutions

Cost: 500 Gold

Production Time: 20 days

Twenty days. That was the killer, wasn't it? Twenty days to produce once you had the funds. On top of that would be all the time to make whatever new units – or research unit types – that came from it.

It was almost certain none of his other opponents had purchased that building in the previous battles. How could they have and how would they even be considered a threat if they did? The same problem with unit and gold production would plague them, even if they had a bit of a head start. Now, however, if he chose not to acquire it, what kind of disadvantage did he put himself in in the future?

In some ways, no way to know. Until he got it, he probably wouldn't.

So. Evolutionary choices next, all while building up his secondary army down here. And hoping that Braskar didn't find anything dangerous.

***

Global Status Report

Day 64 (End of Day)

Pooled Gold: 249.75 (+42.75 Gold per day)

Total Units: 6 Woodlings, 5 Firecracker Flowers, 2 Saakal

Cooldown: None

Unit Organisation

Town 1: Irvine, 3 Woodlings, 3 Firecracker Flowers

Town 2: 1 Firecracker Flower, 1 Woodling, 1 Saakal

Army 1: Braskar, 1 Firecracker Flower, 1 Saakal (en-route)

Village 1: 1 Woodling

Village 2: 1 Woodling

Town 1 Status Report

In Production: 1 Woodling (3/4), 1 Firecracker Flower (1/5)

Structures Completed: Grove, Road, Stall (II), Ranged Copse, Harbour, Village #2 – Watch Tower, Blacksmith, Fishing Dock

Structures Available: Grove (II), Basic Greenhouse, Watch Tower, Tavern, Marketplace, Ranged Copse (II), Stone Harbour, Shipyard, Trading Post, Temple, Blacksmith (Upgrade), Fishing Wharf

Town 2 Status Report

In Production: (None)

Structures Completed: Den (II), Tavern, Wall, Temple, Stall (II)

Structures Available: Den (III), Javelin Range, Training House, Watch Tower, Blacksmith, Temple (II), Granary

Chapter 65

A day later and Matt finally had an army worth calling, well, an army. No sign of a cavalry or any other kind of enemy thus far, which was all good and fine. Matt could take a few quiet days, though he was growing more concerned each moment there wasn't a problem.

Still, with four woodlings and three firecracker flowers, he felt he could split some off for his expeditionary army. Obviously a little risky, but keeping two woodlings and a single firecracker flower behind that would be reinforced in a few days should be fine, especially since he was sending the army in the direction of the most likely problem. More than that, he could always pull the Village 1 woodling back if things got tricky. He was almost tempted to do that right now, really.

Resolved to start out the second army, the only question was whether to send it right along the coast like before or swing a little north of the coast. He'd already mapped the coast, so it made little sense to repeat the same trail – other than to hunt down his enemy immediately.

"What do you think?" Matt asked the team during their morning meeting. "If we keep them just slightly north of the coastline" – he gestured at the map that only Irvine and he could see – "we'd be charting more hexes. See a little more of what's out there, which isn't a bad thing, I think."

"I'd agree that it's not a bad thing, but…" Irvine hesitated, then added, "But I'm still not convinced we should be removing so many of our units. What if they do get routed? Then what?"

"Hopefully, they'd retreat in time," Matt said. "We know they can retreat."

"And yet have almost never seen it," Irvine said.

"I must agree that the risk you're running seems a little high, my lord," Braskar said, echoing the Alchemist. "Are you certain this is what you wish to do?"

"I am," Matt said firmly. "I can't keep hiding. We can't keep hiding."

"There is nothing to be ashamed of, in admitting you are afraid," Braskar added.

"I'm not..." Matt hesitated, then slowed down and exhaled. "I'm not saying I'm not afraid. But I'm not doing this to show I'm not scared. I'm doing this because it's the right thing to do."

"If you are certain… my lord."

"And I'm not being asked," Irvine grumbled, arms crossed.

"You going to say anything other than not to do it?" Matt raised an eyebrow at the Alchemist who just shrugged. "Yeah, didn't think so."

A flicker of his fingers had the units moving, pulling away from the walls and their Grove and marching out the open doors. He also pulled the saakal that had been completed and sent it down to meet with the burgeoning army, knowing it was necessary.

Now, hopefully, they'd not run into any major obstacles…

***

The next decision was how much more to add to his people. In the end, he had chosen to hold off till the most recent Firecracker Flower was finished. He could have added another Saakal but he was still trying to save money for the Greenhouse.

Of course, three days after that, apart from a few random encounters with angry wildlife by Braskar, they had yet to see signs of further opponents. Irvine had, thankfully, created extra potions before he had begun researching, allowing them to stock the units leaving with at least a single Potion of Strength each. On the other hand, that had led to quite a bit of complaints from the Alchemist – even if he continuously increased his experience.

Matt figured that in a few days, Irvine would finally decide to just utilize Burst Production just to have a chance to do research.

It was the next day that the second army ran into the first enemy unit.

No real surprise, it was a cavalry unit. What was a surprise – and frustration – was that the entire incident had happened without any member of the team noticing the battle beginning or ending. Irvine had been working on his potions, Matt on a new crossbow. No notification had appeared for either and by the time Matt had returned to the map room later that day, only a notice that the fight had begun and ended had been there.

Of course, he'd called a meeting with Braskar soon after, the orc quite irritated at the lack of his own encounters.

"It seems you were right. The combination of our ranged units and the saakal are quite effective," Braskar said.

"How'd you come to that conclusion?" Matt asked.

"The minimal loss of units, even though you encountered the cavalry in the most disadvantageous of conditions," Braskar explained.

"And that is?"

"Open plains."

"Right…" Matt found himself nodding, recalling some nerdy arguments about the use of cavalry and how movies never did them right. Still, if that was the case, would woodlings be considered heavy or light infantry? Perhaps just medium. "Any other insights?"

"Perhaps one," Braskar said. "Stop producing units."

"I thought you were complaining about me not being sufficiently safe before."

"That was before. You should be sufficiently covered for now."

Matt considered, wanting to object. He had held off on buying another unit yesterday already after all, though he had been playing with the idea of adding more saakal and woodlings.

"Why?" he finally asked.

"Our current moving mixture seems effective. Till we have a better idea of our opponent, it is best to wait."

"Fine," Matt said with a long sigh. He had four hundred and sixty-eight and a half gold right now, plus a small trickle coming in from the battle. Another forty-two and change to be produced the next day. That literally put him at the point where he'd be able to get the Greenhouse. Which was the point. After that though, he had meant to add more to the army. If he chose not to do that though, well…

There were other buildings to be made, gold production buildings, a Hero that he'd ignored for too long…

Options, basically. Options he'd ignored because he might have swung too far into security.

"Yeah, fine. I'll stop doing a CMA maneuver," Matt said. "Hopefully, nothing new arrives."

"Hopefully."

***

Global Status Report
Day 69 (End of Day)
Pooled Gold: 468.5 (+42.75 Gold per day)
Total Units: 7 Woodlings, 6 Firecracker Flowers, 2 Saakal
Cooldown: None

Unit Organisation

Town 1: Irvine, 2 Woodlings, 2 Firecracker Flower

Town 2: 1 Firecracker Flower, 1 Woodling

Army 1: Braskar, 1 Firecracker Flower, 1 Saakal

Army 2: 2 Woodlings, 2 Firecracker Flowers, 1 Saakal (en-route)

Village 1: 1 Woodling

Village 2: 1 Woodling

Town 1 Status Report

In Production: (None)

Structures Completed: Grove, Road, Stall (II), Ranged Copse, Harbour, Village #2 – Watch Tower, Blacksmith, Fishing Dock

Structures Available: Grove (II), Basic Greenhouse, Watch Tower, Tavern, Marketplace, Ranged Copse (II), Stone Harbour, Shipyard, Trading Post, Temple, Blacksmith (Upgrade), Fishing Wharf

Town 2 Status Report

In Production: None

Structures Completed: Den (II), Tavern, Wall, Temple, Stall (II)

Structures Available: Den (III), Javelin Range, Training House, Watch Tower, Blacksmith, Temple (II), Granary

Chapter 66

When it rained, it poured. Confirming production of the Greenhouse the next day was a quick and simple matter, though watching all five hundred of his hard-earned gold disappear with the click of a notification was a little painful. Still, it had begun and in twenty days he would know what it was that he had bought. This was what it must have felt like, buying something from a late-night shopping channel. Thinking and dreaming of how good the product you're purchasing would be, the anticipation of some marvel, even if you knew deep down it would be nowhere near as good as they had promised.

Of course, that had not been the only thing that'd happened that day. To start with, Braskar had yet to locate a new opponent. Over twenty days of travel back and forth had seen him confirm that the mountain range on the west continued into the distance. He had spent a few days moving along the range and even entering one pass, only to find it stymied by a lack of passage, all the while complaining about sore feet. The good news was that the mountain range at least meant that attacks from the west could be stopped if they ever figured out where the passes were.

On the other hand, other than a singular mountain he'd spotted almost due north of the second town and another series of mountains to the east, the majority of the land he'd found was comprised of flat plains or forest hexes.

Checking against the border of the mountains and traversing the hills had given hints that the mountain range might end eventually – or just have a passage – much further north. They'd had quite the debate if he should verify that, but in the end, the orc had then shifted east, moving across the plains through forest and then plains and then more forest in search of additional trouble. It was when he was in the northeast – as oriented from the second town – that the orc finally ran into trouble.

***

The snap of wings opening was the only indication of a coming attack. Braskar threw himself backwards moments before large claws reached out to grab at him. Even as fast as he moved, the edges of those claws ripped along the edges of his armour, sending a long screech through the air. Hitting the ground hard, Braskar still managed to roll over and come up with his knife, his axe slung over his back in a bad position for easy retrieval at that moment.

His own attack had just been the precursor, for all around him, the snap of wings and the screech of their enemies resounded. The cry was strange, like an orc trying to imitate a bird, which was not too surprising when one considered their attackers. Braskar knew, instinctively, these were harpies, though he had never seen them before. A piece of information granted to him after his death, which would have been distracting if he was not in a fight for his life.

Even so, staring at the attackers, Braskar could not help but catalogue their features. Creatures with arms extending from the back that were covered in feathers and ended with long clawed fingers. Not actual feet, but bird feet beneath, tucked up under a shorter torso and large tail-feather plumage at the back. Those clawed feet were being used to great effect as they grasped and tore at the firecracker flowers.

Clear sap flowed from deep wounds, some of the harpies having landed on the ground and using their clawed fingers to strike at their targets. Others were hovering in mid-air, desperately flapping their arms as they attempted to kick and tear at their opponents. As always, the wood elementals were unnervingly silent in their struggles, leaving the all too mortal noises to others.

In this case, that included the saakal. Returning from scouting ahead, the group ran on all fours to rejoin the battle. Soon enough, they'd close in on the harpies and launch themselves with their Charge ability. However, they were not as quick as the firecracker flowers. The explosions from their water-generated ranged attacks sent seeds spiralling out of their arms. They were deafening, causing Braskar's ears to ache. The flowers leaned backwards as they attacked, seeds flying through the air to pierce flesh and feathers alike.

Harpies dropped, some thrown off bodies by surprise or a lucky blow, others flapping desperately as their wings were pierced or they attempted to dodge. On the ground, the charging saakal met the few that stalked forward with ferocity, tearing into them and leaving nothing but a mess of blood and feathers.

A few remaining members of the unit lifted off, gaining altitude quickly as they dodged the explosion of flying seeds. One dropped, peppered so badly it could no longer keep itself aloft. However, two of those members survived, leaving the range of the firecracker flowers and winging off into the distance. Any of the creatures that stayed on the ground were lost, torn apart with ease.

Braskar stared at his unbloodied knife before he sheathed it angrily. Trained eyes roamed his own units, finding that he had lost only three members of the firecracker flowers. There was other damage, a long claw mark on a saakal, an arm torn off.

Not a bad result, all things considered.

So why was he furious still?

***

"Twelve units. You're sure?" Matt was saying later after Braskar had filled him in.

"I am, my lord. Ten fallen to my people, two who managed to retreat," Braskar said. "Three firecracker flowers lost."

"Good job," Matt muttered absently as he stared at the information.

Battle Report (Hero Braskar vs Enemy Unit)
Result: Victory! 1 Unit Escaped
Rewards: +0 Gold, +1 Reputation

"No gold this time," Matt said. "I wonder if that's because we didn't destroy the unit entirely?"

"It stands to reason, my lord."

"And we know units regenerate, right?" Matt said slowly.

"Yes, my lord."

"Crap."

"My lord?"

"You might want to pull back," Matt replied.

Braskar stayed silent at first, Matt allowing the orc time to catch up. He had realised the warlord liked to come to his own conclusions. "You fear they will conduct hit and run tactics, wearing my people down? I do not believe that is as much of a concern as you believe."

"They have more individuals per unit than you."

"But are more fragile," Braskar grunted. "If we retreat now, it only allows them to roam unopposed. Better to hunt down their city. And we have the Woodling coming."

"However, you can't hurt them but they can you. If they keep rotating units out, they'll slowly win. Depending on how many they have, this could be bad. This time around, they hit all of you. Next time, they might focus on your ranged units. And"

"I do not believe they can target so carefully. Not without a Hero."

"No guarantee they won't arrive either."

"Are you ordering me back, my lord?"

Now Matt had to hesitate. Arguing pros and cons with Braskar was one thing, but in the end, the question was whether to listen to the Warlord's instincts and push ahead or pull back? He knew Braskar was aggressive and he himself a little defensive.

How much was too much? At what point did he have to just accept that being aggressive was the way to go?

"Fine. Keep going. But I'm sending another unit of my firecracker flowers after you," Matt said.

"Very well, my lord."

Funny how Braskar sounded so happy to have nearly been killed. Still, the matter was resolved. If the harpies were as weak as mentioned, this might be an easy battle.

Of course, that was before the next problem cropped up later that evening.

***

Global Status Report

Day 70 (Middle of Day)

Pooled Gold: 11.25 (+42.75 Gold per day)

Total Units: 7 Woodlings, 6 Firecracker Flowers, 2 Saakal

Cooldown: None

Unit Organisation

Town 1: Irvine, 2 Woodlings, 1 Firecracker Flower

Town 2: 1 Firecracker Flower (en-route from Town 1), 1 Woodling

Army 1: Braskar, 1 Firecracker Flower, 1 Saakal, 1 Firecracker Flower (en-route from Town 2)

Army 2: 2 Woodlings, 2 Firecracker Flowers, 1 Saakal

Village 1: 1 Woodling

Village 2: 1 Woodling

Town 1 Status Report

In Production: Basic Greenhouse (0/20)

Structures Completed: Grove, Road, Stall (II), Ranged Copse, Harbour, Village #2 – Watch Tower, Blacksmith, Fishing Dock

Structures Available: Grove (II), Watch Tower, Tavern, Marketplace, Ranged Copse (II), Stone Harbour, Shipyard, Trading Post, Temple, Blacksmith (Upgrade), Fishing Wharf

Town 2 Status Report

In Production: None

Structures Completed: Den (II), Tavern, Wall, Temple, Stall (II)

Structures Available: Den (III), Javelin Range, Training House, Watch Tower, Blacksmith, Temple (II), Granary

Chapter 67

It came, of course, from the east. Matt had not noticed the issue until he'd checked in later that night, only to stare down at the new hex blinking at him. He leaned forwards, poking at the details, and watched as information on a third village popped up. There were tiny pennants on the graphic of the village, not the grey-brown of what Matt had labeled as neutral but a dark brown with a slash of red in-between.

"What do you think?" Matt said softly. "This the source of the attacks?"

"Looks like it," Irvine said, arms crossed. He leaned forward, as though getting closer would provide more information. "Those cavalry units seem to be the same."

"They are," Matt said, gesturing to call up the unit information.

Type: Raider Unit

Tier: Lesser Tier I

Number: 12

Movement: 2

Melee Attack: High / Very Low

Melee Defense: Low

Ranged Attack: None

Ranged Defense: Low

Hit Points: Low

Speed: High

Special Abilities: Charge, Unknown

Vulnerabilities: Unknown

"The fact that they have militia units to back them up isn't great though," Matt said.

"Militias are no concern," Braskar rumbled.

"Not the ones you fought. But these guys are upgraded."

Type: Militia Unit (II)

Tier: Lesser Tier II

Number: 8

Movement: 1

Melee Attack: Low

Melee Defense: Low

Ranged Attack: Very Low

Ranged Defense: Low

Hit Points: Low

Speed: Medium

Special Abilities: Unknown

Vulnerabilities: Unknown

"They have a ranged attack?" Braskar said, surprised.

"Yes. I'd guess crude bows or slings of some form. Maybe a mix even," Matt offered. Wasn't as though he could tell, not from the information given to him. "Nothing too worrisome."

"Except there's two of those units and two raiders," Irvine said. "Doesn't seem like a fight worth taking on."

"We could still win…" Matt said slowly. "I can't believe our units, upgraded and more numerous, couldn't beat them."

"Agreed," Braskar rumbled. "Five units against four? Should not even be an argument."

"Even if they have a lousy post fence defense helping them," Matt said. He was kinda jealous of that, actually. Stakes driven into the ground, covering the entrance, were not the most innovative defensive encirclement, but since they were all tied together by poles, it did require his units to either jump them or hack them down. Either that or be funneled into a kill zone.

Better than his own makeshift attempts at least. Though he might look into making some of these himself.

"So what's the problem?" Irvine said.

"No problem, I guess." Matt shook his head. "But why did this village improve and upgrade but not Village 2? Did we just hit this one too late? That doesn't seem right. The raiders have always been there."

"Perhaps the raiders were destroyed by our enemy?" Braskar offered. "And we just missed them."

"Perhaps." Now Matt felt bad for not checking the militia unit that Braskar had fought. They'd rolled over them so easily that he hadn't gone into the details. "Or maybe this one was always designated as a little tougher?"

"It's possible." Irvine shrugged. "The ways of this world are strange and different after all."

Braskar rumbled his agreement, and Matt sighed. "Truth. So we hit it tomorrow, grab another village, and then, what? Keep sending more units north?"

"That seems the most prudent option, my lord."

"No objections here. If you're done…" Irvine glanced out the door, obviously impatient to leave.

Matt waved the man away, already making notes about other options so he could think them over again. This seemed like the right choice to make. So why did he feel so worried?

***

No surprise that Matt spent the whole of the next day wandering back and forth inside the tactics room. Map room. He still hadn't chosen a term for it, though control room seemed apt. Even so, the one thing the room at the top of his keep had was a lack of entertainment. Once again, Matt found himself longing for the mind-numbing balm of app games, clicking his way through hours of spirit-destroying existence. Though such luxuries might waste one's life away, it was perfect for times like this when distraction was all too desired.

It was after a dismal lunch – one where the meal tasted like cardboard – that the army finally clashed with the village. Matt could only watch the flashes on his board, reading the obtuse information that trickled in as woodling and firecracker flower unit members died.

He could have taken action, used one of the spells that were his only method of interacting with a battle. But each use put him on a lengthy cooldown. If his concerns about attacks on Braskar held out, it could very well be that the orc would need his aid soon enough.

Though even that was limited. He could heal the Warlord, but the damn Lightning Bolt technique was constrained by the distance between himself – or the towns he owned, he was yet to ascertain that – and the Heroes.

"Nothing to do but watch, which is just…" Matt sighed. "It was a lot easier when the damn sprites were just sprites and not actual units. And the biggest penalty was that I had to reload a saved game."

No answer, because of course there wouldn't be.

More unit members fell, then, as suddenly as it began, a new notification appeared.

Battle Report (Army 2 vs Village Militia)
Result: Victory! 0 Units Lost, 4 Units Defeated

Rewards: +6 Gold, +1 Reputation, Control of Village #3

Matt automatically flicked away the request for him to name the village. There wasn't much new in the conquest of the village, though there was something interesting when he brought up the new build options. He had to admit, he was curious.

New Build Options Available

- **Road (10/+0.25 Gold/increased movement speed by 50%)**
- **Watch Tower (15/+1 hex view)**
- **Horse Farm (50/Access to new building upgrades)**

"Damn. Horse Farm it is!" Matt muttered. That was an easy option to purchase, what with the potential for cavalry. How cavalry and his wood elemental build would work together though, Matt had no idea, but he was looking forward to finding out.

If, that was, it actually worked.

On the other hand…

"And a Road too, I think…" Matt muttered to himself. His town was a little weak right now, but again, the concerns were only if they managed to punch through his army. So, better to spend money linking it up and reduce the amount of time he needed for reinforcements than worry about potential new enemies. He'd also start a new woodling when he had the money tomorrow, just to bolster his army. That or send it off to the new village.

He'd see. Just depended on what the enemy chose. The enemy he had yet to find.

***

Global Status Report

Day 71 (End of Day)

Pooled Gold: 0 (+43.75 Gold per day)

Total Units: 7 Woodlings, 6 Firecracker Flowers, 2 Saakal

Cooldown: None

Unit Organisation

Town 1: Irvine, 2 Woodlings, 1 Firecracker Flower

Town 2: 1 Firecracker Flower (en-route from Town 1), 1 Woodling

Army 1: Braskar, 1 Firecracker Flower, 1 Saakal, 1 Firecracker

Flower (en-route from Town 2)

Village 1: 1 Woodling

Village 2: 1 Woodling

Village 3: 2 Woodlings, 2 Firecracker Flowers, 1 Saakal

Town 1 Status Report

In Production: Basic Greenhouse (1/20), Village #3 – Horse Farm (0/7), Road to Village #3 (0/3)

Structures Completed: Grove, Road, Stall (II), Ranged Copse, Harbour, Village #2 – Watch

Tower, Blacksmith, Fishing Dock

Structures Available: Grove (II), Watch Tower, Tavern, Marketplace, Ranged Copse (II), Stone Harbour, Shipyard, Trading Post, Temple, Blacksmith (Upgrade), Fishing Wharf

Town 2 Status Report

In Production: None

Structures Completed: Den (II), Tavern, Wall, Temple, Stall (II)

Structures Available: Den (III), Javelin Range, Training House, Watch Tower, Blacksmith, Temple (II), Granary

Chapter 68

"Braskar, why exactly are you heading further north without more backup?" Matt asked crossly. At first, he thought the orc had just been moving around, checking nearby. That had covered the first day. Even two. Three days later, it was quite clear that the orc had no intention to slow his search for their new enemy.

"It will take too long for reinforcements to arrive," Braskar said firmly.

"We have roads built," Matt said. "It'll take half the time to get there."

"Still at a minimum another six days, depending on where I am." Braskar shook his head. "And saakal, if you even sent some, would be useless. We need ranged fighters."

"I can buy those… I'm planning on buying those," Matt protested. It was entirely the reason he hadn't bothered making more saakal right now, instead reserving the gold for the ranged saakal units when he had enough. Of course, it would take two hundred gold to do that, so at best he had another four days before it was possible.

He did consider picking up more gold-producing buildings, but the need for troops that could deal with the harpies and were closer to the vector of attacks was causing him to reconsider that. A four or five day difference in a troop being created could mean all the difference. It was why adding ranged units to Town 2 had suddenly become important.

Troop logistics, who knew it would be so important?

"I understand, my lord. But in the meantime, our enemies have a chance to regroup. The last attack was plain enough," Braskar said. "I believe the enemy is low on combatants too."

"Because you had two scouts attack you instead of, like, five?" Matt said. "You know, they might just be luring you in. And you lost a lot more units that time."

"Two firecracker flower saplings and a saakal pup is not that significant."

"Saplings? Pup?"

"I felt it was better to designate some terminology to individual units."

Made sense, of course. Didn't make Matt any less upset. "You don't have any backup either in terms of potions."

"Understood. If I believe we are in danger, I will retreat. But pushing ahead is my recommendation, my lord."

Matt pursed his lips and looked over to Irvine, who had been quiet thus far. "What do you think, man?"

"That I have nothing useful to add to such discussions," Irvine said. "Push or don't. The orc is always going to charge. You must make the decision."

"And what do you think?"

"I think you have been forgetting your other options," Irvine said.

"I've looked over all the build and unit options repeatedly." Matt crossed his arms. "We just don't have that many choices with the gold we have."

"I was not speaking of units or buildings."

"Then…" Matt trailed off, realizing what Irvine was speaking of. "The Hero."

"The Priest."

"I…" Matt hesitated, considering. There was a lot to be said about getting a Priest. For one thing, their ability to heal units would be a significant advantage. So why did he hesitate?

Memories. Of calling death from the sky. Of screams and a flash of light, the roar of thunder. A body smoking in the distance, a body that had been alive and living and moving a short moment ago. His first true kill…

His first…

"My lord?" Braskar's voice rumbled, bringing Matt back to the present. He blinked, realizing that Irvine was looking at him, face filled with concern and compassion.

"I…"

"It won't be the same person," Irvine said softly. "They won't even be here…"

"I know that," Matt said firmly. Or tried to, but his voice came out weak. He hated how he sounded, but guilt clutched at him, reminding him of what he had done. Killing someone should not have been that easy, should not have been so simple. There should have been something more, some payment, some effort. It should have been harder.

Then again, he had died once before. Perhaps there wasn't a hell to send him to anymore because he was there already.

If this was hell, it was a little tacky.

"You're… right. We could use a Healer. Priest." Matt shook his head. "I'll… look at it later."

"It is not necessarily the best option," Braskar added. "More ranged units close by would also be advantageous, my lord."

"In the future, yes. Not as much as a Priest healing you immediately, I think." Matt hesitated, trying to run the scenarios through his mind. He couldn't get the math to come up right. "I… think. I'll try to game out the scenarios and math a bit maybe?"

"Do not forget levels," Irvine said, smirking. "As we get more experience, we can do more."

"Oh?" Grabbing at any distraction, Matt focused on Irvine. "You have something to say? A new level?"

"Not yet. But close." Irvine reached into his jacket and pulled out a potion, pushing the purple liquid towards Matt. "I have, however, a new potion."

"Ooooh!" Matt grabbed at it, holding the potion up and watching the information flash upwards.

Item: Potion of Greater Strength
Use: +5 Melee Attack

"Oh, very nice," Matt said.

"What is?" Braskar grumbled, not being able to see anything, of course. Matt let Irvine crow about his success, a factor that made the orc add, "I am nearing my own level increase, my lord. A few more battles and I too shall be stronger."

"Balanced accounts!" Then Matt frowned. "Is that why you're pushing so hard?"

"It is not!" Braskar sounded offended. "There are good reasons for my decisions." There was a slight hesitation before he added, "Though more levels are not not a consideration."

"I see…"

"It's for the overall good, my lord!"

"Which is why a Priest earlier rather than later is important, boy." Irvine leaned in. "I'd bet that Heroes will be what make the difference in our battles in the future."

"More than units?"

"Aye." Irvine crossed his arms. "If not, why even have us? You could fight all this with just your units. They added us for a reason."

"Could be they just like resurrecting and torturing us." Matt cocked his head to the side. "You know, we still don't know why you two. Or why your histories are so different."

Unfortunately, both Heroes admitted to no further knowledge on that matter. Matt was, he admitted privately to himself, beginning to suspect some degree of mental manipulation by the gods who'd recreated them. But…

Even if he suspected that, what could he do?

Not a whole lot from the way he saw it. Other than what he was doing now, which was trying to win the game. And that meant…

"Fine. Take your risk, Braskar, but be smart. Don't push too far ahead of the Priest and my reinforcement. But if you think you can take out more of those harpies or find their keep, so be it."

"Thank you, my lord."

"And you." A finger rose and pointed at Irvine. "Crank out some more of those potions. We're going to need them and whatever level up you get."

"Don't tell me how to distill potions, boy. I know."

Matt snorted, then leaned back, staring at the tactical map that hovered before him. "Now let's just hope that nothing else shows up in the meantime."

***

Global Status Report

Day 74 (Start of Day)

Pooled Gold: 111.25 (+43.75 Gold per day)

Total Units: 7 Woodlings, 6 Firecracker Flowers, 2 Saakal

Cooldown: None

Unit Organisation

Town 1: Irvine, 2 Woodling, 1 Firecracker Flower

Town 2: 1 Firecracker Flower, 1 Woodling

Army 1: Braskar, 1 Firecracker Flower, 1 Saakal, 1 Firecracker Flower (en-route from Town 2)

Village 1: 1 Woodling

Village 2: 1 Woodling

Village 3: 2 Woodlings, 2 Firecracker Flowers, 1 Saakal

Town 1 Status Report

In Production: Basic Greenhouse (4/20), Village #3 – Horse Farm (3/7), Woodling (2/4)

Structures Completed: Grove, Road, Stall (II), Ranged Copse, Harbour, Village #2 – Watch Tower, Blacksmith, Fishing Dock, Road to Village #3 (3/3)

Structures Available: Grove (II), Watch Tower, Tavern, Marketplace, Ranged Copse (II), Stone Harbour, Shipyard, Trading Post, Temple, Blacksmith (Upgrade), Fishing Wharf

Town 2 Status Report

In Production: None

Structures Completed: Den (II), Tavern, Wall, Temple, Stall (II)

Structures Available: Den (III), Javelin Range, Training House, Watch Tower, Blacksmith, Temple (II), Granary

Chapter 69

The last thing a general ever wants to fight is a two-front war. Well, except maybe a four-front war. But since Matt was facing only two, he was going to accept that what he had was just really bad luck overall. Which, considering he was killed by aliens when he foolishly accepted a pronouncement in his head during an existential crisis, was just about the right speed.

Knowing he was unlucky did nothing for the unappealing fact that an army had shown up the next morning right on the edge of Village 3's vision, which was two hexes away from it.

At least Matt wasn't mentally complaining about the lack of coffee anymore. The shot of adrenaline that he'd received when he'd seen the army after wandering in this morning had substituted just fine.

Just. Fine.

Enemy Army Sighted!
Quantity: 3 Units

"Any idea why we can see unit quantities now when we couldn't before?" Matt muttered, quietly hoping that Braskar or Irvine would know.

"The Watch Tower?" Irvine offered.

"The keep upgrade," Braskar said.

"Yeah, those are my two guesses too," Matt said. "Unfortunately, no way to tell which one it was at this time. What I'd do to be able to RTFM. I'll never complain about reading a manual again."

"Manual, my lord?"

"A book of instructions."

"Ponderous and slow."

"And prone to errors," Irvine said, shaking his head. "You cannot believe the number of mistakes I find in even supposedly well-written alchemy texts."

"Not that kind of manual," Matt said, then paused. "Though you're both not wrong."

"The enemy, my lord."

"I know, I know. But I'm not sure there's much we can do." Matt waved his hand at the table. "We could try to meet them, but we can only move a single hex. If they choose to meet us, great. If they're fast-moving like the saakal, they could choose to avoid us. If they're smart, they might even try to lure us away from the village."

"For what reason, my lord?" Braskar asked. "The villages only provide a small increase in gold. Though the increased view is useful…"

"There's that. But I've also been wondering…" Matt shook his head. "Tangent. The question is, what can I do?"

Braskar fell silent while Irvine poked at the images. He was trying to get more details from the map, but unfortunately, neither the notification nor the map provided further details. Matt could have told him that but figured the Alchemist needed something to do while the Warlord was thinking.

"I think your instincts are right, my lord. Wait to see how they act. If they try to bypass the village, you will at least know that and can act against them. With the new Road, you can return your army to the town first."

"Unless they're super fast, like a speeding bullet."

"My lord?"

Matt sighed but left it. "Watch Tower, you think?"

"In the new village to expand our coverage?"

When Matt confirmed, the orc rumbled his agreement. Watch Towers were not very expensive but did set their builds back. Still, at their low cost, the additional view they offered – even if they lost the village shortly after – was worth the trade-off. At the least, they'd be able to tell if the army was moving closer.

"How about the other village? The first one?" Irvine asked, curious.

"No point." Matt gestured to the map. "With one more from the Watch Tower, that puts Village 3's base surveillance to a three hexi radius. With the two Village 1 gets, we've got the entire area covered."

"And from the west?"

"Nothing's come from that way." Matt reached forward and rapped the table, just for luck.

"Yet," Irvine said.

Again, he struck the table. "Don't put up any more flags, will you?"

"What do you mean, boy?"

"Remind me to explain it later," Matt said, dismissing Irvine's question. "What do we do if they decide to avoid us entirely?"

"Do, my lord?"

"I'm trying to count hexes, see if we can get back in time. Annoying that Roads work for both sides." Matt really did wish that the system made Roads one-way. It'd make life simpler.

"I see."

Matt grunted, ignoring the comment. They were three days' movement from his own fort. However, to make use of his own Roads, they'd have to join them. Which, depending on how fast the other army was, might mean he couldn't catch them from behind.

The issue was more what they would do now and how effectively they might pin his forces down if he was intent on keeping the village in his control. If he left his army inside till he had enough to bolster the defences, he would be stuck once more.

Just as importantly, he only had four or five days left before the army arrived. Maybe less depending on how fast these new opponents could move. That meant that he'd need to consider what he could build. Saakal and firecracker flowers were five days each, which meant that in the worst case, they might be too late.

On the other hand, if he waited, he would have enough for a Hero in two days.

And, of course, the most important question, where the heck was the new enemy keep?

"If that is all," Irvine spoke up, breaking Matt's contemplations, "I'll get back to making potions."

"Yeah, you do that. And I'll..." Matt frowned.

"Watch the map and work out if there's anything else we can do?" Irvine said.

"I guess..." Matt let out a huff. He wished he could do more, but digging was right out. Or mostly out. He could maybe do about half an hour of that before his side ached so badly, he had to lie down and wait for the agony to fade. As for making crossbows...

Well, unless he could figure out how to get the blacksmith, who refused to interact with him, to actually provide real metal and not steal scraps, the crossbows he had were the best he could do. Now, he might, if he got particularly inventive, manage to Home Alone a bunch of them together to make additional traps, but contrary to movie expectations, such things were rather difficult to set up properly. And just as prone to hurt the trapper as the trappee.

Frankly, he'd be better off just building a giant hammer to smash into someone's face when they opened a door than to crank a crossbow, leave it loaded, and tie the trigger to an elaborate rope pulley system.

In fact…

"Boy, what are you thinking and smiling so evilly for?" Irvine said, bushy eyebrows drawn low.

"Nothing… nothing at all." Matt grinned.

"Uh huh. So long as it's no more of those crossbows or random traps. Remember, the servants aren't going to remember to step strangely just because you want them to. You're just lucky they don't clean up your scraps."

"Fine, fine…" Matt threw his hands up and then winced as the wound in his chest tugged tight. He lowered them again. He ignored the concerned looks the Alchemist gave him as he nursed his side. "I'll go do something else. Maybe build more movable obstacles or something."

"You do that. And keep thinking of what we can do, eh?" Irvine said.

"Yes, sir." Matt even threw a mocking salute as he watched the Alchemist disappear. He stared at the information for a moment longer, running the math. Just about enough… A quick flicker of his fingers and he added a firecracker flower to the queue.

Then he turned away to head for the stairs.

One way or another, he was going to find a way to be useful.

***

Global Status Report

Day 75 (End of Day)

Pooled Gold: 115.25 (+44 Gold per day)

Total Units: 7 Woodlings, 6 Firecracker Flowers, 2 Saakal

Cooldown: None

Unit Organisation

Town 1: Irvine, 2 Woodling, 1 Firecracker Flower

Town 2: 1 Firecracker Flower, 1 Woodling

Army 1: Braskar, 1 Firecracker Flower, 1 Saakal, 1 Firecracker Flower (en-route from Town 2)

Village 1: 1 Woodling

Village 2: 1 Woodling

Village 3: 2 Woodlings, 2 Firecracker Flowers, 1 Saakal

Town 1 Status Report

In Production: Basic Greenhouse (5/20), Village #3 – Horse Farm (4/7), Woodling (3/4), Village #3 – Watch Tower (0/1) Firecracker Flower (0/5)

Structures Completed: Grove, Road, Stall (II), Ranged Copse, Harbour, Village #2 – Watch Tower, Blacksmith, Fishing Dock, Road to Village #3

Structures Available: Grove (II), Watch Tower, Tavern, Marketplace, Ranged Copse (II), Stone Harbour, Shipyard, Trading Post, Temple, Blacksmith (Upgrade), Fishing Wharf

Town 2 Status Report

In Production: None

Structures Completed: Den (II), Tavern, Wall, Temple, Stall (II)

Structures Available: Den (III), Javelin Range, Training House, Watch Tower, Blacksmith, Temple (II), Granary

Chapter 70

"They're pinning us," Matt groused the very next day.

The moment the Watch Tower had appeared, Matt had been able to tell more details about the units that had appeared at the edge of his map. That had been the only good news of the day.

Enemy Army Sighted!
Quantity: 3 Cavalry Raiders

Through the rest of the morning, he had watched with bated breath for the enemy to move. When half the day had come and gone and the units had just stayed in the same spot, he knew for sure that they they had chosen not to shift locations.

Two hexes away from his village. Just far enough that Matt could not move his own units to meet them, not without them leading him on a wild goose chase. Too close for him to leave the village at all, because then they'd take it.

As it stood, if he tried to even chase them down, they had the option of reinforcing with more units from another direction. If he had saakal, he might have stood a chance, but his wood elemental army was just too slow.

"What do you think? Should I split my army?" Matt asked Braskar. The orc was quite a distance away now, nearly half again the size of his original map and seven days away from the second town, right next to a large lake. If not for the lake, Matt assumed the orc would have explored even further, going back and forth as he had, slowly revealing more and more of the land. Thus far though, he had yet to encounter another raiding party.

Maybe the orc had been right that their enemies had only a few units. That seemed strange to Matt, considering the sheer number of units he had acquired himself. Spread out, he had to admit, but his harpy enemy should have more. That sense of incongruity was why he wanted Braskar to hold off. If he kept pushing ahead and they launched an attack, there was nothing Matt would be able to do.

Especially since Braskar couldn't run very well.

"You could, my lord. But it would not be recommended," Braskar said. "We know not the strength of those cavalry units. If they are significantly upgraded, they could win against the smaller part of your army. Perhaps even the bigger."

"If they're upgraded," Matt pointed out.

"Yes."

Staring at the stone roof and wooden buttresses, Matt worried his lip before looking down. He had a way of checking, one that the opponents could not stop. But it would mean he'd lose the unit, something he preferred not to happen.

On the other hand… knowing the strength of his enemy might well be worth it.

"What if I let out one of my units as bait?" Matt said. "The saakal or a woodling would work if they chose to attack."

"To ascertain the strength of their army?" Braskar hesitated. "Certainly a viable option. Though you will lose the unit, and we've stopped producing saakal already."

"For the Priest, yes." Matt sighed. "I still don't see a way around it. If this army is significantly upgraded, it'll be necessary to reinforce our army. I already have the woodling that I just made on its way, but that's not enough, especially if we need to reinforce."

"It is a risk, I agree." Braskar fell silent and Matt waited for his analysis. "Use the saakal."

"Why?"

"We know units can retreat. If we can have them engage and then retreat…"

"That's assuming I can give the command to the saakal in time," Matt replied. "That assumes I can even get the information in time before the battle is over."

"True, my lord. But I have faith in you."

Matt grunted, but after a moment's further thought, he triggered the saakal to move forward the next day. If he did this right, he'd force a battle with the hostile army.

"About your reinforcements," Matt said once that was done.

"Yes, my lord?"

"You should get the second firecracker flower in the next few days. I'm debating how to move the second Hero. Assuming they're already present and come out immediately, I can either strip the town further or send them alone. Thoughts?"

"Reinforcements would be good."

"Agreed, but I don't have anyone. So I best get to building more firecracker flowers. Maybe turn the second one back and have them meet in the middle?"

"A wise decision."

It amused Matt that they were smart enough to be given a simple order like 'join with first army,' while at other times, the system seemed incredibly dumb. He'd have to forcefully group the Hero and the unit, but he debated pulling even more units from the second town.

He'd have to decide tomorrow how much he was willing to risk things.

Fighting a two-front war sucked.

***

Braskar sighed, staring at the lapping waters of the lake. He thought, if he squinted hard enough, he could see the other side of the watery impediment. It was not a massive lake, unlike the other one he had once found. This one ran north to south, forcing him to skirt sideways. He'd decided to follow it northward to see where these harpies might be coming from.

All indication was that they'd come from north of him somewhere. At first, he'd thought north-east, but now, he assumed it was just north. Unless the opponent was purposely throwing him off by sending the scouts north first before breaking east or west or even around.

Frustrating that he didn't have a better method of watching for enemy units. Perhaps another Hero might have some ability to do so, but for him, he was locked to only seeing a single hex away from his unit.

It was another reason he wanted the harpy town. If they could conquer that, not only would they gain a significant advantage in gold production, but they'd also finally have aerial scouts. The Warlord in him salivated at the thought.

The saakal were good but too fragile. Too easily destroyed. Much like those cavalry raiders down south.

Braskar wondered what kind of unit mix his lord might face. If the land to the east was mostly plains, then cavalry and other mounted units would be very dangerous. Assuming they had a proper general or Warlord in charge, his lord might not even be able to force a fight. Perhaps he should suggest upgrading their firecracker flowers – or even acquiring the long-range versions of their units.

Doing so, of course, meant that they wouldn't be able to acquire the saakal's equivalent of a long-range team. What they might be, he did not know. Perhaps it was something he should push his lord to review. However, such action was potentially dangerous.

He had noticed that his lord had a tendency to get distracted all too easily by a new building or unit. Whatever interested him at the time was what he often chose to focus upon, which made him highly adaptable on one hand. Unfortunately, that also left him and Irvine scrambling at times to keep track of what his lord was thinking of next. And worst of all, it meant that previously good plans and strategies were discarded in lieu of the next bright idea.

Like his initial plan for a lot of small units – his zerg rush – that had now become building out lots of gold-producing areas and a Hero. Of course, Braskar understood that gold producers were required, but somehow, it seemed that his lord should have been more focused.

He thought for a moment longer before reaching out to his lord again.

"My lord."

"Braskar?" Matt answered immediately. "What's up?"

"I wonder, could the numbers we see of the harpies and the cavalry… Is it because they are more expensive?"

Silence from the other end. Braskar waited patiently as he walked along the lakeside with his army. He kept half an eye on the water, the other half on the skies. The saakal were also closer to his main units now rather than ranging far out front.

"Makes sense," Matt said slowly. "I don't think there's a way to tell, but it's possible that the harpy scouts are the cheapest units. And still probably expensive." Drumming noise, presumably from fingers playing on a wooden table, came across the link. "If that's the case, expect their actual units to hit harder."

"Stronger but more expensive and faster?" Braskar frowned. "This seems like an unfair advantage when one includes their ability to fly."

"Yeah. Maybe not all those things, except the expensive. They might be slower and more heavily armoured or something. I'm imagining armoured harpies, which is…" Matt trailed off. "Well, kinda cool. I wish I could see that."

"I'm sure you will, my lord."

"So long as they're on my side." Softer, quieter, he repeated the sentence.

Braskar ignored the whispered words. It was likely his lord did not expect him to hear them, nor would he shame the young warrior in that manner. Fear of death was nothing to be shameful of, though many young warriors refused to take the wisdom of their elders.

They would learn soon enough.

Even the mightiest warrior cried.

Even the greatest died.

***

Global Status Report
Day 76 (Start of Day)
Pooled Gold: 159.25 (+44 Gold per day)
Total Units: 8 Woodlings, 6 Firecracker Flowers, 2 Saakal
Cooldown: None

Unit Organisation
Town 1: Irvine, 2 Woodlings, 1 Firecracker Flower
Town 2: 1 Firecracker Flower, 1 Woodling

Army 1: Braskar, 1 Firecracker Flower, 1 Saakal, 1 Firecracker Flower (en-route from Town 2)

Village 1: 1 Woodling

Village 2: 1 Woodling

Village 3: 2 Woodlings, 2 Firecracker Flowers, 1 Saakal, 1 Woodling (en-route from Town 1)

Town 1 Status Report

In Production: Basic Greenhouse (6/20), Village #3 – Horse Farm (5/7), Firecracker Flower (1/5)

Structures Completed: Grove, Road, Stall (II), Ranged Copse, Harbour, Village #2 – Watch Tower, Blacksmith, Fishing Dock, Road to Village #3, Village #3 – Watch Tower

Structures Available: Grove (II), Watch Tower, Tavern, Marketplace, Ranged Copse (II), Stone Harbour, Shipyard, Trading Post, Temple, Blacksmith (Upgrade), Fishing Wharf

Town 2 Status Report

In Production: None

Structures Completed: Den (II), Tavern, Wall, Temple, Stall (II)

Structures Available: Den (III), Javelin Range, Training House, Watch Tower, Blacksmith, Temple (II), Granary

Chapter 71

It was early morning the next day and Matt was up at the tactics room, eager to see what had transpired overnight. He knew, of course, but he still scanned the map for any additional problems. Not that he expected them, not immediately. If someone was moving in, unless he'd missed it late at night, they'd only appear midday at best on the map.

No, that wasn't the reason he was up early.

What he was looking forward to was buying the Priest. Hiring them. Initial fear was washed over with the anticipation of a dopamine hit from going shopping. A quick check on the Tavern had him pause for a moment before he remembered that that was not where he picked up Priests. Still, now that he had the notification open, he paused to look it over just in case he had more slots.

No such luck.

Name: Tavern

Building Type: Hero Managements

Tier: Lesser Tier I

Heroes Available to Recruit: Warrior, Ranger

Number of Available Hero Slots: 1

Though the available Heroes had him blinking.

"Huh. They changed." Matt stared at the pair of options. The Warrior was quite clear – they had already run into one before. Individually stronger than the Warlord, but without the unit control that Warlords were able to provide. Weighing the two, Matt preferred a Warlord like Braskar over a plain Warrior.

Perhaps when he had more Hero slots, but he needed generals, not soldiers, right now.

That was probably the same problem with the Ranger. If they were at all like the Dungeons and Dragons class or even Sir Tolkien's work, individually they were strong, but mostly as scouting units. Not particularly useful in this case.

"Though, if I get Aragorn, I bet I could make him glower at the female Heroes and they'd be all 'oh, Aragorn, please ravage me with your stringy, unwashed hair and manly, manly scruff.'"

Perhaps Matt had issues with the character after a particular bad college relationship, when his ex had complained about his lack of facial hair and had compared him to said ranger. Like, how was he supposed to compete against an imaginary and perfect king?

Well, in that case, the answer had been not at all.

Yeah, no Ranger for him. For a lot of reasons.

"Priest, Priest, Priest. Time to grab a Priest," Matt said softly to himself. A flicker of his fingers and the Temple was called up. No changes there, so confirming the purchase was quick. Two hundred gold disappeared out of his treasury in moments and a new notification came up.

The first of its kind in a while.

Lasya (Level 1 Acolyte)
Specialty: Theology
Skills: Aura of Inspiration, Minor Healing
Experience: 0/100

Attack: 09

Defense: 07

Power: 14

Knowledge: 19

"Damn, those are good stats," Matt said, eyeing the numbers. "Though… the skills are different? Didn't the other one have things like curses and healing?"

No answer. He could poke at Irvine to get an answer. The man had a better memory than him. But it didn't matter. After all, he had something more important to do, especially as he eyed the portrait that came with all the information. The Priest – who was a female, it seemed – was cute in the stern, soil-muddled way of her skin and dark hair.

"Lasya."

"Sir." Her voice was silky smooth, a lilt to it that suited her skin. He'd call her Indian or Pakistani or something from that portion of Earth, but if things carried out…

"How are you doing? How did you know to appear on my map?"

"Appear, sir?" She sounded puzzled now. "I was in the Temple. Serving the… the…" She trailed off, confused. "I… no. I was on the field, tending to the sick, during the battle. And then…"

"You can remember your past?" Matt said, surprised. "Your death?"

"Yes… no." She struggled for a moment, her voice pained. "I remember the field but not my end. I remember the line breaking, the men charging, and that was it. No more."

"I see. And your arrival?"

"I just remember being in the Temple. That time, it's hazy. Like I wasn't really there, just… drifting through my days."

Matt gulped, leaning back. He stared at the door where a servant came by every once in a while. How they drifted through the keep, taking care of the basic tasks, feeding, chopping wood, cleaning. He could not help but wonder if each of those servants was just like Lasya.

How many of them were just… drifting… until called upon? Some of them? All of them? Were the militias that were being sent out to fight his own units – were his own units – made up of real individuals too? Just not called upon, not real, because they were not needed yet?

"Sir?"

Matt blinked, shaken out of his contemplations. "I'm sorry, what?"

"Do you have orders for me, sir?" Lasya said. "Why did you call me?"

"I…" Matt shook his head, pushing his thoughts aside. He could not say how many of those here were Heroes-to-be. He believed, had to believe for his sanity, that not all of them were like that. That most were just mindless automata.

And if that was a lie, he was still going to believe it. Because otherwise, well… Otherwise he wouldn't be able to function.

That was the human condition, wasn't it? Lying to oneself to function?

"I'll send the orders through the map, but I want you to meet up with one of my other Heroes. Braskar." Matt hesitated then added, "He's an orc."

"A what?" Lasya said.

"Orc. Brown-skinned, tusks. Big fella. My Warlord." Matt exhaled. "Just wanted to warn you."

"I… see. A demon, but on our side?"

"I wouldn't call him that."

"Of course, sir."

"We've got a harpy problem – flying units, raiders so far – but we're worried there might be more. We want you to link up, find the fort or keep or whatever they're using, and take it," Matt said.

"I can do that, sir," Lasya said. "Do I leave now?"

"In a second. You should meet your fellow Heroes."

"Of course, sir. I look forward to it."

Somehow, Matt actually believed that she did. Disoriented or not, there was a gentleness and kindness to her voice. Or perhaps he was just hoping for it. After all, she was the first female he'd met here who wasn't trying to kill him.

***

Global Status Report

Day 77 (End of Day)

Pooled Gold: 3.25 (+44 Gold per day)

Total Units: 8 Woodlings, 6 Firecracker Flowers, 2 Saakal

Cooldown: None

Unit Organisation

Town 1: Irvine, 2 Woodling, 1 Firecracker Flower

Town 2: 1 Firecracker Flower, 1 Woodling, Lasya

Army 1: Braskar, 1 Firecracker Flower, 1 Saakal, 1 Firecracker Flower (en-route from Town 2)

Village 1: 1 Woodling

Village 2: 1 Woodling

Village 3: 2 Woodlings, 2 Firecracker Flowers, 1 Saakal, 1 Woodling (en-route from Town 1)

Town 1 Status Report

In Production: Basic Greenhouse (7/20), Village #3 – Horse Farm (6/7), Firecracker Flower (2/5)

Structures Completed: Grove, Road, Stall (II), Ranged Copse, Harbour, Village #2 – Watch Tower, Blacksmith, Fishing Dock, Road to Village #3, Village #3 – Watch Tower

Structures Available: Grove (II), Watch Tower, Tavern, Marketplace, Ranged Copse (II), Stone Harbour, Shipyard, Trading Post, Temple, Blacksmith (Upgrade), Fishing Wharf

Town 2 Status Report

In Production: None

Structures Completed: Den (II), Tavern, Wall, Temple, Stall (II)

Structures Available: Den (III), Javelin Range, Training House, Watch Tower, Blacksmith, Temple (II), Granary

Chapter 72

Mid-afternoon the next day, he was upstairs, biting his lip. He was wondering what would happen when the saakal met the enemy units. It also might answer some questions on how this world worked, at least in terms of non-Hero-controlled units.

For example, he had given orders for the saakal from Village #3 to exit and charge his opponents the night before. That meant that in the morning, they had exited the village and moved to the first hex throughout the first hours of the day. They were loping well ahead.

Now, the question was, did his opponent have to set up their orders beforehand? Were they watching his units so that they could, in the middle of the morning when it was clear that the saakal were coming out, back their own units off?

Or did he have to do it the day before or at the start of the day? Exactly when could they get this information and when could they make use of it? Obviously, the answer only came if they actually took action. If they stood there and accepted the saakal's charge, he'd have no new information. He didn't know if they could make decisions on the fly, could only do so when someone was watching – and no one was – or could only do so when a Hero was present.

Impossible to prove a negative, which was aggravating. Of course, he knew what he could do theoretically. He'd seen the option to alter the choices for the saakal mid-day, which was why he always tried to get up here just before noon so that he could make adjustments if necessary.

Then again, it wasn't as important for him. He only had one unit type that could move two hexes a turn. His opponent on the other hand seemed entirely made up of cavalry. Which meant they should, if they were forced to deal with the same constraints, be up in their tower.

Assuming they were constrained in the same way.

Too many damn questions, no manual. Pretty much the human existence really, though when there were meant to be random and arbitrary rules, there should at least be a manual. It was ever more aggravating without one.

All of which meant that Matt could only watch, leaning against the table, drumstick for lunch in hand, and wait. It didn't take that long for the time to pass. The saakal appeared on the other side of the hex and his opponents disappeared from the hex at the same time.

„So, we're playing ring around the rosie, are we? Or is it chairs?" Matt muttered.

It was good news. He had learnt something new. Specifically, he'd learnt that his opponent either could set up more complex commands for units to keep them away without a Hero to intervene or was like him, coming up to check on their units regularly. He leaned towards the second, really. He'd already seen how unresponsive enemy units were when there were no Heroes in play and only marginally better when those Heroes weren't Warlords or commander units of some form.

No reason to believe that it would be any different for the enemy. If the gods and their enemies were making them play that slanted a game, he would have hoped they'd let it be known beforehand.

So.

„Guys..." Matt spoke up, calling the Heroes interface upwards. He filled them in quickly, answered the few questions there were, jumped when Layla spoke up and he remembered she was part of the team, and then dismissed them all.

The question was, what to do next turn? Other than inputting tomorrow's movement to chase after the unit, he wondered if they were going to be rushing around the village. If so, did it mean he was stuck and pinned still anyway? If both armies had the same movement rate, it certainly seemed that way.

Matt sighed after a moment, putting his feet up on the desk. Time to do some math again and figure out what to do. He wasn't going to make a decision yet though, what with the new build coming up tomorrow.

And his lack of gold, of course.

Chapter 73

Matt was up early the next day since he was looking forward to the completion of the Horse Farm. Lasya was on her way to meet with the firecracker flower and Braskar eventually while he had started another woodling yesterday. Right now, he intended to continue building up a gold reserve, if for no other reason than to get more gold-producing buildings.

Still, that was not the excitement. Today was Horse Farm day. It still seemed strange to him that he'd have horses for his wood elementals, but what did he know? The entire killing-people-and-resurrecting thing was also strange, but it worked.

First things first though. He dumped his funds into a firecracker flower in his own fortress to get them going. Then, and only then, did he take a look at the information that came up on the Horse Farm.

Name: Horse Farm

Building Type: Unit Upgrades

Tier: Lesser Tier 0

Benefits: Allows Creation of Cavalry Units

"Kind of on the nose name, isn't it?" Matt muttered, staring at the name. Ah well, no one was winning awards for naming here. He still only used numbers for his villages and towns. He pulled up his original town and found the new addition easily.

Structure Available: Brisk Nursery

Building Type: Barracks

Tier: Lesser Tier I

Units Available to Produce: *Walking Palm Trees, Tumbleweed Riders, Dandelion Troopers*

Cost: 300 Gold

Production time: 8 days

"Well, that's interesting." Matt stared at the options once more and flicked his hand sideways. He knew Irvine probably would not care, and a quick check confirmed it. On the other hand… "Braskar. Got a moment?"

"I do, my lord."

"Got the Horse Farm built, and now I've got the option to build a 'Brisk Nursery.' Three units available, just like with the Ranged Copse, but this time they're a little weird," Matt said.

"Tell me. I will listen." Matt heard some shifting around, a loud grunt, and then silence. He could not help but wonder what that was all about, but he was much more excited about the idea of checking out the available units.

Unit Name: Walking Palm Trees

Type: Wood Elemental

Tier: Lesser Tier I

Number: 6

Movement: 1

Cost: 50 Gold

Melee Attack: 15

Melee Defense: 18

Ranged Attack: 0

Ranged Defense: 20

Hit Points: 12

Speed: 10

Special Abilities: Armoured Charge

Vulnerabilities: None

Growth Potential: Low

"Damn. That attack and defense," Matt said after he finished reading it. The palm trees were weird, with long trunks and multiple roots that lifted them off the ground, making them look like vertical centipedes. They even had a layered, almost scalemail-like bark. Multiple 'arm' limbs too, all the better for beating. "This feels and looks like they're the wood elementals' heavy cavalry equivalent. Not much movement, but decent speed, and they've got a charge ability."

"Heavy cavalry. Armoured knights, or in this case, hardened trees that can break a set line. Powerful, not particularly maneuverable," Braskar said.

"We got the saakal for that, don't we?"

"In a sense. The saakal are what I would consider light cavalry for their armour. Medium cavalry in their ability to break lines due to their lack of fear. We should continue before making decisions."

"I know, I know!" Matt grumbled, but he did pull up the next unit.

Unit Name: Tumbleweed Riders

Type: Wood Elemental

Tier: Lesser Tier I

Number: 8

Movement: 2

Cost: 50 Gold

Melee Attack: 10

Melee Defense: 8

Ranged Attack: 2

Ranged Defense: 12

Hit Points: 12

Speed: 12

Special Abilities: Charge, Expansion

Vulnerabilities: Fire (Medium)

Growth Potential: Medium

The tumbleweed riders were the most alien-looking of the group. The walking palm trees were trees with glowing eyes and moving bodies, but in the end, they were just trees. This, though, was just weird. The tiny glowing illustration of the tumbleweed riders sat before Matt, making him shudder a little. Tumbleweed riders were as though someone had bulked out your average tumbleweed, added a solid core in the center of dense branches, and then made sure to add some glowing, burning eyes within.

Weird and creepy, what with the green-brown, almost dead portions of its outer body.

"Very high hit points," Braskar rumbled. "And this ability of Expansion. I do not know what it does."

Matt hummed, trying to remember what he knew of the plant from his home world. All he could recall were bad movie references, where the hero and villain stood across from one another till someone flinched. Not particularly useful, really.

"I got nothing. Low defense… I guess because it's mostly dead?" Matt said slowly.

"It's dead?"

"Yeah, mostly. The outside of the tumbleweeds, the part that, umm, tumbles. It's all dead material, dried branches and the like, when it pulls apart. I guess in this case it's not entirely dead, since they actually need to move, but mostly. So, hard to kill but easy to damage. Tiny branches."

After a little more prompting and Matt's hesitant description of what he saw, Braskar added, "The attack seems sufficient for base attacks. But I do not see how it provides any advantage over the saakal. They are both light cavalry."

"They have some ranged attack?" Matt offered. Two was weirdly low. Maybe the shards from their bony protrusions could explode outwards or get carried on the wind or something?

"Negligible amount unless you have a large number."

"Yeah, you have a point," Matt sighed. It would have been nice, but not knowing what Expansion meant plus the low stats, he couldn't see how the tumbleweed riders added to their current army build. No point in having two of the same unit type. Even if they were kinda cool looking in the 'looming over your bed as you wake up from a nightmare' way.

"Last one."

Unit Name: Dandelion Troopers

Type: Wood Elemental

Tier: Lesser Tier I

Number: 12

Movement: 2

Cost: 50 Gold

Melee Attack: 10

Melee Defense: 8

Ranged Attack: 0

Ranged Defense: 8

Hit Points: 8

Speed: 14

Special Abilities: On the Wind, Propagation

Vulnerabilities: Fire (Medium)

Growth Potential: High

The dandelion troopers were… walking dandelions. No face, no eyes, just blobs of white on thin stalks that didn't look like they'd be that dangerous. Of course, their melee attack numbers indicated otherwise, which meant he was likely missing something.

"High growth potential but the lowest numbers overall, it seems," Braskar said. "Not much better than our woodlings, other than greater speed."

"And numbers of units…" Matt frowned. "Number of units? Unit numbers? Spores? Number of dandies." He nodded firmly, having chosen what he wanted. "Yeah, there's a dozen dandies there."

So what if he grinned when he said it, knowing no one else was going to get it? This was a weird hellscape he might as well have fun with.

"I believe the dandelion troopers are unique due to their special abilities, but I do not know this plant. Nor do I understand this 'white ball of poof, kinda like a cloud stuck on a branch' description you have offered," Braskar complained. "Do you have insight into this unit, my lord?"

"I actually do know these dandelions," Matt said. "I guess I should be grateful they are drawing from Earth plants?" He shook his head after a moment, dismissing the idea of weird alien wood elementals. And wasn't that a mouthful? "Dandelions basically are made up of floating seeds. You blow on that cloud, the puffy white bit, and the seeds float up into the sky, dispersing and propagating that way."

"Propagating?" Braskar questioned. Matt shook his head, clarifying for him. Sometimes he forgot that certain words might not translate well. Or that the Warlord might not have the education to understand it. No matter what kind of weird magic made it possible for them all to speak English.

"I see, my lord. So do you think then that the first skill allows them to travel in the air?"

"Looks like it, though how it helps across the battlefield..." Matt shrugged. "Could be useful. But that also is confusing, because propagation is just the same. You know?"

"Different uses for the same ability?"

"I guess?" Matt sighed. "It doesn't really matter, since I can't buy anything. Not yet."

"True enough, my lord. Will you consider the matter then?"

"Yup. Backburner while I try to figure out where else our gold has to go." Matt let out a sigh. For all the excitement of getting some cavalry units, truth was, he probably needed to focus on getting more gold first. He'd avoided that for a bit, and if he didn't keep adding to his daily gold production, he would fall behind.

Even if this looked all too tempting.

"Any other news, Braskar?"

"Nothing, my lord. Not as yet."

"Alright, good luck. Lasya's on the way to you. Don't take any risks till then, will you?" Then Matt winced. He'd forgotten to talk to her about this entirely. Something to check since, well, he did want her on the team.

"Yes, my lord."

Content with that, Matt cut the connection and braced himself for another conversation. Maybe he could lie and say that he just wanted to have these conversations individually?

Or perhaps, if he was lucky, she just wouldn't ask.

Chapter 74

The conversation with Lasya had gone as well as could have been expected. She had not had any insights to offer him, so Matt wandered off for breakfast. By the time he came back in the afternoon, little had changed beyond the proximity of his own unit next to the raider units and their continued movement away. With the village in a hex, they were circling at a distance three hexes away, going in and out of range of the village. Close enough to be a real threat either way.

For all that, and all his thoughts about what to buy next with his gold, it had been Irvine who had come upstairs, smelling of acrid chemicals and nutmeg, and noticed the change.

"What are these Running Kennels?" Irvine said, poking at the map.

"The what?" Eyes wide, Matt prodded at the information. From the name, he knew it had to be in the second town. A quick highlight brought up the information. Quietly, Matt cursed himself for missing this.

Apparently, creating and accessing the horses around the third village had opened the options in the second town for a cavalry too. Suddenly, the importance of what Braskar was doing exploded. If the new fort had other villages and resources to access, what else would he be able to build? What new units?

For that matter, were there new gold-producing buildings?

Structure Available: Running Kennels

Building Type: Barracks

Tier: Lesser Tier II

Units Available to Produce: *Warg Riders, Saakal Vanguard, Outcasts*

Cost: 300 Gold

Production time: 6 days

"Well… that's different," Matt found himself muttering.

"What is?" Irvine said.

"The breakdown. At least one isn't an entirely new type but an upgrade?" Matt raised a hand, cutting Irvine off. "Let's do this right, shall we?"

"What?"

"Braskar. Lasya." Matt sent a tendril of thought out, pushing for the two to connect with him. When they finally did, their responses had him smiling a little.

"My lord?"

"Sir?"

"Irvine found a new building option. Running Kennels," Matt said. "Faster build time at six days, same cost. Three options again."

"The Horse Farm allowed you to build kennels? Sir?" Lasya added belatedly. He didn't blame her at all. The entire system was all kinds of confusing after all.

"Yes. Let me get through the readout and we can discuss world magic weirdness later, eh?"

"Of course, my lord." Similar choruses of agreement rang out.

Unit Name: Warg Riders

Type: Beastkin

Tier: Lesser Tier II

Number: 8

Movement: 3

Cost: 65 Gold

Melee Attack: 12

Melee Defense: 10

Ranged Attack: 0

Ranged Defense: 14

Hit Points: 8

Speed: 16

Special Abilities: Mounted Companion, Charge

Vulnerabilities: Sonic (Low), Fear (Low)

Growth Potential: Medium

Of course, Matt described the unit image that came along with the warg riders. He had to smile a little since it reminded him a little of a famous fantasy movie but was also different since the saakal were more animal-like than the orcs. In this case, they looked more like children holding on to their much larger parents, riding body pressed to fur, than actual riders with stirrups and the like. On the other hand…

"It sounds as though the companions are the wargs? Or are the riders the wargs?" Braskar hummed.

"Wargs are the wolf-like creatures," Matt confirmed.

"The wargs then seem to be an additional unit for combat. It's possible the saakal – the riders – dismount after a charge and continue the battle with their companions," Braskar said. "My people used to do the same, though we used horses and our horses did not fight unless pressed."

"Why not?" Matt asked curiously.

"Beasts of burden are expensive to upkeep and raise, especially war-trained ones," Lasya spoke up. "The smell of blood, the noise, the screams can unnerve your average beast. If you do not raise them properly, they will flee such situations immediately."

"Yes. And we needed our animals for retreat later," Braskar added. "Better to save them for the future."

"So, basically, the wargs are even faster-moving saakal who can really pack a punch. Probably great for flanking maneuvers or patching a hole in a line," Matt said. "But, with the way the units move, are they even smart enough to do that?"

"It seems even sillier than normal if they don't allow at least some additional intelligence in their deployment," Irvine said. "After all, even the raiders knew better than to walk into your open holes."

"Open holes?" Lasya's voice rose. "What kind of holes are they speaking of, sir?"

"Pit traps." Matt rolled his eyes at Irvine, the older man grinning back unapologetically. "And you have a point. So probably some basic intelligence, but again, something we'll likely be better able to use with Braskar. And they're fast. Like much faster than anything else we have. Might be useful for scouting. Or chasing down cavalry."

"Yes. Three hexes could make quite the difference in our operations, my lord."

"Unless we get something better with the harpies," Matt said. "Also, they're expensive."

"True, my lord."

"Moving on…"

Unit Name: Saakal Vanguard

Type: Beastkin

Tier: Lesser Tier II

Number: 8

Movement: 2

Cost: 50 Gold

Melee Attack: 16

Melee Defense: 15

Ranged Attack: 0

Ranged Defense: 15

Hit Points: 10

Speed: 12

Special Abilities: Rage, Line Breaker

Vulnerabilities: Sonic (Low), Frenzy (Medium)

Growth Potential: Medium

"They look like the big, big brother version of the saakal. Except, you know, with heavy plate armour and a bunch of axes. Though, those claws look nasty enough I'm not even sure they need the axes," Matt said, staring at the pictures.

"Those are truly frightening visages. And all of them bear scars." Irvine shuddered. "I do believe these are their elite members."

"Heavy infantry line breakers, meant to be the front line of any attack. I would not be surprised to see a saakal berserker option come up if we continue to upgrade the saakal barracks," Braskar said musingly. "Combined, this would be a fast-moving, heavy-hitting infantry army if they were by themselves."

"I agree," Lasya said. "Their ranged units are likely stone throwers or javelins if the armies are like those we faced before. On my world, that is." She made a small humming noise in her throat as she thought, then added, "Powerful, but is this not the same as your plant hands?"

"The palm trees?"

"Yes, sir."

"Yeah, except faster. Lower defense though." Matt then nodded. "Good point though. No need to double up on them if we get the palm trees. Or vice versa."

"These Rage and Line Breaker skills… one builds up, I assume, like our own orc. But what does the second do?"

"No idea," Matt said. "A projected attack? A super short-range charge?" He shrugged. "Won't know till we buy it, or see someone use it on us."

Braskar grumbled a little, joined by Irvine, but Matt was already reading the next option. No point, in his view, to continue complaining.

Unit Name: Outcasts

Type: Beastkin

Tier: Lesser Tier II

Number: 4

Movement: 3

Cost: 25 Gold

Melee Attack: 8

Melee Defense: 12

Ranged Attack: 4

Ranged Defense: 8

Hit Points: 8

Speed: 16

Special Abilities: +1 Hex View

Vulnerabilities: Sonic (Low), Fear (Medium)

Growth Potential: Low

"Mangy curs," Irvine said, even before Matt could describe the image.

"Sir?"

"Irvine's right, if not politic. They're ugly, dirty creatures. Very few in number, they look like what they're called. Outcasts, individuals who live on the outskirts of society." Matt hesitated. "If anything, I'd be more worried about meeting these guys in an alley than the vanguard."

"Aye, I'd agree on that. The vanguard might kick your ass for fun, but these boys will shank you in the ribs for the clothes on your back and the boots on your feet," Irvine said. "I vote no."

"I say yes. These are the scouts we have spoken of requiring before. Even a single unit, with an army, could make a significant difference. Nevermind their ability to range independently of the army."

"And cheap too," Lasya said. "The cheapest unit by far."

"Not exactly," Matt said. "The unupgraded woodlings are only twenty gold still. But the cheapest cavalry unit for sure."

Lasya muttered a thanks to him, which Matt waved away. She was still learning after all, barely a day birthed in this world, unlike the rest of them. What with their grand old age of nearly eighty days.

Babies, all of them, in so many ways.

"Four scouts. They'd be killed the moment they encounter anyone," Irvine said.

"Remember the option to retreat. And see their speed? I think they are meant to be able to retreat at any time. Along with the additional hex view…" Braskar huffed. "These are good units, my lord."

"I'd agree, except it's going to cost an arm and a leg to just get the kennels," Matt said. "And don't forget, we also need the money down south. And for more gold-producing buildings."

"I…" Braskar fell silent.

Eventually, Irvine got fed up and spoke up. "You what?"

"Apologies. I shrugged. My lord is right. I am sure he will make the right decision, but I will say that scouts will make a big difference."

"More than the dandelion troopers or hand trees?" Lasya said.

"Depending on what we face, yes."

"Hmmm…" Lasya seemed doubtful but chose not to speak further.

"Thanks, guys. I'll let you get back to it. And I'll… do some thinking, I guess." Matt sighed. There wasn't anything else he could do anyway, not now.

Not until they knew more of what they faced.

***

Global Status Report

Day 79 (End of Day)

Pooled Gold: 71.25 (+44 Gold per day)

Total Units: 8 Woodlings, 6 Firecracker Flowers, 2 Saakal

Cooldown: None

Unit Organisation

Town 1: Irvine, 2 Woodlings, 1 Firecracker Flower

Town 2: 1 Firecracker Flower, 1 Woodling

Army 1: Braskar, 1 Firecracker Flower, 1 Saakal

Army 2: Lasya, 1 Firecracker Flower (en-route)

Army 3: 1 Saakal (chasing raiders)

Village 1: 1 Woodling

Village 2: 1 Woodling

Village 3: 2 Woodlings, 2 Firecracker Flowers, 1 Woodling (en-route from Town 1)

Town 1 Status Report

In Production: Basic Greenhouse (9/20), Firecracker Flower (4/5), Woodling (1/4)

Structures Completed: Grove, Road, Stall (II), Ranged Copse, Harbour, Village #2 – Watch Tower, Blacksmith, Fishing Dock, Road to Village #3, Village #3 – Watch Tower, Village #3 – Horse Farm

Structures Available: Grove (II), Watch Tower, Tavern, Marketplace, Ranged Copse (II), Stone Harbour, Shipyard, Trading Post, Temple, Blacksmith (Upgrade), Fishing Wharf, Brisk Nursery

Town 2 Status Report

In Production: None

Structures Completed: Den (II), Tavern, Wall, Temple, Stall (II)

Structures Available: Den (III), Javelin Range, Training House, Watch Tower, Blacksmith, Temple (II), Granary, Running Kennels

Chapter 75

"Ring around the rosie, pocket full of posies. Ashes, ashes, one falls down, we all go around." Matt frowned, then shook his head. „No, that's not right. It goes a different way." He drummed his fingers on the table. "Something, something, plague, death, children's game? Or has that been disproved?"

Idle thoughts. Useless ones. He did not have a lot to do, not right now. Even if he wanted to get the new units building, he needed three hundred gold for either the Brisk Nursery or the Running Kennels. He could rebuild the Ranged Copse and get a squirting cucumber, though how much more range they had he was uncertain. That cost two hundred gold.

His other option was purchasing gold producers. Those basically meant the Marketplace, the Fishing Wharf, the Harbour, or the Trading Post, all of which were two hundred to two hundred and fifty gold pieces to build out. That was, if he didn't spend a single gold piece for a minimum of three days.

Of course, he could try to get a few more units, but the only thing he could buy right now was a saakal. Unfortunately, he saw no point in buying them, not when they offered no major advantage. Not when he could purchase actual scouts or faster units soon. Well, soon as in twelve to fifteen days, give or take a bit.

All of which meant that for the next few days, while he was waiting for his gold to refill, the only thing he really had to do beyond healing slowly was watching the map. After all, the last thing he wanted to happen was for Braskar or Lasya or his saakal unit to end up in a fight and him not notice.

The major question for Matt right now was what to do with the various gold-producing building options available. He knew he needed to buy another gold producer, and there wasn't a huge difference in what was being offered beyond build times. And what they could potentially offer afterwards. On that note, he made sure to pull up the information on the Marketplace and Trading Post.

Structure Available: Marketplace

Building Type: Treasury

Tier: Lesser Tier II

Benefit: +10 Gold Per Day

Cost: 200 Gold

Production Time: 12 days

Structure Available: Trading Post

Building Type: Trade

Tier: Lesser Tier II

Benefit: +1 Gold Per Day per Connection

Cost: 250 Gold

Production Time: 6 days

The good news was that the Marketplace was the cheapest option by far for the amount of additional gold it gave. It made the most sense, except for the huge amount of time required to build it. If he wanted something to boost him immediately though, the Trading Post was faster to build than anything else by a full day. The Stone Harbour was the worst of all options, being slow to build and expensive as well as producing not much more gold, while the Fishing Wharf just added to what they had before. A decent middle of the road alternative, but not useful right now.

The question was what they did. The Trading Post obviously made sense in the long-term, depending on what 'connection' meant. He assumed it had to do with the roads and, maybe, the Harbour and Shipyard. But were villages connections or just other towns? If it was just a town, then he was adding just one gold for a 250 gold price.

If, on the other hand, it included the villages, he would be standing at +4 right now. And probably a lot more as things built up. The Trading Post would automatically add to his gold, though right now, it just wasn't as good. Except, of course, it would start giving him gold before the Marketplace could.

„So, build the Trading Post first and get gold from it, and then save up to build the Marketplace?" Matt muttered to himself. „Or build the Marketplace first and then get the Trading Post because it takes longer so we should get started immediately?" That assumed he wouldn't need more units, which he was certain he was going to. So whatever decision he made, it would affect him for the foreseeable future. He might not even get a new gold-producing place for a while if the pace of combat increased.

„Marketplace then, I think. More gold now..." Except, one other factor niggled at him.

The building tree. What other new and cool buildings or units would appear if he got either of those places? He figured the Trading Post and Marketplace both added the next level up of their building tier. He might even get out of Lesser Tier and get to... Less Lesser? Less Tier? Middle Tier? Middling?

More importantly though, what random combination would there be? He assumed he needed something like the Shipyard before ship building became a thing, but with a Harbour and a Trading Post, was there a cool combination there? Or Granary and Marketplace as he'd thought of before? How about the Horse Farm and Marketplace? Would he then be able to build a rodeo? Or, less silly, a Colosseum?

There were so many options involved. Maybe even the Marketplace and Trading Post might cause things like a Merchant Guild or a Bank to appear.

Those were just some options he could see coming along if he knew anything about such games. Which, Matt liked to think, he did a little.

In the short-term though, the question was which of the two had the most chance to get an upgrade and what kind? The Marketplace had been available the longest, so by that theory, it made him think that it might have the most symbiotic configuration with his current builds. In particular, a Fishing Dock and Marketplace combination might get him something. Also, at some point, he was sure stuff like the Granary would be viable, or even a Pottery. After all, there seemed to be quite the lack of artisan-based items.

Thinking it over, Matt sighed. It made perfect sense to go with the Marketplace. That extra ten gold was going to be a major boon, and if things went well, he'd have a chance to get the Trading Post soon after. And if not, even if it took longer to come out, he'd have it started rather than waiting for things to play out.

No, the Marketplace was the way to go. Now he just had to hope that the team didn't run into anything too troublesome before he could buy it.

***

Global Status Report
Day 80 (End of Day)
Pooled Gold: 90.25 (+44 Gold per day)
Total Units: 8 Woodlings, 7 Firecracker Flowers, 2 Saakal
Cooldown: None

Unit Organisation
Town 1: Irvine, 2 Woodlings, 2 Firecracker Flowers
Town 2: 1 Firecracker Flower, 1 Woodling

Army 1: Braskar, 1 Firecracker Flower, 1 Saakal

Army 2: Lasya, 1 Firecracker Flower (en-route)

Army 3: 1 Saakal (chasing raiders)

Village 1: 1 Woodling

Village 2: 1 Woodling

Village 3: 2 Woodlings, 2 Firecracker Flowers, 1 Woodling (en-route from Town 1)

Town 1 Status Report

In Production: Basic Greenhouse (10/20), Firecracker Flower (0/5), Woodling (2/4)

Structures Completed: Grove, Road, Stall (II), Ranged Copse, Harbour, Village #2 – Watch Tower, Blacksmith, Fishing Dock, Road to Village #3, Village #3 – Watch Tower, Village #3 – Horse Farm

Structures Available: Grove (II), Watch Tower, Tavern, Marketplace, Ranged Copse (II), Stone Harbour, Shipyard, Trading Post, Temple, Blacksmith (Upgrade), Fishing Wharf, Brisk Nursery

Town 2 Status Report

In Production: None

Structures Completed: Den (II), Tavern, Wall, Temple, Stall (II)

Structures Available: Den (III), Javelin Range, Training House, Watch Tower, Blacksmith, Temple (II), Granary, Running Kennels

Chapter 76

„My Lord."

Matt hunched his shoulders as he heard the voice. He groaned a little, putting down the hand axe that he had been utilising to chop down a wood branch into a spike. He was working in the courtyard rather than his self-appointed workshop since he had no desire to haul the… obstacles… out of the way.

There was a word for it, he was sure. But whatever it was, he couldn't remember it and Irvine had been no help. Braskar might know, but he always forgot to ask the orc.

„What is it, Braskar?" Matt said tiredly.

„Is there something wrong, my lord?" Braskar sounded worried after hearing the exhaustion in Matt's voice.

„Just you calling me in the middle of the day. Just before you'd sight trouble if someone was moving at two hexes a turn, in fact. Give or take an hour or two," Matt answered.

„Ah, I see you have gotten ahead of my report."

„He's pretty smart, isn't he?" Lasya said, surprised.

„He can hear you."

„Oh! I apologise, sir. I..."

„It's fine. When you're as good looking as me, you realise that most people think you're pretty dumb," Matt said.

„I have never..." She hesitated, then added, „You were giving me an excuse and a way out, weren't you?"

„I was." Matt shrugged. „It's fine. We can discuss my sense of humor later. When Braskar doesn't have something dire to report."

„It is not dire, my lord. As you know, I am to meet with Lady Lasya in two days. However, it seems I have drawn out our opponent at last."

„You found their base," Matt said.

„Yes, my lord." Braskar said. „You can see, of course, that the force facing me is somewhat... well..."

„Spit it out." Matt brushed his hands and pants off, dropping wood shavings to the ground, and turned to the door. He would need to be in the map room to tell, and right now, that seemed more important than making a proper abatis.

That was the word! Abatis. He knew watching all those Roman history documentaries for Ancient History 201 would come in useful at some point. Well, that and knowing how to make a road, though that was - it seemed - less important here.

„Total of five units, my lord. I can't see the exact composition. They move around in a very disordered fashion, it seems to me. None of this flying in V-formation like proper avians." Braskar sounded almost insulted by that, which amused Matt to some extent. It did make him wonder why if it wasn't for magical reasons. Or if their opponent had sacrificed a degree of endurance to confuse matters. But why bother confusing matters at all...

Unless.

„Hero. They might have a Hero in that group."

„Sir?" Lasya could not help but ask.

„No reason to give up the advantage of flying in formation, even if it's a magical world. The V is an aerodynamic property. There's a way that the lead duck breaks the air that makes it easier for every other duck - or bird - behind it to fly. Physics hasn't changed, so common sense shouldn't either. If they aren't flying like that, it's because they're trying to hide their numbers." Matt shook his head. „No reason to hide numbers if you've got equal number units or types of units. Unless there's a standout one."

„Like a Hero," Lasya said.

„Like a Hero." He went up the stairs, taking them two at a time and then stopping to slow as he began to breathe hard. He hated not being able to exercise, especially as breathing hard meant the wound in his chest hurt even more. Why he couldn't get magical healing like the rest of the group, he didn't know. Not important.

„Can you retreat?" Matt said.

„I..." Braska's voice was troubled, and then he made a little humming noise. „Maybe."

„Then do it. Get out of there. Link up with Lasya if you can. Then you can push ahead."

„You think the five units are enough to deal with my army?" Braskar said. No ego in his voice and no challenge, which was good.

„I think if they force the fight, we'll learn something just as valuable," Matt said. „And if they don't let you back off, we'll learn something else too." He paused, then added, „Just make sure to call for help if you need it." Upstairs now, Matt went to the table and poked at the new flying unit notification on the table.

Enemy Army Sighted!
Quantity: 4 Harpies, 1 Hero

„And there we have it." Matt frowned. "Why bother with all that then if I just needed to get up here? Unless the Hero is stupid or…"

"We only started recognizing Heroes when we got Watch Towers, my lord," Braskar rumbled.

"That's what I figured too," Matt said. Or at least, it was around that time they started spotting enemies with the aid of the Watch Tower. Before that, they'd had no quantitative data. So, that meant… "The Watch Towers are boosting our information-gathering ability even when you aren't near them." He grinned savagely. "And our opponent has never bothered building them."

„Why would they not?" Lasya stopped, then muttered softly, „I should stop talking before I think. They don't because they have flying units, is that not right, sir?"

„That'd be my guess. Probably figured they range out far enough so there's no point in getting Watch Towers. They probably can get within the next hex, or even launch an attack, get the information, and then fly off. No harm, no foul." Matt sighed. „Not sure they're wrong."

„Except they're taking actions that offer no benefit," Braskar pointed out.

„Does it hurt them?" Matt shook his head. „I guess it doesn't matter. Though it does make you wonder what mistakes we're making that we don't know we're making."

„It does make one wonder," Lasya echoed. „I shall pray for an answer."

„My lord?" Braskar's voice interrupted the pair once again.

„Yes?"

„Things might become hectic. So if there's nothing else…" the orc rumbled.

„No, go for it." Matt shut his mouth and took a seat, leaning back in his chair. There was nothing else to do but wait. Wait to see if they were going to attack and if so, support Braskar as best they could.

The answer was slow in coming. It was always going to be, but time still dragged on for Matt. The former accountant found himself doing his best to keep himself busy, querying Lasya about her background, doing occasional sit-ups, squats, and a single, ill-conceived push-up, and even stretching in-between. The only thing he could do that was of help was send a firecracker flower running after Lasya and move up a unit from here to Town 2.

It was only when the hour was late in the afternoon, when it was clear that the enemy was not closing in from the distance, that Braskar was confident in declaring, „They're not attacking." Matt finally relaxed.

Until he remembered this was just the first day. They could still choose to attack later.

And there were still two more days to go before Lasya could join up.

***

Global Status Report
Day 81 (End of Day)
Pooled Gold: 134.25 (+44 Gold per day
Total Units: 8 Woodlings, 7 Firecracker Flowers, 2 Saakal
Cooldown: None

Unit Organisation
Town 1: Irvine, 2 Woodling, 1 Firecracker Flower
Town 2: 1 Woodling
Army 1: Braskar, 1 Firecracker Flower, 1 Saakal
Army 2: Lasya, 1 Firecracker Flower (en-route to Army 1)
Army 3: 1 Saakal (chasing raiders)
Army 4: 1 Firecracker Flower (en-route to Lasya)
Army 5: 1 Firecracker Flower (en-route to Town 2)
Village 1: 1 Woodling
Village 2: 1 Woodling
Village 3: 3 Woodlings, 2 Firecracker Flowers

Town 1 Status Report

In Production: Basic Greenhouse (11/20), Woodling (3/4), Firecracker Flower (1/5)

Structures Completed: Grove, Road, Stall (II), Ranged Copse, Harbour, Village #2 – Watch Tower, Blacksmith, Fishing Dock, Road to Village #3, Village #3 – Watch Tower, Village #3 – Horse Farm

Structures Available: Grove (II), Watch Tower, Tavern, Marketplace, Ranged Copse (II), Stone Harbour, Shipyard, Trading Post, Temple, Blacksmith (Upgrade), Fishing Wharf, Brisk Nursery

Town 2 Status Report

In Production: None

Structures Completed: Den (II), Tavern, Wall, Temple, Stall (II)

Structures Available: Den (III), Javelin Range, Training House, Watch Tower, Blacksmith, Temple (II), Granary, Running Kennels

Chapter 77

It was mid-day the next day when Matt groaned. He was checking things over, having moved up a project from downstairs along with some paper and charcoal and big plates of refreshments, knowing he'd be up here for the foreseeable future. After taking care of adding a Woodling to the mix, he had not much else to do. All of which meant that while his saakal kept chasing around the other cavalry units, he could pay attention to the real problem – Braskar. And the two armies he faced.

Enemy Army Sighted!

Quantity: 3 Harpies, 2 Harpy Archers

"Archers," Matt muttered out loud as he saw the details appear. „That seems intensely unfair."

„My lord?" Braskar said.

„Extra range, which means even if we had snipers, we'd be outranged. No way any of our ground troops can shoot them before they can shoot us."

„Why?" Lasya asked.

„Physics," Matt replied.

„Greater height means greater range," Braskar said simultaneously. Then, he added, „That assumes, of course, that their bows are of decent quality. There are quite a range of such instruments after all."

„Oooh, good point." Now that he wasn't wincing at the thought of the new enemy units, Matt was envisioning the archers and realising something else. „They're also likely to have limited ammunition."

„Yes. So, greater range probably, first strike ability almost certainly. But they might not be able to provide on-going support," Braskar rumbled. „Frustrating, but like any skirmishers, they cannot turn the tide of battle unless they have sufficient numbers. Two units are nothing."

Matt nodded in turn. That was all too true. He could not imagine that they were bending the rules of physics that much that they were going to magically teleport or replenish arrows for the archery units. Which also meant...

„They might not be able to sustain more than one or two attacks before needing to retreat," Matt said. „Unless the system magically replenishes their stockpile."

„Mmmm... I would hesitate on believing that, my lord. Like my rations, it might be replenished each evening," Braskar said.

„What?" Matt hesitated, then frowned. „You get magical food?"

„Yes. Did you not realise that, my lord?"

„Uhh, not really. Didn't think of it, actually." He shrugged, then winced. He really should have considered it. After all, logistics was the job of the general, right? „That's good, I guess. Also bad. Yeah, I can see how they'd recreate the arrows. But not in battle, right?"

„No, not in battle, my lord."

Lasya was silent, as was Irvine. The Alchemist had little to add, at least to this side of things. And Lasya, while on her way to join the orc, was still getting an understanding of this world. Nevermind the fact that she was a Priest and not a Warlord.

„So, what now?" Matt said.

„They must converge on this hex. Or launch attacks."

„Separate ones?" Matt said, frowning. „Can they do that? Does the system let that happen?"

„Perhaps." Braskar sounded uncertain too and Matt didn't blame him. Understanding where reality stopped and the weird rules of this world began was confusing enough. In reality, co-ordinating attacks across dozens of miles couldn't be easy, even if both parties were flying groups. If they could co-ordinate at all, they might need to slow down and speed up and make sure they all arrived within minutes, if not seconds, of one another.

Otherwise, the firecracker flowers could reset and open fire. And that was the major concern, making sure the ranged attackers they had weren't ready to pepper them before they landed, before the battle began. Which meant co-ordination in the real world.

Or the world might force them to hold off, stop there from being interference. Maybe even stagger the battles. That would be the worst case scenario for the harpies, forcing them to fight twice over with brand new groups. If that was the case, Matt would have held back and grouped them into a full army.

„Odds of them joining together to fight?" Matt said.

„Uncertain."

„Then..." He hesitated, staring at the table and gauging what was happening, and then sighed. „I guess then we wait. I'll go piss and we can see what happens in a few hours. Because that's when we'll know, right?"

„Yes, my lord."

Best case scenario, they attacked and the two armies would be forced to fight separately. That would allow Braskar to beat back both armies, with injuries but potentially no major unit losses. Second best scenario, the two enemy armies chose not to fight right now, held off till they joined up in the hex that Braskar was within. They'd form a giant army, which would not the best thing, but they'd still have to rush over to meet Braskar. And by tomorrow - or later today even - Lasya would be only a hex away.

***

They didn't attack that day.

That was the good news. The bad news was in the updated army information.

Enemy Army!
Quantity: 7 Harpies, 2 Harpy Archers, 1 Hero

Compared to that army, Braskar was rather badly outnumbered. One firecracker flower, one saakal. Even when it had been just the four harpies and the Hero, he did not think they could have won that without major damage. Admittedly, the firecracker flower that Braskar was running was a veteran with upgraded stats but still...

Now, there was no doubt in his mind that when they caught Braskar, he was going to lose. Badly. His only hope was to meet up with Lasya and that together, the pair of them could survive the attacks. Two firecracker flowers were powerful, able to do enough damage to the flying harpies. Even if the saakal weren't of much use.

Which meant this morning, it was all about who could make it to one another first.

„Come on, come on, come on..." Matt found himself chanting under his breath, watching the little units hover on the magical map. Nothing moved, for it never truly updated the actual movements till units were in another hex. So all he had were verbal reports, none of which were particularly useful.

Worse, the area that Braskar was marching through was all fields and plains and some rolling hills. Not much in terms of trees, which meant they couldn't even use them for aerial cover. All they could do was march and hope that Lasya would reach them in time. Since they only needed to meet,

Lasya was marching to the edge of her hex and Braskar his, so that together they could meet up. Except, of course, their opponent was faster.

All of which meant that Matt had no idea who had order of priority for the battle. If there was an order of priority.

„This is an insane world. It really is." Matt sat back down, put his head in his hands, and let out the biggest sigh he'd ever had. „I'd say I wish I was back home, but anything's better than trying to balance an account. Literally anything." Melodramatic a bit, perhaps, but then trying to figure out where that extra $0.02 was missing could drive even the most sane person, well, insane.

Even if, most of the time, you just shoved it in an adjustment account and called it a day.

Unless you had an anal-retentive boss that was trying to punish you for not wanting to work longer hours.

„You know, Irvine, if there's one thing this world is good at, it's work-life balance."

„Balance?" Irvine growled. „And you know, I could be doing something more productive than listening to you narrate your boredom."

„You could, but you yourself said you're a little nervous for our friend. And yes, balance. Like not working eighty hours a week kind of thing. Here, you get about ten hours of productive daylight, and then you're done. Finished. No more updates, come back tomorrow. Can't even make it give you more work if you want it to."

„What's the point of balance if you like what you do? If you love what you do?" Irvine said. „I worked for three days straight once, making a potion. Best three days of my life." A slight pause. „Might have been the mushrooms that I was using too. They made everything more... fun."

The look Matt gave him was all very skeptical. He knew Irvine well enough to know the man's version of fun involved more chemicals than was wise. Then again, he'd died once.

„Maybe we can have one of those parties after Braskar survives,” Matt said.

„Now that's a-” Irvine shut up as another voice cut in.

„My lord, I see Lasya. However, I fear we will not make it. I must have our people set up if we are to survive at all.” A slight pause, then he added, „It has been an honor to dance the blades with you, my lord.”

„And you,” Matt said somberly. „One last thing.”

„Yes, my lord?”

„Don't die. That's an order.”

He could not see it, but he could imagine the orc's big, savage grin. Then, all Matt could do was sit back and wait.

***

Global Status Report
Day 82 (Middle of Day)
Pooled Gold: 158.25 (+44 Gold per day)
Total Units: 8 Woodlings, 7 Firecracker Flowers, 2 Saakal
Cooldown: None

Unit Organisation
Town 1: Irvine, 2 Woodlings, 1 Firecracker Flower
Town 2: 1 Woodling
Army 1: Braskar, 1 Firecracker Flower, 1 Saakal

Army 2: Lasya, 1 Firecracker Flower (en-route to Army 1)

Army 3: 1 Saakal (chasing raiders)

Army 4: 1 Firecracker Flower (en-route to Lasya)

Army 5: 1 Firecracker Flower (en-route to Town 2)

Village 1: 1 Woodling

Village 2: 1 Woodling

Village 3: 3 Woodlings, 2 Firecracker Flowers

Town 1 Status Report

In Production: Basic Greenhouse (12/20), Firecracker Flower (2/5), Woodling (0/4)

Structures Completed: Grove, Road, Stall (II), Ranged Copse, Harbour, Village #2 – Watch Tower, Blacksmith, Fishing Dock, Road to Village #3, Village #3 – Watch Tower, Village #3 – Horse Farm

Structures Available: Grove (II), Watch Tower, Tavern, Marketplace, Ranged Copse (II), Stone Harbour, Shipyard, Trading Post, Temple, Blacksmith (Upgrade), Fishing Wharf, Brisk Nursery

Town 2 Status Report

In Production: None

Structures Completed: Den (II), Tavern, Wall, Temple, Stall (II)

Structures Available: Den (III), Javelin Range, Training House, Watch Tower, Blacksmith, Temple (II), Granary, Running Kennels

Chapter 78

Things weren't as dire as they looked at first glance. All that meant was that it went from impossible to nearly impossible to attain a victory. There were a few reasons for the cautious optimism that Braskar was feeling. The first among them was the stand of trees – a small one but a stand – that he had spotted a short hour ago. He'd traded distance to meeting Lasya for angling towards the trees, because the additional cover it would offer his people was worth it.

Of course, his opponents had spotted the problem as well and had sped up. For the last ten minutes, he had been dealing with the archers loosing arrows at his units. Which, he had to admit, was the other optimistic portion.

They just did not have the accuracy to fire over that distance. They sent the arrows high into the sky and were unable to actually hit their targets with any degree of regularity. Sure, by the time the arrows, which were coming in on a long-lobbed flight, arrived, the striking power from falling from so far above was significant, but they'd also lost most of their forward momentum at that point. With the firecracker flowers' higher than normal defense, the few that did strike did little to kill his saplings.

In the meantime, other harpy units were flying in as fast as they could, trying to catch up. They were closing in and Braskar was forced to glance back every once in a while to gauge the distance. Hanging behind, next to the much slower harpy archers, was the Hero, too far back for Braskar to tell what kind as yet.

"We won't make it…" Braskar muttered to himself. Not before the first of the harpy units hit them at least. Which led him to wonder if he would be better off utilizing the firecracker flowers in a set position to fire back, dealing as much damage as possible, or if he should keep running, hoping they wouldn't be picked off.

In the end, he made the best choice he had. After all, he'd promised his lord.

"Turn around and retreat slowly to the tree line. Hold and fire when the harpies attack, retreat when they are gone," he commanded the saplings, then his eyes narrowed in thought before he added, "Use the Potion of Defense now."

Their only potion. He wished they had managed to get more copies, but that was all they had. In fact, he wished Irvine had learnt that Potion of Speed. It would have come in useful right about now. What was it that his lord liked to say? Shoulda, woulda, coulda?

As always, the wood elementals had no reply. Yet, he felt there was a moment of connection, a way that those burning eyes in the bark focused upon him, the sway of the arms and branches hanging around them that said they were ready. In their own way, the wood elementals were true warriors.

He held their gaze one last moment, offered them a nod, and then took off, waving the saakal after him. Time to go, time to make it to the trees with his melee fighters. It would force the harpies to come down, allow them to do battle where his fighters held the advantage.

swings. He glanced back as he loped forward, keeping his strides long so that he could cover the ground fast without tiring himself out completely. The saakal were all around him, keeping pace with the slower orc.

The harpies were in the air, already in the stooping plunge with their wings tucked in. Ready to crash into their enemies. Braskar cursed internally, thinking the firecracker flowers might open fire too soon. They didn't though, instead holding back till the creatures were at the optimal range.

The first crack of exploding seedlings flying into the air was punctuated by the striking of flying projectiles impacting fleshy, feathered bodies. The first attack was always the worst, and in this case, nearly half the units of harpies leading the way fell. That, of course, left another unit right behind to keep coming and the first half still angling down.

Resolutely, Braskar turned away and focused on running. He knew how the rest of that fight would continue, for the firecracker flowers had another pair of arms. They would launch that attack at near point-blank range into the remaining harpies, which would see most of them fall.

However, there would be barely enough time - maybe not at all - to get a single volley on the second unit flying down behind the first. Those might see a few more who fell, but by that point, the weight of fire would be less because some of the firecracker flowers would be dealing with the surviving members of the first harpy unit. Even if they didn't manage to kill any of his own saplings, it would be enough to throw them into disarray.

When the second unit hit, he would start losing saplings. After that, the third would do even more damage, the fourth...

There was no point thinking about it. Braskar had something more important to worry about on a personal level. When he had glimpsed back, he had noted that not all the harpies had stopped to attack their rearguard. Enough of them, of course, to make sure the firecracker flowers were lost.

The other three units were winging their way to them now, coming straight for the group. And worse, the archers had shifted the direction of their attacks, targeting him and the saakal instead. If there was one piece of good news, it was what he had seen when he had looked at the other Hero. He was sure his lord had also seen it.

Azimma (Level 1 Winged Scout)
Specialty: Scout
Skills: Greater Sight, Forced March
Experience: 78/100

Attack: 4

Defense: 6

Power: 6

Knowledge: 9

A Scout Hero. Their Flying and Greater Sight abilities probably were the reason they'd found them, but the fact that they had such a low attack and power meant that in battle, they were a non-issue. Braskar could crush the other with one hand behind his back, he was certain. No, the major advantage for the other Hero was that trying to run or hide was out of the question. It was likely that his Flying skill was the reason for the lower overall numbers everywhere else, same as with the rest of the harpies.

Musings about the problem were ripped away as an arrow glanced off Braskar's armour, bouncing off the pauldron to hit the ground. He grunted, hearing a pained yelp that turned to whimpering. He spotted the saakal that was hit as he glanced back, seeing them hobbling along, injured.

The orc didn't stop. He knew better than to slow for a single unit, especially when there was nothing he could do. When the opponent had ranged fire and you didn't - or you were outnumbered - the only reasonable course of action was for every orc to look out for themselves and run. Run till you hit your goal and then hunker down and wait.

The world was cruel, the battles they fought even worse. Better to save some of the clan than lose them all.

„My lord," Braskar called out, his voice firm. He had been thinking, considering the best options. „If the flowers survive the first run, if you can..."

„Heal them. I'm already watching..." Matt let out a long hiss as he thought.. „I might do it before the fourth unit. They're down to one unharmed, two injured now."

Braskar hesitated, then grunted in agreement. He chose to let his lord decide on the matter as he was too busy running. The longer they could keep the firecracker flower active, the better. It was the only unit that could do significant damage to the flying units, and it would buy them time if the enemy focused on it.

The screams of the harpies, the flap of their wings, he could sense them behind. Coming closer and closer.

All he could do was run.

By the time they reached the trees, he had lost a second saakal pup. He himself had gotten a wound, a cut along his forearm when an arrow had managed to find a gap between his elbow guard and his bracers. Luckily, it had deflected enough that it had not lodged deeply and wiggling it out and tossing the remnant had left him with a bleeding but minor wound.

Only when they were in the rough center of the small number of trees - barely even a dozen of them all together - did he spin around, putting one of the trunks between him and his opponents. They had slowed their attacks with the bows, hovering in place, the last couple of units having landed to finish his injured saakal.

They'd made it. Barely, but they'd made it.

Now the question was, what would their enemies do?

Chapter 79

„Hurry, Lasya. Hurry..." Matt chanted softly. He had already repeated those words once to the Priest. He could not do anything else, and so he watched the firecracker flowers do their thing. They were surviving, barely; the increased defense, their higher level and thus increase in firepower and defense, it was all making a difference.

Not enough.

So far, his opponents had yet to lose a full unit. The first one had been savaged badly, but he had no time to call the firecracker flowers to attack the single harpy left behind that was flying away. Strategically, even if he sacrificed total damage output, taking out the unit now and not letting it heal and regenerate new unit members was the smart thing to do.

But that would mean less damage now, less of the harpy units in total in this battle. And if Braskar had any hope of surviving, they needed the max amount of output of damage. He wished he could have tossed a Lightning Bolt, but they were too far away from the Town. Too far to offer any aid but healing.

So he watched, lower lip worried between his teeth as he saw the numbers of the firecracker flowers drop. The second harpy unit fell, nearly losing half their number. They took out two flowers though before they winged away and only lost one of theirs in the clash. Then, the third unit hit and he lost three more flowers, only one unit somehow managing to escape harm by sheer luck.

The chaos of battle and all that.

It was so strange, so remote. Watching numbers flash up and disappear on the map. The temperature up here was a little cold, but nothing too bad. He was comfortable, even as a rainstorm raged outside his window, the occasional rumble of thunder breaking through. The smell of falling rain, of the comfortable drumming of raindrops on the roof. Perfect gaming weather, where no one complained if you didn't leave the house to see the great outdoors.

Complete nonsense when others were dying, at his behest, on the other side of the map.

The third saakal unit broke away, a couple of harpies staying down long enough to savage one of the damaged flowers and end them.

Time.

He stabbed his finger on the spell, watched light play over the firecracker flowers. Hoped it was enough.

Because that was all he could do.

***

She could see them. She knew they could see her. The horse she was riding was being pushed harder than any animal that she had ever ridden before, and Lasya was cursing her lack of riding experience. If she was a little better at it, perhaps she could remember how to stay on the horse better, make it easier on the poor animal. If she was a little better, maybe they could have reached Braskar already.

Not that she was the only hold-up. These moving trees, these swaying stalk and trunk and branch creatures, unnerved her. More than she liked to admit, though they had never done anything to make her worry about them. No, her nerves were entirely due to their alien nature.

What kind of mind looked at something so different and decided that it was the best choice for allies? She did not know and was worried that she might never know. He was so different, and it angered her that she failed to understand. After all, that was one of the major tenets of her faith.

Understand, sympathise, guide.

Control.

And this. This mad rush of clopping hooves, hard breathing horse, and the silent creak of wood and plants; what kind of control was there to be had? They were dancing to the tune of their faster opponent. An opponent that watched her coming, that had full knowledge of her arrival and control of whether to engage or flee.

It was maddening, it was frightening, it was ridiculous.

„Faster, faster, faster!" she chanted over and over again under her breath. She could feel her god reaching out through her, touching the horse, the creatures beside her. It sped them up a little. Gave them energy when they would have flagged.

All for the best, even as the harpy units stooped through the air, flying slowly into the small copse of trees. They couldn't do their divebomb attacks, not without risking life and limb. So they were coming in slowly, turning to tear at the saakal who lay waiting on the ground. The saakal and the orc.

Whatever that was.

The saakal she saw soon enough. It had been described to her, so when she saw the loping creature come tumbling out of the woods, holding on to a harpy with its mouth as its clawed hands gripped and ripped. The pair tumbled end-over-end for a time before the saakal came up on its feet, tearing its head sideways and ripping a hole in its prey. It threw its head back to howl its victory, only for a pair of harpies that had been patrolling the copse on the outside to fall upon it.

Another brief skirmish, this time the creatures coming down in a swooping attack that left long tears across flesh and knocked the saakal over. It attempted to stand, managed to make it to its feet and begin retreating only for a pair of arrows to land, finishing it off.

It was clear that anything outside of the copse would die.

Anything… but the firecracker flower that still stood, farther away. Staggering back, one tree-limbed hand gripped the body of a harpy to wave off its attackers. The other remaining arm grew in size so that when the second harpy attempted a flanking maneuver, it was greeted by an explosion of seeds. The attack was timed and angled so that another harpy, coming in from the side and higher up, was caught too, the creature forced to flap and back off as it was trailed by falling feathers and blood. Unlike the shredded remains of the other.

Even so, there were at least eight of the harpies left and a single sapling. The outcome was clear.

Making a snap decision, she reached forward with her faith. She tried to envelope the other wood elemental with it but failed. If it was a true believer…. But of course it was not.

Again, she spurred on her horse. Urging it to go faster, to cover the ground necessary. She kept reaching out, trying to feel the connection that was necessary, all the while watching the flower fight on valiantly. It should have died, if not for the shrill cawing, the notice that her presence and that of the new unit brought. She saw some of the units turning away, coming for her.

No rhyme or reason, no indication of why these other units were attacking her. She could see the Hero waving its wings, desperately calling forth, and she realized perhaps this was not a matter of control. Not a matter of choice.

She was sure Matt would have a reason, a way to explain it. All she could think was that she was in trouble if those harpies reached her before she had backup. Yet, she kept pushing onwards, rushing ever closer until she felt it.

Like something snapping into place, a wood joint sliding together neatly. She threw the full strength of her ability at it, calling upon her god to assert its dominance over this world. Healing – or a version of it – as reality returned to what her god willed it.

Firecracker flowers reappeared all around the surviving one. One, two, three, four. Five saplings, all standing there together, hands raising as water filled the flowers and they aimed their arms at the descending birds.

Then she was reining in her horse, trying to back off before the other harpies fell upon her.

Chapter 80

"Yes!" Matt hissed, watching the saplings repopulate on his map. He did a little dance, knowing that meant that Lasya was finally in the fight.

Now, now they had a real chance. The harpies had taken quite the beating, though they had only lost two whole units so far. They managed to pull back some of the units when they got too injured, somehow able to selectively call for retreat. Perhaps it was a racial thing or some other finer method of control for the enemy.

Matt leaned towards a racial trait, just like their flying. An ability to preserve their numbers where otherwise they would be forced to fight to the end. He did wonder about the first battle, why they had not fled, but could come up with a million reasons and never know it for truth.

After all, not all the units had retreated when they should have. So it might just be a percentage chance thing, and his own units might have that as well. A morale break, which wood elementals just didn't need. A break, that was.

The archers were still flashing once in a while but much more slowly. Whether they had run out of arrows or were close to it, they rarely did anything. All but for the one angling for Lasya, that was.

***

Lasya cursed as she fell off her horse. She managed to roll enough so that when she hit the ground, she only drove most of the breath out of her body. For a moment, she lay stunned before an arrow landing just in front of her face made her twist and scramble upwards. A shuddery, indrawn breath allowed her to breathe, sucking in air through a bruised chest.

Cursing, she reached sideways and almost tugged the arrow in her side out. She paused as she remembered her training, then felt another arrow cut through the air and strike her shoulder, bringing more hissing pain. Resolved, she pulled hard, screaming a little as the arrow emerged and ripped open her wound.

Then, she forced her Healing through her body, fixing the problem. It was dangerous to extend her faith so often, though it was easier when it was her body, her faith. After all, she was closest to her god.

No time to consider it though, no time to wonder for too long. Instead, she twisted and ran to the side, trying to dodge the arrows. She was thankful that they were slowing down, even as another arrow tore into her, lodging in her arm. She stumbled from the pain and impact, cursing internally.

She realised she would never make it. Not to the copse of trees. Not when more harpies were on the way, were already fighting within. She had given the others a chance to win, but she wondered if it had been worth it.

After all, she had just come back alive…

Then, a crack. A rippling series of large cracks coming from behind her. Shrieks of harpies, the screams of the dying. Turning around, she realized the firecracker flowers were firing on the archers, ignoring the trio of harpies launching their attacks on them.

Why? How?

"Don't just stand there. Run!" Braskar roared, waving at her from the trees.

Now, she realized what was happening. He must have used his command ability, made the firecracker flowers guard her rather than themselves. She sprinted again, hissing with each jolting step as the arrow in her arm moved, but she did not stop.

By the time she got under cover, the firecracker flowers had the full attention of the archers and the remaining harpy units. Only two harpy members, circling around came flying towards her. Braskar grinned widely, his eyes glimmering with hunger as he hefted his axe.

"Good timing. We might just survive." A hesitation, then he looked back around. After a moment, he seemed to come to a decision. "Support the flowers. We need to end some of their units."

"Of course. I just need… a moment…" She exhaled, shifted away deeper into the trees. She realised he was ignoring her already, eyes focused on the harpies winging their way down.

She had no weapon. A mistake, a foolish one. She should have brought one, but she had not been thinking. Hadn't thought she would be risking herself so directly. Hadn't realized she would be forced to do this. Now, she was useless. Glancing around, she grabbed for a stick she saw not so far away. She stumbled over to take it and turned to help Braskar. She immediately lowered it again.

By the time she had done all that, the fight was over. The first creature had been killed, bisected by a strange red light that had appeared around the orc that she had caught only a glimpse of. It shot out and killed the flying creature, giving the giant bark-skinned, muscular orc time to kill the other.

The skin colour bothered her but only a little. The colour was unusual, for sure - black, yellow, and purple were more appropriate. The tusks were a bigger issue, for she had never seen that before. But seeing flying humanoids and wood elementals and half-animal beings already… it was less of a concern.

Second monster dead, he stalked over to her and pointed behind. She spun around and saw the firecracker flowers she had come to save down once again. To only two. She felt within, realized she had maybe one cast left in her. She threw her faith at the creatures, watching them bloom.

"Focus. We'll talk later."

Lasya could only grunt agreement as a wave of exhaustion took her. He didn't even pause as he bent down and picked her up, carrying her further into the trees. He set her down as a saakal came trotting up next to them.

This battle was not over. Even if, in her estimation, they had a real chance of winning now.

Chapter 81

What was that saying? There's nothing worse than a battle won except a battle lost? Matt sort of understood it now, though he still felt a rising sense of jubilation deep within as the notification appeared.

Battle Report (Heroes Braskar and Lasya vs Enemy Units)
Result: Victory! 1 Saakal Unit Lost, 3 Harpies Defeated, 6 Units & 1 Hero Escaped
Rewards: +6 Gold, +3 Reputation

They had won. More than that, they had just laid a crushing defeat on their enemy. Even when their enemy had double their units in total, they had lost. He had won a staggering victory, and a part of him just did not believe it.

"Everyone okay, right?" Matt asked once again.

"We are fine, my lord. Lasya has healed herself and has begun the process of healing the rest of our units," Braskar said.

"She can heal them outside of battle?" Matt said, eyes widening. If that was the case, the Priest was much more powerful than he had thought. At the rate she could heal, it would be literal hours before their units were back to full strength.

And it was very clear that the individual units needed it. They had lost their last saakal via an unlucky shot by the retreating archers, ending them as a threat. That left the firecracker flowers who were still alive but desperately needed more melee help. Weak as they might be, if the harpies just landed en-masse and fought close quarters, he had a feeling he'd lose units again.

"Not exactly, my lord. She says she can feel her connection to her god is frayed. She will be able to heal them slowly, but not to the same extent. Not if we wish her to be of any use," Braskar clarified.

"I see. Alright. Still, accelerated healing is good…" Matt trailed off.

"Is it me or did we win that a little too easily?" Lasya said. "Not that it felt easy, but…"

"No, you are correct," Braskar rumbled. "This was easier than I was expecting. They are much more vulnerable to our firecracker flowers than expected. They fall too easily to attacks."

"Tell me about it," Matt said.

Braskar relayed the battle from his viewpoint, Lasya interrupting and adding her own thoughts, few as they might be. In the end, Matt could not help but mutter, "A bad choice or a bad usage of the enemy race's benefits?"

"Sir?"

"We get to choose our races." Lasya made an affirmative noise, and he remembered that the Heroes gained some innate knowledge upon their resurrection. He pushed that thought aside, or his own curiosity about why he didn't have any, and continued, "So perhaps the harpies were a dud race. One of those that look great on paper, but their disadvantages are worse than you'd expect. Or it could be that they're being used badly."

"How would you use them, my lord?" Braskar asked.

"Separate armies from you guys, I think. Priests with them, for sure. Maybe a Warlord, but you can't fly, so… eh." He licked his lips, thinking out loud. "Larger groups. No scout teams but groups of, say, four. You use them to harry attackers. Hit and run. It seems the harpies can retreat, so you let them do that. Hit once, pull back. Hit again the next turn with the Priest healing. Maybe even rotate between armies, so that you don't just have one army. Combine that with a slower, normal army below."

"You might lose units."

"Yeah, but if you can retreat with most of them intact, you can build up experience. Become tougher, force your opponent to take losses. Then, hit them with the anvil when they've gotten confident." Matt shook his head. "Maybe I'm overly optimistic. Maybe you would lose too many for it to be good."

"Perhaps, my lord. But I concur. Harassing tactics to wear down an opponent seem to be their optimal strategy," Braskar intoned.

"They were just basics, was that not right, sir?"

"What?" Matt said.

"Basic units. Not like our cavalry options," Lasya clarified.

"Yeah. Not even sure they're upgraded…" Matt trailed off, eyes widening. "Jammed printers!"

"My lord?"

"They're basics. And we're not in the basic end of the game anymore." When there was no expected reaction, Matt continued in a hurry, "They're going to be upgrading with others. Vanguard harpies, harpies that might do more damage. Better ranged units. Something…"

"Ah…"

Matt's gaze dropped to the map, biting his lip. He drummed his finger, then spoke. "Let me know tomorrow if you're going ahead or pulling back till reinforcements are arriving. But I'm sending the Woodling we have from the second town to you." He bit his lip, thinking. "I'll get one more from the second village to you too."

"If you're stripping the town…"

"I'll send a Woodling from mine. Wish I could pull a woodling from the other village back here, but they're pinned. We'll be short but not horrendously so." Matt hesitated, then nodded. "But whatever happens, we need to hit that army. Finish them before they upgrade. Or at least before they can field heavier units."

"Agreed, my lord." A slight pause. "Saakal?"

Matt bit his lip, debating. They were useless against the harpy units. Too soft, too easily taken down. Potentially useful against the cavalry units, but those were stuck, his army pinned down. If he created them, he'd be waiting a little, pulling back on his other cavalry options.

Then again, he was busy building as much as he could.

"I'll start now," he said. "Alright then. Get rested. And let me know your decision tomorrow." Matt hesitated, then added, "Good job."

"Thank you, my lord."

Killing the connection, Matt turned back to the map, adjusting marching orders. He hated it, but it had to be done. Especially when he saw his armies spread out all over the map. If those raiders ever decided to get serious, if another cavalry army showed up, he could be defeated in detail.

He was gambling and he knew it. And deep in the pit of his stomach, he could not help but think that at some point, he was going to roll the devil's eyes.

***

Global Status Report

Day 82 (End of Day)

Pooled Gold: 139.25 (+44 Gold per day)

Total Units: 8 Woodlings, 7 Firecracker Flowers, 1 Saakal

Cooldown: Spell Casting (0/7)

Unit Organisation

Town 1: Irvine, 2 Woodlings, 1 Firecracker Flower

Town 2: (Empty)

Army 1: Braskar, Lasya, 2 Firecracker Flowers

Army 2: 1 Saakal (chasing raiders)

Army 3: 1 Firecracker Flower (en-route to Army 1)

Army 4: 1 Firecracker Flower (en-route to Town 2)

Army 5: 1 Woodling (en-route to Town 2 from Town 1)

Army 6: 1 Woodling (en-route to Army 1 from Village 2)

Village 1: 1 Woodling

Village 2: (Empty)

Village 3: 3 Woodlings, 2 Firecracker Flowers

Town 1 Status Report

In Production: Basic Greenhouse (12/20), Firecracker Flower (1/5), Woodling (0/4)

Structures Completed: Grove, Road, Stall (II), Ranged Copse, Harbour, Village #2 – Watch Tower, Blacksmith, Fishing Dock, Road to Village #3, Village #3 – Watch Tower, Village #3 – Horse Farm

Structures Available: Grove (II), Watch Tower, Tavern, Marketplace, Ranged Copse (II), Stone Harbour, Shipyard, Trading Post, Temple, Blacksmith (Upgrade), Fishing Wharf, Brisk Nursery

Town 2 Status Report

In Production: Saakal (0/5)

Structures Completed: Den (II), Tavern, Wall, Temple, Stall (II)

Structures Available: Den (III), Javelin Range, Training House, Watch Tower, Blacksmith, Temple (II), Granary, Running Kennels

Want to see two pieces of exclusive character art of Matt? Or maybe a behind-the-scenes peek at the map Tao drew for the series?

Subscribe to his newsletter on Tao Wong's author website and receive the pieces of art or the map in your inbox!
https://www.mylifemytao.com/bonus-epilogues

Join my Discord (https://discord.gg/ZYjwf5kBWe) or Facebook Group (https://www.facebook.com/taowongauthor/) to talk all things Magic Kingdom with other readers.

Climbing the Ranks

The World Changes. Dreams Don't.

Mystical towers changed the world twenty years ago. Now, Arthur Chua faces the beginner tower in Kuala Lumpur, Malaysia, looking to change his destiny.

What was once a puzzling mystery has become a necessary part of economic growth. Climbing the Tower is the only form of escape available for one like Arthur, without money or connections. He's not looking to be a hero or famous, just a survivor.

Fate, on the other hand, has other plans for him. At long last, the reason for the arrival of the Towers will be revealed, and humanity will once again experience a seismic shift when the truth appears.

Of course, Arthur's going to have to survive long enough for that to happen...

https://starlitpublishing.com/products/climbing-the-ranks

Author's Note

Thank you for reading the first collection of Magic Kingdom at War. If you enjoyed reading the book, please do leave a review and rating. Not only is it a big ego boost, it also helps sales and convinces me to write more in the series!

Follow Matt's adventures in *Magic Kingdom at War Volume 5*.
https://www.mylifemytao.com/?page_id=9258

For more great information about great LitRPG series, check out the Facebook groups:

- GameLit Society
  www.facebook.com/groups/LitRPGsociety
- LitRPG Books
  www.facebook.com/groups/LitRPG.books
- LitRPG Legion
  www.facebook.com/groups/litrpglegion

About the Author

Tao Wong is a Canadian author based in Toronto who is best known for his System Apocalypse post-apocalyptic LitRPG series and A Thousand Li, a Chinese xianxia fantasy series. His work has been released in audio, paperback, hardcover and ebook formats and translated into German, Spanish, Portuguese, Russian and other languages. He was shortlisted for the UK Kindle Storyteller award in 2021 for his work, A Thousand Li: the Second Sect. When he's not writing and working, he's practicing martial arts, reading and dreaming up new worlds.

Tao became a full-time author in 2019 and is a member of the Science Fiction and Fantasy Writers of America (SFWA) and Novelists Inc.

If you'd like to support Tao directly, he has a Patreon page - benefits include previews of all his new books, full access to series short stories, and other exclusive perks.

www.patreon.com/taowong

Want updates on upcoming deluxe editions and exclusive merch? Follow Tao on Kickstarter to get notifications on all projects!

https://www.kickstarter.com/profile/starlitpublishing

For updates on the series and his other books (and special one-shot stories), please visit the author's website:

www.mylifemytao.com

Subscribe to Tao's mailing list to receive exclusive access to short stories in the Thousand Li and System Apocalypse universes!

https://www.mylifemytao.com/book-club/

About the Publisher

Starlit Publishing is wholly owned and operated by Tao Wong. It is a science fiction and fantasy publisher focused on the LitRPG & cultivation genres. Their focus is on promoting new, upcoming authors in the genre whose writing challenges the existing stereotypes while giving a rip-roaring good read.

For more information on Starlit Publishing, early access to books and exclusive stories visit our webshop: https://www.starlitpublishing.com/

You can also join Starlit Publishing's mailing list to learn about new, exciting authors and book releases:

https://starlitpublishing.com/newsletter-signup/

To learn more about LitRPG, talk to authors including myself, and just

have an awesome time, please join the LitRPG Group!

https://www.facebook.com/groups/LitRPGGroup/